The Drowning Place

FREE PROOF COPY – NOT FOR RESALE

This is an uncorrected book proof made available in confidence to selected persons for specific review purpose and is not for sale or other distribution. Anyone selling or distributing this proof copy will be responsible for any resultant claims relating to any alleged omissions, errors, libel, breach of copyright, privacy rights or otherwise. Any copying, reprinting, sale or other unauthorized distribution or use of this proof copy without the consent of the publisher will be a direct infringement of the publisher's exclusive rights and those involved liable in law accordingly.

Also by Sarah Hilary

DI MARNIE ROME SERIES

Someone Else's Skin
No Other Darkness
Tastes Like Fear
Quieter Than Killing
Come and Find Me
Never Be Broken

Fragile
Black Thorn
Sharp Glass

The Drowning Place

SARAH HILARY

HARVILL

1 3 5 7 9 10 8 6 4 2

Harvill, an imprint of Vintage, is part of the Penguin Random House group of companies

Vintage, Penguin Random House UK,
One Embassy Gardens, 8 Viaduct Gardens, London SW11 7BW

penguin.co.uk/vintage
global.penguinrandomhouse.com

Penguin
Random House
UK

First published by Harvill in 2026

Copyright © Sarah Barratt 2026

The moral right of the author has been asserted

Penguin Random House values and supports copyright. Copyright fuels creativity, encourages diverse voices, promotes freedom of expression and supports a vibrant culture. Thank you for purchasing an authorised edition of this book and for respecting intellectual property laws by not reproducing, scanning or distributing any part of it by any means without permission. You are supporting authors and enabling Penguin Random House to continue to publish books for everyone. No part of this book may be used or reproduced in any manner for the purpose of training artificial intelligence technologies or systems. In accordance with Article 4(3) of the DSM Directive 2019/790, Penguin Random House expressly reserves this work from the text and data mining exception.

Typeset in 12/14.75pt Bembo Book MT Pro by Six Red Marbles UK, Thetford, Norfolk
Printed and bound in Great Britain by Clays Ltd, Elcograf S.p.A.

The authorised representative in the EEA is Penguin Random House Ireland,
Morrison Chambers, 32 Nassau Street, Dublin D02 YH68

A CIP catalogue record for this book is available from the British Library

HB ISBN 9781787305397
TPB ISBN 9781787305403

Penguin Random House is committed to a sustainable future for our business, our readers and our planet. This book is made from Forest Stewardship Council® certified paper.

MIX
Paper | Supporting responsible forestry
FSC® C018179

To Lisa Shannon

Joe nearly didn't catch the school bus that Friday, the day that changed everything. He woke to the sound of his parents fighting, not shout-fighting but the dark hiss of whispers. He wanted to stay in bed; if he got up, he'd be part of the fight. Mum would make breakfast, or Dad, whoever wanted him on their side today. Joe was eleven and already knew there were sides, to everything.

'Joe! Breakfast!' Dad's football voice: *'Quick kick-around, champ. Come on!'* Joe hated football. The only sport he liked was swimming.

'Joseph Ashe, get down these stairs!' Mum cutting to the chase.

He dragged himself to the bathroom. His face in the mirror was bony, his grey eyes wary. He thought of Sammi's brown eyes lit with laughter; that helped. He wished they didn't have to wear uniform for the trip. Black trousers, green sweatshirt. He looked like a green-and-black soldier fly. If they were lucky, they'd see soldier flies today: broad centurions that bred in rotting vegetation. They were going on a trip to Bamford Edge which had millions of millipedes. Joe and Sammi had a bet on for who'd see one first.

Downstairs, Mum was microwaving porridge. Dad had made toast, 'Nutella, champ?' Joe had never eaten Nutella in his life. Mum threw him an eye-roll as she served up the porridge he hated but which he'd eat when there wasn't a choice. She'd won this round. Too bad Dad was on the school run; Joe had to listen to him criticising Mum's breakfast choices all the way to the bus stop.

Luckily, Sammi was waiting, which meant Dad was happy to drop him and go. On days when they beat Sammi to the stop, Dad (like Mum) insisted on staying so Joe wasn't waiting on his own. It'd been embarrassing when he was ten, worse now he was eleven. Seth Morton's brother Des said it was because of perverts. Seth and everyone else would be on the bus already; only Sammi and Joe got on here, at what his gran called the arse-end of Edenscar. Mum said it was a miracle the bus still ran out here. Dad agreed but when he said Joe should get a bike, Mum said, 'With the state of the roads?' Even when they were agreeing they argued. Joe's gran said it didn't mean anything, but she didn't have to live with them, or anyone, since Granddad Ashe died before Joe was born.

Sammi stamped his feet. 'Too cold for millipedes.'

'Just means they'll be slower. Easier to spot.'

'Dead, you mean.' Sammi started doing a dance he'd picked up, feet moving in complicated patterns. He was always moving and thinking, figuring stuff out. Some days, Joe was sure he could hear Sammi's head ticking.

'Fruit flies were the first living things sent into space.' Sammi flipped on his heel. 'Most died but twelve survived to be parachuted back to Earth.'

'What did they feed the flies, in space?'

'Fruit. Or dog turds.' Sammi pulled Joe into the dance. 'Turds in space!'

Joe tried to keep up but Sammi's moves were too good, three for every one he managed, so he settled for watching and laughing. By the time the bus came into view, they were out of breath.

'We need the back seat,' Sammi said. 'Don't look at Seth. Or Devin.'

Joe nodded, sobering at the mention of the two boys. Devin was okay on his own but Seth had a way of making people pay attention; a busload of classmates could be a busload of bullies before they reached Bamford Edge.

On the bus, Seth was bullying Hayley Stratton by pretending to help with her bag. Miss Roache hadn't noticed because Seth was great at pretending to help with people's bags. When Hayley's ended up at his feet, Joe bent to get it. Her sleeve rode up, new bruises on her wrist. She caught him looking – 'Piss off' – angrier with Joe for seeing the bruises than she was with Seth for throwing her bag about. Seth kicked at his feet – 'Yeah, piss off, perve' – as Joe made his way to the back of the bus where Sammi was waiting: 'Told you not to look at him.'

'I didn't. Just helped Hayley with her bag.'

'Well don't. It's not brave to get stung by a tarantula.'

Ellie Howden was drawing on the window with her finger, a picture of her little brother, Theo. Her best friend, Zoe Cooper, drew a cat at Theo's side. She saw Joe watching and pressed her lips into a shy smile, drawing whiskers on the cat before Ellie added claws. Zoe was nice. Joe wasn't friends with her the way he was with Sammi, or with Paige Blackwall who was in the seat in front of theirs, next to Molly and Tyler. Sammi said Zoe's mum wouldn't let her hang out with boys, and anyway Paige had the forest behind her house where they could build dens.

Miss Roache came down the aisle, checking everyone was settled for the trip. She had a red streak hidden in her hair like a secret. You only saw it if she tucked her hair behind her ear like now, smiling at Joe and Sammi. 'Do you two have your packed lunches?'

Joe's mouth opened but Sammi said, 'Yes, Miss Roache,' and she nodded, returning to the front of the bus.

'I don't have anything. I forgot.' Joe felt sick. He'd be hungry all day and it meant a fight between Mum and Dad over who'd forgotten the lunch.

'Joe . . .' Sammi nudged him in the ribs. He opened the neck of his bag, showing two sets of sandwiches, two apples, two bags of Wotsits. 'Mum thinks I'm on a growth spurt.'

Joe was too grateful to feel awkward. Impossible to feel awkward with Sammi anyway, who never noticed or pretended not to. He was watching from the back window as the road sloped through woods where they built a camp last summer before Des Morton found out and told Seth who told everyone Joe and Sammi were shacked up in Fairy Woods. The memory brought a hot throb to Joe's throat. Des could *piss right away*, as Joe's gran told wasps that found their way inside her house. He reached for Sammi's hand and held it. Sammi raised one black eyebrow at him, his eyes laughing, lit to honey by the sun.

Seth wasn't the first to see them holding hands. That was Hayley. She hissed at Seth, 'Look at that!' and Joe knew she did it to get Seth's attention off her for a bit, but of course it all kicked off then. Seth stood up, calling to Mr Edison, 'Sir, there's perverts on the bus!' and Miss Roache turned and the driver did the same and the bend in the road did the rest.

The bus hit the edge and went over, wheels spinning in thin air before finding the trees. Giant cobwebs cracked across the windows as they splintered and smashed. Everyone screamed as a rush of green came through – sharp branches grabbing like hands – but the slope was made of mud, nothing could hold them.

The bus raced towards the reservoir like a rocket.

It hit the water, hard. Went under, fast.

Waves of broken glass rolled from the front of the bus to the back, the force of it jerking Joe's shoulder so hard it broke. Somehow he kept hold of Sammi's hand, their fingers twisted into a fist. Sammi's eyes were wild. He was shouting something Joe couldn't hear because water like thunder was filling the bus, roll after roll of it, black and angry. Suddenly, unstoppably, they were drowning.

Everyone on the bus – Seth and Devin, Molly and Tyler, Hayley, Ellie, Zoe, Paige, Joe and Sammi, Miss Roache, Mr Edison, the driver – everyone. *Drowning*.

That whole time Sammi's hand was in his and all Joe could think was, *Don't let go, don't ever let go*.

I.

Joe stopped running when the rain came, and because his phone was buzzing. *Work.* It was his day off but it'd been drummed into him that 'off duty' was for uniforms. Detective sergeants should be ready for anything.

'DS Ashe. I'm going to take a wild stab and say you're leaning into a drystone wall, flexing your hamstrings. How far are you from Edenscar?'

'Forty minutes out?' Joe shook rain from his head, exaggerating the estimate to be certain of exceeding expectations, a thing that generally kept his boss in a good mood.

'Powderhill, number 28. Backs on to the woods. You know it?'

'Yes.'

'Well, in your own good time. Not an emergency.'

DCI Saxton rang off, and Joe pocketed the phone.

Below him, the reservoir seethed before settling into a flat expanse of water, 464 billion litres of it, rippling into a Y-shape fringed by forest.

'Rain'll bring out the sting bugs.' Sammi hadn't joined him on the run, but he'd been waiting for Joe when he reached the reservoir. 'Took you long enough. Getting slow in your old age.'

'I'm twenty-eight.' Joe checked his watch. 'Same as you.'

Forty minutes, he'd told Saxton. In reality, it would take him twenty. He could do what he'd come up here to do, spend time with his best friend.

'How come you never run with me?'

'Don't need the exercise.' Sammi flexed his biceps. 'In great shape, aren't I?'

'For someone who's been dead for seventeen years? Not bad.'

The water flung back Sammi's laughter in a hundred pieces, bright and brimming, unchanged after all these years.

Behind him, the Upper Derwent Valley ran in folds and pleats towards Win Hill. The summer was long gone, but it wasn't yet winter with its rash of brown grasses, bracken and bilberries, the sun slung low in the sky. Mist was coming down, rubbing out the forest ranges. At the horizon, a single tree like a woodcut held out. The mist hadn't reached it, but it would. When it got to work, the mist swallowed everything. Joe often thought if he stood still long enough the mist would take him, wipe him out.

'It's busy today.' Sammi was looking down into the reservoir, where Joe rarely looked. He'd tried staying away from this place, but it was here Sammi was at his sharpest, most solid. Which made sense, Joe supposed, if he let himself think about it. About the fact he saw ghosts and that Sammi, unequivocally dead, had never left his side since that morning.

'Five minutes, then you need to get going.' Sammi pulled himself on to the wall, sitting with his back to the reservoir. 'What's in Powderhill, d'you think?'

Of course, being alone up here also meant less chance of anyone noticing Joe talking to himself. 'I'm about to find out.'

'What if she's there?'

'Paige?' Joe shook his head. 'I'll deal with it. It won't get in the way of whatever Saxton needs doing.'

'No,' Sammi agreed. 'None of us ever gets in the way of that.' He beat his heels against the wall in time to the rhythm of the water.

Nine children drowned on the bus that day. Joe still saw them: Paige and Zoe, Ellie and Hayley, Molly, Tyler, Seth and Devin. Only Sammi aged, growing with him, a man of twenty-eight now. Strange comfort, since it made Joe miss him more. None of the others grew up, or spoke, or joked with him. None of them came to crime scenes, helping him crack cases, feeling so real he had to pinch himself.

'Three minutes,' Sammi said. He never let Joe run late.

Rain had turned the Snake Pass into one long hiss. As he turned in the direction of his car, Joe caught a flash of white in the field above. A mountain hare come too soon for snow, its white coat winter-ready, black tips of its ears twitching in the wet grass. He watched the hare until Sammi said, 'Better get a wriggle on,' then turned and headed for Powderhill.

'Here he is, Britain's Most Haunted . . .'

Ted Vicars was on the scene, which meant Saxton had despatched two detective sergeants out here, where the gritstone edges of the Dark Peak rubbed up against the houses. Saxton liked to challenge Joe to improve his team-working skills, and hanging out with DS Vicars was widely acknowledged to be the most challenging aspect of life with the Derbyshire Constabulary.

'What's up?' Joe asked.

'Dunno, but it looks like kids.'

Ted thought kids responsible for ninety per cent of crime on their patch. Part of it was laziness, hating to exert himself until the evidence gave him no choice, but often kids *were* involved, bored pre-teens the principal offenders.

'Been inside?'

'Guv said to wait for you.'

'Backup?'

'Do me a favour.'

He'd be doing Ted a favour soon enough, should Saxton decide to turn up with the expectation of at least one of them doing his job properly.

'Have you secured the scene?' Joe could see plainly enough that no, DS Vicars had not secured the scene, and had been enjoying a sly cigarette all over its perimeter. 'What do we know?'

'Nosy neighbour spotted movement inside, late yesterday, owners haven't been down in weeks. Second-homers, raved about how "real" it was, nature on their doorstep, then discovered the arse-ache of keeping the place habitable. You'll enjoy this: they reckon those woods are haunted. Kept seeing shadows. What d'you think?'

'Opaque objects placed in the path of light will cause shadows. So, yes. Trees, light, shadows. Highly likely.'

'That's what you tell Tyler and Molly's mum and dad, is it? That they're seeing shadows?'

Joe didn't tell anyone anything, not any longer, but even so Edenscar loved to whisper about ghosts. His fault. He should've kept his mouth shut from the start, as soon as Sammi appeared – 'Surprise!' – opening his hand to show a ladybird crawling in his palm, the one bright spot in Joe's room.

'Haunted woods,' Ted was saying, 'you'll fit right in.'

Number 28 Powderhill wore the bland face of most cottages around here, repurposed as holiday homes. Proximity to the woods was attractive in daylight, but no estate agent would encourage viewings after dusk when a tide of shadows crept in, bringing Edenscar's familiar brooding menace. Brutal, visitors called it, that sense of the landscape biding its time.

'All right, Egon Spengler. We going in, or what?'

Joe started up the path to the front door. 'Egon Spengler? Is that a *Ghostbusters* reference?'

'Don't tell me you've never seen it,' Ted grumbled. 'Can't believe I'm working with a Zoomer. How old was your dad in 1984?'

'Five. How old were you?'

'Eight. Bloody hell.'

'Was Egon the nerdy one with the glasses?'

'Yeah. I was more of a Venkman fan myself.'

'The sceptic? Of course you were.' Joe nodded at the path leading around the side of the cottage. 'Watch where you're walking. Broken glass here.'

They followed the trail of glass to what was left of the small kitchen window, more smashed glass on the counters inside.

'Kids,' Ted said. 'Told you.'

'How many kids would fasten the latch after themselves?' Joe walked back to the front, knocking on the door, 'Police,' running through the formalities, but the place was empty. Empty houses always gave off the same chill.

'You could fit through that window,' Ted said. 'You're a whippet, thanks to all that running.'

'There's a simpler solution.' Joe looked at the litter of rocks by the porch. He pulled on a pair of nitrile gloves before crouching to pick up the least convincing rock, taking out the key concealed in its base.

Ted grunted. 'People're still doing that? Hiding the key in a fake rock?'

'Because no one believes it. You didn't. Neither did whoever smashed that window to get inside.'

Joe flicked on the hall light, illuminating an expanse of hardwood floor. Black leather sofas, indifferent art; no books, not even a bookcase. The stale scent of a place unlived in. He'd been here when it was a proper home, smelling of chips and ketchup, Paige Blackwall's mum making sandwiches while Paige, Sammi and Joe watched TV together, crammed on to a flowery sofa.

'No one here.' Ted was in the kitchen, gloved-up. 'That window's smashed from the outside. Can't find whatever they used to do it.'

Otherwise, the kitchen was spotless and characterless. Plastic pot plants on the windowsill, chalkboard for shopping lists with 'Retreat, Relax' chalked on it.

'The neighbour who called it in. Was that Sandra Buck?'

'Who else? Assumed it was holidaymakers, worked herself up to a lecture about the septic tank. When no one showed, she was only too happy to call us.'

Joe searched the kitchen for a likely missile. The latch being fastened on the inside said chuck-and-run. But where was the stone, or brick?

Ted straightened from peering under the table. 'Could've been ice like last winter. Kids taking the tops off frozen puddles, using them like frisbees. Little sods thought it very clever when the ice melted and got shot of the evidence.'

'No frozen puddles in October.' Joe turned a slow circle, looking from the window to the range. 'I don't think this was kids.'

'Getting that special feeling, Egon? Shivers up your spine?'

Sammi leant his shoulder into the wall. 'Tell this joker to shut up, Joe.'

Joe just said, 'Bedrooms. Come on.'

He led the way up the staircase, Ted close behind. Sammi was waiting for them on the landing, scuffing one foot at the carpet, a warning in his stare. Joe had the strong sense if he turned he'd see Paige in the Dalmatian onesie she wore after school, unembarrassed

9

to sit with two boys in their uniforms, tucking into chips because it was Mrs Blackwall's turn to watch them that afternoon. When it was Sammi's mum's turn, they played in the big garden at his house, eating the fancy cakes she'd baked. Here there was only the forest, and Mrs Blackwall said it wasn't safe to play there. They'd played all the same.

'Pick a door,' Ted prompted. 'Only three, and that one's open.' He nodded at the bathroom, moving to push past Joe, who said, 'Is that a mountain bike?'

Spoked wheel, fat tyre rearing up from the bath. They'd found stolen bikes in stranger places, but this one set a ticking in the back of Joe's skull. When Ted switched on the light it glinted from the pristine carbon frame. 'Weird place to keep a bike. Surprised the little sods didn't take it.'

'Why didn't they?' Joe wondered.

'Too heavy for them? Jax's not much bigger than an eight-year-old.'

Jaxon Grice was Edenscar's most prolific bike thief. He and his friends lifted a total of six over the summer, sawing through bike racks, covering the damage with duct tape so owners caught on too late.

Joe eyed the contents of the bath. 'That's a Trek Procaliber. It weighs about ten kilograms and it's worth the thick end of four grand.'

'Nice,' Sammi agreed.

A better prize than any of the bikes Jax had pinched back when a heatwave was starting wildfires on the moors, laying bare the bones of villages drowned under reservoirs. Joe had got into the habit of trekking up to Ladybower to see the shallow wash of water where the bus went in. He'd thought there might be answers at last, but in the end the drought gave them nothing new.

Ted turned on his heel. 'Bedrooms.'

Sammi said sharply, 'Better stop him, Joe.'

He strode after Vicars. 'Hang on, don't—'

As Ted opened the bedroom door, a flick of sound was followed by a *yark* – Joe grabbing Ted's elbow, snatching him back as the bolt sped past to land with a fleshy thud in the thick plaster of the wall. Ted closed his open mouth.

Sammi said, 'That shut him up,' but he was out of breath all the same.

'Police! Put your weapon down.' Joe waited. 'Tell us when it's down.'

Silence. No one was in the bedroom, he'd put money on it. The bolt had somehow been rigged to fire when the door was opened.

'Put it down, you little shit! That's attempted murder. Forty years for that! You'll be older than I am when you get out.'

Ted was convinced this was kids, but Sammi wasn't and nor was Joe. Four grand's worth of bike in the bath, a crossbow rigged in the bedroom . . . This wasn't kids. But there was a kid here. He'd been trying not to think about her, telling himself it was hypervigilance, a detective's instinct for danger. If he turned in the direction of the bathroom he'd see Paige in her school uniform, dripping with water and chips of windscreen, face white with death, eyes black—

'Dial it down, Dramatico.' Sammi telling him to get it together. Do his job.

'How the hell did you *know*?' Ted glared.

'I didn't, just heard it, same as you.'

Ted shook his head, adrenaline making him angry. 'You're uncanny, mate, you know that? Bloody *I see dead people* . . .'

'I don't see dead people. For the simple reason they don't exist.'

'Better,' Sammi said approvingly.

Joe took out his phone and opened the camera, reversing the screen to see into the bedroom. The crossbow was strapped to a chair, nose pointing through the slats, rail empty. The room was deserted, unless someone was hiding under the bed; Joe could really do without that. He pocketed the phone and took out his ASP baton, nodding at Ted to do the same. They went into the bedroom weapons drawn, their shadows cartoonishly large on the lime-washed walls. Few hiding places. Just a recess around the chimney breast repurposed as a wardrobe, empty.

Ted swept under the bed with his baton before squatting to look, 'Dust bunnies, that's it.' He joined Joe by the chair, staring down at the crossbow.

Not a modern weapon. Agricultural. Its back end was fashioned from a shotgun, the kind found in any farmhouse around here, an old rat-catcher's gun; the front end was pieced together from yew and iron. Ted pivoted to stare at the bolt bristling from the wall. Had it hit its intended target, he'd be wearing it through his neck.

'Still think it was kids?' Joe asked.

'Maybe. Some sick little shits out there.'

Ted followed him in the direction of the second bedroom, waiting while Joe unlatched the door with his baton, the pair of them standing well back. No bolt this time, just the door swinging open into an empty room. Well, empty unless you counted the assorted weaponry, making the crossbow look like an afterthought.

On the bed: a dozen traps, some designed to save the farmer reaching for his ratting gun, others large enough to take a man's foot off. On the floor: lengths of wood hammered with nails, spike-side up as a nasty surprise for anyone strolling in here with their eyes closed or their shoes off. A matching length of wood was fixed to the inside of the windowsill, a maniac's idea of home security. Hanging from the light fittings and wardrobe doors: wire snares, assorted chains, manacles. The room reeked of iron and engine oil. A few of the traps were ancient but Joe had the feeling each had been lubricated to make certain it would work; this wasn't a gruesome museum but a fully operational, lethally efficient arsenal. And a threat. Cold-blooded, full-throated, shouting at them from the bed and floor and walls.

'All right, Spengler. You win. This isn't kids.'

'He's catching on.' Sammi prowled the room.

'So what is it?' Joe asked Ted.

'Messed up. No wonder those second-homers hate it here.' He poked his ASP at the bed, snatching it back as a trap snapped. 'Welcome to the Dark Peak . . .'

Thudding from inside the wardrobe brought their heads round, steel snares skittering against its shut doors. Sammi put his ear there, listening.

'Police,' Joe said. 'You'll want to come out now.' He used his lightest voice because whoever was in the wardrobe had run out of options. If they were armed, they wouldn't be hiding. They might, however, be afraid. Fear did funny things to a person, could make you dangerous in ways courage could not.

Ted said, 'Come out or we'll wire those doors shut and wait for an Armed Response Unit. Your choice.'

More thudding. The sound was low down, not heavy enough for an adult. Joe's blood prickled, coldly. *A child?*

Ted rapped his baton on the side of the wardrobe. 'That's your choice — ARU? Give us a hand with this wire, then, Detective Sergeant.'

Joe used the baton's end to open the wardrobe's door.

'Oh, shit.' Ted took a step back reflexively.

Sammi did the same. Joe didn't blame them; the smell from the wardrobe was black and bloody, like the mess inside. Two red pinpricks glared up at them. *Eyes.* One of the traps had caught a rat, a big one down from the forest. Its back was broken, eyes glazed, mouth flecked with wet.

Joe shone his phone's torch, looking for a place where it might've chewed its way inside. 'It was put in here.' He crouched, looking at the rat. He should end its misery, but didn't know how to do that without making more mess and this was a crime scene, that'd been clear for the past half hour. Whoever did this was dangerous. Bloodthirsty. Capable of worse.

'Far worse,' Sammi agreed grimly.

'*Put in here?*' Ted echoed.

The start of something, not the end. Joe held the rat's gaze. 'They set a trap and then put the rat inside the wardrobe. Recently. Otherwise it'd be dead by now.'

'Nice.' Ted sounded sickened.

'Like you said. Welcome to the Dark Peak.'

2.

'Where's the Wi-Fi?'

Laurie's phone wasn't happy, letting her know what it thought of damp stone houses built between hills where even the sheep looked lost.

'Adam?' she called down the stairs. 'Where's the home hub? I can't find it and I need to be online!'

'In the back bedroom,' her husband shouted. 'Wardrobe!'

'I'm *in* the bloody back bedroom,' she said under her breath before shouting, 'No wardrobe in here!'

'Behind the curtain on the right!'

She stubbed her toe on the foot of the bed because of course it stuck out at an angle like everything else in her father-in-law's house. Nothing was straight, not the window frames, nor the floors. It was like the house in a fairytale, one where witches suck the marrow from small children before spitting out their bones to make a bracelet.

Behind the curtain was a set of shelves crammed with mouldy shoeboxes. She crouched to where plug sockets might be expected to lurk, finding a black box with an ominously unlit display. When she tested the socket, half of it came loose from the wall, the other half staying put only because damp had made the plaster spongey. They'd need an electrician to sort it. She held the socket in place with her foot and wrestled the plug free, looping it around the box before carrying the whole lot downstairs to where Adam was unpacking in the ferociously unfitted kitchen.

'Dead on arrival.' She dumped the hub on the nearest surface. 'If you're trying to murder me just know electrocution can be tricky for the pathologist. A challenge to prove it was murder, although easier when the victim's found face down in a house mostly made of death traps. Where's the coffee?'

'In another box. If I was going to murder you, I'd use the silage trench at the farm.' He nodded at the field behind the house. 'Let the pigs get rid of the evidence. That'd fox even DCI Reza.'

Laurie slid her arms around his comfortable waist. 'Rez would work it out. He knows I'd not be caught dead near a silage trench, or pigs for that matter. Made me promise I'd make it out alive, wants me back in one piece.'

'His best detective inspector?' Adam kissed her. 'Of course he wants you back. Might happen sooner than either of you planned since Dad's in worse shape than I'd thought from what the girls said.'

His sisters, Helen and Esther. They'd asked Adam to come home and help with his dad's decline. Laurie hadn't seen much of her father-in-law during the last two decades, but she'd signed up to see a lot of him now. Dementia. Peter needed all the help he could get. Team effort.

'I'm here for you,' she reminded Adam. 'All of you.'

Adam hugged her, resting his chin on the top of her head; Laurie was tall but she'd married a man who was taller, even on those rare occasions when she wore heels. 'Not as if you're going to be twiddling your thumbs,' he said. 'This's deepest Derbyshire but it still has a crime rate.'

Crime rate? She wasn't convinced it had a pulse rate.

'Stolen tractors and badger baiting?'

She was joking, but Adam tensed. He'd worked hard to persuade her this secondment wasn't a step down, just a temporary sideways manoeuvre. Greater Manchester Police to Derbyshire Constabulary. And because he was a trauma counsellor, he'd pitched it as a chance for Laurie to regroup; the last two years had been tough. He was taking a sabbatical, his dad his priority right now. Derbyshire Constabulary was welcome to her for as long as Adam needed to be here. Family came first; she'd learnt that lesson the hard way.

'You'll thrive,' her boss had told her back in Salford.

'I don't know, Rez. The Dark Peak? What'm I going to be doing? Ticking off ramblers for trespassing on the Duke of Devonshire's many sacred acres?'

'You might get lucky – body in a septic tank.'

'It'll be mine if I don't find a way back here, and fast.'

Adam eyed the dead hub. 'I'll find someone to fix this.'

'Get them to check the wiring while they're at it. I wasn't kidding about the death trap up there.'

'Chris Miles's the local electrician. Funny, when we were at school he nearly blew up the science lab by sticking his finger in a socket.'

'Great. Let's definitely get him in.'

Their heads turned at a tortured sound from outside. 'Jesus . . .' The last time she'd heard a noise like that it was coming out of a man whose battered wife had stopped him with a pair of scissors. Impromptu gelding.

'Pigs,' Adam said. 'You'll get used to it.'

He'd given her ten years while she was moving up the ranks to DI, never complaining about the long days and nights, how little they saw of one another, jokes about what a good wife he was: hot meals on the table, a shoulder to cry on. This was her chance to repay that favour. She'd get used to the forests and peat bogs, bloody rocks as far as the eye could see. Pigs, much closer to home.

'You'll thrive on it, Bower.' Rez had listened to her offload these thoughts with his customary show of patience. 'You love a combat zone.'

'Why'd you think I don't want to leave Salford?'

'Because you're a madwoman. In any case, you'll be back. Probably with a commendation under your belt.'

Laurie had looked out of Rez's window at the long unlovely skid mark that was the Manchester Ship Canal. Last summer, she'd led the team responsible for pulling four fridges from the canal, each weighing 250 pounds, leaking blackly as it was lifted to the path. Two held nothing worse than fetid water, but the others had a nightmare apiece: severed human hands. Not even a matching pair. That was a slog, three arrests at the end of it, winning her team a commendation of the kind she would never come close to here. Not that she needed commendations, or severed body parts, to make her job worth doing. Just the chance to put thugs and drug dealers behind bars, bring a little peace to the families they'd ripped apart.

'Coffee.' Adam put a hot mug into her hands. 'I'll run you into town tomorrow, find you a phone signal.'

'I'll go myself. Put in an appearance at the station, meet DCI Saxton and the team.'

'Not until Monday morning, surely.'

'Early reconnaissance. With luck, they'll be in a better mood on a Friday. And I should get to know Edenscar.'

'Enscar,' Adam corrected her, not for the first time. 'It's spelt Edenscar but pronounced *Enscar*. Locally anyway.'

'*Enscar*. Need to find my feet. Saxton's expecting me to pitch straight in.'

'The girls'll be great for adding local colour. Unlike yours truly, they put down roots here. Anything you need to know, ask them.'

Laurie nodded, but she wanted to see for herself how the land lay here. Population fewer than four hundred. Sheep outnumbered people, she bet.

'They're going to love you,' Adam said.

'They're not. But I don't need them to love me, just to let me get on with it. When I'm not helping you put this place in order.' Her eyes went to the artwork on the walls. Adam's dad had some deeply dodgy taste. The picture over the dresser looked like a still from a snuff movie: a very dead dog with its head in a boy's lap.

'Magnus Saxton's going to latch on to you just as hard as Rez. You know they called him the Edale Viking?' Adam grinned at her wrinkled nose. 'Not a lot of Magnuses round here. He runs a tight ship, that's what my spies tell me.'

His sisters, he meant. She sipped her coffee, thinking about what she'd heard of Saxton's tight-knit team. 'There's a rumour one of them sees ghosts.'

'Joseph Ashe, you mean?'

'You know him?'

'Knew him. *Shit*—' Adam had moved his dad's toaster to make space for their air fryer, crop-dusting the floor in the process, burnt toast crumbs everywhere.

'Don't tell me you were at school with him too?' Laurie said.

'Hardly. He must be sixteen years younger. But you couldn't live around here without knowing about Joseph Ashe. Hand me that kitchen roll?'

'Leave it, I'll hoover it up. Living around here when, exactly?'

Adam pushed the crumbs into a heap with the toe of his shoe. 'For the last seventeen years. All anyone ever talked about back then. Some still do, Esther says, especially those who've lost someone—' He swerved, changing the subject. 'When they're not bitching about the state of the roads or whose kids've gone off the rails. You want to make a name for yourself, sort out the juvenile crimewave. To listen to my sisters, half of them are dealing and the rest robbing bikes.'

Back in Salford, the kids were killing one another. If all they were doing here was lifting bikes, she'd be bored within a week. Bored and thankful. What kind of DI – what kind of *person* – wouldn't be glad of a break from finding kids as young as eight stabbed in the street? Edenscar was a chance to shake loose a little of her city scepticism, remind herself most people were kind and considerate. Most people were like that in Salford, too. She was already missing them.

'You don't need to do that, by the way.'

'Do what?' Adam asked.

'Tread on eggshells. I'm a big girl. My sister died, but that doesn't mean I don't want to talk about her. Sometimes I really do.'

'Of course. That's natural. I understand.'

Her husband, the trauma counsellor. Tricky, though, given how little Isabel had liked him. Nothing personal, just an addict's aversion to the caring profession. For years, Laurie had played peacemaker. Until Izzy blew it all up at their wedding. No going back from that, although she'd kept hoping. Had she given up, grief would've drowned her long before death stepped in to take matters out of her hands. She pulled out a chair and sat at her father-in-law's table. 'Tell me about Joseph Ashe.'

'He's a local celebrity.' Adam refilled their coffee cups. 'Even when I was still living here. Before the bright lights of Salford lured me away.'

'I thought that was me,' putting her chin in her hand, giving him eyelashes.

'I was talking about you.' Adam grinned. 'Who sent Jim the Lad to jail?'

Sooner or later, the shine would wear off her success with that crook Jim Chancellor, solving a cold case that'd foxed the force for two decades. Reputations rested on current solve rates, not once-in-a-lifetime lucky breaks. Not that it was a lucky break, since she could've ignored her gut feeling. Digging had made her unpopular with plenty of people, just not the CPS.

'What makes Joseph Ashe a local celebrity?'

Adam stirred sugar into his coffee. 'First of all, and sorry, this sounds brutal, but he should've drowned like everyone else on the bus. Nine kids, three adults. None of them made it out of the bus, let alone to the surface. This wasn't like crashing into a lake, or even the sea. That reservoir is a death trap. The currents alone . . . Depth of the water. *Coldness* of the water. Add that to the length of time he was submerged. No one could believe it. Everyone said it was unsurvivable.'

'How did he survive?'

'Found his way out of the back of the bus and swam. Overflow current must've caught him.' Adam set the spoon aside. 'Christ, Lore, if you ever see that place. You won't believe it any more than the rest of us. A skinny eleven-year-old with a broken shoulder. Sole survivor.'

Laurie thought about that, about meeting DS Joseph Ashe, looking him in the eye, knowing what she knew. 'What caused the crash? Brake failure?' She'd seen enough of the roads around here to guess how that could've been catastrophic.

Adam shook his head. 'Nothing wrong with the steering or brakes. But the second the bus went into the water, it was going to be fatal.'

'Yes, but why'd it go into the water?'

This time Adam hesitated, playing with the sugar spoon. 'That was the hardest thing for everyone to get their heads round. It was Joe.'

The words made no sense. Laurie stared at him. 'What?'

'He distracted the driver. Well, him and another boy, Sammi Torre. They were mucking about on the back seat.'

'Oh come on!' She felt a flare of anger like heartburn in her chest wall. 'Which eleven-year-old hasn't done that? We're talking about a traumatised, bereaved *kid*. People didn't really blame him, did they?'

'Well that's the thing, Lore. How'd you think they found out?'

She recognised the careful look on Adam's face. He'd given her the same look after Isabel died, for months afterwards. Eggshells, and cotton wool.

'Joe was the sole survivor. No witnesses.'

'You're saying he *told* them it was his fault?'

Adam nodded. 'He told them.'

'Same question, in that case: he'd just survived a major trauma; why would anyone take what he said at face value?'

'I don't know, but they did. Some of them still do.'

She tried to picture that. The town closing ranks, pinning a tragedy of that magnitude on a lad who'd lost all his mates. 'Friendly place you've brought me to.'

'It is, actually.' Adam lightened the mood with a grin. 'You'll see. From what I've heard, Joe gets on okay with most people now. Just a few outliers who're convinced he's a *conduit to the beyond*,' doing a spooky thing with his hands.

'Because he sees ghosts?'

'Because *they* do, or think they do.'

'Where? By the crash site?'

'By Joe. Or with Joe. Like I said, mystical conduit.' Adam stood, taking their empty cups to the sink. 'Mass psychosis, if you want my professional opinion. Some sort of emotional contagion triggered by shared trauma.'

'Go on.'

'It's not uncommon in close-knit communities, especially where social or physical isolation is a factor. Add a major traumatic event and you've the perfect breeding ground for mass hysteria.' Adam stood the cups to drain. 'Don't bite my head off at this next bit, but studies show mothers and older women can be a catalyst for this phenomenon.'

'So not eleven-year-old boys?'

Adam dried his hands on a tea towel, taking his time to answer. She got the impression he was treading softly for her sake rather than Joe's. Her sister cast a long shadow. 'Right after the crash, Joe told his mum and dad he saw ghosts. Word got around. Next we knew the mums of the dead kids were seeing their ghosts at Joe's side. Hannah

Cooper saw her little girl Zoe. One or two of the others were the same; some convinced their husbands to join in. The smart ones moved away.'

'That must've been tough.' It'd taken Laurie three years before she was ready to clear her sister's stuff from the spare room. 'Moving, I mean.'

'Most of them didn't. Joe didn't.'

She couldn't identify the expression on her husband's face. On a stranger's, she'd have called it censure, or envy. But that wasn't Adam.

'You think he should've done that? Moved away?'

'I don't know.' Adam started unpacking another box. 'Maybe.'

'And he didn't just stay. He joined the police, became a detective. What's your professional opinion about that?' She thought of that half-drowned boy pulled from the water. 'Complex PTSD?'

'At the least. But he worked past it, must've done, to be allowed into the police. Too many checks and balances, otherwise.'

Adam avoided her eyes, both of them remembering the grief counselling she'd endured after Izzy's death. Seven years ago but permanently on her record, triggering regular checks. And she wasn't a child at the time. Her life had been hopelessly tangled with Izzy's thanks to the sticky nature of addiction, but she'd only lost one friend, not nine. 'Seventeen years is a long time. I'm going to assume he's solid, unless you've heard anything to the contrary?'

'I've prejudiced your first impression enough as it is. See for yourself. Monday, or tomorrow if you're serious about getting stuck in early.'

'Oh, I'm serious. *Ow*—' A crumb of burnt toast stabbing her socked foot. 'Where's the hoover likely to be?'

'You're the detective.' Her husband was loading plates into the cupboard. 'I'm sure you'll figure it out.'

3.

Merry's house smelt of hot wax and essential oils, some less essential than others; his grandmother had repurposed an old chip pan for her latest hobby of candle-making. Like all her previous hobbies, this was less about mastering a craft, more about giving her an excuse to curse around the clock (her words). Joe was six when he discovered not everyone's grandmother liked to curse. Of those that did, none could hold a candle to Merry.

'Look at this fucking rubbish.' She pointed Joe at the kitchen counter where candles were arranged like a clutch of knuckled fists. 'Meant to be bloody roses.'

'Well, they do look bloody.'

She laughed, reaching to pinch his chin. 'You look a little beaten yourself, kiddo. But still beautiful.'

'Not glamorous, though. Not like you.'

'Oh, hush.' She flicked at his cheek with affection. 'Have you eaten?'

'Not since lunch.'

'Apple pie in the fridge, if you fancy it?'

'Oh go on, then.'

Joe reached their cups down from the pegs above the stove. He fetched the milk and pie from the fridge, watching Merry drop teabags into the pot. She wore a shapeless man's cardigan over a pair of denim dungarees, thick socks on her feet. She didn't look like anyone's grandmother, more like a senior civil servant along the lines of those dreamt up by John le Carré. Miriam Anne Ashe (Merry for short) was his dad's mum. Eighty going on eighteen.

'Seen much of your mum and dad lately?' She cut wedges of Wensleydale, adding it to the plates.

Joe pulled out a chair to sit at the table. 'Not in a while. You know how it is. Mum was on a retreat, last I heard. Dad's busy with his work.'

'That quarry's his happy place. He's a practical man, always was. Give him tools, things to do with his hands, and he's contented. Anything else . . .' She shook her head, excusing her son's long silence.

Joe wasn't a stone to be quarried or broken down, there was no practical solution to him. He'd survived what he should not have survived. Dad struggled with that. Mum too. In the end, it'd been easier to lose touch than to keep trying and failing to make contact. He stretched in the chair, working the day's stiffness from his shoulder. He'd been watching Merry make tea for as long as he could remember. When he was sent home from hospital, not knowing Sammi and the others had died, it was Merry who made him feel safe. His parents squabbled as soon as he was home. Fighting, he found out later, over whether it was better to tell him or keep him in the dark. He lay in bed listening, wondering what was so terrible no one would talk to him about it. His left shoulder was strapped; he had to keep the arm in a sling, take painkillers three times a day. If he forgot to take them, the pain was like a snake twisting itself tighter and tighter. He wanted to talk to Sammi about what sort of snake it was, boa constrictor or python. He hadn't worked out yet that Sammi was in his head. Mum cried when Joe asked if he could see him, Dad saying angry things about the school, the bus company. Joe couldn't follow what was said, partly because the painkillers made him foggy. A week after the crash, he took himself to Merry's cottage – 'I need to know what's going on, will you tell me what's going on?' – and she sat him with a cup of sweet tea and told him Sammi drowned, everyone on the bus drowned except him. It made sense of the pain in his chest which had nothing to do with the snake in his shoulder. When he told his parents he wanted to stay with Merry, they didn't put up a fight. In some ways they seemed relieved, as if they hadn't known what to do with him. All the other parents were planning funerals and memorials, while his were drawing curtains and looking furtive, even ashamed.

'I'll get in touch,' he promised Merry now. 'You're right. It's been too long.'

'Do what you think best, my darling. But don't go lonely.'

It was one of her sayings. She'd advised him, soon after the crash, to stop telling people about Sammi. She'd seen the way people stared at him, heard the whispers. For his own protection, she said, don't dig their dead.

Joe filled his mouth with cold apple pie. He hadn't come to talk about his parents. He'd come for peace and quiet, his head full of what they'd found in Paige Blackwall's old home. 'So Pru broke up with me.' His girlfriend of eight months.

'About fucking time.'

'Gran!'

'What? She was making your life hell, from what I can gather.'

'Well, in fairness—'

'Oh fuck fairness, kiddo. She was always too good for this place, wanted everyone to know it, too. Swanning around, nose in the air. That brother of hers is a nasty piece of work but at least he doesn't give himself graces.'

Merry thought magpies who failed to nest in the same tree twice were disloyal. Pru had escaped Edenscar briefly for university. When she broke up with him, she said she wished she'd stayed away, everyone here was stuck in the past, Joe included. He wasn't present enough, she said. There was some truth in that; hard to concentrate when half his head was taken up with Sammi, who saw his relationship with Pru as a betrayal. Sammi had never forgiven Merry for warning Joe to be quiet about the ghosts; he refused to come to her cottage even now.

'Good riddance,' Merry was saying of Pru. 'Now you can find yourself someone who appreciates you for who you are, not what you do.'

Joe finished his food. 'I don't mind being appreciated for what I do. Although from all accounts I'll have my work cut out impressing my new boss.'

'Laurie Bower? Another one who's only here under duress, I expect.'

'Meaning?' Merry had the inside track on everyone in Edenscar.

'Adam Bower was always a temporary fixture. Turned tail as soon as he could. Mind you, his dad was just the same. Peter Bower.' She said the name as if it left a bad taste in her mouth. 'Thought himself too good for us, set his sights higher.' She gave a grim little smile. 'Got his wings clipped for his troubles.'

'In what way?'

'Oh, I don't know the details.' She waved his question aside. 'A highbrow business venture that went awry. You'd think his son would've taken a warning from that, but he couldn't wait to get away.'

Joe had a vague memory of Adam Bower, who'd been in his late twenties at the time of the crash. 'Well, he's home now. Adam, I mean.'

'About time he showed his face. Imagine going to the trouble of training as a trauma counsellor and not coming home where you're needed.'

Edenscar, she meant. This brutal, brooding, blighted place. *Home*.

'Life's not as simple as that,' Joe said.

'Simple enough for you, wasn't it? You joined the police because you knew this place was in need of some law and order.'

'Yes, that is not why I joined the police.'

She ignored this, pinning her proudest look on her face. 'My grandson saw a way to make things a bit better for those of us who've no choice but to live here. And he stepped up. Now look at him, working all hours, coming home half-starved because he's never put himself first in his life.'

'I don't know who you're describing.' Joe drank his tea. 'But he sounds like an absolute arsehole.'

'DI Bower doesn't know how lucky she is.'

'We'll see. You don't know the couple who bought 28 Powderhill, do you?'

'Second-homers,' Merry said promptly. 'Why?'

'We need to be in touch with them. Someone broke in there.'

'Set a fire, did they? Or trashed the place?'

'No, not that. I can't talk about it, only wondered if you knew the owners.'

'Lawlor, that's the name. Cottage that backs on to the woods? Abby Blackwall's old place. In a mess, was it?'

Joe thought of the crossbow bolt quivering in the wall, oiled mantraps, dying rat. Paige's ghost counting down like a clock, dark patches of water spreading under her school shoes. 'It was a mess, yes.'

'One for your DI Bower to get her teeth into, then.' His grandmother started clearing their plates. 'I expect she likes a challenge. Can't see why she married Peter Bower's boy, otherwise.'

4.

Friday dawned like a Poundland apocalypse. Rain, wind and not a single shop open other than the 'General Store' that stocked six kinds of fruit cake but not batteries or hoover bags, and whose owner was pleased to tell Laurie, no they didn't have Wi-Fi and even if they did it wouldn't be free to anyone wandering in off the street.

'Is there a coffee shop somewhere? Costa, maybe?'

'You want to take yourself over to Edale for that.'

She really didn't. 'And you've no hoover bags?'

'Co-op in Bradwell, best bet.'

She'd wrestled the hoover from a cupboard in the house where Adam was waiting for Chris Miles to come and fix the dodgy wiring. *Wrestled* because her father-in-law had devised an under-stair assault course involving brooms and mops, walking poles, tennis rackets and worse. 'Seriously, Adam?' Holding up a shotgun. 'The safety isn't even on.'

'Well put it on, and stop pointing it my way.'

When she told him the gun wasn't loaded, her husband – *her husband* – replied, 'Never, never let your gun, pointed be at anyone. That it may unloaded be, matters not the least to me.'

'Does your dad have a licence for this?'

'I'll ask the girls, but I expect so. Everyone round here does.'

Laurie had stashed the gun in the boot of her car. Then she'd washed her hands at the sink before fixing Adam with her Salford Stare, the one she gave boys with knives and men who thought they'd try their luck because she was a woman and not bad-looking, at least according to that little scrote Chaz Lester.

'Next time you feel the urge to go full yokel, leave out the poetry, all right? I've enough to contend with, without that.'

Adam put a finger on the side of his nose: 'Keep your place and silent be. Game can hear, and game can see.'

At which point, she'd thrown a tea towel at his head, telling him he was lucky it wasn't the toaster, before heading out in search of civilisation or the part of it she needed to get online. It took forty-five minutes to discover 'full fibre' were words locals associated with breakfast, not broadband, and to decide she may as well head to work, which would presumably have an internet connection, even if it was single-digit megabits per second.

From the outside, the police station was grey-faced and breeze-blocky, with a jaunty dash of Tardis-blue. Touched up, Laurie suspected, ahead of a visit by the High Sheriff of Derbyshire. She could've talked for a week about the reasons why the High Sheriff (a role that should've died out a thousand years ago) was a waste of space and time, but since no one was likely to listen, she restricted herself to dark thoughts about the waste of money, before giving thanks for the fact Edenscar had a fully operational police station. Too few places had. No station meant no on-site custody suite, for starters. She'd heard every argument from budgets to bureaucracy, but the bottom line was that asking local police to transport offenders to Ripley or Manchester meant each officer had around two hours less per shift to do their job. As far as she'd been able to discover, Edenscar's station survived thanks to a local connection to the almighty police and crime commissioner himself. Who or what this connection might be, she'd yet to discover. With luck, she wouldn't be around long enough for it to matter, politics being her least favourite part of the job. Probably, Adam said, why she hadn't made DCI yet. 'Come on,' she'd argued, 'I'm not even forty-five yet.' That didn't wash with Rez, who'd made DCI when he was a year younger, although he put it down to positive discrimination – 'Not that my old mum minds, since it's got me where she wanted her first-born to be.' Rez was the best DCI she'd worked with. It made her furious to think he'd won the promotion because his mum's side was from Karachi. His dad's was from Kearsley, which should've evened the odds but didn't if you were a bigot, and there were still far too many of those in the police.

She parked in one of the station's bays, pulling down the mirror to check her reflection. *First impressions, Bower.* The face looking back at her was the one that'd asked for hoover bags and been given Edenscar's equivalent of the middle finger. She made the necessary adjustments, adding a swipe of lipstick. A nice face according to her mum, heart-shaped with light brown eyes and mid-brown hair, cut short despite Adam liking it long (she'd convinced him long hair was asking for trouble in her line of work, an excuse for offenders to pull her face into a kicking). Good teeth and bones. Great skin even with fine lines creeping in. She'd been lucky with her genes. She put up the mirror, taking her bag from the passenger seat. Too late to regret her choice of outfit and anyway, she regretted nothing. Jeans and biker boots, jumpers and jackets were the clothes she owned, the ones she wore to work. She'd hung a couple of suits in the wardrobe at Peter's place, but doubted she'd be wearing them.

The station was as grey inside as it was out. Also too hot, radiators eating a hole in whatever budget the local connection had bought or bribed from the PCC. No desk officer, and the door unlocked. Great start. She pushed through the swing doors, walking up a deserted corridor. More swing doors, into an open-plan space where operations presumably took place, unless six empty desks was normal. At the seventh, a young woman half Laurie's age was frowning at a monitor, oversized white headphones clamped across her head, one leg curled under her, the other dangling from the seat of her chair. Black tights, black Docs, a man's blue-and-white-striped shirt worn as a dress with an elasticated belt of the kind that carried shotgun pellets. Laurie, who'd been expecting some variation on Barbours and wellies, liked her on sight. Even more when she said, 'Fuck,' and dragged the headphones from her head. Dark hair, all fringe and undercut, eyes wide and black as a pony's. 'I mean, Hello?'

'Fuck's fine.' Laurie pulled out a chair to sit facing her. 'Don't suppose you were expecting anyone at this hour. Fort Knox at the front. Where's everyone?'

'You're . . . ?'

'DI Bower. You thought I was arriving on Monday. Don't worry, I'm not expecting cake and balloons.' She sat back as the young woman stood to attention. 'Well maybe Monday. But this way you get notice. You are?'

'DC Shaw, ma'am.'

'Good to meet you. Are you often on your own here?'

'Everyone's out at Powderhill. Well, Dash is. And he took Theo. Doubt Ted's out of bed yet.'

'Dash?'

'DS Ashe. Joe. And Theo's DC Howden.'

'Right. I'm Laurie.'

Her face cracked into a grin. 'Milla.'

Laurie had told herself, given how short a time she'd be here, the best approach was steely indifference, all formalities observed. She'd even resolved to submit to 'ma'am', if it meant the team keeping its distance. DC Milla Shaw made it tricky to be ma'am or even guv. *That's how they'll get you, Bower. With their stealth DC in her Docs and bullet belt.*

'Is DCI Saxton also in Powderhill? Where is that?'

'Out by the woods. Guv's headed over at some point, but he has meetings today in Ripley.'

Out by the woods could be anywhere around here. Laurie unpocketed her phone. 'What's the Wi-Fi password?'

Milla told her, adding, 'Powderhill's about twenty minutes north of here. I can give you a postcode, if you like?'

'How's DS Ashe going to feel about me wading in on his crime scene? I'm assuming it's a crime scene?'

'He and Ted were out there yesterday. Sounded grim.'

Laurie looked up from checking her emails. 'Bodies?'

'Just one. In the wardrobe, poor little bugger. Joe said there was nothing he could do.'

'A child's body?' She froze. 'In a wardrobe?'

'Oh god, no.' Milla looked appalled. 'A rat. Joe says there's traps all over the place, and Ted says he was nearly shot by a crossbow.'

Laurie listened as she related the story of DS Vicars' narrow escape. 'So, to wrap up. No one was hurt, and the house was empty?'

'Well, not empty. All these weapons and traps, like I said.'

'But no arrests. They're up there bagging evidence, hoping for prints?' She nodded at Milla's monitor. 'What're you doing?'

'Trying to reach the owners, boss. Mr and Mrs Lawlor, second-homers.'

'You get a lot of those around here?'

'Too many. At least according to Ted.'

The twinkle in her eye invited Laurie to make fun of Ted Vicars. 'A local place for local people?'

'He wishes.'

'And DS Ashe?'

Milla's expression became guarded. 'Dash is good. I mean, he's lived here all his life. But he's good.'

'Why *Dash*?'

'DS Ashe – *Dash*. Saves time. Better than the one Ted came up with.'

'Which is?'

'Britain's Most Haunted.' She pulled a face, grinning. 'Ted's a bit of a joker. You'll see what I mean when he gets here.'

'I'll try to contain my excitement.'

Powderhill really was out by the woods, in a shadowy scrub of land where the road fell off at the foot of the trees, tarmac giving way to pine needles, an outbreak of bracken. Laurie parked behind the unmarked pool car where police tape twitched in the breeze, the first sign of what she'd call 'normality' since she landed. Mist everywhere, smelling dank and dangerous, not unlike the quays on a winter's morning. Only two houses, neither in danger of exciting anyone addicted to property porn. She hid a shiver as she approached the fair-haired schoolboy guarding the door to Number 28. 'DC Howden? DI Bower.' She showed her card before he could ask to see it. 'Is DCI Saxton here?'

'No, ma'am. Just me and DS Ashe.'

'And the rat. How's it doing, do you know?'

'It's dead, ma'am. At least' – he frowned, not wanting to give a misleading answer to her question – 'I think so. Joe will be able to confirm.'

He looked about twelve, with a soft round face and soft blue eyes, and was that peach fuzz on his chin? Laurie was tempted to ask Saxton if he was child-snatching from the local secondary school. 'I'll head in. If you've no objections?'

'Of course, ma'am.'

He stood aside, eyes front. Laurie slid past into the tiny cottage, overstuffed with leather sofas, its expensive floors silent under her feet. In the doorway to the kitchen, a man stood with his back to her. A shade shorter than Adam and leaner, with a narrowness that said he was pure muscle under his clothes. She'd dated a gymnast like that once. Five foot ten, fantastic in bed. Well, the sex had been fantastic. Afterwards it was like trying to spoon an ironing board. 'DS Ashe?'

He turned, cool grey eyes fixing on her face. 'DI Bower?' He looked exactly right, in a mid-dark suit neither bespoke nor ill-fitting. Clean-shaven, dark hair cut short but not aggressively. Good-looking but not head-turning like DS Chaz Lester, that arrogant sod from Salford who got himself shot by a jealous husband and now worked in PR, pretending he'd taken a stand against police corruption rather than caught a bullet in his backside. Joseph Ashe looked as if bullets would bounce off him, that sleek muscle definition like body armour. Or else the bullets would halt in mid-air, *Matrix*-style, before falling at his feet. She'd never seen anyone with such striking gravity, as if he existed inside his own force field. She began to see how he might've held the whole of Edenscar in his thrall, even as a pre-teen. What was it Adam called it? *Emotional contagion*. She made a decision there and then, to be impervious. Bulletproof, the pair of them.

'I'm hearing something about a crossbow?'

'Yes. Sorry, is it ma'am? Or guv?'

'Boss, if you must. Ma'am if you want to piss me off.'

He processed this without blinking. 'Upstairs. The crossbow. Rigged to fire when the bedroom door was opened.'

'Nifty. But no one was hurt, is that right?' She waited to see if he'd claim credit for saving Ted Vicars from a bolt through his neck. This, according to Milla, was the story Vicars was putting about. Fitting, since he looked like something Dr Frankenstein had dreamt up after a long night short on sleep: skin in five different shades, mouth lined like a smoker's, teeth to match. Laurie had met him on her way out of the station. 'I was told DCI Saxton might be here?'

'He was. He had to leave for a meeting in Ripley.'

'About this?' Laurie nodded at the shattered window.

'About the next firearms surrender,' Joe said.

She thought of Peter's shotgun in the boot of her car. 'Lots of surrendering around here?'

'Less than you might think.'

'They should widen the scope to include crossbows.' She pushed her hands deeper into her pockets. 'Show me where the rat died?'

Joe led the way up the staircase. He nodded at the landing wall – 'The bolt –' then at the bedroom – 'The crossbow.'

Laurie registered how solid the bolt was before entering the room, circling the chair where the crossbow was mounted. She'd seen a few in her time, and more than enough repurposed shotguns to know this weapon was deadly. The fact it hadn't killed anyone (that they knew of) should have made it easier to look at than weapons that had murdered or maimed, but it didn't. She crouched to sniff at the rail between the riser and the stock at the rear.

'This was well lubed. The flight rail and the trigger.' She peered at the wire used to rig the bolt. 'Whoever did it meant it to land.'

Joe was tracking the wire between the trigger and door, studying the way it had scored the handle. He was seeing this scene for the third or fourth time, at a guess, but he kept looking. And he let her look without interruption, not feeling the need to put his stamp on her first impression. She liked that about him.

'Flight rail,' he said. 'That sounds technical. Are you an archer?'

'No, but my sister was. Won a few medals for it. Show me the other room?'

She blinked Isabel away. *Bulletproof, remember?*

The other room was worse in lots of ways. Laurie studied the heavy metal on the bed before opening the wardrobe to find the dead rat. The whole set-up gave her the cold creeps. More than that, it tweaked her antennae, the way a bedroom full of bullets would've done back in Manchester. 'TripAdvisor, one star.'

When Joe made no comment, she raised an eyebrow at him. 'You've seen this sort of thing before?'

'Most of it, yes.' He pointed to the spikes on the windowsill. 'Similar to bike traps set in the woods last summer. And rat traps shouldn't be used but badger baiting's been outlawed and that doesn't stop every farmer. Snares are allowed, for the most part. You'll see a lot of those.'

Laurie turned a slow circle, making a mental map of the room. 'Someone's coming to dust for prints, bag all this up?'

'Eventually. DCI Saxton's put in a request, but with no evidence anything was taken from the house?' Joe shook his head.

'That crossbow looks a lot like attempted murder, doesn't it?'

'Funding priorities, the usual thing.' He was studying the configuration of traps on the bed. 'We'll bag it ourselves, I expect.'

'Let's get to the station, see what DC Shaw's heard from the Lawlors.' She let a little Salford steel into her voice: 'And you and I can have a chat.'

Joe turned to look at her. She saw the fingers of his right hand twitch into a fist then flex to let the shape go.

'You're not telling me you haven't worked up a couple of theories already. You've the look of someone who's trained his brain to do that in his sleep.' She waited to see if he'd smile. He didn't. 'That's a compliment where I come from. Saves on overtime too, which should please DCI Saxton, or at least the PCC.'

'The PCC, perhaps. DCI Saxton didn't give the impression he was ecstatic about the situation here.' Joe scratched his cheek. 'The dead rat didn't help.'

They left the room for the landing.

'Saxton doesn't like rats? I thought that was a prerequisite for living here. Rats, sheep, pigs. Is that a bike in the bath?'

'A Trek Procaliber, yes.'

Laurie looked from the gleaming bike to Joe. 'You're a mountain biker?' It would explain the physique.

'Thefts over the summer.' He shook his head. 'The bikes ended up in the reservoirs, our job to fish them out.'

'Sounds like an exciting summer.'

At last, he smiled. 'We had a couple of wildfires, that spiced things up. One was on Saddleworth Moor. I expect you saw that from Salford.'

Not 'Manchester'. *Salford*. He'd been paying attention.

★

At the front of the house, DC Howden was standing like a tin soldier. 'Ted's got the evidence bags sorted,' he told Joe. 'He's on his way. I'll lend a hand.'

'If that's what DI Bower wants.'

DC Howden didn't look at Laurie, his round eyes fixed on Joe.

'Sure.' Laurie nodded. 'Stay and help. You can bring the pool car back when you're done. DS Ashe, you're with me.'

When they were in the car, she said, 'He *can* drive? How old is he?'

'Twenty-three.'

'He looks ten years younger.'

'I expect it's the fresh air.' Joe fastened his seat belt. 'A prerequisite of living around here.'

Her lips twitched. 'Was that a joke, DS Ashe?'

'It was an attempt at humour, certainly. Boss.'

'That reminds me –' she swung the car in the direction of the station – 'who do I have to kill to get a decent cup of coffee around here?'

'I'll get you one. Flat white?'

'Is that what they mean when they call you spooky? No, don't answer that.'

'I wasn't going to.' He was watching the road suddenly, his profile as taut as the rest of him.

The route back to the station took them between slices of woodland where fog rose like steam, trees breathing hotly in the day's chill. She ran the car's wipers. The weather at least was familiar, not that different to Salford, smash and grab sunshine at best. Joe was used to it, probably ran in the rain and mist, bathed in tarns, found his way across peat bog without losing his composure let alone a shoe. She'd managed to slip three times already in the yard outside Peter's place. She'd wanted to call Rez to hear him laugh – 'Imagine surviving four decades of Salford's worst winters only to end up flat on my arse outside a pigpen' – homesick for her city, its terraced streets and tower blocks, polluted sunsets, sharp eyes on every corner, warm hearts. Even those mean little bars where Isabel loved to drink and dance, dance and drink. She missed it. And all those secret, intimate details that made her good at her job. Out here, she was starting from scratch. Theo Howden knew more than she did of Edenscar.

At the station, she climbed from the car, springing the boot to pull out Peter's shotgun. 'Guessing you'll know what to do with this.'

Joe didn't bat an eyelash. He took the gun and pointed its muzzle at the ground, checked it was empty and left it open. 'Do you have the paperwork for this, by any chance?'

'Somewhere. Belongs to my father-in-law. I'll see what I can find.'

Joe handed the shotgun to the desk officer before following Laurie to her office where she perched on the edge of the desk, nodding at him to close the door. He was wary; it showed in the set of his shoulders. She wondered how much he'd been told of how she did her job, what he'd learnt online or from Saxton. Peter was a local man. No doubt everyone had an opinion about that, and about Adam too.

'Two of you despatched up there yesterday, according to Milla. Is that usual? Two detectives for a domestic?'

'More usual than not,' Joe said. 'DCI Saxton likes a police presence, makes people feel safer. If there'd been other priorities it might have taken a while before we got around to it. But if you're asking whether whoever set that trap knew we'd be the ones walking into it, I'd say yes, quite likely.'

She hadn't in fact been asking that. It sounded outlandish, but he used the same cool tone from before, when he was pointing out death traps. 'Bit of a stretch, but I'll bite. How long's that list? Many enemies out there?'

'More than enough. But I'm struggling to think of one with the patience or skill to pull off a set of stunts like that. It felt performative.'

'Yes it did. And where I come from that generally means a distraction. If we're stretching, tell me what else was going on here in the last couple of days.'

'I'm not aware of anything, but I'll ask Milla to take a closer look.'

'I'm guessing we need to factor in animal cruelty and how that tends to escalate. He's killing rats now, might go for cats or dogs next.'

'True,' Joe said. 'Although I should point out we get a lot of it around here, more than the national average. Rural areas do. Dog fights, cat cruelty, poaching. Not everyone ends up a serial killer, thankfully, or we'd be knee-deep in them.'

'What's DS Vicars' theory? He has one, I'll bet.'

'He thought it was kids, until the crossbow put paid to that.'

'Nearly put paid to him, way he tells it.'

She was pushing for a reaction, something to give her the measure of Vicars. But, 'It was a nasty moment,' Joe agreed, peaceably.

She got the impression he did that a lot: agreed for the sake of peace or to move things along. It made her want to shake him up. 'Is DS Vicars a lazy sod?'

When Joe blinked, she lightened it with a smile. 'Come on, help me out here. I need to get up to speed, can't waste time dancing around office politics.'

She watched him reconstruct the cooperative expression. 'Ted's a good detective,' he offered. 'I like working with him.'

'Bet you say that to all the detectives.'

'All the ones I've worked with.' His voice matched his eyes, cool as steel. 'It helps to be a team player, or so I'm told.'

They locked stares until Laurie found herself smiling again. Damn it, she'd always had a weakness for the ones who fought back. 'All right, next question. Do you trust DC Howden to make a proper job of bagging up that horror show?'

'If I didn't, I'd have stayed and done it myself.'

'Would you?' She put up her eyebrows. 'Seem to remember telling you to come back here with me.'

'I'd have found an excuse to stay. And you'd have let me. Because you might like a few shortcuts, but not when it comes to crime scenes.'

'Are you second-guessing a senior officer, DS Ashe?'

A tiny pause but this time he didn't blink. Fast learner. 'I've never second-guessed anyone in my life, boss. Just did my homework. You have a reputation—'

'Everyone has a reputation, detective.'

Tempting to hear what he had to say about hers, but it could wait. Work to do. He'd reverted to the neutral expression that had irked her earlier. She suffered a moment of vertigo, as if she'd been scaling his defences only to find herself right back where she started. She'd had more luck reading cops in riot gear.

'When's DCI Saxton due back?'

'After lunch, he said.'

'Right. Let's see how much progress we can make in that time.' She moved to the seat behind the desk. 'Check in with DC Shaw about the Lawlors, see what progress she's made. And let's get the neighbour in, find out about this prowler.'

'That could be tricky. Mrs Buck doesn't like to leave her home.'

'None of us likes doing that.' Too prickly. She made herself smile.

Joe wasn't falling for it. 'I'll see what I can find out about the crossbow, if you're happy for me to pursue that?'

'Knock yourself out.' She began opening drawers in the desk. 'Hand me that biro?' He did and she used it to fish a face-mask from the bottom drawer, dropping it in the bin. 'Any point asking you about DI Broomfield?' whose desk she was raiding. Extended leave, some gossip there. But she'd asked the wrong man, her question bouncing clean off him. 'Forget it. I'll ask DC Shaw.'

After a beat of silence, Joe said, 'DCI Saxton will be able to give you the information you need. We're a small team—'

'You're *my* small team for the foreseeable.' Opening another drawer. 'This isn't going to work if we're being mysterious with one another.'

'There's no mystery. I just feel it's unfair to put Milla in that position. Not conducive to team relations.'

The chilly way he said it brought a flush to Laurie's cheeks. 'You need to wind your neck in, DS Ashe.'

'Yes, ma'am.' He'd not forgotten what she'd said about pissing her off; he was using *ma'am* to deflect, wanting her attention off Milla. *Protecting* Milla. As if Laurie were a threat; it raised every one of her hackles.

'You've one another's backs, that's evident. And I'm only here for half a year, but if you'd really done your homework' – she returned the biro, mucky end first – 'you'd know I can make a lot of trouble in six months. Just so we're clear.'

'We're clear.'

5.

Joe waited until Ted was back from bagging up Powderhill before he headed out to Middlestone Hall. Hard now to believe the hall, built in 1765, had been about to fall into disrepair when Nelson Roache swooped in to save its bankrupt owners. The purchase made local headlines, 'Hero of the hour'. Merry was among those who applauded Nelson's loyalty to his home town. 'Mind you,' she told Joe, 'he always was a canny one.' When he asked her to elaborate, she told him to stop being a detective and eat the cake she'd baked him.

Middlestone Hall had two entrances, both involving long crunches of gravelled drive, timber gates, stone pillars. Visitors were treated to glimpses of sunken gardens and summer houses, wide lawns, acres of parkland. Inside, the place rang with echoes, front door opening into a hall large enough to house the whole of 28 Powderhill. Joe had been coming here since before he joined the police. The hall was too grand to feel welcoming, although cleverly concealed central heating meant it was warm even on a winter's evening. The real welcome came from Nelson, who was never less than pleased to see Joe, even when he came, as today, in the guise of Detective Sergeant Ashe.

'How are you, Joseph?' He led them into the green drawing room where a fire was lit. 'You're looking well, if a little tired. Magnus working you hard?'

'Always.' Joe returned his smile. 'But it's what I signed up for. How are you, sir?'

'Very well indeed. Sit down. You'll have coffee?' He was already pouring it from a cafetière on the sideboard.

'Thanks. It's kind of you to give me your time, especially at short notice.'

'My door's always open for you. I thought that was understood.' He put the cup and saucer into Joe's hands, settling in an armchair.

At seventy-four, he had the broad shoulders and powerful build of a much younger man. Six foot with a full head of greying hair, beard cut square like a sailor's, wearing cords, checked shirt, tweed jacket. He'd been born in a house smaller than 28 Powderhill, to a father injured out of work and a mother who died while he was a child. His grandfather worked in the last of the coal mines to operate in the Dark Peak. Nelson did reasonably well at school, stratospherically well after leaving aged fifteen to start his own business: a mail-order company selling rare books and antiques bought as bargains in house clearances. By the age of eighteen, he owned two local shops, and had since opened more in Sheffield and York. His daughter, Maggie, had been Joe's favourite teacher. Photos of her were all over the house. In the one on the desk at Nelson's side, Maggie was aged about eight, dressed for horse riding, standing with her hands behind her back, chin tilted at the camera.

'How can I help?' her father asked Joe. 'You have your detective face on. I'm guessing this isn't a social visit.'

'The cottages up at Powderhill. Do you know them?'

'Near the woods?' Nelson cradled the cup and saucer in his large hands. 'No trouble, I hope?'

'We found a number of traps, improvised weaponry. I wondered if you could put me in touch with Tom Sangster.'

Sangster was a local historian, and an expert in IEDs. He spoke passionately in support of the firearms surrender, and knew a great deal about medieval weaponry.

'Tommy's in Italy, I think.' Nelson reached for his phone. 'I can message him your number?'

'It's good of you, but not urgent. Let me ask DCI Saxton first.'

'It's important, I can see from your face. Whether or not Magnus agrees, let me message Tom. You came for my help, let me help.'

'You heard him, Joe, let him help.' Sammi was on the fireplace fender seat, his elbows on his knees, chin in his hand. He liked to tease Joe about coming here, calling Nelson his 'inside man'. 'If DI Bower could see you now.'

Joe shook that image away, accepting a second cup of coffee. The room was comfortable, the weather locked out. He and Nelson talked for a time about nothing of importance. Nelson was a close friend of the police and crime commissioner, Alan Worricker, but even had he not been, Joe would've stayed away from police business in Middlestone Hall.

'Because you're an idiot.' The fire gave Sammi a rosy halo, almost angelic but for the scowl he was directing at Maggie's dad. 'What's the point of having an inside man if you don't empty him out?'

As he was leaving, Nelson said, 'I'm told you have a new boss. DI Bower? Quite the reputation, from what Alan Worricker says.'

'So I'm led to expect.'

'It's good for Peter Bower to have his family close at this time. A diagnosis like that can tear a family apart.'

The pair of them crossed the reception, footfall echoing on the stone tiles. Joe was always surprised he sensed no ghosts here. He'd have liked to see Maggie but never had, here or elsewhere in Edenscar. Nor Mr Edison, nor the bus driver. Only the kids haunted him, and Sammi, who was his age now. 'Old enough to know better,' Sammi agreed. He was pacing, keen to leave. For whatever reason, Middlestone Hall put him on edge. Maybe *he* saw ghosts. Joe had never asked him.

Nelson paused to deadhead one of the roses on the hall table. 'These're flowering late this season. I'd take the credit, but my gardeners deserve that. The impetus for rewilding was mine, however. They weren't convinced at the outset, not as easy as it sounds to make space for wilderness, I'm told. But it's paying dividends at last.'

Outside, he indicated the garden sprawling to their left, where the lawns grew long and unruly, threaded with wildflowers. 'Always a war out here, between us and nature. We should know our place, don't you think?' He held out a hand, eyes twinkling in a smile. 'How's your grandmother, Joseph? You'll give her my best? She was always the one we boys were chasing. Peter Bower and Terry Doyle, all of us. Merry Tadwell, that minx. I was three years younger than Peter and Terry, didn't get a look-in. She ran rings around the lot of us. Remember me to her, won't you?'

He always ended their chats with this request, as if Joe might've forgotten to pass on his last message, or as if Merry was often on his mind.

He turned the pool car in the direction of the police station, stopping when he reached the huddle of houses at the bottom of the valley, where he parked up to stretch his legs. 'Joe . . .' Sammi's voice was full of caution.

'Just a look, that's all. Three minutes. Then I'll get back, see if Laurie's managed to put Saxton's back up yet.'

'Nelson had stories about her. You should've asked him, he'd have shared.'

'Unprofessional, though.'

'You need all the help you can get. She's going to ride you, otherwise.'

They'd stopped at the top of the road, looking down at the garden shed where they'd set up camp when they were seven. A third of the garden was orchard now, branches burnished by plums, the remains of an old treehouse half-hidden by leaves and fruit. 'Remember when we—'

'Shut up,' Sammi said softly. 'Bad enough you keep bringing me here. When're you going to give it up, Joe?'

'When I'm ready.' He leant into the fence, looking at his best friend. Sammi stood with his face tipped to the afternoon's sun. Not the boy of eleven who'd danced at the bus stop, warned him it wasn't brave to be stung by a tarantula. A man of his age, brown-eyed, beautiful, and dead. 'You're staring.'

'No one out here to notice.'

'Yes there is. Dad's right there.'

Joe turned towards the garden, seeing Adrian Torre raise a hand. 'All right, you're right. Come on.' He began walking, ignoring the protest from behind.

By the time he was at the front door, Sammi's dad had come up the path, brushing soil from his hands. Even in his gardening clothes, Adrian was neat. Not expensively turned-out like Nelson, but quiet and tidy in old moleskin trousers and a navy fisherman's jumper. In his late fifties, slim and fit, greying at the temple. He didn't look like his son for the simple reason Sammi had been adopted by Adrian and Anna Torre when he was four years old. They'd loved him for seven years before losing him to the reservoir that lay east of their house, just beyond the bend in the road. 'It's good to see you, Joe.'

'You too. How are you both?'

'We're well. We don't see as much of you as we'd like.'

'I'm sorry, work doesn't always make it easy to get up here.'

'Yes, we're out on a limb, rather.'

His eyes went over Joe's shoulder but he wasn't seeing Sammi, just the slope of road that ended in the water. Joe wondered how they were able to stay so close to where it happened. His parents had done the same, but their son survived. A shadow moved inside the house, curtains swinging at the window. Sammi's mum wouldn't come out, wouldn't even look at him on those rare occasions when they met in the street, or the shops. As far as he knew, neither of the Torres saw their son's ghost. For Sammi's mum, Joe was a painful reminder of what she'd lost, her grief compounded by guilt. Had they not adopted Sammi, he'd still be alive.

'Take care, won't you, Joe?' Adrian reached for his shoulder, sensitive fingers resting for a second before he released his grip.

'I will, thanks. You too.'

Back at the pool car, Sammi was waiting, eyes narrowed at the unlit stretch of woodland that marked the horizon. 'You feel it too, don't you?'

Joe watched the wind bear down on the tops of the trees. A hedge-cutter was at work somewhere; he smelt the split green scent of broken branches. 'I feel it,' he told Sammi. Someone or something out there, waiting. Whoever set those traps in Powderhill. Or a bigger danger, as yet unseen. Crouched and clawed, bloodthirsty between the trees.

6.

In the station's evidence room, Laurie considered the bags brought back from Powderhill. The traps weren't any friendlier sealed inside plastic, the crossbow looking like a mail-order murder weapon. Ted held up the bolt dug from the wall. 'Doesn't look much, does it? But it nearly had my eye out.'

'Yes, you said. What did you do with the rat?'

'Ice box.' He nodded down at what looked like a family-sized picnic box with a jaunty red stripe up the side.

'Where's DS Ashe? Said he was chasing down a lead on the crossbow.'

'Could mean anything round here.'

She was starting to wonder if there was a local word for *urgency*, if maybe she was pronouncing it wrong. 'If you had to hazard a guess?'

'He might've gone over to Yeaveley . . .'

Like questioning a farm animal. 'What's in Yeaveley?'

'Big estate. Shooting, archery, that sort of thing.'

'How far from here?'

'An hour, give or take.' He drummed a tune with his hand on the ice box. 'Hovercrafts, too. Took my sister's kids in the summer.'

She'd be gone by the summer, thank God. 'Get hold of him, will you? And find out when DCI Saxton's due back.'

'Lunchtime, boss. We could go to the pub, grab a beer and a bite, meet the rest of the team? We promised we'd keep the guv's pew warm until he gets back.'

Proximity to the dead rat hadn't put a dent in Ted's appetite then. 'Another time. Let me know when you've worked out where DS Ashe is.'

Back in Broomfield's office, Laurie told herself she could've handled that better, but she didn't waste time regretting her decision. Adam had texted to say his dad was coming home from respite care a day earlier than anticipated – 'Any chance you can pitch in?' She told him she'd do her best. She stood where she could watch Milla work, her fingers a blur on the keyboard. Ted wasn't at his desk, presumably in the pub. She pulled on her jacket, heading in Milla's direction. 'Anything new?'

'Not yet, boss. Left a couple of messages for the Lawlors. Trying the letting agency now. Friday's changeover day so they're bound to be busy.'

Laurie asked. 'Where's Joe, do you know?'

'On his way back from Middlestone, boss.'

'Not Yeaveley?'

Milla wrinkled her nose. 'Why'd he be in Yeaveley?'

'Why was he in Middlestone?'

'Nelson Roache lives there. He's a big deal, locally. Lots of connections. Good for opening doors, you know?'

If Roache was the link between this station and the PCC, she needed to ask DS Ashe why he'd spent the last two hours sucking up to the local palm-greaser. 'Friend of Joe's, is he?'

'Everyone likes Joe.' Milla's phone rang and she reached for it. 'Mr Lawlor, thanks for calling back. I've a few questions about your property in Powderhill?'

Laurie was tempted to stay, but didn't want to make Milla self-conscious, knowing she'd bring her an update as soon as she had one.

'DI Bower?' From the corridor. DCI Magnus Saxton didn't look overly surprised to find her here three days before the start of her service. Suited and booted, fading fair hair brushed back from a wide forehead, ice-blue eyes. She could see where the nickname had come from. Every inch the Edale Viking. 'We weren't expecting you until Monday.'

'Thought I'd show my face, guv.'

They shook hands. Saxton's grip was chilly from the outdoors, but friendly enough. 'Have you had lunch?'

In the Tollgate, Ted was tucking into a sandwich with a side order of onion rings and a pint. Saxton raised a hand in his direction, nodding Laurie towards the snug at the other end of the bar. 'I'm assuming you've met DS Vicars?'

'And DCs Shaw and Howden, yes. Also DS Ashe.'

'You've been busy. What'll you have? My treat.'

'Whatever you'd recommend. And a Diet Coke, thanks.'

She found a table in the snug. The bar was a hammered length of brass sporting rubber beer mats: Beavertown, Buxton, Brewdog. A tap for Brixton pale ale, another for Neck Oil. All of which she could smell, to varying degrees. She hated these places. City bars were bad enough but it was in a local like this she'd lost Isabel, started to lose her. She blinked, focusing on the clientele. *Come on, Bower, let's see those detective skills at work.*

Magnus Saxton was trusted, well liked. Of the four men at the bar, three were relaxed around him, shoulders down, pints in hand. Farmers, from the look of them, ruddy-faced and weather-beaten in hard-wearing clothes. The fourth man was unhappy with life in general and Saxton in particular. In his thirties, brickie build, tough-chinned. Could've been bravado, but Laurie didn't think so; she'd seen a lot of bravado in her time. This man wasn't afraid of being seen, might even welcome the chance to flex his muscles. In a pale hoodie stained with what looked like brick dust but might've been dried blood. A job in an abattoir? Jeans, trainers. Reddish hair scraped into a short fringe, which, with his long oval face, gave him the look of a thuggish monk. Brother Buckfast.

Saxton returned with the drinks and a dimpled pint glass of cutlery. 'Food's on its way. Fish and chips, since it's Friday.' He settled into the seat opposite.

They'd spoken before, of course, when this relevant service was first being negotiated. Rez said Saxton was a good man. Well, he said he'd heard only good things, which wasn't the same but a fair indication in Rez's case, given how close to the ground his ears liked to be. Saxton had brought two Diet Cokes. She suspected he was an ale drinker like the locals, didn't want her uncomfortable. Or he knew about Izzy. Decent of him, either way. They chinked glasses and drank.

'How're you settling in? You're up in Peter's place, I think?'

'That's right. Still sorting out the broadband.'

'Ah, that's why you came into work early. Not just for the lay of the land.'

'You got me.' She put up her hands. 'But it's been good to meet the team.'

Saxton drank a mouthful of Diet Coke. 'What d'you think?'

'Early days, obviously. I wouldn't want to make any assumptions.' She could've used a visual cue but he wasn't giving her anything other than a look of polite curiosity. 'DC Shaw seems very capable.'

'Very. She'd be our tech wizard, if the tech was up to scratch. As it is, most of her wizardry comes in the form of cranking up the hardware at dawn so we can check our emails before midday.'

'Sounds familiar. Salford could use her skills most mornings.'

'DC Howden – what's your verdict there?'

She returned his smile. 'Much too early for verdicts. Still hearing opening statements.'

'You aren't going to ask if he's as wet behind the ears as he looks?'

She was saved from answering by their food being brought to the table by a woman of her age who set the plates down with a wide grin for Saxton and a nod for Laurie. 'Any sauces-ketchup-vinegar?'

'All of the above please, Liz.' Tucking in, Saxton said, 'You've had plenty of time to come up with a diplomatic answer to my question.'

'*Is* DC Howden as wet behind the ears as he looks?'

'Not remotely. Highest score of his intake year, and determined to make a success of it. Underestimate him at your peril.'

'Grateful for the warning.' Laurie ate a chip with her fingers. 'Anything else I should avoid at my peril? Overtime requests, that sort of thing?'

Saxton shook vinegar over his plate. 'I'd like to promise you less paperwork than Salford but you know how it goes. You said you'd met Ted?'

'Briefly.' She ate a forkful of fish. 'Seems solid. And comfortable. Not a criticism. Every team has someone like that.'

Mostly men, but she kept that thought to herself. If it wasn't for all the men too lazy to go after detective inspector, she'd have had a harder fight on her hands to get promoted.

'That leaves Joe, then.' Saxton sat back, wiping his mouth on a paper napkin before reaching for his glass. His smile was more serious than before; they'd reached the crunch point in the conversation.

Inevitable, really. Not only was Joe a local celebrity, he was the best detective on Saxton's team by a country mile; that'd struck Laurie as soon as she'd seen him at work in Powderhill.

'I like him. A cool head, from what I saw.'

Saxton hid a look of relief by reaching for another chip. 'Very cool. Best DS I've worked with. Smartest, too. He's headed for great things. DI by the time he turns thirty, mark my words.' Pushing hard, in case she'd fallen for the local gossip.

'Looking forward to working with him. What's the story with Nelson Roache?'

His eyebrows went up. 'You work quickly. What've you heard?'

'Only that he's helpful from time to time. Joe was over there this morning. After we'd been looking at what was found out by the woods.' She ate mushy peas messily, wiped her chin. 'In Ordsall, we'd call it a cache.'

'Oddsall?'

'Spelt Ord, pronounced Odd. Something we have in common with this place.' She realised as she said it that she'd put a foot wrong. Not *we* and not *this place*. She was here in Edenscar for the foreseeable, needed the locals as relaxed around her as they were around Magnus. Well, all except Brother Buckfast at the bar there, watching with the narrowed eyes of a snake.

Saxton twisted in his seat. 'Des Morton. Have you met?'

'Not had the pleasure.'

'You may find you want to defer it. If you get the choice.'

Laurie picked up a chip, resisting the urge to use it in lieu of a middle finger in Morton's direction. 'Des looks intimately acquainted with the custody cells. Or is it me?'

'It's not you.' Saxton crunched batter between his teeth. 'If you think he's unfriendly now, wait until he sees you in Joe's company.'

'What's he got against Joe?'

'An imagined grudge. He's not the only one. I'm hoping you brought your famously sharp wits with you.' Saxton fixed her with his Icelandic stare. 'We may look like a sleepy backwater but looks, as I'm sure you know, can be deceptive.'

7.

In Powderhill, Sandra Buck opened her door with a smile for Joe and a look of sharp suspicion for Laurie. 'Who's this then?'

'Detective Inspector Bower.'

Joe didn't need to prompt his new boss to produce her card for Sandra's close inspection, although he did wonder what she made of the Lawlors' diminutive neighbour in her velour tracksuit and *faux* Ugg boots, miniature bull terrier on a rope lead. Nancy was a muscular white dog with one black eye and a striking egg-shaped head who stood about thirty-five centimetres tall, weighed thirteen kilos and hated visitors. This should have made her a good watchdog but Nancy refused to bark or growl, preferring to communicate her hatred with her eyes, which were small and crimson and contained all the furies of hell.

'She's going deaf,' Sandra said. 'Didn't hear you knocking. I'll lock her in the back. Then I suppose you'll want to hear about what I saw across the way.'

'Number 28, yes. We really need your help there.'

Sandra scooped Nancy into her arms, nodding them inside the house. When she was out of earshot, Laurie asked, 'Who shrunk Bill Sikes's dog?'

'Bull's-eye,' Joe said.

'Are you agreeing with me or . . . ?'

'That's the dog's name in *Oliver Twist*. Bull's-eye.'

'His girlfriend was Nancy, wasn't she?' Laurie pulled a face. 'The one he clubbed to death. Nice choice of name for the dog.'

Joe watched her weighing up the front room with its dirty floor and shabby furniture. The three-bar fire was switched off but still managed to give out a smell of singed fur. White had not been a good colour choice for the sofa. Half-eaten dog biscuits added to the carpet's mad swirl; Nancy had digestive issues. Not long ago, Sandra had called the station in a flap about the burglar who broke in to defecate all over her kitchen. He'd been tempted to delegate that one to Theo but Sandra insisted she needed Joe, so he and Theo came armed with rubber gloves and crime-scene masks to clear up Nancy's mess. He wondered what Laurie would say about that particular use of police resources. Or the fact Sandra had several times been cautioned about nuisance phone calls, the nature of which Joe had no intention of sharing. Laurie was bound to run Sandra's name through a database when they were back at the station, in any case. Best to leave her to find out for herself.

'Coward,' Sammi grinned against his ear. 'Oh look, biscuits.'

Sandra had returned with a tray which she set down, tucking herself into an armchair. Her velour tracksuit, child-sized, was flesh-pink with rhinestones. 'Drink up.' Her voice, deep and distinctive, was one of the reasons she shouldn't make nuisance phone calls, or not to the police.

Joe handed a mug to Laurie, taking the other for himself. The tea was the colour of pina colada and tasted of what it was: watered-down milk. 'We're hoping you can tell us what you saw. You saw someone moving around inside, on Wednesday?'

'Place's empty for weeks on end. Houses need people in them, else they'll turn to damp. Stands to reason.'

'When was the last time you saw the Lawlors?'

'Summer.' Sandra dug herself deeper into the chair. 'She's no better than she ought to be, and he's daft thinking sunflowers'll grow in that garden.'

Joe left a pause for Laurie to ask questions. When she stayed silent, he took it to mean she wanted him to lead. That was the tactic they'd discussed on the way over here, Laurie having established he'd drawn a blank at Middlestone Hall — 'Still, nice to spend time with local royalty' — fixing him with that city stare of hers until he had trouble sitting still. He'd never squirmed in his life but she brought it out in him, without any perceptible effort on her part. 'Like itching powder,' Sammi said.

Not much chance of Sandra squirming, with her attention firmly on Joe. 'You're looking thin.' Nodding at the biscuits. 'Keep your strength up, pet.'

'Take one for the team, Joe.' Ginger nuts were Sammi's favourite biscuits.

Joe took one from the tray. 'Can you remember what time it was that you saw someone in the house?'

'Late. Closer to nine than eight. I was waiting for Nancy to finish her business. Takes her longer and longer with all the rats down from the forest. It's why I wanted to talk to them. Their rubbish's a disgrace, all dumped in the same bin, no proper lid. Never seen so many rats, all these years I've lived here.'

'Was there a car parked up on Wednesday?' Joe asked. 'Or a van?'

'Just the usual car,' Sandra said airily. This was the first time she'd mentioned a car.

'And what's that?' Laurie asked. 'The usual car.'

'You know the one.' She flapped a hand at Joe. 'Always parking where it shouldn't, getting towed.'

Sammi straightened, alert, snapping his fingers at Joe.

'I'm not sure I do know,' Joe said. 'Can you remind me?'

'Oh, you *know*!' Sandra giggled coquettishly.

He'd been praying she wouldn't do that. Laurie shot him a look like the crossbow bolt, landing with roughly the same impact. 'Should've ducked.' Sammi was watching Sandra. 'Walk her back.'

'Forget the car for a minute. Tell us what you saw in the house. The lights must've been on, if it was after dark.'

She creased her face. 'I don't think they were, come to think of it.'

'But you definitely saw someone inside the house.'

'Oh I definitely did. You can tell her majesty that, straight up.'

'Her majesty?'

'Her ladyship, if she prefers. That's what Teddy's calling her.' She gave Joe a wink as if they were the only two in the room. 'Lady Bower.'

For a second, the air felt frozen. Sammi gave a long, low whistle of incredulity. The only thought in Joe's head was, *That was fast work, even for Ted*, before he pulled himself together.

'DI Bower needs your statement as the witness to a crime. We're

51

taking it very seriously. Please extend us the courtesy of doing the same.'

Sandra turned such a vivid shade of pink she clashed with her tracksuit. It was Laurie who saved the situation. 'How long have you lived here, Mrs Buck? A few years, I expect. It's a lovely house.'

'Forty-two . . .'

'Forty-two years. I wasn't much more than a nipper then. And Joseph wasn't even born. You'll have seen some changes in that time.'

'More than you'd think.'

'Tell me about this car on Wednesday?' Laurie fell into a comfortable rhythm, extracting answers from Sandra like a magician pulling coloured handkerchiefs from a very small, tightly sealed pocket.

'Shouldn't even be on the road. Untaxed, I'll bet. Teddy says they ought to take it for scrap.'

'DS Ashe?' Laurie asked. 'Whose car are we talking about?'

'Des Morton's, I imagine. Des is—'

'Brother Buckfast.'

Joe blinked. 'I'm sorry?'

'*Brother Buckfast.*' Sammi laughed. 'She's funny. You've never had a funny boss before.'

'He was in the pub earlier.' Laurie's tone was arid. 'DCI Saxton pointed him out. Make and model?'

'Black Golf GTi. Convertible, late eighties, collectable by now if he hadn't driven it into the ground.'

'It's in a right state,' Sandra agreed. 'Half the roof ripped away, last I saw.'

'And this was on the Wednesday just gone?' Laurie levelled a glance at Joe. 'Parked outside Number 28?'

Sandra's face screwed into a walnut as she fished for the memory. 'Didn't I mention it when I called the station?'

'Not then, no.'

'There *was* a car. And someone in the house. Nancy heard them. She'd have been barking, if she could.'

'She can't bark?' Laurie said.

'Vet says no reason why not but she never has. Doesn't mean she's not a good watchdog. You should've seen her hackles go up. If I hadn't put her on the lead, she'd have gone for whoever climbed out of that window they smashed.'

No one at the station had mentioned the broken window to Sandra. 'You've been over to take a look?' Joe asked.

'Too right I have. Need to know what I'm up against, don't I? Teddy says there's all sorts in there. Traps, you name it.'

'Teddy should keep his own trap shut,' Sammi said.

Joe was fairly confident Laurie was thinking the same thing. 'You didn't hear the window being broken?' she asked Sandra.

'No . . .'

'And all this was Wednesday?' Joe said. 'You've not seen or heard anyone in the cottage since then?'

'Only you and Ted, yesterday. And DC Howden. That poor lad still misses his sister, sticks out a mile. No wonder he stays close to you, pet.'

Joe kept his expression neutral, aware of Laurie's close attention. She'd have armed herself with the facts when she heard she was going to be working with him. 'That's a waste of good paranoia.' Sammi wanted to be searching for a back route into Powderhill. Whoever brought the crossbow and traps came quietly, unseen and unheard. Through the woods, Joe was sure of it.

'Prove it,' Sammi challenged him.

When they left Sandra's place, Laurie stood for a time looking at Number 28. The forest crowded behind the cottage, treetops like teeth. What was left of the light hung from the windows like pale yellow blinds.

'Check one thing, quickly?' Joe started towards the cottage.

Laurie glanced at her watch, aware of the promise she'd made Adam to try to be home in time to lend a hand with Peter. 'Use your words, detective.' She strode after Joe. 'What're we looking for?'

'Whatever broke that.' He pointed at the boarded-up window. 'A branch, or a pole. We ruled out bricks.' He dropped his stare to the ground, following the traditional pattern of a sweeping search, tracking right, towards the woods where there were plenty of branches, most of them attached to trees.

Laurie joined him. 'You think someone did it on purpose? *After* they laid those traps, rigged the crossbow. They didn't break the window to get into the house. They did it on the way out. To be sure the police would be called?'

'There isn't any way a crossbow fitted through a window this size, let alone a mountain bike. They had a key. Either the one from under the rock, which we've bagged with the rest of the evidence, or a copy.'

Joe was at the foot of the trees. Within the next hour, it'd be too dark to search without floodlights. Laurie missed the city's light pollution. It never got properly dark in a city. Not like here, where the darkness never really retreated.

'Didn't we have this discussion earlier? Too much of a stretch, isn't it? Whoever did this wanted the police inside the house, that's what you're saying. One of you with a bolt through his neck.'

'It nearly happened,' Joe reminded her.

'In Salford, we keep tabs on who hates us enough for a stunt of that kind. Who's top of your list? Des Morton? Assuming his car was out here. Actually, scratch that. Let's look at theories that make sense, shall we? The assassination angle has too many holes in it. And don't say *like Ted's neck nearly did*.'

Joe was busy shining his phone's torch into a dense fist of bracken. 'Hold this, would you?' He handed her the phone, pulling gloves from a pocket and reaching a long arm into the bracken to extract a slim pipe with a dent in its middle.

'What's that?'

'A skim stalk. Attaches the skim point and mouldboard to a plough.'

Laurie didn't understand more than two of those words, but she knew a weapon when she saw one. 'Looks handy.'

'It would be, in the wrong hands.' Joe angled it to demonstrate how neatly it could've been used to smash the window. 'In the car?'

'Boot. Use a couple of carrier bags to keep it clean for SOCO.'

Joe deposited it according to these instructions, stripping off the gloves and pushing them into the opposite pocket to the one he'd taken them from.

Laurie turned a slow circle on the gravelled death trap that passed for a driveway. 'So someone sets up that agricultural assault course, dumps a pricey bike, then breaks a window to be certain it gets reported and investigated. Who'd go to that kind of trouble? And how'd they get inside? All very well saying they had a key but presumably that limits our suspect pool. Tenants, cleaners; I want to know who's been here in the last six months, and how they feel about the police.'

'All good questions,' Joe agreed.

'Here's another one: who'd know how to rig a crossbow like that? I wouldn't. Would you?'

Joe shook his head. 'That crossbow's old, an antique. I'm hoping our local weapons expert can shed light on that. Tom Sangster.'

'Friends in high places?'

'It helps, sometimes. Let's see if it's of any use in this case.'

Laurie looked back at the woods, wondering how empty trees could feel more threatening than a council estate full of criminals. 'You believe in this car, last Wednesday? Des's car?'

'Not readily. Sandra would've mentioned it when she made the call to us.'

'Makes a lot of calls to the station, does she?'

'Quite a few, yes.' His tone didn't change, but Laurie was learning Joe could be a closed book and an open one at the same time, at least where the locals were concerned. She'd learnt a lot watching him with Sandra Buck. The care he took to put her at ease then the snap in his voice when the woman strayed into the minefield of Ted's nickname; Joe had Sandra on a shorter lead than the one on her own dog. Ted was going to catch it from both directions tomorrow, Joe more pissed off about the nickname than Laurie, and she wasn't exactly overjoyed.

'I thought *Teddy* was her favourite. But it's you, isn't it, pet?'

'Were you to waste time examining the call log, you'd find she's overfond of requesting my presence, yes.' Joe rolled his left shoulder. 'She's lonely.'

'Few marks for modesty, and none at all for being soft-hearted. I like my detectives like you lot like your rocks – granite.'

In the car, Joe fastened his seat belt. 'You were fairly soft with her yourself.'

'Tactical. She wasn't going to give me anything while she was making doe eyes at you.' Laurie fired the engine. 'Does that dog of hers really not bark?'

'If she does, I've never heard her.' Joe was scrolling on his phone. 'Milla says the Lawlors don't own a bike. The letting agency's sending over a list of recent guests.'

'Let's see if one of them's an expert archer. Wouldn't that be nice?'

'It's an idea,' Joe said politely. Wishful thinking wasn't his style, or hers.

She catalogued what she'd learnt over the course of the day. Magnus Saxton had been keen to impress on her what a great team she had here, possibly because he'd figured out what it meant for a city-bred DI to find herself dumped where the sharpest knives were served in dimpled glasses in the local pub. Ted Vicars was going to be a pain in her arse. *Lady Bower*. She'd show him how ladylike she could be. All because she wouldn't go to the pub with him. She thought of nights out in Salford at the end of a shift, or when a case closed the right way. *Camaraderie*. That's what Ted wanted, a shortcut to a decent working relationship. Hadn't she been looking for shortcuts herself? Still, it rankled. *Lady Bower*. Milla was more her cup of tea, savvy and smart. Saxton said Theo was sharper than he looked, which'd better be true. All these sweet young things with their bright eyes and shiny noses did her head in. In Salford, they were called HVPDs. High Voltage Partial Discharge. She wasn't looking forward to working with Theo. Apart from anything else, the kid kissed the ground Joe trod on.

Which brought her to Joseph Ashe, currently seated alongside her in the car whose suspension was nursing a noisy grievance. Sandra had the hots for Joe, not unusual in little old ladies living alone, although in Salford they tended to be cheekier about it, copping a feel when they could. Joe had known how to handle her, known the name for that improvised weapon stashed in the boot. Every place had its secret language, a way of holding strangers at bay. Salford was no different to Edenscar in that regard, although the smaller the place the tighter the ranks, in her experience. Edenscar had every door locked shut, that's how it felt, Joe her best chance of unlocking them. Trouble was he'd stashed the bloody key under a rock, hadn't he? That cool grey stare of his repelling unwanted questions. He'd had his fill of celebrity by the time he turned twelve, which was fine by Laurie, who'd had her fill of detectives who loved the limelight. She could've done without the strong silent act, even so. 'You've gone quiet on me. Tell me what you're thinking.'

'This has been a long day for you,' Joe said dutifully. 'Given you weren't supposed to start until Monday.'

'Stop sucking up.'

'I wasn't aware I was, boss.' He wound his neck in, fast.

'Forget it. Long day, like you said. Where can I drop you?'

'Anywhere you like, but we should put that skim stalk into evidence.'

'Station it is, then.'

8.

Adam was outside when Laurie parked up, looking like he hadn't slept in a week.

'Sorry, time ran away with me. Is your dad here?'

'The girls are getting him settled. Helen had to bring Rory straight from school. Could really have used your help, Lore.'

She locked the car. 'I'm here now. What can I do?'

'Help me fix supper for six? Dad's got the idea we're all here for a celebration. Easier than trying to explain to him, again, what's really going on.'

Laurie walked with him to the porch. 'What've we got in?'

'Sod all, but Esther's on her way from the Co-op, with Bella.'

Bella was Rory's age, a pair of pre-teen cousins. Laurie hadn't seen them in four years, between work and precious holidays with Adam. In the sitting room, she found Rory stuffed in an armchair, in thrall to his phone. She'd remembered a skinny boy with freckles. This lad was big, with hair that skated scarily close to a mullet, and a mouth he had difficulty closing by the slack way he was mouthing along to the phone; she heard the familiar irritation of a TikTok soundtrack.

'Hi, Rory,' got her nowhere. She followed Adam into the kitchen. 'Where're we going to eat?'

'Back room. God, I hope Es brings wine.' Adam sent an apologetic smile across his shoulder. 'Sorry, I'm going to need that tonight.'

'Go ahead. I'm guessing the kids'll want Diet Coke. I'll have some of that.'

'How was work? Is it going to shake down okay?'

He needed her to say yes, not even to qualify it. A simple, emphatic *yes*. He'd enough uncertainty to deal with right now. She gave her best smile. 'It's going to be great. Why don't you freshen up? I'll deal with supper when Esther gets back. Take a moment.'

'Thanks, I could use one. It's been worse than I was expecting.' Adam gave a small gesture of pain. 'He hardly knows me, Lore. I knew it'd be tough but he's angry, disappointed, I don't know. Horrible.'

'Let it go.' She pulled him into a hug. 'Breathe, yes?' When he started to relax she turned him towards the stairs. 'Take as long as you need.'

'Es is running late. Was the traffic bad?'

'No, but the roads are terrible. Potholes deep enough to dive in. Don't worry about supper. If it comes to it, we'll steal a pig from next door.'

He laughed, like her husband again instead of the shadowy-eyed stranger who greeted her on the doorstep. A spasm of guilt gripped her for having abandoned him so soon into their new lives. *Do better, Bower.*

Esther arrived with two bags of shopping: everything needed to make shepherd's pie from scratch. She couldn't have done them all a favour and bought the ready-meal variety (the Co-op did a decent one) to save time and sanity? Laurie unloaded the bags into the fridge and cupboards. Watching Esther chop onions, she was reminded of the last time they were in a kitchen together: a failed attempt at New Year's Eve that'd left Laurie wishing she'd accepted the glass of champagne Peter pushed at her all evening. Seven years ago, not long after she lost Isabel. Laurie had made no secret of her sobriety, still adjusting to the idea that grieving for her sister was going to be a lifetime's work. New Year's Eve felt like a slap in the face, Peter's expensive champagne pinging its pale bubbles inside the flute he pressed into her hand – 'Just a sip to see in the New Year' – and she was tempted, not to please him but because she'd been made aware over the course of the day that she'd never please him, no matter how happy she made his son. The champagne wasn't a treat or a celebration. It was a test. To see if she was like her sister who drank herself to death, loudly and messily. Izzy spent the last year of her life crashing from crisis to crisis, hostile phone calls to family members, doorstep confrontations, stealing from her own family and Adam's – a meteor burning through everything, lighting it all up with her rage and sadness. 'One sip won't kill you' – Peter's eyes like marbles loose in their sockets. It'd crossed Laurie's mind to wonder if he was unwell, but she'd said nothing. Now here they all were, Peter dying a slow death and his youngest daughter weeping, either from the onions or with grief. 'How can I help?' she asked Esther.

'Peel some spuds? Where's Addy?'

'I told him to take a break, freshen up.'

Esther's eyebrows went up at *I told him*, as if Laurie had used an obscenity. Good wives didn't tell their husbands what to do, certainly not after they'd been absent all day. And never under their father-in-law's roof. 'Are you looking forward to starting work on Monday?'

'I am, yes. They seem a nice bunch.'

'They are.' Esther's smile was tight-lipped. *Insider knowledge*, the smile said. *Local* knowledge.

Laurie told herself to stop being a bitch and show some sympathy. 'I'm sorry about your dad. It must be so hard.'

Esther scraped onion into a pan where butter was browning. 'Bella and Rory have been knocked for six. Bella, especially.' She rinsed her hands in hot water, rubbing her fingers on the tap – 'Gets rid of the onion smell' – before shaking them dry. She was a big woman but the easy way she moved around the kitchen made Laurie feel clumsy. 'Save those peelings. They'll be glad of them next door. I'm sure Addy said, but we're pretending we're here for a party. White lie, easier for Dad. We'll likely be doing it a lot.'

Laurie's teeth clenched. She'd had her fill of lies while Izzy was alive. About why Laurie never went to the pub any more, why the car keys weren't where her sister left them, why Laurie was taking time off work to hang around Izzy's place, how she should loosen up and what was fifty pounds anyway to a *detective*. She reminded herself of Adam's stoicism during that time – the worst of her life – and renewed her vow to help him now. Sweeping potatoes into a pan, she added water and salt, set it on the rear of the stove before Esther moved the pan forward. 'This ring's better.'

Six months of passive aggression; get used to it. She gave Esther her best smile. 'I'll check on Adam, then lay the table.'

'Bella's laying the table. She's a good girl.'
'She's great. Be right back.'

Adam was sitting on the edge of their bed, on his phone. Laurie closed the door and slid behind him, wrapping her arms around his chest, her legs around his waist.

'I love you –' she kissed his ear – 'Adam Ross Bower.'

He closed the phone down quickly, but not before she'd seen what he was studying: statistics on dementia, rates of decline, life expectancy.

'Hey.' She kissed his neck. 'I've got you. You know that, right?'

Adam rubbed the phone on the leg of his trousers before setting it aside, sliding until he was under her on the bed, Laurie straddling his waist. 'Put your hands on me,' she instructed.

Adam flexed his fingers at her hips. 'What're these, chopped liver?'

'Gross. But even so, put them on me.'

'How's supper coming along?'

'I peeled the spuds. Esther's hit her stride so I said I'd get out from under her feet and look after you.'

Adam's hands pushed inside her shirt, until a sound from the next room made him tense. Helen's voice, murmuring. Laurie wondered what it took to keep Peter calm, realising she had no idea. Her husband's head was turned towards the wall, his whole body rigid with listening. She wanted to pull his hands against her bare skin, kiss the shadows from his eyes, bring him back from *their boy* to *her man*. If she hadn't cut her hair, she'd have let it down, remembering how he used to pull on it, gently but firmly, until their lips met.

'We should help downstairs,' he said.

'It's all under control. Esther and Bella—'

'No, Lore. Come on. They've been doing it for months. My turn. It's why we're here, remember?'

'Tough audience.' She eased off, pulling the bedcovers straight, wishing she'd brought their duvet. Peter's bedding was slippery, felt like a fire hazard. She was gripped by a desire to be in the woods with Joe, hunting for discarded plough parts. Anywhere but here in this too-small house where she felt outnumbered and underqualified for the task she'd signed up for. She picked a pillow feather from Adam's fringe. 'Go and chat with Rory. I'll give Bella a hand with the table.'

Adam nodded, his eyes downcast, phone back in his hand. His socks were mismatched, one blue, one black, like a child who'd dressed in the dark. How many hours in six months? She was tempted to pull out her phone and check, but decided she didn't need the extra gut punch. *Buckle up, Bower, it's family time.*

After Adam's sisters and their kids left, Laurie thought it would be easier, just the three of them. Adam insisted on doing the dishes – 'You stay and chat with Dad' – a plea in his eyes as he left them together, Peter staring at Laurie – 'Who the hell are you doing here?'

Who not what. *Your son*, she was tempted to quip, *the one doing the washing-up because he's had enough of your temper for the night.* It would've been cruel, drawing attention to his mistake. Instead, she did her best to mirror Helen's calmness. 'Adam and I are staying for a while. We don't see enough of you. I'll try not to get under your feet. We're here to help.'

'Help with what?' He peered at her. 'Who the hell are you?'

'I'm Laurie. Adam's wife.'

He pointed. 'Adam's in the kitchen.'

'He is, yes. Would you like a cup of tea?'

'I'd like a glass of wine in my own bloody house.'

Helen had warned them to keep the wine out of his reach. It didn't mix with his meds, or his moods. 'No wine, sorry. I could get you a ginger ale. Or a coffee?' Decaf, but he didn't need to know that.

He thumped the table with his fist. 'I'll go up the place myself.'

'The Co-op? It'll be closed now. It's late.'

'This isn't late.' He snorted. 'Plenty of day in it yet.'

How was she going to get him to bed with none of Helen's knowledge or Peter's trust? Frightening for him to feel among strangers in his own home. Family gatherings always filled her with horror, raising the spectres of failed interventions, the pattern repeating until that last time, one final phone call before blue lights circled her sister's shattered life. She felt a sudden panicky urge to see the city, to be anywhere but here in the middle of nowhere with this man who didn't like her, even if he'd forgotten why. He hadn't forgotten, though. She was wrong about that. As she began folding the cloth from the table, he leant forward, screwing his face into an insult. 'I know you, you little bitch. Who you are. Adam'll know too, when I'm ready to tell him.'

9.

Joe was cooking supper when his phone rang. Unknown caller. Sammi craned his neck at the screen. 'Don't pick up, you're off duty.' But Joe wiped his hands and took the call. 'Hello?'

'Joseph? Tom Sangster. Nelson asked me to call.'

'Mr Sangster, thank you for making the time for this.' Joe turned off the heat under the rice. 'Sorry to disturb you on your holiday.'

'Not a holiday. I've a house over in Italy, we've been putting it to bed for the winter this past fortnight, catching some late sun while we're at it. Nelson said you'd found a weapons cache?'

'That's right. At least, very little of what we found was weaponry in the strict sense. But there was a crossbow, fairly old. Home-made, at a guess.' Joe sketched a few details. 'Rigged to fire a bolt when a door was opened.'

'A booby trap?' Sangster sounded intrigued. 'Was anyone hurt?'

'Fortunately not. I was wondering if you could help me understand how easy it is to rig a crossbow in that way?'

'Depends on a number of factors. I'd need to see the crossbow in question.'

'I'm assuming it's not common knowledge, setting that sort of booby trap?'

'Well, yes and no. It depends how dedicated one is to doing such a thing. Finding the information isn't difficult. My website, as just one example, has a rather neat set of notes around that precise subject.'

'Rigging a crossbow?' Joe said in surprise.

'Any number of improvised weapons. Historical details, to be clear, but anything from victim-operated devices to command-operated via a pull string, say. A few timed explosive devices up there, too; you'd be surprised how long those have been around. Any century you fancy putting your finger on will throw up something deadly and ingenious. Certainly a crossbow or two in that mix.'

'I don't suppose your website has a paywall? Or a subscriber base?'

'Afraid not. I couldn't monetise that sort of thing, haven't the technical know-how apart from anything else. It's a hobby, for other hobbyists.'

'Does it get a lot of traffic?' Joe asked.

'It used to. Let me send you a link so you can see for yourself. Might be worth getting your tech team to dig around, see where the traffic's coming from, how much of it's local.'

'Thanks, that's going to be helpful. I appreciate you making the call.'

'Always happy to do Nelson a favour. He speaks very highly of you. I've no doubt you'll get to the bottom of this quickly.'

When the call ended, Joe returned to the kitchen, impatient for the ping from his phone – Sangster's text about the website. He didn't have to wait long.

Keep Your Distance was a serious endeavour, its detailed content easy to navigate, organised by century and weapon type. Joe started searching, only stopping when Sammi said, 'Will you please eat something? You're making *me* hungry.'

Joe set the phone aside and finished the meal he'd intended as a Thai curry but which became tinned tuna and rice, for speed. As he ate, he scrolled the site, making notes. He found a short historical account of how in 1760 a crossbow was rigged using wire and a door handle, a black-and-white sketch showing how it was done. Not quite the blueprint for Powderhill, but not far off. Sammi said, 'DI Bower's going to want Sangster in for questioning.'

'Unlikely, since he's been in Italy for the past fortnight.'

'He wanted you to know that. *This past fortnight*. Odd, don't you think?'

'He didn't need to call me if he was being evasive.'

'Nelson told him to. People tend to do as they're told by Nelson Roache.'

'That's true.' Joe was deep into the website.

'I mean, look at you.' Sammi's voice was innocent. 'What was it DI Bower called it? Sucking up to local royalty.'

'She'll be doing it herself soon enough.'

'Doubt it, not the type. Not Nelson's either, come to that. Can you see her on his brocade sofa?'

'Can you shut up and let me concentrate?'

Sammi was silent for a time, stretching his long legs under the table at Joe's side. He'd kept his distance while Pru was here, although not always. In the end, she'd accused Joe of still being in love with his best friend.

'You were in love with me, weren't you? I was in love with you.'

'You're right about Sangster.' Joe thumbed through his notes. 'I'll need him to take a look at that crossbow.'

'Joe.'

'Mmm?'

'Is this going to be a problem? I thought Pru not being here would make it easier.'

'Did you? I didn't.'

He set the phone aside, looking at his dead friend. The light sat on Sammi's shoulders and shone from his eyes. The realness of him was shocking. Joe would never get used to it. Never. The others might've been made of water from the way the light passed through them. Paige and Zoe, and Ellie Howden. All in his mind, a symptom of his guilt and grief. Sammi too, but that was harder to accept because he was so real. And because no one but Joe ever saw him.

Theo Howden was the first to say he saw ghosts too, pointing at Joe's side – 'Ellie's with you.' His sister. Theo was just a kid at the time, twelve years old. Joe was sixteen, hadn't mentioned the ghosts to anyone in a long time. 'She's with you –' pointing – 'Ellie,' and Joe denied it but Theo kept saying it. He must've said it to others too, because suddenly Molly and Tyler's mum was seeing the twins, and Hannah Cooper was seeing Zoe, and everyone was staring again and whispering about Joe. When Merry asked what'd happened, he said, 'It isn't me, it's them,' which Sammi took badly, staying away. At first, Joe was glad. He just wanted to be normal, or as normal as a sixteen-year-old with complex PTSD could be.

But he quickly began to miss Sammi, ended up begging him to come back.

'We can do stuff now Pru's gone. Talk, whatever . . .'

'We've been through this,' Joe said. 'I have to work, I need a clear head. Not even for work – to stay the safe side of a psych ward. I'm not supposed to see you, or anyone. I'm meant to be one hundred per cent recovered. No complications. Regular health checks.' He rolled his left shoulder. 'You know all this.'

Sammi rubbed his thumb at a scorch mark on the table. 'I miss you, that's all. Thought you missed me too.'

'Every day. But there's nothing I can do about it, is there? Not if I want to stay sane. You wouldn't want a madman for a best friend, would you?'

'Zoochosis,' Sammi murmured. 'Animals in captivity get depressed and anxious. Most zoo-kept animals are on antidepressants. They executed Tip the elephant in Central Park Zoo, with cyanide.'

'The things you know.'

'The things *you* know.'

'Conceded. Help me concentrate?'

He ran an internet search for Thomas Sangster which uncovered among other things a history of wild game hunting. Locally, but also in Poland. Joe blinked when he saw Sangster's name paired with Nelson's on the trip advertised as 'Wild Boar Trophy Hunting' and described as 'thrilling and formidable'.

'The wild boar,' Joe read aloud, 'also known as the "king of the forest", is a challenging, intelligent and worthy adversary, requiring skill, strategy and precision to track and bring down. A true test of a hunter's abilities.'

Sammi hummed the tune from *Psycho*'s shower scene. 'Hello, Thomas Sangster.'

'And Nelson was with him.'

'You know, he didn't actually say he was in Italy right now. *This past fortnight* might've been past tense. Decent solicitor could get him out of that, no problem.'

Joe zoomed in on the two men with their sickening 'trophy'. Big smiles, lots of blood. Pints of blood. 'You have to wash with special soap before you go on a hunt of that kind.' Sammi was feeding him facts from the backroom of his brain. 'Scent and sound are enemies of the hunt. Macho ritual bullshit.'

A shot sounded, a mile to the west, then a second, soon afterwards.

Joe lifted his head, listening. The sound, at a guess, had travelled from Higher Bar Farm where Chris Miles lived with his young family. Chris had a firearms licence; not the first time Joe had heard shots fired from up there. He shut the laptop, sitting in the sudden silence. 'Sammi?'

Sammi was gone, not scared so much as vanquished, Joe's head emptying him out so he could focus on the gunshots. A common noise around here, but he never got used to it. Never wanted to; the day he ignored the sound of shots would be the day he stopped being a detective. The silence retreated into the normal soundtrack of Friday night, but Sammi stayed away. Joe missed him, the loss a nagging pain under his ribs. He tidied the kitchen before climbing the stairs to his bedroom, looking west from its window towards Higher Bar, wondering why he had the feeling tomorrow was going to bring trouble. Saturdays were generally peaceful in Edenscar. The kids took themselves off into Sheffield or Manchester. Too soon for Laurie to be back at the station, unless she decided to put in another impromptu appearance. Too soon to see the Lawlors or the letting agency. So why was the back of his neck pricking, his thumbs along with it? He couldn't get that website image out of his head: Tom Sangster and Nelson Roache kneeling either side of the bloodied, gored head of a boar. Laurie would call a strong stomach a *prerequisite for living around here*, and she'd be right. He'd seen worse things, even if he couldn't remember beyond a smear of white faces, branches grabbing at the bus as it rocketed into the water.

'You let go, Sammi. I lost you.'

He leant his head against the window, thinking about the shed at Sammi's old house, the look on Adrian Torre's face when he wished him well, the warm weight of the man's hand on his shoulder. The photo by Nelson's armchair of Maggie dressed for riding. How Laurie stared at the skim stalk before telling him to put it in the boot. Sandra saying Des's car had been in Powderhill when it was up on bricks the last time Joe saw it. Tom Sangster saying he'd been in Italy for the past fortnight when Joe hadn't asked for the information. Something in all that disturbed him. He wished Sammi would return so they could talk it over, find whatever was hiding in the day's work. Left to his own devices, Joe was a decent detective, methodical, precise. But it was the instinctual stuff that made him exceptional. Sammi was pure instinct.

From the window, he watched high beams in the west, travelling down the hill from Higher Bar. The car turned north when it reached the junction, taking the road away from Edenscar towards the distant glow of Manchester.

10.

The sound of violence had Laurie tumbling from bed. *Bin day*. Taking away the fallout from the weekend's family meals. The rusty edge of a storm in the air, like a blade. Monday, at last. Lorries faded into the noise of the farm next door. Adam stirred, turning towards her with a confused look. 'Lore?'

She kissed him. 'Pigs.'

'Morning to you, too.'

Joe and Milla were already at their desks, Milla smothering a yawn with a bagel – 'Boss'; Joe saying, 'One of these is for you,' holding out an insulated cup of coffee. Double-walled, copper-coloured steel, the kind of reusable cup she'd have bought herself. She took a sip. Flat white, strong enough to wake a sleepy koala. 'Thanks. Anything exciting on the horizon?'

Joe stayed on his feet. 'Another neighbour reporting a disturbance. Up at Higher Bar Farm. I'm heading that way, if you'd like to come?'

'Love to. But I'm in a meeting first thing, with DCI Saxton.'

'Of course. In that case, I'll take Theo.'

'Who lives up there?'

'Chris and Odette Miles, and their baby Eric, which might account for the disturbance. The neighbour was a little unclear on the detail.'

Another Sandra Buck, in other words. Laurie didn't blame the neighbours; there was so little to do around here she might start making nuisance calls to the police herself. 'Chris is an electrician, isn't he?'

'That's right. Do you know him?'

'Adam does. They were at school together. He's meant to be fixing our wiring this morning. How long's it going to take to free him up for that?'

'I haven't been able to get hold of him, or Odette, but that's not unusual on a Monday. Early starts for everyone.'

'Well, try not to delay him. It's driving me up the wall having no Wi-Fi.'

'I'll do my best,' Joe promised.

Ted rolled up shortly afterwards with Theo, who'd been busy in the evidence room, bringing records up to date. When the team was gathered, Saxton made formal introductions – 'Most of you had the pleasure of meeting DI Bower on Friday' – before inviting briefings about the day's work. 'There's something new in evidence? From Powderhill?' He looked to Laurie for an answer.

She could picture what Joe had found in the bracken, couldn't remember its name. In Salford, they'd have called it 'pipe improv', any weapon fashioned from a piece of pipe.

'Skim stalk,' Joe said into the silence. 'We think it may've been used to break the window at Number 28.'

'Correction.' Laurie felt wrong-footed, going on the defensive. 'DS Ashe thinks that. I'm yet to be convinced.'

She met Joe's grey gaze across the room, conscious of the others judging the tension between them, Ted mouthing *Lady Bower* at Milla.

Joe said peaceably, 'It's just a theory at this stage.'

'And Mrs Buck? How much help was she?' Saxton smiled at Laurie. 'Or did she rub you up the wrong way? She's a habit of doing that.'

'Except Joseph here.' Ted gave a dirty laugh. 'She'd love to rub you up any way she can. Right, Romeo?'

Joe laughed along with the others. Saxton steered the conversation to the Lawlors, the team's attention switching to Milla. Had Laurie not kept her eyes on Joe, she'd have missed the look that came and went in a heartbeat and made her aware, again, that there was a hell of a lot more to Joseph Ashe than he let people see. The 'Romeo' joke was old, but it stung. He must've sensed her attention because he looked up, meeting her eyes with an impartial expression that dared her to ask him if he was okay. She didn't have time to waste puzzling over who the real Joe was, but nor did she like the idea of not knowing what to expect when the pair of them were in the field together.

A literal field, in all likelihood; she needed a proper pair of walking boots.

Saxton was saying, 'What about the car seen outside Number 28?'

Laurie was able to answer this: 'Golf GTi, convertible, eighties model. Des Morton's, we think.'

'Ted can take that one.'

'Right, boss.' Vicars cracked his knuckles. 'Been a while since I had an old ding-dong with Des.'

'How was your weekend? Did you do anything nice?' Theo smiled hopefully at Joe as they headed out to the pool car.

'I saw my gran, on Sunday.'

'She'll have liked that.'

Joe didn't reply because Theo didn't mean Merry. He meant Ellie, his dead sister. He'd convinced himself she was a permanent fixture at Joe's side; he begged him not to go running up at Ladybower Reservoir – 'She hates it there' – as if Joe could feel any more responsible for what happened. He didn't know what to tell Theo half the time, other than to keep his thoughts to himself around Ted and the others. Laurie too, now. Luckily Sammi was there: 'Get a grip. Higher Bar Farm.'

Joe let Theo drive, so he could check his texts. Nelson had been in touch – 'Tommy says you're all set' – so he replied to that with thanks. He'd prepared notes he could share with Laurie, checking these for typos or colloquialisms, anything likely to wind her up.

'Cars are still here.' Theo pointed. 'I'll have to park on the verge.' He did, settling the car's tyres into the deep grooves left by a tractor.

The farmhouse stood alone at the end of a dirt track, a three-bedroomed stone-built house that shouldered the winds coming down the Derwent Valley, multiple drainpipes running the rain from its roof. Two cars were parked in the driveway: Chris's white Nissan and the green Honda Odette drove. Bobby German, who'd reported the disturbance, lived in a semi-detached at the other end of the track, some distance from the Miles's front door.

Joe turned that way, seeing smoke trailing from Bobby's chimneys. No smoke from Higher Bar's. Its windows gave back the sky's glare, washed with cloud. He was aware of a familiar percussion in the rear of his skull. Theo was waiting for him to make a move, face blankly expectant. Joe wanted to tell him to wait in the car, but he couldn't. They had a job to do. 'Come on.'

Up the path to the back door; everyone used the back around here, better to track mud across quarry tiles than carpet. The farmhouse had a short stone step to its windowless door. Inside, Joe knew, a narrow hall led to the kitchen; he'd been in the house, but not recently. A garden rake was propped at the side of the door, the exterior wall newly pointed in places where Chris was working to keep the weather out. Rain had a habit of finding its way through most structures around here.

Joe knocked on the door, waited. Silence, like at Powderhill. No, not like that. This silence was sticky.

'Gloves,' Sammi said.

Joe unpocketed a pair, pulling them on while Theo watched, frowning. He tried the door and it opened, the smell sending him back a pace.

Theo's face was white at his shoulder. 'What *is* that? Joe?'

A gun fired twice, on Friday night. High beams taking the road away from here, towards Manchester, or Sheffield.

'Go back to the car,' he instructed Theo. 'Find tape, secure the scene. All the way from the gate. I'll call it in, as soon as I know what it is.'

'But it's . . . just a disturbance. Isn't it?'

'Go to the car. Find the tape. Secure the scene.'

'Don't,' Theo said. 'You'll scare her. Joe, please. Don't take her in there.'

'DC Howden.' He used his least flexible voice. 'I need you securing the scene. From the front gate. You're in charge of making sure no one comes in who isn't police. Can you do that?'

Theo turned on his heel and went.

Sammi stayed with Joe, the pair of them staring at the kitchen door. Joe knew the layout, had sat with Chris and Odette drinking tea last summer after Chris reported his bike missing from the garage. The kitchen had a red quarry-tiled floor and blue walls, a range. Pine cupboards, matching table and chairs. A traditional farmhouse kitchen, with sophisticated lighting because Chris was an electrician. And dead. Joe knew he was dead, from the smell alone. Everyone in here was dead. He took out his phone, brought up the number for the station and opened the door into the kitchen.

For a second, the body on the floor seemed to reach for him, stretching one blackened arm until it dissolved in a fizz of flies that rose, seething, from the chest cavity. The body lying across its legs was no better and in some ways worse, a wet spill of blond hair around a deep head wound where more flies were walking, delicately.

The call connected. Milla said cheerfully, 'Dash, what've you got?'

'Two bodies. Chris and Odette Miles, by the look of it. Both dead.' He stayed where he was, conscious of preserving the crime-scene. 'We need everyone here. Forensics. Sal Thomas. The whole lot.'

Milla didn't waste time asking questions; she hung up so she could make the necessary calls. Joe pocketed the phone, moving his stare from the floor to the rest of the room. The table was laid for supper, three places, two chairs, a third with a booster seat strapped to it. Where was Eric?

'Dead,' Sammi said. 'Murder weapon?'

'This wasn't an airgun.' Joe was looking at what was left of the back of Odette's head. 'Shotgun, by the look of it.' He glanced at the table. 'Nothing's been knocked over, or smashed. No struggle. Where's Eric?'

'Dead,' Sammi repeated. 'Back door was unlocked. No forced entry. They let whoever it was in. They knew him.'

'Or he was already here. Or she was. Where's Eric?'

'Murder-suicide?'

'Maybe. Doesn't look like it, though.'

'Doesn't it?' Sammi scanned the room. Joe, watching him do this, made a mental note to be certain he wasn't seeing Sammi when DCI Saxton arrived. He had to assume Saxton would come, unless he despatched Laurie. 'Something to get her teeth into,' Sammi agreed.

'Stand down, would you?'

'Better check on Theo.'

'I need to find Eric first.'

'No one's alive here, Joe. You can see that – *feel* that.'

'Even so, I need to check upstairs.'

'You'll have to cross the floor to do it. That's Saxton's crime scene.'

'Doesn't matter. Eric's more important.'

But Joe was already retreating, knowing he could find a way upstairs through the front of the house without walking his footprints all over the kitchen.

Outside, Theo was standing by the tape he'd tied across the front gate. His fists were clenched like his face. 'Joe?'

'Help's on its way. Stay there.'

The front door was locked, solid. Half-glazed and ultra-modern, mortice deadlocks. No sign of anything unusual in either of the front rooms. Baby toys on the floors, but no blood. No Eric, either.

Joe strode back to the kitchen, calculating ways in which he could minimise the impact of his path to the stairs. He could no longer see Theo, thought he'd gone into the house, then spotted him on the verge with his head between his knees. He crouched close. 'Just breathe. Four-seven-eight, like in training.' He breathed with Theo to make it easier: in for four seconds, hold seven, exhale eight. He could hear sirens on the road below. 'The team's coming. Try to be on your feet for that.'

'Where'll you be?'

'Inside.'

'Don't. Joe, *please*—'

'Keep breathing.' He stood, stepped away. 'And do your job, detective.'

Joe was in the kitchen when Laurie joined him. 'What's wrong with DC Howden?' she demanded, her quick stare scanning the scene.

'His first time with dead bodies.'

'He seems to think you're the one with the problem, told me to take you out of here. Said it wasn't safe.'

'Do I look as if I need to be taken out of here?'

She scrutinised him. 'No, you look good.'

'Let's operate on that principle then.'

She nodded, turning her attention to the bodies. 'Tell me what I'm looking at.' She winced, correcting herself: '*Who* I'm looking at.'

'Chris and Odette Miles, almost certainly.' Face down, but he recognised the watches and rings they each wore. 'They have a one-year-old. Eric.'

'Have you looked for him?'

'Not upstairs.'

Laurie stared at him. 'Why the hell not?'

'Front door's locked. Staircase is that way.' He pointed across the slaughterhouse floor. 'I don't have the right crime-scene clothes in the car.'

'A child's safety takes priority, don't you think?'

She was deeply pissed off. He didn't blame her, couldn't say what he was thinking, what he *felt*. That Eric, if he was in the house, was dead. Joe and Laurie were the only living people here. She turned on her heel and walked out, down the hall and into the garden, taking up the rake in one gloved hand.

Joe followed her around the side of the house, watching as she used the rake's handle to break the lower pane of the front door. It took effort, the glass reinforced. She reached inside and threw the locks, pushing the door wide. 'Stay here' – she handed him the rake – 'until I say otherwise.' Her voice was chilly.

Joe wanted to defend his decision, but he kept silent. She was the senior officer. Her crime scene, not his. He waited as she went up the stairs, one gloved hand on the baton in her belt.

Time ticked by. More sirens, further down the valley, a full team on its way. The silence unsettled him. A blur of light on the staircase moved like water. He stepped inside, shattered glass creaking under his boots. Footfall overhead. Then Laurie was coming down the stairs towards him – 'I told you to stay outside' – and he took another step, smelling lake water, fierce black rot from the kitchen. Laurie's face was pale in the half-light. 'DS Ashe. I need you to stay down here.'

Joe looked past her, to the stairs. 'Eric?'

'Yes.'

'In the bedroom?'

She tidied the cuff of her shirt, keeping her eyes on his. 'The bathroom.'

A toy dinosaur sat halfway up the stairs, purple tail turned to the wall. When Joe climbed a step towards it, her voice tightened. 'Stay where you are, please.'

'Tell me.'

She searched his face before nodding. 'He drowned. In a foot of bathwater. You don't need to see that. Let me look after him. You stay down here.'

Laurie waited until Joe was outside before she let herself feel the impact of what she'd found upstairs. That poor little baby. She'd been furious with Joe for failing to search for Eric the second he saw the bloodshed downstairs, but he'd been dead at least forty-eight hours. The whole family had. She stood breathing their deaths, wishing for her team from Salford. Not that sickly boy by the police tape. And not Joseph Ashe, who'd prioritised a pristine crime scene over a vulnerable child. She walked through broken glass back into the fresh air. No sign of Joe. When she reached the kitchen, he was using a tablet to record details of the scene. All right, then.

'Tell me what you see.'

'Shotgun fatalities. I heard a gun being fired up here, late on Friday.' Joe didn't look up, recording a clean sweep on the tablet. 'Assumed it was Chris shooting at vermin. Everyone does it out here. Everyone with a farm, licensed firearm. Two shots. One after the other, perhaps twenty seconds between the two.' He turned to face her. His eyes were dark, mouth wrenched with regret. 'This looks as if it might be two days old but I apologise, for Eric. You're right, that should've been my priority.'

He'd been with DC Howden, she bet. Making sure the kid didn't faint. He'd never admit that, though, too much of a team player.

'You couldn't have saved him, not today. No one could.'

Joe's gaze flickered then switched back to the scene. 'No gun here, unless it's under one of the bodies. Back door was unlocked. No defensive wounds that I can see, but it's hard to tell.'

'One for the pathologist,' Laurie agreed. 'Who will it be, do you know?'

'Sal Thomas, if we're lucky. She's the best around here.'

'When's the last time you saw something like this? Here in Edenscar?'

'Never,' Joe said. 'Bodies, from time to time. But road or farm accidents. Elderly people living alone. Wholesale slaughter? Never.' He frowned at the blood spatter on the dishwasher. 'Before my time, though . . . there was a killing like this. The Frith family, about a mile south of here. Parents, two kids. Never solved.'

Laurie watched the way he made himself take in every last wet, rotten detail of the scene. When a fly hovered by his cheek, he didn't flinch. 'The Frith family. When was this?'

'1965. Farmhouse, like this. Isolated, no immediate neighbours. John Frith and his wife, Liz. Their six-year-old Sean, baby Alice. Found by a farmhand the next morning. I'd have to dig out the details to be sure, but I think it was the next morning. Parents died from gunshot wounds, children were stabbed. The shotgun was recovered, but not the knife. My gran remembers it; everyone of her generation does. We might find that makes this more difficult.'

'Let's leave that for the DMC.' Directorate of Media and Communication. 'I'll alert the coroner. Saxton's on his way. You and I should finish the log, make a start on the briefing. Theo can handle essential access. Can he?'

Joe nodded. 'Yes.'

'Once the examiner gets here, we'll talk with the neighbour. Is it someone you know?'

'Bobby German.'

'More use than Sandra Buck, I hope.'

'Probably.' Joe nodded again. 'Yes.'

'No CCTV here? Chris was an electrician. That's odd, don't you think?'

'Not really. He's more likely to have it where he keeps his van. There's a big garage, more of an outbuilding, we could check there.'

'The Nissan and Honda out front?'

'Chris's, and Odette's. The van will be in the garage, unless whoever did this took it.'

They looked again at the slaughter on the floor.

'This might have been a robbery,' Laurie said. 'But it looks personal.'

'Yes, it does.'

'And that's a positive ID on our victims? Chris and Odette Miles.'

'I'd need to turn them over, to be certain. But based on height and weight? Yes. I've seen those watches on them, and the rings too.'

His first time seeing people he knew murdered. Savagely, too. As bad as anything she'd seen in Salford. That was the biggest contrast between her job and his. In Salford, the victims were rarely people she'd known well. These murders were going to rip through Edenscar; the whole town would be grieving. Her biggest fear coming here had been boredom. It hadn't even crossed her mind to be afraid of death sliding in under cover of darkness to lay waste to a family.

'DS Ashe. Joseph? Look at me.'

He did, unblinking, knowing what she wanted. She checked his pupil responses, and nodded. 'You're good. All right. Let's get to work.'

II.

Dr Salome Thomas was five foot six. Late fifties, striking, black. She didn't waste time on introductions, nodding at Laurie as she suited up for the scene. 'Odette?' she asked Joe. 'And Eric?'

'And Chris. Looks like.'

'Jesus.' She reached a gloved hand for his elbow, stopping short of contact. She'd been the attending pathologist when the bodies were pulled from Ladybower Reservoir. She'd looked out for him that day: saw the police questioning an eleven-year-old in the back of an ambulance and stepped in, told them to back off and let the paramedics do their job. One of them asked why she didn't do hers – 'Dead bodies are all yours. We'll deal with the live one, thanks.' Joe hadn't thought of that in years. It made him wonder why he'd been so keen to join the police. 'You know why,' Sammi murmured, but Joe tuned him out. He was angry with Sammi, or rather with himself, for failing in his first duty to Eric Miles. It'd never happened before, his instinct overriding the rules.

'He was dead, wasn't he?' Sammi insisted.

Not the point. It was my job to check. I failed.

After they'd briefed Sal and her team, and with DCI Saxton in attendance at the farmhouse, Joe and Laurie were free to find out what had prompted Chris and Odette's nearest neighbour, Bobby German, to contact the police. They walked the single-track road to the top, where police tape was stretched to prevent anyone turning down in the direction of Higher Bar Farm.

'This's quite a distance,' Laurie said. 'Must've been some disturbance to be heard up here, but no one took any action at the time?'

'Bobby only reported it at 6 a.m. this morning.'

'Gunshots, and whatever else went down? Screaming, I'm

guessing. He doesn't think that's important? Only gets suspicious when it goes quiet?'

Joe considered how best to explain to her how Edenscar operated, without taking up the rest of their day with PowerPoints and graphs. 'People round here notice patterns. Blame it on the landscape, or weather, or farming. They know seasons, behaviours. What's considered normal or not normal depends on those patterns. It's normal to hear rifle shots, especially at this time of year when the rats are coming down from the forests.' He turned to look back at the farmhouse. 'What wasn't normal was seeing no smoke from the chimneys this morning. No cars leaving for work. That's when Bobby called it in.'

Laurie shielded her eyes to stare at the house where Sal and her team were at work. 'Everyone around here knew they had a baby.'

It wasn't a question but Joe nodded. 'Common knowledge.'

'So even if they didn't go upstairs, if whoever did that turned and left, they knew they were leaving an unattended one-year-old.'

'If it was a local, yes.'

'I can't see a one-year-old staying quiet through a killing of that kind.' Anger under the surface of her voice. 'It was murder. Not just theirs. Eric's, too.'

Joe nodded. He should have been the one to see the drowned boy in the bath. As it was, she'd shielded him from that. 'Let it go, Joe.' Sammi's eyes were on the road ahead, his long body angled away from the deaths.

Laurie said, 'Let's see what Mr German has to say.'

The houses facing them could not have been more different, despite being built as a pair a century ago. The empty house was the smarter of the two, gutted and modernised, freshly pointed and painted. Low-maintenance garden, flowers in planters, expensive outdoor storage container for bikes or buggies. All done in the expectation of Bobby selling the neighbouring house. At eighty-nine years old, the developers must've calculated he wasn't far from social care, no family to pass the house to, but Bobby clung to his health as stubbornly as he did everything else, including the home he'd allowed to fall into what was politely called a state of disrepair but looked, from the outside anyway, like an act of vandalism. The exterior, pebble-dashed some time in the 1970s, suggested an alien life form had taken root. The garden was a junkyard of thorn bushes, bricks and broken furniture at the heart of which a pleather 'La-Z-Boy' sat like a beaten and bleached throne. On warmer days this was where Bobby was found, with a four-pack of beer, happy to share his thoughts with passers-by, if they were local. For tourists and developers, he had a licensed firearm and an ancient collie, Isla, who could sometimes be stirred into showing her teeth. Joe liked Bobby, but he was not looking forward to introducing Laurie to this incomparably rural part of their patch. Bobby and Isla were the tourist board's idea of a nightmare, not the postcard-perfect image of the Peak District they wanted to show the world. Mostly Joe came up here to talk Bobby into handing over his gun, or at least putting on clothes when he was sitting outside.

'Shit.' Laurie had slipped again, on the cobbles leading to Bobby's front door. 'Is there anywhere in this bloody place that isn't covered in moss?'

On the assumption this was a rhetorical question, Joe didn't answer. He knocked on the front door, summoning a sound of fury from Isla.

'Oh, good,' Laurie said. 'A dog that can bark. Does it also bite?'

'Not if she knows you. Isla's her name.'

'Right. Well, you tackle Isla. I'll deal with Mr German.'

'Good luck', Sammi said, 'with that.'

Joe knocked a second time, without any answer other than an escalation in Isla's spirited bid to break down the door from the inside. 'Let's try the back.'

He'd only tried the front to give Bobby the chance to get dressed should the mood take him. It hadn't, unfortunately. He was poking around the garden in nothing but a pair of greasy suit trousers held up by garden string and the width of his arse, a fair portion of which was on display as he bent to work a lug wrench under the base of the metal dustbin where he liked to burn garden waste, along with letters from the developers and their solicitors. 'Bobby, this is Detective Inspector Bower. We've come about the disturbance at Higher Bar.'

'Why Isla's fitting, is it?' Bobby gave a grunt, poking the wrench deeper under the bin. 'Think she'd have your scent by now.' He gave up on the bin, chucking the wrench into the grass before turning with a broad grin.

Laurie didn't recoil but it was a close call; Bobby had very new teeth. They gave him a smile any Hollywood film star would've been proud of, almost luminous in their whiteness. In Bobby's face, which wore every one of his eighty-nine years heavily, they looked like a torch shining from the mouth of a partially collapsed cave. No one knew for sure where the money had come from or why Bobby chose to spend it on lavish dental work, but here they were: The Teeth. Laurie's composure, under the circumstances, was impressive. 'Mr German. We need to talk about what's happened at Higher Bar Farm.'

Bobby worked his trousers to his waist then let them drop. 'Kicked her out, has he? Her and the kiddie.'

'Why would you think that?'

'She's no better than she ought to be. Kiddie doesn't even look like him.'

'Bobby,' Joe said, 'can we talk inside? It's not that warm out here, and it'll help Isla settle down.' The dog hadn't stopped barking.

Bobby led them through the back door into the kitchen, not the cleanest room in the house but Joe happened to know the sitting room was worse. Laurie, to her credit, gave no impression of noticing the rancid state of the stove, sink and counters. Isla barrelled through from the front of the house to circle Joe, a better-looking dog than Nancy, and friendly enough. She ignored Laurie since Bobby was doing the same, flopping at Joe's feet as the three of them pulled out chairs to sit at the kitchen table. Like Nancy, Isla took no notice of Sammi, who pulled himself on to a cleanish corner of the counter and sat listening to what Bobby had to say.

'You reported a disturbance,' Laurie said, 'early this morning?'

'Last Friday,' he corrected. 'That's when it was.'

'But you only reported it this morning.'

'No point calling your lot over the weekend. Busy catching boy racers, or else keeping churchgoers in check.' He grinned. 'I'm joking. Tell her, Joe.'

'No time for jokes, Bobby. I'm afraid what's happened at Higher

Bar is very serious. We need you to tell us exactly what you heard on Friday night.'

Bobby searched his face, the light leaving his eyes. 'He's not killed 'em. Not that, Joe.'

Isla looked up with a whimper, alert to the distress in the room. Not just Bobby's. Joe was emitting a low-frequency distress signal; Laurie, too.

'Would you like a cup of tea? Or a glass of water?'

Bobby nodded, his stare going through Joe to the wall behind. No tears in his eyes but he made a sound like weeping, deep in his chest. Sammi didn't take his eyes off him. Joe stood to fill the kettle, letting Laurie pick up where he'd left off.

'Mr German, can you tell us what happened on Friday? What made you think something was wrong at the farmhouse?'

'He were out in the lane.' Bobby didn't look at Laurie, staring dead ahead. 'Miles. With his gun. Didn't think anything of it, other than foxes or rats. Joe knows. I've had 'em out back for weeks now, worse than ever. Isla won't be out on her own, will you, girl?' He reached blindly for the collie.

Joe made a cup of sweet tea and brought it to the table.

'I told him, "Wish you'd come and shoot some of mine," but he's too busy. Too much work on, that's what he says. Didn't stop him doing the wiring next door, mucking up my circuits while he's at it.' He jerked a thumb in that direction. He was starting to recover from the shock, enough to glare at Laurie. 'Who's this, then? She's new. Where's Saxton?'

'He's on his way. This is DI Bower. What kind of gun did Chris have with him, when you saw him in the lane?'

'Ratting gun.'

'What time was this?'

'Teatime. I'd put a pie on. Six-ish. Getting dark, but he's a light in his hat.' Bobby lifted a hand to his forehead. 'Here.'

'Did you speak to him?'

'Raised a hand. Got an eyeful of his torch, but we didn't speak. Looked like he were searching for summat. Murderous, that's how he looked.'

Joe could feel Laurie's stare on him but he waited it out, not wanting to put words in Bobby's mouth, or ideas in his head. Sammi maintained a similar silence.

'The kiddie's not dead, Joe. Is he?'

'Why would you think that?' Laurie asked.

Bobby took up the tea. 'He's like a pup with fleas, that baby. Unsettled. And she's no better. Pair of them like cat and dog up there, all hours.'

'They fight a lot?' Laurie glanced at Joe, who shook his head. This was the first he'd heard of unhappiness in the marriage. 'Is that what you heard on Friday?'

'Shooting. Then shouting, when he got back to the house.'

'How many shots, Bobby?' Joe asked.

'Two or three. Maybe more.'

'And was it definitely a ratting gun?'

'What else would it be?'

'You didn't hear a shotgun on Friday night?'

Bobby went pale. He made a tough shape with his mouth as if to steel himself against whatever Joe was going to say next. No wonder. The images from that kitchen were bursting so brightly in Joe's skull he was surprised he wasn't projecting them on to the walls, red and black, lurid with loss.

'I'd the telly on later. Didn't want to listen to him taking potshots all night.'

'And the shouting?' Joe said. 'What was that about, could you tell? You heard it over the television?'

'Heard her wanting him to come and help. That kiddie's a handful. That's what spooked me, this morning. He's often quiet on weekends, but never on a Monday.' His eyes were wet. 'Couldn't hear him bawling. No fires lit. Cars sat in the drive. That wasn't right. It wasn't right, Joe.'

'You did the right thing, Bobby, calling it in.'

'Too late, though.' His hands shook. 'Wasn't it?'

Laurie said crisply, 'We'll need your prints, Mr German, and a DNA swab. To help us narrow a few things down. The clothes you were wearing on Friday night would be helpful too. Is that going to be a problem?'

12.

At the station, DCI Saxton gathered the team for an update on what was unfolding at Higher Bar before beckoning Laurie and Joe into his office. 'I don't need to tell you how big this is going to be.' His face was drawn, his eyes bleak. 'I've put in a call for additional manpower from Ripley. DI Bower, this isn't the start either of us thought you were walking into. But I know you'll step up. Not your first murder.'

'Not by a long stretch.' Laurie kept her face blank, everything held under the surface. The team needed to see her coping, focused on the task in hand. No benefit to anyone if she let out the howl that'd been crouched in her chest since she stepped into that bathroom with its cheery yellow walls. A foot of bathwater, that's all it took. No shotgun, no red. The worst room in the house. She was glad she'd kept Joe out of it. But it meant she was carrying it all by herself.

Saxton said, 'Joe, you were first on scene. That can't have been easy.'

Fearing he meant to offer Joe counselling before the investigation was even underway, Laurie said, 'DS Ashe dealt with everything exactly as I needed him to. I'd like him to be on this with me.'

'Joe?'

'I want to be on it, guv. Glad of the chance to work with DI Bower.'

He looked as calm as she was pretending to be. It was a decent disguise, no obvious tells, but she'd caught him blinking in the car as they left Bobby German's place, those grey eyes trying to get rid of what they'd seen. She needed to stick close for the foreseeable, make certain he didn't unravel. Some excuse about her car, she decided, so they'd be joined at the hip for a while. She didn't have time to learn another set of quirks and Joe, for all his mystery, was a good detective.

'We want to keep this tight,' she told Saxton. 'I'll need all the insider knowledge I can get. Give the grunt work to Ripley, but the important stuff stays with the team here.'

Back to the incident room. She'd tasked DC Shaw with setting up summary boards where Milla had pinned photos of Chris and Odette, and Eric. Bobby's name was on the board, with his contention that Chris was jealous of his wife, suspecting her of being unfaithful. At a gut level, Laurie disliked this as a motive, but at this early stage it went on the board. If Chris had sneezed in the General Store, it went on the board. Nothing demotivated a team faster than staring at an empty expanse of white, waiting for inspiration to strike. The gunshots Joe heard were on the board. Around 9.15 p.m., he'd said. Two shots, probably the fatal ones, but they couldn't discount acoustics, the way every sound round here bounced off water or trees or stone. Laurie nodded at Theo, who was poised with a marker pen. 'An airgun was found on the property. We know Chris had a licence for an airgun, but we need to check make and model. DC Howden, you're on that. From what we saw at the scene, and going by Dr Thomas's initial findings, we're missing one shotgun. The murder weapon. Joe, you saw high beams around the time you heard the shots on Friday, thought they might've been from a vehicle driving away from Higher Bar towards Manchester or Sheffield?'

'Possibly.' Joe was being as cautious as ever. 'We've put in a request for ANPR, in any case.'

'Good. DS Vicars, you're on that. Point of entrance was the back door, which'd been left unlocked.' When Theo didn't add this to the board, Laurie raised her eyebrows at him. 'DC Howden?'

'It's just . . .' Deferring across her. 'Joe?'

Laurie needed to stamp on that, right now. 'You two can play Batman and Robin in your own time, not on mine. DC Howden, was the back door unlocked when you arrived on the scene or wasn't it?'

He reddened. 'It was, ma'am.'

'So write it on the board.'

While he did this, Joe said levelly, 'Everyone's back door is left unlocked around here. That was the point DC Howden was wanting to raise. It might be less significant than you think.'

'Thank you.' She froze her voice. 'I'll let you know when I stumble across anything of insignificance in this triple homicide investigation.' The back of her neck prickled. 'DS Vicars, instead of mouthing nicknames at DC Shaw, give me what you have to add to this incident board.'

'Chris's van was in the garage.' Vicars squared his jaw, trying to blank his face. He didn't have Joe's knack for it, like trying to blank a slab of raw steak. 'Far as we could tell, everything was intact. Lots of valuable kit in there. Think we can rule out robbery as a motive.'

'Do you? Just because nobody nicked his cable cutters or cordless drill doesn't mean it wasn't a robbery. Thieves might've been after something very specific, about which we know nothing.' Laurie waited until everyone in the room was looking at her. 'Joe and I are going to speak with Chris's parents, and Odette's mum. I want a list of possible suspects, and motives. Who was driving up there on Friday night? Full ANPR report. Where's the murder weapon? Who were the last people to see Chris and Odette alive? Together, or separately. What were their movements on Thursday, and earlier in the week? And all the rest of it. Medical records, bank records, historical evidence, similar crimes.' She waited as Theo wrote on the board, watching the team's reaction.

Everyone was tense, unhappy, focused. Milla looked much older, a frown pinching her face. Ted had folded his arms, tucked in his chin. Joe was too pale but otherwise mirroring Laurie's calm, his eyes dark and serious.

'Let's find who killed these poor people, and quickly.'

13.

Keith and Beverley Miles lived in a two-bed terrace behind a shallow stone wall, iron gate guarding three steps to the front door. A second, interior door led into the sitting room where Keith was feeding wood to a log burner. It was Beverley who'd opened the door to Joe and Laurie – 'You'll want to come in' – all her grief in her voice, lying low in her throat. In the sitting room, she began patting cushions into shape on the smart grey sofas. Shelves along every wall, photos and souvenirs: a resin tiki statue, illuminated Hollywood sign, Swiss cowbells, Venetian glass. Keith thumbed at invisible dust, aligning each souvenir more precisely. The only shelf he didn't touch was the one with the photos: Chris as a new dad, arms full of baby blanket, beaming; Keith and Beverley in their best clothes, flanking Chris and Odette at their wedding; a recent photo of Eric showing off a new front tooth. The room smelt of sweet wood, fig or apple, sour notes from the split timber stacked at the side of the log burner. Beverley finished with the sofa cushions, standing back with a nod to let Laurie know it was safe to sit down. She tried to smile at Joe but it slid from her face, leaving her mouth crooked.

'I know you've spoken with your family liaison officer,' Laurie said. 'We're here because we're leading the investigation. We'll answer as many of your questions as we can. We have questions of our own, but we're not here to make things harder for you.'

Keith made a noise that said she couldn't if she tried, things were already as hard as they could be. His son and daughter-in-law, dead. His grandson, dead. He was the only one still standing, as if the sofas offered comfort he wasn't ready to accept. His face said he'd yet to weep; he looked more vulnerable than his wife with her raw-rimmed eyes. They'd been somewhere sunny a few weeks back, their tans jaundiced. Beverley smoothed her dress, a big woman with a comfortable lap (easy to picture Eric nestled there), but she looked brittle, angular. Keith held his pain in his shoulders and elbows, a fighting stance, no target in sight. They each wanted a proper use for their hands, grief making a mockery of whatever they usually did to keep busy, the small actions that made up their everyday existence. No more *everyday* for Eric's grandparents.

'You'll want us to tell you who did it,' Keith said. 'Who might've done it. You'll want quarrels, grudges, whatever pushed whoever over the edge. Except he didn't live like that. A quiet lad, always. Quiet-living family man. Hard worker, was Chris, kept his head down, nose clean.'

'His room's the same,' Beverley said quickly, as if she feared where her husband's speech was headed, had heard it before and knew it ended in buckled knees, broken sobs. 'You'll want to see that.'

'Please,' Laurie said.

The bedroom was at the back of the house, small and square, unmistakably a boy's room. Shelves of treasure: Lego, cars, action figures, an assortment of litter scavenged by the magpie-eyed little boy Chris had been; maybe Eric would've had played with them. Pebbles and shells, shiny screws, bleached bones belonging to mice and birds. A desk with a small library of textbooks, the wall above pinned with arty photos in black-and-white, a handful of pen-and-ink sketched faces, young. On the window, decals pointed out star constellations. Laurie recognised Orion. A jolt of memory: Isabel's tattoo, home-made with a sewing needle and biro, on the inside of her wrist where her watch-strap would cover it. Spidery starburst, Libra, their shared birth sign – 'balance, harmony and justice' – Izzy enjoying the joke, sucking on a cigarette, her breath tequilaed.

Laurie turned from the window to see Chris's mum watching the room the way a prey animal watches its predator, anticipating teeth and claws.

'We keep meaning to clear this out, make a guest room.' She touched a white pebble on the shelf. 'Chris didn't want it changing, said it'd be perfect for Eric when he was old enough to stay over.'

Keith had stayed downstairs, clamping his jaw around the idea of detectives in his boy's bedroom. Laurie looked at the textbooks on the desk. 'My husband Adam was at school with Chris. From the sounds of it, he was a lively lad.'

'He could be, when he was trying to fit in. School's a hard place until you make friends.'

'How did he and Odette meet? Was that in school?'

Joe was studying the photos and sketches tacked to the wall, staying silent to make space for Laurie's questions and Beverley's answers.

'She wasn't at school here. She's from Macclesfield. They only met seven years back, when Chris was doing a job for the shop where she worked. He was here with us until he was thirty-eight. Most families don't get that long.' Her eyes moved over Joe, travelled the room. 'Six years since they were married. All of us starting to think they'd be no kids, until Eric.' Her voice broke on the boy's name, a hand coming up to ward off sympathy; too soon and too soft, an insult, almost, when grief had thrown a handful of stinging gravel.

'He was made up when Odette fell pregnant, we all were. He wanted a big family. If you'd known him, you'd have said he was happy being an only child. But he hated it. That's what he told me after Eric was born.' Her eyes went to the single bed, stripped to a blue mattress under a green blanket. 'The loneliness of it.'

Laurie had never been lonely growing up with Izzy snapping at her heels, not even two years younger although there were nine between them now, between Laurie's nearly forty-four and Isabel's for ever thirty-five.

'Did Odette want more children too?'

'She didn't talk about it as much as Chris, but she'd her hands full with Eric. I told her once he's walking and talking, it'll be easier.'

Her voice was numb, as if she'd reached the bottom of a pit. She'd start trying to climb upwards soon, looking for handholds. Murder was different, though. With murder, the pit kept opening under your feet.

'Have you spoken with Odette's mum since it happened?'

'Not properly, but yes. We're all trying to make sense of it.' She wiped her eyes. 'It's worse for Keith. Eric had two grannies but only one granddad.'

Worse for Yvonne than Keith surely, since she was alone with her loss. But Laurie knew better than to try to fit someone else's pain into a shape that made sense to her. Instead, she walked over to the window to give Beverley a rest from the weight of this moment, hoping older memories might be less painful. 'Chris was into stargazing?' She indicated the decals. 'Is that a hobby he had as a kid?'

'Cameras of all kinds. Photos, pictures . . .' Her eyes went to the desk and she gave a sudden airless gasp. 'Oh! No. Let me . . .' Snatching at the sketches, pulling them from the wall, metal tacks falling through her fingers. 'I'm sorry.'

Laurie took a step towards her, unable to see what was so alarming in the squares of paper she was pulling down, piling in her palm. Joe made a small movement with his head, bringing Laurie to a halt. 'Mrs Miles,' he said, 'it's all right, please don't upset yourself.'

'I should've thought. I'd forgotten these were here.'

The wall was pricked where tacks were pulled, photos shuddering in scales of black-and-white. Beverley's fingers trembled around the handful of paper. She tipped the pile on to the desk, wiping her palm on her wrist. 'I'm sorry.' Her voice was hushed, scared.

'It really doesn't matter.' Joe stood very still and spoke very steadily. 'Please don't worry. None of that's important right now.'

Chris's mum ducked her head in a nod. 'I'd better get back to Keith.' Almost running from the room.

Laurie stared at the sketches, stirring them with the tip of one finger. 'What is this?' Children's faces. Older than Eric. Ten or twelve years old, girls and boys. She separated the faces across the surface of the desk, her finger halting on a dark-haired boy, his eyes pencilled grey, staring straight back at her. 'This is you.' She looked up at Joe in surprise.

He moved his hand near to hers, making more space around each of the sketches. 'Paige Blackwall. Ellie Howden.' A glimpse of Theo in the girl's face. 'Molly and Tyler Hall.' Twins. 'Zoe Cooper.' He spoke their names lightly, carefully. 'Seth Morton. Devin Andrews. Hayley Stratton.' He paused before placing his thumb on the final sketch, of a lovely boy with mischief in his eyes. 'Sammi Torre.'

Laurie knew that name, from Adam: *'He distracted the driver. Well, him and another boy. Sammi Torre. They were mucking about on the back seat.'*

'Chris drew these?' she asked Joe.

'That's what it looks like. From photos published in the papers, after the crash.' His thumb rested on the last boy's face. 'The whole town was in shock. Chris must've been . . . mid-twenties?'

'Twenty-seven. Same age as Adam.' The ends of her fingers itched. 'That makes these a bit ghoulish. Don't you think?'

Joe didn't answer. She'd no way of knowing whether he agreed with her or found the sketches moving in a way she couldn't appreciate. Nothing overtly sensational in Chris's art. He hadn't hidden these away in a drawer, or taken them with him to the farmhouse. His mother had found nothing upsetting in the sight of them all these years, until Joe was standing here. 'You never had any trouble with Chris, personally? Unwanted attention, that sort of thing?'

'Never,' Joe said. 'I'd have told you if I had.'

'He's well liked, local. I'd understand if your instinct was to protect him.'

'By withholding information that could help us find his murderer?' Joe shook his head. 'No.'

Laurie looked again at the cheap treasures, single bed. 'He was living at home until he married.'

'Not unusual,' Joe said. 'Families are close here.'

'He was thirty-eight.'

'I'm twenty-eight, still stay with my gran a lot of the time.'

'You don't think it's odd?' She turned a circle. 'This is a kid's room.'

'Could be he took all the serious gear with him. It's not that different to my room at my gran's, to be fair.'

Laurie looked again at the sketches, trying to imagine a grown man sitting here, big shoulders curled, concentrating on recreating the faces of dead children. Whatever Joe said, it was odd. Voyeuristic. 'He didn't draw the adults who died, only the kids—' She stopped, frozen with shock.

A third hand was on the desk, between hers and Joe's. Petrol-black nail varnish, thin fingers stained by cigarettes, silver snake ring with its ruby eye long lost, blue spidery starburst . . . She looked up, dizzy, caught the snatch of her sister's smile in a shadow lying to the left of Joe's mouth, hazel eyes challenging her. She blinked and it was just Joe. 'Are you all right?' A note of concern in his voice.

She moved away, staring from the window across narrow gardens until her pulse returned to normal. *Emotional contagion.* She wanted Adam's arms wrapped around her. Not for comfort but ballast, to hold her down, keep her here in the present, not spiralling into the past.

'What is it you're thinking?' Joe asked quietly.

'That we'd better get back down to his mum and dad.' She toughened her voice, back to business. 'Keith needs time to come to terms with this. But we need answers to our questions. Let's tread carefully, see how far we get.'

Keith was loading more wood into the log burner. 'This was Chris –' shutting the door on the burning wood – 'and this –' pointing at the sofas – 'all the holidays where we got these –' the souvenirs – 'all Chris. Whatever you're writing on those boards of yours at the station, entering in your logbooks . . . he never forgot where he came from or what he owed. Man of his word, always.'

Beverley said, '*Keith*,' on a worn-out note of despair. His stare bounced off her, skittering across the floor, climbing the walls. 'Wanted the best for us, always. Just like for her and Eric. Family first. Always.'

'He was a good son,' Laurie summarised. 'A good provider.'

The air in the room was incendiary, the log burner sending a shower of sparks sizzling against the glass, crazing Keith's face to orange as the skin under his eyes sagged, his mouth falling into the same destroyed shape as his wife's. 'Best son a man could have.' His breath shattered. 'Best dad, too.'

Beverley reached out, gathering the pieces of him, sitting the pair of them on the sofa. 'More questions.' She looked pleadingly at Laurie. 'You'll have more questions.'

'About Higher Bar Farm, yes.' Laurie and Joe sat together on the sofa facing Chris's parents. 'When did Chris and Odette move there?'

'Right after the wedding. They wanted to be married out of there but the house wasn't ready, so much more needed doing than the surveyors said.'

'Money pit.' Keith stared straight ahead. 'From the off. They wouldn't be told. Chris said he'd sort it. He did, too.'

'Not an easy first home,' Laurie suggested.

'No such thing. But Chris wasn't a dreamer. Things needed doing, he did.'

'It was a lovely home.' Beverley insisted. 'They both made it that. A lovely family home.'

Her fingers whitened around her husband's hand and he nodded as if she'd tugged it out of him: 'He did a good job. No one ever found fault with his work.'

'He was very busy with work,' Joe said.

'In demand, yes.'

'We were worried he was working too hard. Weren't we, love?'

'Nothing wrong with hard work.'

'No, but with Eric so little . . .'

'He wanted the best for his boy. What dad doesn't want that?'

'Yes, but all the same. We wished he didn't work so much.'

'Man of the house. That's what we do.'

It was a strange, sad stand-off. The pair of them pulled apart by the murders, stranded either side of its landslip, no easy way to reach one another. They'd told the FLO they weren't aware of any problems in the marriage, or with Chris's work, or in Odette's life. Everything was going according to plan, they'd said, until Friday night brought a killer to Higher Bar.

Silence ran the length of the street outside, all ears, cautious as a cat. In the house opposite, curtains twitched. Everyone was waiting for what came next. An arrest, or a reason to hope this horror was contained, no danger of it infecting more families.

'You can take the lead with Odette's mum.' Laurie checked her reflection in the car's mirror, avoiding Joe's eyes. She hadn't looked at him since whatever unsettled her in Chris's bedroom. Sammi propped his chin to the back of Joe's seat. 'She saw someone.' *Who?*

'No idea.' Sammi sounded intrigued rather than troubled, studying Laurie's profile. 'I couldn't see them.'

'Change of plan.' Laurie had her phone out, checking messages. 'Yvonne's with Odette's sister in Newcastle. We'll have to catch up with her tomorrow.' She pocketed the phone, wiping her fingers. 'Pub tonight. Chance to regroup.'

'The team's a bit shredded,' Joe agreed. 'But I don't see it going down well. Everyone's heard the news, they'll want us hard at work, not downing pints.'

'Just you and me, then. Not drinking.' Sand in her voice, dry and abrasive. 'Letting the locals know we're available. Community support.'

Joe glanced at her. 'Is everything all right?'

'Debrief first.' She ignored the question. 'I want Milla digging into Chris's financials. Six years since he took on that farmhouse, sinking money into it from what his dad said. But he's buying sofas and sending them off on pricey holidays? Maths isn't my strong suit, but something doesn't add up there.'

Joe didn't argue. From the back seat, Sammi said, 'The pub's because she doesn't trust you out of her sight. You're in for a session, like it or not.'

14.

The Tollgate was doing a brisk trade for a Monday night, busier than Laurie had anticipated. Heads swivelled at Joe's arrival. She'd thought that sort of thing only happened in films: drinkers falling silent at the advent of strangers or in this case a stranger and a local celebrity. Had the doorway been less narrow, she'd have missed the way Joe tensed. She didn't blame him, had been in blizzards more welcoming. From a table in the corner, a man in his fifties climbed to his feet, coming towards them with a hand held out. 'How are you, Joe? This must have been an impossible day.' Quietly spoken, handsome but not in a showy way, shielding Joe from the curiosity coming from the punters at the bar.

'Mr Torre, this is DI Bower.'

'Laurie, please.' She shook his hand.

'Adrian Torre.' His hand was dry, his grip neither too firm nor too soft. Up close, she recognised the grief in his eyes, knew he'd lost someone. *Torre.* Sammi's dad, had to be. He didn't look like a Monday-night drinker. She wondered if he'd made a point of being here in case Joe called in. 'Come and sit with me,' he said. 'I'll get the drinks in.'

'Thanks.' Laurie nodded. 'Diet Coke for me.'

'And me,' Joe said. 'Thanks.'

When she turned to watch Adrian pay for the drinks, Laurie caught sight of Brother Buckfast with his forearms on the bar, such undiluted antipathy on his face she had to contain a flinch. Not directed at her but Joe, the facial equivalent of a machete launched in his direction. 'What is that dickhead's problem?'

'Ignore him.' Joe kept his eyes on his phone. 'He won't go away, but at least you won't be wasting your time wondering what his problem is.'

'Why's that a waste of my time?'

'Because even he doesn't know what that is. Not really.' Joe was scrolling. 'I need to talk with you about Tom Sangster's website.'

'What's that got to do with the murders?'

'Nothing. It's about the crossbow in Powderhill.'

'I get it, you're multitasking. Holding it in separate boxes, whatever. As long as you know what happened up at that farm takes precedence over everything. Forget the crossbow. These are *murders*. I need all of your attention on—'

She broke off because a pale-faced woman was standing by their table, twisting her hands into a fist. 'Is there any news, Joe? Of what happened?'

'Not yet. We're doing everything we can.' Joe climbed to his feet. 'This is DI Bower. She's leading the investigation.'

The woman barely glanced at Laurie. Everything about her was pale – face, hair, eyes – like looking at a film negative. She wore a white anorak, bleached jeans. 'Another child, Joe. Were you with him? Was there that, at least?'

Joe looked across the woman's shoulder, prompting Laurie to do the same. A man was making his way towards them, tight look on his face. *Trouble*. Laurie put her chair back, straightening to her full height. The woman shot her a fast, frightened look then shut her face down as the man reached the table and put an arm around her shoulders, 'Come on, love. Let's leave it. Not tonight.'

Joe said, 'Mr Hall, this is DI Bower.'

Hall. Molly and Tyler's mum and dad. Laurie's throat clenched. This pale, shattered-looking woman had seen her kids with Joe, and it'd emptied her out.

Mr Hall jerked his chin at Laurie then led his wife to a table by the door. Adrian Torre had been waiting at a discreet distance with their drinks. He brought them to the table now. 'It's a difficult day, for everyone.'

Joe nodded, reaching for his glass. His fingers were white. He kept his eyes down. Mr Hall and his wife were out of earshot, but Laurie could see other people in the pub staring at Joe. Why hadn't he warned her it'd be like this?

'It took courage', Adrian said quietly, 'to come in here. I'm glad you did. It's important for people to see the team working on this case.'

'It was DI Bower's idea,' Joe said. 'And for exactly that reason. DCI Saxton will be doing the same, I'm sure.'

And DS Vicars, if only to keep his guv's pew warm. Laurie felt a pulse of frustration, largely at herself. Joe wasn't the guilty party here. She'd more or less strong-armed him into coming. Now he had to put up with eye-knives being thrown by Des, Mrs Hall smothering him with her grief. Adrian, at least, was treating him like a normal human being, 'If there's anything I can do, you only have to ask.'

'Could you call on Bobby? He was in a bad way when we left him.'

'Of course. I'll do it first thing tomorrow.'

The moment felt weirdly intimate, as if Laurie had no business being here. *A local place for local people*. Bobby gave her the dry heaves – those trousers, those *teeth* – but Joe had been gentle with him, and with Beverley too. Her mind kept skipping to those sketches in Chris's bedroom, the children's faces, her sister's hand. Izzy's hand. *Izzy's smile*. Fear flooded her, at a primal level, outside her control. Some joker at the next table was chatting up the waitress. Travelling salesman, hawking his services – 'I did a stint with the Royal Marines, know all about challenges.' She wanted to challenge him to fix this: a family killed like cattle, a town in thrall to the man who left a drowned baby in a bathtub. Her phone pinged with a text. Adam, asking if she was okay. He'd heard the news, of course, his sisters' jungle telegraph working overtime. What answer could she give? *I'm fine, just dead bodies, what I do for a living, remember?* She had a flash of Izzy's face bruised by death, had to pinch her wrist to ground herself. She thumbed the phone off, pushing it into her pocket. Adrian Torre was talking about Anna. His wife, by the sound of it. Making excuses for her, why she wasn't with him. This had been Laurie's bad idea, wanting Joe off duty so she could convince herself everything was normal when everything was very fucking far from normal; a flash of silver from someone's bracelet and she was seeing the rings on her sister's fingers. *Enough*. She drained the Diet Coke, nodding thanks at Torre, telling Joe she was off. 'See you early tomorrow.'

He stood when she did, walking with her to the pub's narrow doorway.

'No need for you to come. Stay and chat with Adrian. He obviously enjoys your company.'

Joe gave her a curious look, following her through the door into the dark outside the Tollgate. 'You need a lift home, don't you?'

Shit. She'd forgotten about the shared car, her excuse to keep him close. 'Fine. Wait for me, in that case.' She went back inside the pub, to the toilets. She'd thought she'd have time to compose herself on the drive home, but if she was being chauffeured she'd need to get herself together before she left. Her reflection in the mirrored wall confirmed this. She was wild-eyed with anger, or fear masquerading as anger. She washed her hands, held her wrists under the tap. Pressed wet fingers to her cheeks then dried them in her hair, smoothing it into shape. After that she rolled her neck, counted to twenty, and went outside in search of Joe. He wasn't by the car. She heard the familiar sound of a fight brewing – voices hissing, feet scuffling – and stalked in that direction, aware she was in the mood for a scrap, wishing she hadn't left her baton in the car.

At the side of the pub, Brother Buckfast and a mate were facing off with a third man. Nothing physical but it was warming up in that direction, the air bending around them, making dangerous shapes. A thump of surprise: the third man was her DS and instead of reading the riot act, Joe appeared to be waiting for Morton and his mate to bore and move on with their evenings.

'Oi! Wankers.' She took her fists from her pockets, approaching at a clip, not running in case she slipped but fast enough for them to stiffen alertly. She had her phone in her hand, camera running. 'Des Morton? Looks like you're about to be under arrest for assault. I hope your lawyer likes late nights.'

Joe stood wide as both men made an exit. She let them go, more interested in knowing what he thought he was playing at. 'Can't leave you alone for five minutes? At the start of a murder investigation?'

Joe rolled his left shoulder, coming out of the shadows into the light. His eyes were fathomless, his mouth firmly shut.

'I asked you a question. What the fuck was that? Dancing with the locals when I need you in one piece? Oh, don't look pissed off with *me*! I'm not the problem here.'

'I'm not pissed off,' Joe said in his usual voice.

As if she hadn't witnessed him gearing up for a scrap at the end of a long day marked by death. As if this were any other night of the week. They eyed one another. The air was thick, unbreathable. Storm incoming. She didn't trust it or like it but she'd no power over it, that's how it felt. 'If you're not angry, what's that?' She nodded at the half-formed fist he'd made of his right hand.

Joe shook the shape from his fingers. 'Not what it looks like.'

'No? Because it *looks like* you want to punch someone. Granted, that arsehole needs punching. But you do it a lot — clench your fists. If you've anger issues, I need to know. Call it operational intelligence.'

'I don't have anger issues.' Joe spread both hands, showing their empty palms. 'Send me on a course, if you like. But I'll ace the tests and, anyway, you need me here, don't you? We've work to do.'

'So what is it, then? Some sort of tendonitis?'

'Sure. Yes. Tendonitis.' Joe put his hands into his pockets, shrugging himself narrow. She waited for a look of apology to soften the hard mask he'd made of his face, but it didn't come.

'Des Morton. What's your excuse for him? Tendonitis of the brain? His mate's lucky I left my baton in the car or he'd be lying there —' she jerked her head at the gutter — 'with a broken dick.'

'That *was* lucky,' Joe agreed.

Laurie was spoiling for a fight, could feel the welcome buzz of it in her wrists, better than the fear she'd felt in the pub. 'Why're you putting up with crap like that from jokers like him?'

'I have to live here. You don't. It's clear enough how quickly you're going to leave once these six months are up—'

'That's none of your business, is it?'

'Fine. Just like this' — he gestured at the pub — 'is none of yours.'

'Difference being I'm your DI so maybe show some fucking respect.'

'We're off duty,' Joe said. 'And respect cuts both ways. I'll show some when I see some.'

★

From inside the pub, music played on, uninterested in their drama. Joe turned away, tilting his head at the sky, exasperated at himself for losing his temper, a thing he never did. Coldness crept into the palm of his right hand. *Sammi*. 'All right, look. That was deeply discourteous and unprofessional of me. I apologise unreservedly, ma'am.'

'Boss.'

'I apologise unreservedly, boss.'

'This is your best grovelling, is it?' Laurie dusted down her jacket. 'Because I've seen better from hardened drug dealers.'

'I expect that's right.'

She glared at him. She'd been edgy ever since Chris's room, whatever or whoever she'd seen there. The face-off with Des hadn't helped Joe's cause, but she'd been angry before that happened.

'Better defuse this, Joe. Important work to do.' Sammi was flicking brick dust from his shoulders. Wary of this fight with Laurie, seeing where it was headed more clearly than Joe could. Was this about her exit strategy? She wasn't going to hang around even with three murders to solve on her first full day on the job, wanted to be gone from Edenscar as soon as possible. Which meant taking no prisoners, giving no ground. He had six months of this to look forward to.

'What's that look?' She circled her index finger in front of his face. 'Because it's not "I apologise unreservedly, boss".'

'God, you're hard work.' He waited a beat. 'Sorry, did I say that out loud?'

To his amazement, she laughed. 'You're wasted round here. Why the hell aren't you in Manchester, or Sheffield?'

How was he supposed to answer that to her satisfaction, let alone his own? He shrugged. 'This is my home.'

'The place where you get stared at and talked about? When you're not getting grief from wankers like Morton?' Her stare sharpened.

He had the sense she could see beneath the surface of his skin, behind the mask he wore, right into the back of his head where Sammi was keeping watch, keeping score, 'She's walking all over you, Joe. Stand up for yourself.'

'I'm good at my job. If I didn't have that it'd be different, maybe.

Then, as you're implying, I'd be nothing more than a carnival act. The freak survivor.' He smiled as he said it, because what choice did he have? Laugh or cry. Work or die. Let Des have his fun or fight back, land himself in a law court.

'Jesus, you're cold.' Her eyes flickered. 'Wish I could summon some of that frostiness right now.'

'Well, when you've spent seventeen years being stared at and talked about you get really good at being very boring.'

'I didn't call you boring,' Laurie said. 'I called you cold. How long's Morton been pulling shit like that?'

Since Joe and Sammi were six, their friendship an affront for some reason. 'Did you just friend-zone me, Joe?'

'On and off since I put on uniform. He's bored. A lot of that around here.'

Joe wanted her to say she wasn't bored, just ill at ease. He wanted to say he felt the same, that grief was a nagging pain under his ribs which never went away and today had made it worse. Sharper, deeper. She'd lost people. He could see it, in her eyes. She'd lost people she cared about. 'Careful, brainiac. She won't welcome you digging her dead.' Rain was coming down, making the pair of them shiver.

'I'll drive you home, shall I?' He turned in the direction of the car. 'Early start tomorrow, like you said.'

15.

By the time he reached Merry's cottage, Joe was regretting his bravado. Whether or not she was sticking around, Laurie was his boss. He shouldn't have spoken to her the way he had, or let her see a side of him he never took to work.

'You're wiped out, kiddo.' Merry kissed his cheek. 'But still beautiful.'

'You get any more glamorous, Gregory Peck will whisk you off.'

These formalities out of the way, Joe sank on to the sofa, shutting his eyes. His grandmother reached for his right shoulder and held it hard, until he felt the threat of tears pressing behind his eyes. He didn't want to weep, afraid if he started he'd never stop. He needed to stay frosty, for Chris and his family. 'I made an arse of myself at the pub just now.'

'Did you?' His grandmother moved away, making it easier.

'Mmm.' He blinked, smelling the farmhouse on his clothes. 'Told my new boss she was hard work.'

'She'll have taken it in her stride, surely.' Merry was making a pot of tea, the small sounds a comfort, helping him to stay grounded.

'Maybe, but this was right after I'd been chatting with Des.'

'That little puff adder. What was he after?'

'Nothing new. Laurie caught him at it. Wanted to arrest him, in fact.'

'Good for her. Starting to wonder if she had any wits about her. Knew she must have guts to get herself involved with the Bowers.'

Joe rested his head against the cushions. 'How d'you mean?'

'Peter's poisonous, or he could be.'

Joe's phone was ringing. He shifted his hip, dug it from his pocket, saw the caller display: *Zoe's mum*. His heart sank but he sat up, taking the call. 'Ms Cooper, is everything all right?'

Merry shook her head at him, mouthing, '*No.*'

Hannah Cooper was saying, 'I'm missing her so much tonight. Please, Joe, could you come?'

'I'm running late, I'm afraid, about to sit down to supper.'

'Please.' The pain in her voice was hard to hear. The news from Higher Bar would have reached her by now, spreading like wildfire. He thought of the mood in the Tollgate, unsettled, on the edge of antagonism. Unlike those in the pub, Hannah had no one to turn to or talk with to try to make sense of the murders.

'Just ten minutes,' she was saying. 'Let me see her for ten minutes.'

His grandmother's hand was on his arm. Joe squeezed her fingers then freed himself, climbing to his feet. 'I'll be there as soon as I can.'

'Joseph Ashe, you're a sentimental fool.' Merry waved him away crossly. 'You wear yourself any thinner, you'll be see-through.'

'Keep my supper warm?'

'What else'm I going to do with it?'

Hannah Cooper lived four streets across. To save time and avoid the rain, Joe drove the short distance, parking in the driveway where her car sat bleached by dust. The house was in a similar state of neglect, paint peeling from its door, grimy net curtains hiding the view into its rooms. Neighbours lived either side but rarely saw Hannah. In the case of the Traylors, she refused their help, leaving gifts of food to rot on the doorstep. The Welshes had enough on their plate with two small children, a third on the way. Hannah lodged complaints against the noise the kids made – 'I can't hear myself think' – and after a while the Welshes hit back, saying they were tired of being woken by Hannah wailing her daughter's name. Everyone wanted to be a good neighbour – Edenscar was full of kind people – but it wasn't always possible, or practicable. Hannah had moved here after her dad died, just before Zoe was born. Zoe's dad was never part of the family, a stranger passing through, everyone assumed. Hannah's dad, a farmer, raised her after his wife died. He'd have helped raise Zoe too, if his health hadn't taken a turn for the worse. After his death, Hannah and Zoe were alone but together. Now Hannah really was alone.

'Ms Cooper, how are you?'

She'd put on lipstick, made an effort with her hair. Not for Joe's benefit, although plenty speculated to that effect, asking why a young man who ought to know better, a detective no less, was the only person Han Cooper was ever pleased to see. She wore a short satin nightdress under an oversized brown cardigan. Bare legs, slippers, bruises on her knees. Tall and slender with ash-blond curls, her wide cornflower-blue eyes glazed by grief. 'You're here.' Her eyes went to his left hip. Another reason people talked about the pair of them – 'The way she looks at him! Like she can't wait to get her hands on him' – but it wasn't Joe's body she was interested in, or his mind. She didn't care that he was young enough to be her son, or a detective sergeant. She only cared that he'd been on the bus the day Zoe drowned. 'Come through.'

Joe followed her into the sitting room, seeing her efforts to tidy: photos put straight on the walls, cushions shaken into shape along the sofa. She'd started sweeping crumbs from the sideboard, leaving them in a little heap next to candles and the Bible, the sight of which made him wish he hadn't come. She'd turned to religion once before. It hadn't ended well. It was cold in the house, and damp, with the dead smell of candles scuffing the air.

'Sit here.' She steered him to the right-hand side of the sofa, leaving space on his left where she'd placed a red-and-yellow crocheted blanket.

Joe sat. 'Did you speak with the energy company?'

She shook her head impatiently, gesturing for him to be quiet. She hadn't taken her eyes from the left side of his body. Seeing her daughter there. She'd been seeing Zoe at Joe's side for over a decade. Her face softened into a smile. 'Hello, my little love.'

Joe propped his elbow to the arm of the sofa, resting his head on his hand, overwhelmed by the desire to sleep. It would make no difference to Hannah.

'My darling, I've missed you. I've been wanting to hold you, all week.'

God help him if the neighbours were listening to this. He could lose his job. If he didn't lose his mind first.

'Will you smile for me, darling? Just a little smile.'

Joe shut his eyes, not wanting to see her pain. Hearing it was hard enough, but it was worse on those rare occasions when he refused to come and she strayed beyond a distress call into a full-blown emergency. He knew what Laurie would say, not a million miles from what Merry kept telling him – 'You're not helping anyone, Joseph, least of all yourself' – but he couldn't leave Hannah hanging, not after what she'd done to herself the last time.

'Mummy misses you, so much.' She was on the edge of her seat, elbows gripped in her hands. 'Tell her, Joe.'

He opened his eyes in surprise; she never normally involved him in her communication with Zoe. There was something worse about her tonight, more fragile. She wasn't looking at him; her eyes were fixed on the empty space at his left side. He concentrated until he could feel what she was seeing. Zoe, seated beside him on the sofa. Clothes sodden from the reservoir, barbed with fragments of shattered glass. Skin puckered with cold, goosebumps on her thin legs. The illusion tugged until he had to open his hand, offering it to her. The wet chill of water filled his palm, little icy fingers curling together with his.

'Joe, let her go. *Joe!*' Sammi was angry, the way he always was when Joe gave in to temptation of this kind, letting the ghosts creep close. But Sammi was a ghost too, however much Joe might hate that, wishing his best friend here with him. Sammi was dead. If Joe gave up the ghosts, he'd be giving up Sammi.

'There it is! A smile for Mummy!' Icy fingers evaporating in his grip. 'Such a lovely smile!'

Joe rested his head on his hand, Hannah's delusion draining what was left of his strength, leaving him so tired he shuddered. He shouldn't have come, wasn't helping her any more than the doorstep God Squad who took her money, bruised her knees with their prayer sessions. He could at least catch some sleep. Here in Hannah's prison of a house, where dead leaves drifted and a car sat rusting to nothing in the driveway.

When he woke, Hannah was curled at the other end of the sofa, arms wrapped emptily around her chest, face was blurred by sleep. Joe unfolded himself, pulling the blanket over her carefully. The house smelt of iron, as if the reservoir had leaked in while he slept, receding inch by inch until all that was left were water-damaged walls, the threat of black spores, respiratory difficulties, even death.

'You're a laugh a minute, you are.' Sammi stood biting his thumbnail, head cocked at Hannah as she slept. He looked grim, his face older than it ought to be. He hated Joe coming here, worst of all when he let himself drift into dark thoughts.

'Sorry, come on. Let's make ourselves useful.'

Joe found the meters in a hall cupboard, took photos on his phone so he'd know who to contact about the heating. It wasn't an electrical fault. Chris Miles, at Joe's request, had checked the system a month ago, not charging for the work, calling it his good deed for the day. A hard worker, family man, gunned down with his wife, their son drowned. Joe was acutely aware that in pursuit of their killer he would have to get to know that monster, intimately. Sink his hands to their elbows in the blood and guts of whoever took a shotgun to Higher Bar and blasted Eric's parents to bits. That was their job now, his and Laurie's, learning every last detail of the life that made those deaths. Where the killer lived, what they ate and drank, and read, and wore to bed, what turned them on and off, what they hoped for, what they feared. At the end of this, they'd know the killer better than they knew the Mileses. They'd have to, to catch him and put him away.

In Hannah's kitchen, Joe checked the contents of the fridge and cupboards, finding out-of-date packets of dried pasta, tins of alphabet spaghetti. He made a quick shopping list, hoping Hannah would answer the door if he ordered an online delivery. Otherwise, he'd have to come back himself. The kitchen was a mess of dirty surfaces, dried mud stains from boots discarded by the back door, unopened post, unwashed dishes. He did what he could but he was fighting a losing battle. He shut the front door softly on his way out, walking to his car, waiting for passing traffic to muffle the sound of the engine firing; if she woke, he wouldn't be to blame. Not for that. 'Not for anything,' Sammi said angrily, but Joe didn't believe it. He didn't even believe Sammi believed it.

★

Back at his grandmother's cottage, the rooms were lit warmly, as if she'd known he'd return feeling chilled. Darkness swept the sky, rising and falling in patterns each more intricate than the last. A murmuration of starlings, riding the very last of the dusk. He stood and watched the clouds shift with their swooping, as if a small tornado were gathering and might lift Merry's house from its moorings, spin it into the night. He thought of the floor at Higher Bar after Sal's team took the bodies, blackened shadows left by their murders, blur of light on the stairs as Laurie told him he didn't need to see Eric in the bath. She was right; Eric was the blur of light shifting on the stairs like water—

'Joe,' Sammi warned. 'You're sinking.'

Joe blinked to clear his vision. Above him, starlings jack-knifed, splitting the sky before stitching it blackly together again. He thought of the woman he'd left behind in the unheated house, the magnitude of Hannah's grief. He'd brought her a little comfort. Had he? He wanted to believe it. *Needed* to believe. Didn't let himself think too long about the larger problem – what was missing inside him. How he could face crime scenes and feel everything. Pain, grief, loss. But when he thought of his own trauma – what therapists called his trauma – the feeling was flat and shallow. Unreal, as if it never happened. 'A laugh. A minute.' When he turned to say goodnight, Sammi was already going, a one-handed farewell as he faded.

Merry was on the doorstep, waiting. 'They're leaving.' She nodded upwards. Starlings, freckling the sky. The night murmured around them, bringing the sharp scent of foxes. 'Come inside, kiddo. Supper's waiting.'

16.

'You look knackered, Lore.' Adam folded her into a hug. 'I can't imagine how rotten your day's been.'

Laurie wasn't ready for his sympathy, still in battle mode after parting from Joe. She suffered the hug in silence before stepping back. 'Sorry I'm late. Missed tea, I bet. How's your dad doing?'

'Better today, easier with fewer people in the house. Helen called round, helped him find his feet.' Adam lowered his voice. 'Everyone's talking about what happened at Higher Bar. I can't believe it. That poor family.'

'You were at school with Chris. I'm sorry.'

He put an arm around her shoulders as they went inside. 'I kept some soup for you. Let me heat it up. With a sandwich.'

'Thanks, soup's fine. And a cuppa, if you could pop the kettle on. I'll say hello to your dad, then freshen up. Unless he's best left alone?'

She needed Adam to say, 'Leave him, let's talk about your day.' She didn't even need the second part of that statement, just the first. But her husband gave a grateful smile – 'Would you? He'll like that –' needing to believe she and Peter got on, that Izzy never stormed through this family leaving destruction in her wake. They so rarely spoke about her sister. When Laurie thought of the bodies at Higher Bar, it struck her how cruel it would be if no one ever spoke of Chris and Odette and Eric with fondness, retrieving precious memories from the wreckage of their deaths. *I'm sorry, Izzy.*

Peter was in the sitting room, looking old and frail. She immediately regretted her impulse to avoid him. 'Hello, Dad.' Bending to kiss his cheek.

'How nice to see you.' His voice quavered, afraid of causing offence. Hard to live with only snatches of his mind and memory intact, not knowing whether to greet people as enemies or allies. She sat at his side, taking his hand, large and freckled by age, skin loose over his knuckles. 'Helen,' he said.

'Laurie,' she corrected gently. 'I'm Laurie, Dad.'

'Helen', he repeated in a firm voice, 'told me about the farm.' His hand gripped at hers, eyes moving wetly over her face.

For the first time that day, she felt like crying. The morning's chaos was in her chest, its sour heat in her mouth. The savagery in that kitchen, flies crawling over everything. The little body in the bath. She shut her eyes against the images. 'We'll find them,' she whispered. 'Whoever did that. We will find them.'

'Will you?' Peter sounded scared.

She stared into his face as if it were a fortune teller's crystal and she might find answers there instead of the dimming of the light. He was so different to the man who pulled her aside at his son's wedding, fingers biting her wrist, demanding she take charge of her sister – 'Your responsibility' – as if Isabel were a wild animal and Laurie her keeper. 'We'll find them.' For that baby, if nothing else.

'Lore? What's going on?'

Adam was in the doorway, staring at her in shock. She glanced down at her hand fastened around Peter's. He was trying to pull free, as if he'd been trying for a while but she wouldn't let him. He was weeping, tears running down his cheeks, wetting the collar of his shirt. 'Sorry.' She let go. 'Are you okay?'

He looked terrorised, chin wobbling. 'Addy?'

'It's okay, Dad. I'm here. Everything's okay.'

Laurie stood, waiting for her thoughts to fall into order. When they didn't, she turned and left, climbing the stairs to the room she shared with Adam, standing for a long time looking at her face in the night's windows. Heaviness filled her throat, inflaming her temples. She felt infected, as if she were coming down with something, would wake shivering with fever. What was wrong with her? This place— *Not the place. You.* She stared at her reflection. *You came here thinking you'd be bored rigid and instead you're out of your depth, picking fights, putting off what you need to get done. Grow up. Get to work.* She pushed her hand into her pocket and took out her phone, scrolling for the number she wanted.

He picked up almost instantly. 'Boss?'

'Joe. Let's start again tomorrow. Yes?'

'I'd like that.' He sounded relieved. 'What time d'you want me there?'

'Early. What's that, around here?'

'Seven's when Milla gets in. Not a lot of point being there before her, if we want access to the tech.' She liked the way he clicked into work mode, no hint of grudge or embarrassment in his voice. He sounded knackered, though.

'Seven it is. Get some sleep. We're going to need it.'

'Will do,' Joe said. 'You too.'

17.

Laurie was waiting outside when Joe pulled up at 6.43 a.m., finishing a mug of coffee (he guessed), in dark jeans and an olive biker jacket, the same boots she'd been wearing since she arrived. A broad-shouldered man with bedhead curls stepped out of the house. Adam Bower, creased jeans, red flannel shirt. He looked as if he was going to kiss Laurie, but she intercepted him by putting her empty mug into his hand – 'Got to go' – striding in Joe's direction.

Joe thought for a second before he unfastened his seat belt and climbed from the car, nodding at Adam. 'Morning.'

Laurie shot him a look that asked why the hell he was being polite to her husband when even she didn't have time for that.

'Morning, boss. Thought it was worth checking if you've a pair of walking boots. Rained all night, likely to be a mudslide at Higher Bar.'

'Helen'll have a pair she can lend you.' Adam had followed her to the car, holding out a hand in greeting. 'Joe. Good to see you again. It's been a while.' They shook hands, Adam making a swift study of his face. 'Awful about Chris and his family. I can hardly believe it.'

'It's been a shock for everyone,' Joe agreed.

Laurie was in the car. Adam leant in, empty mug hanging from his fingers. 'I can ask Helen to drop the boots into the station, if you'd like?'

'I'll be fine, but thanks.'

Adam straightened, nodding at Joe. 'I'll let you get off.'

When he was in the car, Laurie said, 'In your own time. No rush.'

He absorbed her eye-roll easily now he knew her a little better. 'Community relations. That's in the job description, isn't it? And Adam knew Chris. Of course you may've talked with him about that already.'

'Inappropriate.' She took out her phone. 'Better if Theo does it. Or Ted. They'll have to come out here, though. He can't leave his dad.'

'How is Peter?'

'He's not getting any better, put it that way.' She set her phone aside with a sigh. 'Sorry. Tricky night. Peter hardly sleeps, the pigs never sleep, and I'm one flat white away from being the boss from hell.'

Joe nodded to where he'd stashed two insulated cups of coffee. She reached for one. 'God, you're good. Tell me where I can buy walking boots.'

'A place out by Bamford Edge. We can detour after the briefing, or go there first, if you like. They open early. Doubt there'll be anything for us at the station before nine. If there is, Milla will call.'

'Thanks. Helen's at least a shoe size smaller than me. Adam means well, but his sisters aren't the answer to everything.' She wrinkled her nose, taking a fresh hit of coffee. 'Not a morning person. Meant what I said last night about starting over. Calculated without the sleepless night, however.'

'It's fine,' Joe said mildly. 'And last night was my fault for not steering you away from the Tollgate. I could've guessed how it was going to go.'

'My bad idea in the first place. I wasn't ready to go home.' She propped her head against the seat rest to smile at him. 'Now that's out of the way, let's get to work. How long until we hear from Sal Thomas, d'you reckon?'

'She'll have a preliminary report for us soon, knowing Sal. Midday at the latest.' Joe waited at a junction where flood damage had torn up the tarmac. 'When's Odette's mum due home?'

'Mid-morning. Nobody's mentioned Odette's dad – is he out of the picture?'

'He died a few years back, prostate cancer.' Joe pulled into a trickle of morning traffic. He'd fallen in with Laurie's need to start early, but realistically there wasn't a lot they could do ahead of Sal's post-mortem report. Interviews would take up the morning, together with ANPR data when it arrived. The search for the shotgun would start up again; Saxton had allocated that to the extra hands from Ripley. Press conference to be organised as soon as they had their facts straight, reassurances given where possible, requests for information; Saxton would want to head that up at a local level. Everyone was itching to get on, admin and bureaucracy like lead weights around their ankles. 'Cary Lawlor's coming into the station this morning. D'you want one of us to take a statement?'

'We should've put him off.' Laurie frowned. 'Can Theo handle that?'

'He can. But he'd be better talking with the mums from the nursery. Odette was there with Eric on Tuesday.'

'Theo and the nursery mums. I can see that. All right, let the desk deal with Lawlor.' She drank more coffee. '*Lady Bower.* What's that about?'

Sammi sat up on the back seat, catching Joe's eye in the mirror, interested in how he was going to answer. *Relax. She needs to know.* 'Easier if I show you. We have time, and it's more or less on the way to the outdoors shop.'

Joe's coffee did what Adam's instant cuppa had failed to do: simultaneously woke Laurie up and eased her into the day. Good to be in the car, sitting in the silence Joe had carved for her, his closed-book act a balm this morning. She was able to pay close attention to their surroundings, imagining the route their killer might've taken on Friday night. 'All the roads like this, around here?'

'More or less,' Joe said. 'The Snake Pass is generally decent, since they have to keep patching it up. Lots of traffic accidents out that way.'

'One of the worst roads in the UK for casualties. Boy racers?'

'And bad weather. People tend to underestimate how hard nature can make things around here.'

Laurie saw what he meant: whole stretches of drystone wall held together by moss, collapsed at intervals under the weight of the weather. Moss was bad enough on its own without any assistance from the rain. When Adam suggested they take a weekend trip to 'Slippery Stones', a popular wild swimming spot, she'd laughed: 'This whole bloody place is slippery.'

The Snake Pass crossed the moor between sinuous stretches of forest. The weather changed three times over the course of the drive – sunshine, rain, mist – while the landscape switched between beautiful and bleak. Easy to imagine their killer on this road, leaving the slaughter at Higher Bar for the shelter of the city. Who'd want to linger? 'Shit – look out!'

Roadkill, *enormous*, but Joe wasn't spooked, swerving before the warning was out of her mouth. He pulled over, cutting the engine. 'I'll be two minutes.'

She watched in the wing mirror as he walked back up the road, pulling on crime-scene gloves, stooping to take hold of the biggest pair of antlers she'd ever seen, easing the deer from the path of any oncoming traffic. He crouched over the dead animal before he straightened and started back in her direction, peeling off the gloves before dropping them into the boot of the car.

'Problem?' Laurie asked.

'I don't think so. Hard to tell. I'll call the district council. They'll send someone to collect him.'

'Him?'

'A stag.' Joe fastened his seat belt. 'Big increase in roadkill numbers lately, especially red deer. Not typical for this time of year. And he was bashed about, not a clean strike from a car.'

'Someone ran it under their wheels?'

Joe angled the rear view mirror to take another look at the stag. 'If you drove over something that size, your car would be off the road.'

'A lorry wouldn't care. Lots of lorries on this road.'

'A lorry didn't hit him, or not only that.' He returned the mirror to its right position, starting the engine. 'He was shot, I'd say. Then the damage disguised to look like roadkill. Farmers do it with badgers all the time since baiting became illegal. Shoot them then toss them into the road, let passing traffic do the rest.'

'That happens a lot around here?'

'More and more,' Joe said.

'Great. I'll look forward to the insurance premium going up on my car when they clock the change of address.'

'Was it that low, in Salford?'

'Different risks,' Laurie conceded.

Joe, she discovered, was accustomed to navigating roads hazardous with corpses large and small, or where sections had been gouged out or gone altogether, lost to landslips that made her shut her eyes. She missed the unequivocalness of the gangs in Manchester, knew where she stood with them, sure of her footing. What had the landscape around here made of Chris and Odette, struggling with the work needed on the house, battling bad weather and isolation? Their killer, too, how was he shaped by this place? Assuming he grew up here and not in the city, a visitor come to wreak havoc before returning to hide on her patch – was that possible? She made a mental note to check in with Rez before the end of the day.

As they crested a bend, the reservoir came into view in a sudden splash of sunrise. They passed a stretch of newly strengthened wall, strung with decaying flowers and teddy bears, before Joe crossed a bridge, turning right, with the reservoir on his side.

By the time they'd parked, the sky was camouflaged in grey, even the clouds had clouds. To either side forests rose in peaks, as if they belonged more to the sky than the land. Laurie followed Joe on foot to where signs were strung across gates: *No horse riding, no drones, no climbing on the dam.* At either end of the reservoir, giant drains were running, twenty metres in diameter, sucking water down circular steps thunderously.

'Bellmouth overflows.' Joe had to raise his voice to be heard. 'Commonly known as the Plugholes. Taking excess water into the river. You won't always see them working, only when the reservoir is full.'

The closer of the two overflows had a sign: *Danger of Death: no climbing on reservoir infrastructure.* The plugholes exerted an irresistible pull, sickeningly hypnotic; Laurie found herself leaning to look deeper. Taking a step back, she indicated the bridge they were standing on. 'What's this part?'

'The tailbay.' Joe shivered. The morning was chilly, neither of them dressed for standing by a body of water before the sun was fully up.

'Where's it go? The water. What's it used for?'

'River control. Producing electricity. Drinking water, eventually.'

A pair of padlocked gates led into low-lying watchtowers built on the water. 'People swim here?'

'They shouldn't. It's a working reservoir. Strong currents, deep water, very cold temperatures.'

The bruise in his voice was the clue she needed to piece it together. 'This is where it happened.'

'Not quite.' He pointed a short distance. 'But yes. This is where the bus went into the water seventeen years ago.'

Laurie glanced at his face but he wasn't looking at her. His eyes were on the water, swallowing it, the way his eyes swallowed everything. 'So *Lady Bower* is Vicars getting at you, not me?'

'Bit of both. Two birds, one stone.'

'Makes sense, lazy arsehole. Callous, too. Picking a nickname for the spot where nine kids died.'

Joe shook his head. 'Ted's not callous. Sometimes humour helps. And let's face it, your surname's a bit of a gift.'

'To a lazy arsehole maybe.'

'He's not lazy either. Wait and see. He'll give this investigation everything he's got, and still find time to look out for Milla and Theo.' Joe gave his slight, serious smile. 'You're not giving him much to work with. *Us* much to work with. It's early days, I know, but . . .'

She couldn't argue with that, or about the ways in which humour helped. 'What d'you recommend?'

'The usual: come out after work, buy a round.'

'That went so well last night. Also, I'm teetotal.'

He blinked, his expression recalibrating.

'Yeah,' Laurie said. 'I should keep quiet about that, shouldn't I?'

'Probably.'

'So if not the pub, then what?'

'Doughnuts,' Joe said promptly. 'Greggs sell them in bulk. There's a concession in the service station. We can stop there on the way in.'

'DS Vicars loves a doughnut. Jammy, I'll bet.'

'Safe bet.'

She waited for him to say more, but Joe lapsed into silence. Fair enough, given where they were standing. She thought of the bus nose-diving into the water, screaming faces at every window. The only survivor. How had he managed to get his head around that? He was watching the road, eyes off in some place she couldn't see. His past, not hers. 'At Higher Bar. With Eric. That wasn't me trying to keep you away from the crime scene.'

'Wasn't it?' Joe turned to face her. 'I preferred it when you were angry with me for failing to prioritise his safety. I don't want protecting.'

'We all want that sometimes. You didn't need to see him, it was obvious he'd drowned. But to be clear? If I'd thought you needed to see him, or if I'd wanted a second opinion? I'd have told you to go up there with me. And I'd've expected you to do it, no questions asked.'

'I'd have done it, no questions asked.'

He didn't want special treatment. Just to be like everyone else. She could never tell him, she realised, about the moment yesterday when she'd imagined her sister was standing with them in Chris's bedroom. Her past, not his.

'Mrs Hall in the Tollgate last night. How often does that happen?'

'Not often,' Joe said. 'But it's bound to be hard for people like her, at least for a time. The murders are shocking enough, but Eric drowned. That's going to trigger a lot of people.'

She was aware of holding her breath, trying not to stare at this man young enough to be her son yet older than she'd ever be, weighted down in the world as if by an extra dose of gravity, a dimension she was missing. Behind him, water stretched up into forest and then to sky the colour of his eyes. Grey as camouflage, clouds hiding in clouds. 'That's why Des has a problem with you,' she realised. 'Because of people like Mrs Hall. He thinks you're exploiting their grief.'

Joe flinched but nodded. 'That's one of his problems, certainly.'

'What else? For operational purposes. I'd like to quantify the threat.'

He dipped his head, as if listening for a sound under the thunder of the reservoir. Then he smiled. 'He has a problem with the fact I'm queer.'

Laurie's turn to flinch. 'Your choice of word, or his?'

'Mine. I can write you a list of his, if you like. But that one's mine.'

'Isn't it more usual to say "gay"?'

'If I was gay, maybe. I'm bi. Prefer *queer*.'

'Right.' She brushed mist from her jacket. 'That was awkward on my part. Give you my word I'm not a bigot. Just semantically inept.'

'It's fine, honestly. I didn't think you were a bigot.' He used his smile to steady her, very good at making space for other people's discomfort. He'd done it with Bobby German, and Beverley Miles, and with Molly and Tyler's mum last night in the pub.

'A lot of conflict, locally. Strong emotions. You get caught in the middle of that quite often, do you?'

'I wouldn't say often. But yes, lots of strong emotions here. I'm not the only one Des has a problem with. He's happy to spread the blame. Hates Nelson Roache because his daughter Maggie was our teacher. She was on the bus with us.'

'Then she died. What's Des's grudge against her dad?'

'Unclear. She should've been able to save some of the kids, maybe. His brother Seth died on the bus. Maggie kept giving Seth second chances for bullying and bad behaviour. If she'd suspended him, he'd have missed the trip. Stayed home when the rest of us . . .' He gestured at the reservoir.

Under their feet, the path was glossy with rain. A stone wall guarded the drop into the water. On the other side, black railings performed the same function. Hard to see how a tanker could've gone over, let alone a school bus. But Joe said it happened on the other side. Rotting flowers and teddy bears.

'Few places it could've gone in. The chances were tiny.' Joe's voice held a thread of puzzlement as if he couldn't stop calculating those odds. 'Two feet either side and trees would've stopped us entering the water, that's what the investigation concluded. They're planted virtually the entire length of the road. The bus found one of the few places where it was a clear ride into the reservoir. Mud bank, no barrier. Daffodils there, in the spring.'

'Did they ever find out what caused the crash?' Laurie hadn't forgotten what Adam said about Joe taking the blame, but she didn't believe for a second it was his fault, even if people like Des Morton took his confession at face value. 'Someone stepping into the road? Driver swerving to avoid a stag?'

Birds rose from the water in a sudden beat of wings. Dark and sleek, a pair of cormorants. Joe watched them climb the sky, his profile drawn, private. 'The driver lost control, that's all they were able to say with certainty.' He said it with so little emotion it was hard to believe it'd happened to him. She'd seen plenty of trauma survivors but few had Joe's steady way of standing, his unflinching eyes on the world. A detective, whose job it was to stare into the ugliest corners, confront the worst realities.

'Why did you do it?' she asked. 'Join the police?'

She thought he'd fob her off, or else refuse to answer. But after a long moment he straightened, putting both palms on the broad lip of the bridge. When he spoke, it was so quietly she had to lean in to listen, her blood chilling at the words he chose: 'I couldn't think what else to do with the guilt.'

18.

The outdoors shop had the boots Laurie needed, after which they headed to the station. She'd been quiet since Ladybower Reservoir. Joe was starting to wish he'd kept his mouth shut, fearing he'd given her a new reason to think his approach to police work was unconventional, at best. But she said, 'I want to get back in that farmhouse. Figure out what the hell went wrong. Between Chris and Odette, or around them. I've not seen a crime scene as bad as that in a long time.'

'Tempting to think everything's more wholesome around here.' Joe guessed she was thinking along those lines. 'But we've our share of problems with break-ins. Drugs, even firearms. A modern weapons arsenal turned up in a Grade II listed townhouse in Buxton not that long ago. I'm not suggesting Chris or Odette were involved in anything like that, but we can't discount it. I wish we could.'

Sammi was silent in the back seat. He'd been silent since the reservoir. Joe was starting to wonder what he'd done to upset him.

'Everyone's a suspect,' Laurie agreed. 'All right. Open minds. Let's see what the day has in store.'

In the station, a fair-haired man in his late thirties was waiting by the front desk. Joe recognised him from research he'd done online. 'Cary Lawlor? I'm DS Ashe. This is DI Bower.'

Lawlor had the subdued shine of someone who'd set off looking London-smart only to be thwarted by the long drive, suit creased by a seat belt, chin in need of a shave. 'I headed up as soon as I could get away.'

'There was no great urgency. Sorry if you were given that impression.'

'No, just that the cottage needs making secure.'

He was nervous. Joe could smell his sweat. Laurie was walking away in the direction of the incident room. He pointed the man at a chair. 'Someone'll bring you coffee. An officer will be with you soon to take your statement.'

Lawlor ran a hand over his unshaved chin. 'I can wait at the cottage? Saw the police tape up the road. Looks like you've a major incident on your hands.'

'I'm afraid that's right. If you don't mind waiting here, it'll make things easier all round. Coffee?'

He'd driven half the night to get here. Joe wanted to know why, but it would have to wait. The briefing about Higher Bar took precedence, over that and everything else.

Saxton was in the incident room with Laurie, the pair of them studying the summary board. Milla was online, Theo checking paperwork. Ted nodded a greeting at Joe. 'Thought you'd be the first in. Well, you and *Lady Bower*.' He curled his lip in Laurie's direction.

'You need to stop using that nickname,' Joe told him. 'The guv wanted to know what it meant, so I explained. She won't want to hear you use it again.'

'Only one *guv* here, and it's not her majesty over there.'

'You're upset. We all are. What happened to Chris and Odette and Eric is terrible. We need to find who did it. We won't if we're not working as a team. What's the news from Ripley?'

Ted stared him down, or tried to. When Joe didn't budge, he shrugged his big shoulders. 'We'll have extra hands. They're back out looking for the weapon. Probably tossed it, but we might get lucky.'

'We might,' Joe agreed. He touched a hand to Ted's elbow, judging it the best way to signal they were on the same side. 'I know you'll be keeping an eye on Milla and Theo. Thanks for that.'

Milla's head was down. Joe saw the stress in her shoulders. It was going to get ugly. How could it not, when people they'd known – seen in the supermarket, spoken to on the street – had been violently killed, and a child's life lost?

Theo looked up when Joe approached his desk. 'I'd like to go with Eric's grandparents for the visual IDs. Unless you or the guv have any objections?'

By *guv*, he meant Saxton. But Laurie was the SIO. The team needed to get behind her. 'Let's wait and see what DI Bower says at the briefing.'

'I heard about what happened in the Tollgate last night.' Theo fidgeted with paperwork on his desk. 'With Molly and Tyler's mum.'

'What did you hear?' Joe braced himself.

'That she wanted to know if you were with Eric. If you'd seen him.'

Sammi was behind Theo's chair suddenly, folding his arms. He'd no patience for Theo's habit of banging on the same drum. That had surprised Joe at first but as time passed, it made more sense.

'Mrs Hall's upset,' Joe said. 'It's understandable. What happened at Higher Bar is shocking. We need to do everything we can to help people come to terms with it. For that, we need answers. That's our job, DC Howden.'

He waited until Theo was looking at him. Felt a familiar tug of tiredness at his inability to let go of the past. Theo had to move on. Joe had, hadn't he? Sammi made a *wrong answer* noise, settling himself on the edge of the desk. Joe ignored him, focusing on Theo. 'You and I need to do our jobs. You're our best family liaison officer. DCI Saxton knows that, and so will DI Bower. So yes, go with the families for the visual IDs. I know you'll be sympathetic, respectful and caring. The same with the mums at the nursery.'

Theo was nodding but as soon as Joe fell silent, he shifted his weight, dipping his voice back down to a whisper: 'You were with Hannah Cooper, too.'

'What?' He saw a flush heat Howden's face. A similar heat was spreading itself across the back of his own neck. Sammi said softly, 'Shit.'

'It's common knowledge.' Theo was on the verge of a stammer. 'That you visit her. And why. Because of Zoe. She asks you over when she wants to see Zoe. It's the same with me, Joe. Me and Ellie. I *see* her—'

'He does see her.' Sammi inspected his fingernails. 'Can't argue with that.'

'I understand.' Joe held hard to his patience. 'But if DI Bower or DCI Saxton hear you talking like this, you'll be made to see a psych counsellor. Me too, in all likelihood. Don't put us in that position. It's not fair on either of us.'

'I just want you to understand', Theo said urgently, 'that *I* understand. What you're going through. But also what you're putting *her* through when you go into crime scenes like that one. How *Ellie* feels—' He gripped Joe's wrist.

Grief ran its fracture up his face. Not for the first time Joe thought, *He's insane, this is driving him insane.* But if Theo was mad with grief for his sister, what was Joe? Because Theo wasn't the only one seeing ghosts. 'Rude. I'm right here.' Sammi had finished with his nails, was reading paperwork on Theo's desk.

'DC Howden? DS Ashe?' Laurie beckoned. 'Briefing, please.'

Theo let go of Joe's wrist and stood, doing as Laurie instructed. Sammi said, 'He was following you last night. Must've been. How else does he know where you went, who you saw?'

Common knowledge, he said.

'Want to know what's on his desk?'

Pretty sure I already know.

A printout from a regional newspaper. Not about the bus crash, or Joe. About Isabel Warden, "Former Champion Archer Found Dead", in Manchester.

'Laurie's sister,' Sammi said. 'Must be. And she didn't tell you. All those confidences you shared out by the water but she kept that to herself.'

Why should she tell me? It's none of my business.

'Or you freak her out. Not everyone's like Theo, wanting their sister's ghost tagging along. I bet that's who she saw in the bedroom yesterday. Isabel.'

Joe told him to be quiet; he needed to focus on the briefing. But now he had something else to worry about. Not whether or not Laurie thought him a freak, but why Theo thought it a good idea to investigate their boss's private life. And how far he'd spread the news of what he'd found. Sammi stood with him, watching Laurie.

Who did this? Joe asked him silently. *Who killed them?*

'We'll work it out,' Sammi said. Then he corrected himself, a little sadly, still watching Laurie. '*You'll* work it out.'

★

Saxton's briefing had been short and to the point. Ripley's uniforms were searching for the shotgun, fast-tracking evidence secured by Sal's team, what Ted called 'tapings and scrapings'. The farmhouse was all theirs, everything logged and listed. Post-mortems were close. Laurie felt it, knew Joe was the same, both of them thinking of the bodies laid out under Sal's lights.

'When did you last see them? Chris and Odette. Eric.'

Better for him to talk than bottle it up, be a tough guy. Murders had a way of wriggling under your skin. If you weren't careful, they took root, spread their shadows down into your bones.

'Chris . . . Ten days ago, on the road out to Matlock. He was driving his van. We nodded at one another in passing, that was it.'

She saw Joe mentally record the moment, making sure he didn't forget. He had the right instincts: not wallowing in the misery but not stepping over it either. Back in Salford, most of her team were hardened to the job's horror which made practical sense, but she sometimes had to remind them where their hearts were. She wasn't going to have that problem with Joe.

'Odette and Eric, earlier in the week, in the Co-op. Odette was buying nappies and baby food.' His face softened. 'Eric was sleeping in his carrier.'

At Higher Bar, Laurie had watched him record ambient temperature, noting the condition of the kitchen: decaying food, crusted dishes, cups of cold coffee. The full log included cell site data, communications from both mobile phones and from the laptop brought into evidence; Milla was developing a timeline to assist in determining time of death.

'We have to look at Chris for this,' Laurie said. 'Same as any other domestic. Bobby thought there might've been an affair in the mix. We should consider that, rule it in or out.'

Joe nodded. Then he said, 'He was underneath Odette, which has to mean he was shot first. Hard to see how that makes it a murder-suicide.'

'Have a think,' Laurie said. 'And get back to me.'

She reached for the log, reading it for a fifth time. She'd taken photos on her phone but preferred the information fixed in her head so she could make connections quickly, later down the line. It was how she'd caught Jim Chancellor: a combination of instinct and instant access to the information they'd been gathering. Kept the crime alive in her head, not as a nightmare but as an orderly set of facts.

Joe said, 'He could've shot Odette then pulled her half on top of him before shooting himself.' He met her eye, nodded. 'I'll keep an open mind. That said . . . no shotgun in the kitchen. So unless a third party removed it for reasons I can't fathom, Chris wasn't the shooter.'

'We'll close that door after the post-mortems, but you're probably right. And, to be clear, you don't need to prove anything.' She held his gaze. 'Not to me. Just keep doing your job. Every angle, all the time. And nudge me if I'm in danger of upsetting the delicate ecosystem around here. I'm counting on you for that.'

She checked her watch, keen to get on. Every investigation moved at its own pace, even murders as savage as these. No point trying to push the local teams to go faster; they'd be moving as quickly as they could. They needed the post-mortem reports; whatever Sal Thomas had to say would guide what they did next. As SIO, Laurie would draw on material generated by the team to support or challenge Sal's conclusions; nothing as simple as a swift consensus. No point telling herself she'd have a lightbulb moment, solve it that way, certainly not ahead of hearing what Sal had to tell them—

A text, pinging. She read it, reaching for her jacket. 'We need to take ourselves to the Northern.' Northern General Hospital, Sheffield.

'From Sal?' Joe nodded at her phone. 'She's ready for us?'

'She is. How long's it going to take us?'

'Half an hour, on the A57.'

'Back on the Snake Pass? Let's go.'

19.

Laurie hadn't been to the Northern in a while, but not much had changed. The hospital ran up against one of Sheffield's roughest neighbourhoods, on-street parking an assault course at any given hour of the day or night. As they stepped from the car, things switched up a gear. Gang of lads, drinking all night by the look of them. No warning, just the sound of a missile approaching at speed.

'Incoming!'

She swerved, her city radar firing in glorious technicolour. The can breezed past her left ear, would've caught Joe square in the side of his head if she hadn't grabbed him. A full can of Carling, open, sharing its contents freely before hitting the road, rolling to a halt.

Joe wiped its wet from his head, shaking froth from his fingers before doing the same with the shoulders of his suit. He didn't turn his head or stop moving. When he reached the can, he scooped it up, depositing it in the nearest bin. Laurie was more impressed than she'd been at any point since meeting him. 'You don't need an anger management class. You *are* an anger management class.'

'No point going full yokel for halfwits,' Joe said.

The Northern smelt of polished floors and breakfasts. Last time she was here, Laurie was with Rez, the pair of them watching a pathologist and APT piece together what was left of a body found in Castlegate, suspected to be that of a dealer they'd tracked over an eight-month operation. The body was nine parts liquid thanks to the heatwave that flattened everything that summer. She remembered the pathologist, Stuart, a redhead with a poker beard, his big hands making sense of the mess, the look on his face as their eyes met. Her questions, his answers. The ringing of steel, everywhere. A joke about soup, another about hiring out the mortuary cold room to anyone desperate for a respite from the heat: 'Two hundred quid gets you half an hour on a body tray, more if you want to slide in the freezer . . .' Humour's half the job, Rez used to say on days when the horror rushed in. When Laurie asked what the other half was, he punched the code for a Diet Coke into the vending machine. She wished Rez could've seen the cool way Joe brushed lager from his shoulders. Crisp customer, DS Ashe.

Dr Salome Thomas was waiting in the exam room. 'One of you smells like a brewery. But you look sober enough.'

'Carling lobby.' Laurie was confident Sal would know what she meant. You didn't need to look like a detective to get cans chucked at you, just someone with a job that didn't involve drinking all night.

'Ah. The urban sophisticates giving you a lukewarm-and-wet welcome. Smells like you took the hit, Joe.'

'Yes, sorry about that. But I am sober, I promise.'

'I've never known you be anything else. Shall we start with Eric? I made him my priority.' Sal spoke without sentiment. 'Thirteen months old. Height and weight average for his age. No sign of illness or neglect, no external or internal injuries, pre- or post-mortem. He drowned.' She rested her hand on the lip of the body tray. 'Ischaemic damage to the brain, kidneys and heart. Cause of death was multiple organ failure consistent with drowning.'

The simplest, least violent of the deaths, but the worst. That poor baby. Alone in a foot of water, crying for his mum, his dad.

'How long was he left?' Laurie asked. 'Can you say?'

'I've known babies drown in under a minute, unattended. He was a strong boy by the look of him, no evidence he was held under the water.' Her factual answers made it easier. 'It was probably quick. I'd expect to see bruising if he struggled. There's nothing like that. Just the usual marks I'd expect on a healthy, lively one-year-old.' She indicated a scab on the child's knee, a scratch on his forearm.

Laurie's head was starting to ache, pressure building behind her eyes. *No tears, Bower, this is spilt milk. Get through it, find who did this.*

Sal smoothed the sheet lightly over Eric, moving to the first of the adult corpses. 'Odette Miles. Thirty-nine. Cause of death was a single shot.' She described the likely weapon: a shotgun, twelve-bore, the kind used to shoot deer. The same weapon had put a hole in Chris's chest. 'I'd love to be able to give you the killer's height, but at best it would be approximate. This could have been someone tall holding the firearm at waist height, or someone short with it mounted on their shoulder. One thing I can rule out: neither Chris nor Odette fired a weapon. No residue. Their deaths occurred very close together but from the configuration of the bodies, Chris was the first victim.'

Not murder-suicide. A tiny scrap of silver lining for Eric's grandparents.

The morning wore on, painstakingly. Clothing was cut and searched, each item photographed and exhibited. The bodies examined for surface fragments – glass, paint, fibres, bodily fluids the killer might have left in the wounds inflicted on Odette and Chris. Sal searched under their fingernails for defensive evidence. Nothing. Everything she did find was secured by the exhibits officer. Laurie knew the procedure by heart: record, seize, package, label, retain. Precise positions of injuries, scars and distinguishing features were recorded on a body map, Sal giving each injury an identifying number for ease of reference. Then the same all over again, for Chris. In each case, cause of death was a gunshot wound. Odette's to the back of the head. Chris's to the heart. Time of death was approximate, but consistent with when Joe heard shots on Friday night.

Sal finished, finally. 'I'd like to be up to speed ahead of the relatives' visit. Who's coming to see the bodies, and when?'

'DCI Saxton will be in attendance,' Laurie said. 'With DC Howden, who's our FLO. Chris's parents. Odette's mum.'

'Eric's grandparents.' Sal gave Joe a watchful nod. 'I'll be careful.'

In the corridor, Laurie checked her phone before tucking it into her pocket, fixing her full attention on Joe. 'You stink. She's right about that.'

'Helpful in there, though. A change from the usual olfactory experience.'

Laurie pulled her face into a smile. Humour had deserted the pair of them. A murdered family could do that, Joe guessed, even to a hardened DI.

'I need caffeine. Vending machine's that way –' she pointed – 'as I recall. Diet Coke.'

Joe nodded, walking away, aware she needed a moment to regroup. 'How about you? You okay?' Sammi, joining him on the quest for the vending machine, dressed as always in jeans and a grey sweatshirt. Joe marvelled again at how real he looked, how real he *was*. Light shone from his hair which smelt freshly washed, brown curls pushed back from his face. His trainers raised a thin sound from the hospital floors, his shadow keeping pace along the scuffed walls. Joe took out his phone as a prop, so he could talk without looking like a madman. 'I'm okay, thanks. You?'

Sammi was peering at the neck of Joe's shirt. 'You're going to need a change of clothes. Carling all over your collar. Sal's not the only one who's going to think you're drunk and disorderly. Can't go interviewing suspects smelling like you spent the night in the Tollgate.'

'Laurie doesn't seem to mind.'

'Oh it's *Laurie* now, is it? One little heart-to-heart and you're on first-name terms.'

Joe came to a halt by the vending machine, wondering what was misfiring in his mind to the extent he was hallucinating his best friend having a strop about his boss's first name. 'What's up?' he said into the phone.

Sammi leant his shoulder into the vending machine. 'Better get her Diet Coke. Wouldn't want to be in her bad books.'

'Seriously. What's up?'

'You told her about the bus crash, but not about me. What'm I supposed to make of that?'

'Well, for starters you could assume I'm not keen to end up on a psych ward when I'm trying to solve a triple homicide.'

'Mad prices.' Sammi studied the contents of the vending machine. 'Who'd pay two quid for a Tango? Actually, I'd love a Tango. And a bag of Wotsits.'

Joe used his credit card for two Diet Cokes, a Tango and a bag of Wotsits. Sammi watched him with shining eyes, turning a neat circle on his heel.

'If it keeps you happy.' Joe put the Wotsits and Tango on the chair by the vending machine. 'Sit this one out. I'll swing back round for you before we leave.'

'I know you will. You don't go anywhere without me. Sooner or later, *Laurie* is going to catch on to that. And then you'll need another heart-to-heart.'

'Not happening,' Joe said, 'if I can help it.'

Outside, Laurie paused to check her phone. 'What's the deal with you and Sal? Definite vibes there.'

Joe checked the street for airborne Carling cans as he took out the keys to unlock the car. 'She was responsible for the post-mortems after the bus crash.'

'Jesus, that must've been tough.' Laurie waited until the pair of them were in the car before adding, 'No wonder she's so protective of you.'

'*Protective* is a stretch. But we do have a connection. It's generally considered helpful, by DCI Saxton anyway. You may feel differently.'

'If it means she's prioritising our stuff, that works for me.'

She was on her phone; Joe wondered if she was messaging Adam. None of his business but he wished she didn't have a tricky home life in the mix. Peter Bower's decline was enough to deal with on its own.

'Yeah.' Sammi lolled in the back seat. 'If only she was going home to an empty flat like you, you lucky loveless bastard.'

'We need motive.' Laurie pocketed her phone. 'Who wanted to kill that couple, and why? Nothing of value taken as far as we can tell. Easy money if this was a robbery. Laptops, phones, TV. Electrical kit in the garage. We're taking a fresh look, though. No disrespect to the local tech team.'

'We need to see for ourselves,' Joe agreed. The thought of being back in that kitchen made his skin clench, but this was the job he'd signed up for.

'Have fun,' from the back seat.

Joe met Sammi's eyes in the mirror: *Don't you dare sit this round out. Stop sulking. I need you in there. Sharpest eyes I've got.*

20.

Sammi was waiting when they reached Higher Bar, shivering by the police tape as if he could feel the blade of wind slicing up the valley. He stood aside for Laurie before stepping close, breath coasting Joe's cheek. 'Someone needs to have your back in there.' Deadly serious. When Joe quizzed him with a look, he said, 'Think about it. And take care, Joe.' He slipped under the tape.

Joe followed, joining Laurie in the farmhouse kitchen where the shadow of the slaughter was horribly bright. Under the tang of chemicals from the tech team, the darker scent of the deaths shimmered, stains on the floor made worse by pale patches where Chris had flung an arm, or where Odette's legs kept the blood from the tiles. The damage had gone wide, pebble-dashing walls and ceiling, leaving savage speckles on the fridge and microwave. Joe was hyper-aware of the bathroom, the small cloud of sadness gathered there. He could taste bathwater, the tips of his fingers wet and wrinkled, roaring in his ears. 'Focus on Laurie. *Joe.* She's solid. Look how solid she is.'

He blinked back the tide of blood, fixing on Laurie. Sammi was right; she wasn't flinching or wavering, just doing her job. She needed the same from him. 'Tell me what you're thinking?' he asked.

'Chris was shot in the chest.' She nodded at the floor. 'Odette in the back of the head. Strong indicator Chris was the primary target. Odette came into it late. Maybe she was running, or trying to run.' She was doing what detectives did at this early stage in an investigation, pulling the evidence in every direction, seeing how far it would stretch, what shapes it made.

Chris on his back, Odette facing in the other direction as if she'd turned, tried to run. The killer taking her down like an animal. How had it felt to be confronted by a gunman in her own home? Nowhere to run, no escape, her child upstairs, alone. Left alone.

'She was trying to get back to Eric. She was with him in the bathroom, wouldn't have left him alone without a good reason.'

'A gunshot's a good reason.' Laurie frowned. 'Although if it were me, I'd bolt the bathroom door and stay with my son, not go to investigate whatever's unfolding downstairs.'

'If she thought it was an accident, Chris had hurt himself—'

'Sorry, no. Same answer. You don't leave your baby unattended in a bath. You take him out, take him with you, or you put him somewhere safe. At the very least you pull the plug, drain the bath.'

'So what would make you leave your child in a foot of bathwater?'

They stared at the stains on the floor, seeing through the nightmare's red membrane to small domestic details layered underneath. It was why they'd come, in a sense, to understand how life was lived here before the killer obliterated it. Fridge magnets in the shape of Lego bricks, a pottery mug – 'World's Best Dad', penguin-printed oven gloves, an upturned sippy cup.

'Let's walk it back,' Laurie said. 'To before the gunshot that killed Chris.' She stepped around the stains, to where stairs stretched up to the floor above.

Joe watched her measure the distance with her eyes, calculating how many seconds it took Odette to get from the bathroom to her death. 'You don't think it was the gunshot that brought her down here?'

'Gunshots are terrifying. Even if you're used to hearing them out there, inside your own home while you're bathing your baby? I don't think she left Eric because she thought she and Chris were under siege. I think she left him because she was sure he'd be safe. Before the killer came, or before the first shot anyway.'

'How could she be sure he'd be safe? You said it yourself: you don't leave a baby in a bath.'

'You might, for a few seconds. Because you'd forgotten a towel and he's a strong one-year-old and it'll only take a tick to get what you need. Come on.'

Joe followed her up the stairs, Sammi staying close.

The bathroom was a good size, yellow tiles, flowered curtains. White units with built-in shelves, bottles and bath toys, splashes of colour everywhere. Acrylic loo seat where starfish and shells sparkled. Heated towel rail on the wall nearest the door, empty. Sammi stood between Joe and the bath, his face grave and vigilant.

'No towels,' Joe said.

'Not in here,' Laurie agreed. 'Towels on the drying rack in the utility room, though. It's in the log.'

He pulled up the details on his phone, wanting to be certain. She was right. 'Utility room's at the foot of the stairs. Facing the kitchen. Both doors were open.'

Laurie nodded. He expected her to head in that direction but she detoured towards the bedrooms. At the front of the house, Chris and Odette had shared a double bed with views towards the forest. The duvet was pulled neat, its cover printed to look like patchwork. The furniture in the room was homely, pine cabinets and wardrobe, dressing table mirror wound with fairy lights, Odette's make-up lined up around a little brass tree, its branches studded with earrings. Chris's bedside table held a phone charger, family photo in a home-made frame: Eric in Odette's arms, Odette in Chris's, small faces sunlit and smiling. Happiness was such a fragile thing, like a cobweb waiting to be torn away—'Depends who spun it,' Sammi said. 'Darwin's bark spider? That shit's tougher than Kevlar.' Places in the pillows where Chris and Odette's heads had rested. *Wish I kissed you when I had the chance, Sammi. Wish I'd taken the trouble to understand my mum's guilt before I let my own get in the way.* 'If wishes were horses, Joe.' Sammi moved restlessly. 'Don't go in the back bedroom unless you have to.' *Have to, it's my job.*

Laurie led the way, the pair of them standing in the nursery among Eric's clothes and toys, counting the ways in which this should never have happened. The box-shaped room was made cheerful by a glowing jellyfish lamp, walls painted ocean-blue and stencilled with fish, a whale blowing a great white cloud of water. The view from the window reached all the way down the Derwent Valley. They stood in silence, shoulder to shoulder, until Laurie said, 'This feels like a decent family home, no monsters under the bed. I'm wary of making assumptions, but I don't sense any neglect here. Do you?'

'None.'

Eric's cot was the kind that converted to a child's bed, a clean scent of fabric softener from its sheets. On a chest of drawers, a monitor designed to record the room's temperature flashed a silent warning that it was too cold. Sammi prowled the landing, impatient for Joe to go; the longer he stood here, the greater the chance of seeing Eric. Part of Joe wanted to see him, as if he could in that way atone for his failure on Monday morning. 'You didn't fail him,' Sammi snapped. 'And you won't. Find his killer, Joe.'

'No towels in either bedroom,' Laurie said. 'Come on.'

They went back down the stairs. In the hall, she nodded at the open door to the utility room where green bath towels hung on a wooden rack. 'I think she dived downstairs to grab a towel and walked in on what was happening.'

They turned to where the kitchen opened its dark jaw behind them.

'And tried to run back upstairs to Eric.'

Joe could see the terror in Odette's eyes, Chris powerless to help her. The shotgun's muzzle swinging between them, settling on Chris. Odette turning to get to her son because her husband was lost. Not trying to escape but to save Eric. Then—A bullet to the back of the head.

'He had to kill her,' Laurie said. 'Because she'd seen him. Perhaps he'd've let her live if she'd stayed upstairs with Eric.'

'Or he was hunting. He was going to kill everyone in this house.'

It took him a moment to register the silence. Sammi said, 'She's staring, Joe. Better try to un-weird that.'

'Might be leaning into my local knowledge a bit too hard.'

Laurie raised an eyebrow. 'Lots of unhinged hunters around here? Only it might've been nice if you'd mentioned that earlier. Say, when we were ankle-deep in gore.'

'An exaggeration on my part. I just meant guns and grouse hunters. Too much late-night Netflix. Sorry, boss.'

'She's not buying it.' Sammi was sitting on the stairs, shoulders braced, barring the way. He didn't want Joe back up there. Or Eric coming down, the way he almost had the last time Joe was here. The house throbbed with death. Joe was aware of his chest filling, heaviness in the palms of his hands. Laurie's voice pulled him back: 'Kitchen door was wide open. She'll have had clear eyes on our killer.'

'Not the killer. Or she'd have run, been gunned down in the hall. Unless it was someone she knew. Someone she thought she could reason with.'

'Keep going.'

'That's all I've got.' Joe shook his head. 'I can't imagine anyone who knew them doing something so savage. To them, to Eric. I can't imagine it.'

Laurie accepted this with a nod. 'She saw Chris, but not the killer. Heard voices, called to him and got no answer. Thought it safe to set foot in the kitchen. All right. Let's take a look in the garage. And at some point I want another chat with Bobby.'

'You think there's something he's not telling us?' Joe followed her through the front door, out of the house.

'He's a watcher, spends a lot of time outdoors by the look of him, knows who comes and goes. Vested interest in being a nosy neighbour, given what you told me about the house next to his.' Laurie was striding in her new boots. 'Get much of that around here? Land grabs? What I'd call turf wars. Those developers want Bobby out; hard to see how they'll make money while he's burning God knows what in that dustbin of his, airing his arse for all to see.'

They crossed in the direction of the garage where Chris had kept his van and business equipment. It was cold outside, punchy, clearing Joe's head.

'Fair amount of poverty in the area, most of it tucked away up side streets. Pockets of wealth, of course, some of it significant. Where we bring in tourists things are easier. Holiday cottages are part of that economy, so it's a problem when people like Bobby get dug in. He's looking after the land, though. Informed conservation, a proper understanding of what thrives around here, what needs tending and what's best left alone. Better than the developers, who managed to rupture a water pipe in the summer, giving us a temporary geyser to deal with. Flooding, road closures. Bobby wouldn't have made that mistake.'

'Holidaymakers are a menace, is that what you mean?'

Laurie hauled on the garage door. A scurry of cold air escaped like a trapped animal, brushing past their legs and away. Inside: an empty parking space for Chris's van, taken for forensics. Cupboards and shelves for the electrical equipment he routinely used, plus three heavy-duty steel storage containers the size of chest freezers, fitted with deadlocks. The tech team had popped the lids, left tags to say which items in Evidence were taken from which container.

'Most of what he kept in here makes sense,' Laurie said. 'For a jobbing electrician. But one thing on the inventory stood out.'

Sammi was sitting on the lid of the nearest storage container, watching her, interested in what she was about to do next. What she did was swing the lid up, dusting Sammi from its surface like a handful of sand. It was starting to mess with Joe's head, seeing the two of them together.

'This', said Laurie, 'is where Chris was keeping a Celestron NexStar Evolution nine point . . . something.'

'Two five,' Sammi supplied, a second before Joe said the same. 'I read the inventory,' he told Laurie. 'A telescope.'

'Not just any telescope. The premium go-to scope for breathtaking views of the night sky. Ten hours of uninterrupted stargazing.'

'He was in a good spot for it. Pricey, I expect.'

'Three grand and counting.' Laurie finished looking inside the container and dropped the lid back down. 'No receipt, no sign of it on the family's bank statements or credit cards.'

'Cash payment? That's not unusual around here. The local used car dealership handles more cash than credit.'

'He shells out for a piece of kit like that then stashes it in a damp garage, albeit in this Fort Knox box?' She rapped the steel lid with her knuckles.

'Not damp. Cold. If it was damp, his gear would be shot. He keeps it dry in here.' Joe eyed the other containers. 'These two were empty, is that right?'

She nodded, dusting her hands, still frowning over the telescope.

'It fits with the window decals at his mum and dad's place,' Joe said. 'A hobby he had to give up when Eric was born, space needed in the house. Back bedroom has the best night views but that's a nursery now.'

'Fair enough. I thought it worth a look.' She stared around the garage as if fixing it in her mind then strode for the door. 'You didn't answer my question about holidaymakers. Are they a menace round here?'

'Not always. As I say, they bring money to the area. We wouldn't have a Spar in Curbar without all the holiday cottages there.'

'Where's Curbar?'

'South of Edenscar. On the way to Chatsworth.'

'His lordship's neck of the woods.'

'Do you know the twelfth Duke of Devonshire?' Joe asked innocently.

'Get lost. We don't all have friends in fancy places.'

Laurie climbed into the passenger seat. Joe looked back at the garage where Sammi was lingering as if he hadn't finished examining the space, or was figuring something out which he'd share with Joe later.

Joe got into the car, fastened his belt and fired the engine.

'That was your cue', Laurie said, 'to tell me all about your pal Nelson Roache, and the police and crime commissioner.'

He checked the mirrors as he pulled away. 'What d'you need to know?'

'Just your basic risk assessment. String-pulling versus brown-nosing. How much time d'you spend on the latter and is it worth whatever favours he calls in higher up the food chain.'

'It doesn't really work like that.'

She studied him with disapproval. Joe was acutely aware of the stains on his shirt. 'So you're sucking up to him for the sake of your pride, is that it?'

'He's been kind to me.'

'In what way?'

'For one thing, he helped me access physio when it looked like this would stop me getting on to the DC programme.' Joe indicated his left shoulder.

'What's wrong with it?'

'Dislocates more easily than it should. Happened in the crash, chronic instability. Physio helps. I'd not have passed the medical without it, and I couldn't have afforded anything like the number of sessions Nelson paid for.'

'Why did he?'

'Not sure. Perhaps because Maggie was on the bus? He took an interest in me after the crash. Lots of people did, but Nelson hasn't asked anything in return. He's given me his time when I've asked for it, opened a door or two, but if you're hoping for scandal, you'll be disappointed. Unlike the Duke of Devonshire, Nelson wasn't born within a hundred miles of a silver spoon.'

Laurie made a sound of suspended disbelief before spending the rest of the journey making notes on her phone. When they reached the station, she sprang her seat belt. 'You've five minutes to find a clean shirt. Then we're debriefing.'

She headed for the incident room, fired with fresh purpose. The visit to Higher Bar had been useful for fitting evidence from the post-mortem into what else they knew, but mostly it'd drawn attention to the gaps in their knowledge. She was keen to get on with the hard work. Past noon on the second day of the investigation. She could feel time slipping away. 'DS Vicars, DC Shaw, DC Howden. Briefing in two minutes. I want an update on ANPR, exhibits, interviews, digital trail – everything you've got. Is DCI Saxton around?'

'With the parents, boss.' Milla pushed the headphones from her head. 'Heading to the Northern.' She glanced at Theo. 'He wanted us heads-down.'

Saxton had decided not to take Theo with him to the hospital, in other words. Probably the right call; post-mortems were light work compared to accompanying families to view bodies. She thought of that baby on the steel tray and hardened her heart for the pursuit of those responsible. 'Two minutes. DC Howden, get your pens sharpened.' She pointed at the summary board.

In her office, she texted Adam to let him know she was back in Edenscar. He'd messaged with an apology for his coldness last night. She tucked the phone away, walking back in the direction of the evidence board.

'Let's crack on.'

Milla propped her iPad on the back of one hand. 'Still waiting on most of the phone data, boss, but I'm able to confirm last calls made from each number. Friday at 7.18 p.m., that was Chris. Friday 7.34 p.m. for Odette. To her mum, who said she asked about dropping Eric with her for the day on Saturday.'

'Who did Chris call?'

'Derek Symonds, local builder. He says he missed the call but Chris left a message saying he had the control panel he'd ordered for a job in Chapel. That's Chapel-en-le-Frith.' Milla watched Theo write the names and times on the board. 'Derek said Chris sounded the same as ever. Last saw him on a job a month ago, in the new-builds over in Swanwick.'

'And Odette's mum? Did she have any cause for concern after the call?'

'She said Odette "seemed edgy" but she'd been that way for a while. She thought it was just how busy they both were, Chris working all hours, Odette alone with Eric, who was boisterous. Her little man, she called him.' Milla blinked, focusing on the iPad. 'I'm waiting for an update on the laptops, and the rest of the phone records. Should have them through soon.'

'Keep on it until you do. Let me know if you need me to put a rocket up anyone. Good work. DS Vicars, what's happening with ANPR?'

'Snail's pace, boss. Calling in a couple of favours to get it through asap.'

'So what else do you have for me?'

'Ballistics failed to recover any casings. Not unusual for a shotgun. I'm getting a list of everyone local with a licence for one of those.'

'Good. Let me know how you get on. Sal Thomas says we're after a twelve-bore. DC Howden, what's the news from the mums at the nursery?'

'Nothing that stands out, ma'am.' Theo stood with pen poised. 'Much like Milla says. Both very busy, Odette struggling a bit with Eric but no red flags.'

'No gut feeling from anyone? People like to speculate when those they know are murdered.'

Theo referred to his notebook, painstakingly. Laurie reminded herself it was useful to have a pedant on the team. Whatever he had to report, it'd be airtight.

'Odette was on about a holiday, saying she needed the sun. Chris was always paying for his parents to go away; she joked her mum-in-law had a better tan than she did. Getting Chris to relax was a full-time job. Everyone agreed she was joking, nothing seriously wrong in the marriage. One thing, though.' Theo put the log down. 'The families came here before the guv took them on to the hospital, and they weren't talking. Yvonne was definitely avoiding Keith and Beverley, and they kept their distance from her.'

'That felt unusual to you?' When Theo nodded, Laurie looked at the wider team. 'Did the families get on, does anyone know? Before this? Any vibes there?'

Milla said, 'Not exactly a *vibe*, but Yvonne was upset about how little Chris did to help out at home, said most of the parenting fell on Odette.'

Laurie nodded at Theo to log this. 'Good work everyone, thanks. One more thing: Bobby German wasn't impressed by the parenting skills on either side. I'm not encouraging that kind of speculation but we need to keep track of it. In DS Ashe's absence, I'll fill you in on what Dr Thomas had for us.' She did this as succinctly as possible. 'Full report incoming. DC Shaw, look out for that, please. Copies to the team when you get it. When I find him, I'll be with Joe, waiting for the chance to speak with Yvonne. DS Vicars, I'll leave you to check in with our friends from Ripley, see what the extended search turned up. Thanks, everyone.'

She found Joe in the corridor, looking no better than he had when they'd walked in here, shirt still stained with lager but eyes clear, focused on something she couldn't see. 'Thought you'd be catwalk-ready, amount of time you've had to smarten yourself up.'

'Cary Lawlor's at the front desk. He's been here all morning.'

'He was giving a statement to the desk officer, wasn't he?'

'He wants to know when he's allowed inside Number 28. Keen to get it cleaned up.' Joe scratched his cheek. 'I've asked him to take a look at the stuff we bagged from the cottage—'

'Get uniform to process the Powderhill case.' She felt a pulse of impatience. 'We've a killer to find, in case that escaped your notice. Priorities, detective. Heard of those?'

'I have, yes. But here's the thing.' Giving her that landing-strip look of his, rock-steady. 'He's just told me the name of the last person inside Number 28. And while it may be a coincidence, I think you'll probably want us to look into it.'

21.

Cary Lawlor stared at the crossbow in horror. The traps provoked a similar reaction, the skim stalk eliciting a blank 'What's that?' while the rat threatened to bring up his breakfast. 'That was in the *bedroom*?' The pricey mountain bike restored some colour to his face. 'Not mine, but I wouldn't mind owning it. That's a nice bike. Did you say it was in the *bath*?' His incredulity exasperated Laurie. Sammi, too; he was pacing behind the chair where Lawlor was seated.

'Let's talk about who last had access to your holiday cottage.' Silence brought the walls closer, making him shift on his haunches unhappily. 'Don't be shy, Mr Lawlor.' Laurie folded her arms. 'We don't have time.'

'It was Chris Miles.'

Sammi put his hands on the back of Lawlor's chair, leaning in to study the man's pallor. In the seat next to Joe, Laurie sat coiled like a cat. 'When was this?'

'About three weeks ago.'

'Be more precise, please.'

Lawlor named a date two weeks and four days before Chris and his family were killed. He had to refer to his phone to be certain. It could have been an act but Joe didn't think so and neither did Sammi: 'He wants to help but he's scared. Triple murder. He doesn't want that touching him.' Except the thing about murder in a place like Edenscar was that it touched everyone.

'Why let Chris into the cottage?' Laurie asked. 'For what purpose?'

'To repair an extractor fan. He rewired the place for us back when we were getting it ready for rental. It made sense for him to fix the fan. He was very reliable but lately he was busy, up to his ears in work, he said.'

'So why not find someone else to fix your fan?'

'We didn't know anyone. This's a small place, and we trusted Chris.' Lawlor was doing his best not to squirm under Laurie's scrutiny, but he was only human. Even Sammi looked a little uneasy, the atmosphere in the room charged with her close attention.

'You trusted Chris,' she said. 'Did you like him?'

Joe had to stop himself looking at her. They'd had no time to discuss tactics, and the question surprised him. Sammi, who had the luxury of staring straight at her, said, 'She's not taking any prisoners today. You want to watch you don't catch yourself on those claws.'

'Like him?' Lawlor echoed. 'I thought he was good at his job. Yes, of course I liked him.'

'He didn't like him.' Sammi straightened to get a better perspective on the man. 'She's good. I couldn't see that, but she's right. He didn't like Chris.'

'I didn't really know him,' Lawlor elaborated into the silence, flushing to the roots of his hair. 'Only – only as an electrician. He was a good one.'

'It's why you wanted him back in your cottage, fixing your fan.' Laurie glanced down at her notes, giving him time to compose himself. 'Did he fix it?' She looked up as she reached the question mark.

Lawlor nodded. 'Later than I'd have liked but it was a good job, all done.'

'You've been inside the cottage, then. Since that work was done, two weeks and four days ago. When were you in the cottage?'

More squirming. Sammi was starting to enjoy it, cocking an eyebrow at Joe, watching Lawlor's gyrations with open admiration for Laurie's tactics.

'I – no, I wasn't actually inside the cottage. I just – he said it was all fixed and I'd no reason not to believe him.'

'Right. What else did he say?'

'Just that. The job was done, everything working again. Nothing about traps or weapons. All that must've been later, after he'd finished.'

'Not much later,' Laurie said. 'Given it was last Thursday when DS Ashe was dodging crossbow bolts. The night before someone took a shotgun to Higher Bar Farm to slaughter Chris and his family.'

145

The words left scars in the air, as if she'd ripped at it with a knife. The murders spilled in, ruined bodies on the floor, a baby crying upstairs.

Lawlor shifted in his seat as if retreating from a tide of blood. 'Terrible. I can't believe it. Just—Awful.'

'Who would do that?' Laurie asked him. 'And why?'

'No one.' He spread his hands. 'I mean, *someone*, obviously. But I can't imagine who, or why. Chris was just . . . He was good at his job. Reliable, tidy. After the rewiring, the cottage was spotless.'

'And after he'd been in to fix the fans?'

'I assumed then too. It's what he said, no reason not to believe him.'

Laurie let him sit with that for a time. 'Are you aware of anyone who went into the cottage after Chris finished the job? Cleaner, letting agent?'

'No.' That flush again, running riot across his face. 'I didn't think anyone was in there. We'd no bookings so the agency was stood down, as it were.' He looked from Laurie to Joe. 'I want to help, really I do, wish there was more I could tell you. Anything, to help you catch whoever did this.'

Once they'd taken his statement, Lawlor was free to go. Laurie didn't want him inside the cottage until the prints Joe and Ted taped on Thursday were checked for a match with Chris. Joe walked Lawlor out of the station, listening to the man's silence with the sense he was churning over the interview, worrying at it.

'It's a long way to come with nothing to show for myself. I do need to get the place cleaned up so we can get it back into rental as soon as possible. Part of me wishes we'd bought the woods instead, which was the original plan.'

'Behind Powderhill? They're for sale?'

'There was a big meeting about it. Gilly wasn't keen; too spooky, she said. Lovely in the summer, though. And spring, when the bluebells are out.'

Lawlor looked spacey, wondering how he'd walked into this nightmare. Medieval weaponry was one thing, a murdered family something else. He'd be lucky if he slept well tonight, or any night for a while. Joe felt sorry for him in spite of his city-bred credulity, or perhaps because of it. 'I'll let you know when we can return the keys to the cottage.'

'It won't take long, will it? I mean, is it worth hanging around? The Tollgate has rooms. I could stay over, see something of the old place.'

'Might be worth looking into that,' Joe agreed. 'But bear in mind this is a murder investigation. Things won't move fast. I'll be in touch when I can.'

By the time Joe linked up with Laurie she was on the phone to the lab, chasing the prints from Powderhill. He waited for her to finish the call before saying, 'Lawlor's taking a room at the Tollgate, should we need him later.'

'For what? Looking pale whenever this place shows its teeth? Crossbows at one end, shotguns at the other. Rats everywhere in between. I'm hoping I can hold on to my ankles for the time it takes us to clear this up.'

Joe kept a respectful silence. She fixed him with a stare. 'What?'

'Not sure the metaphor holds up, boss. But I'll certainly do my best to warn you if I see any teeth near your feet, metal or otherwise.'

'Smartarse. Are you ever going to change that shirt?'

They walked in the direction of the lockers. Joe was on his phone, googling 'woodlands for sale'; Laurie wasn't being nosey, his screen was right there. He put the phone away. 'The wire used to rig that crossbow was bare copper, the kind found in electrical leads. Chris would've been carrying wire in his van. You can get a decent price for it as scrap. Plenty of copper thefts in the area. Could make it a coincidence, but now we know he was the last one in that cottage.'

Laurie thought of the wire used to rig the crossbow, the bolt embedded in the wall, the *violence* of it. Then she thought of the violence committed at Higher Bar Farm. 'Let forensics loose on the wire. I want to speak with Bobby. He accused Chris of messing with his electrics, didn't he? When he was rewiring the house next door. I'd like his honest opinion of what went on there. Lawlor was too nice to say it but something about Chris irked him. I'm thinking Bobby might be the man to help us build a profile of our victims, or one of them.'

'What about Odette's mum?'

'Later,' Laurie said. 'Let's give her the chance to recover from identifying her daughter's corpse.'

Joe stopped at a service station for petrol, pre-packaged sandwiches, drinks. Laurie dropped the Diet Coke into the cup holder, tearing the compostable lid from her sandwich and taking a big mouthful of cheese and celery. Tasted better than the average service station sandwich, either because of the fresh air or the fact she was starving. 'What's your impression of Lawlor? Sensitive soul, or sneaky bastard?'

Joe managed to negotiate the twists and turns of the road while eating his sandwich and answering her question. 'Some of the sensitivity was for show. He wanted us to know he was taking it seriously.'

'Bit over-squeamish about the rat, wasn't he? Must've seen his fair share in London.'

'Bit of transference in the mix?' Joe suggested. 'He'd heard about Higher Bar, knew we weren't talking with him because Chris rewired his cottage. We're investigating three murders. That's what he's really squeamish about.'

'*If* he is. On Friday, we wondered whether that performative set-up in Powderhill was a distraction. Two days before the murders.' She picked crumbs off her jacket. 'Can't ignore that timing.'

'Lawlor doesn't have a shotgun licence, I checked.'

'And he didn't recognise anything in Evidence. Or said he didn't. You had something for me on the crossbow?'

Joe nodded, demolishing another mouthful. 'From Tom Sangster's website. I'll email it to you.'

'Lawlor's sticking around. Doubt he'd do that if he was guilty. I wasn't getting anything serious from him. Were you?'

'Triple-homicide serious? No.'

'Any kind of serious. Well, apart from his hard-on for the bike.' She paused to chew on this. 'What was the point of that? The other stuff makes sense, as a warning or attempted murder. But that's four grand's worth of birthday present. How's that fit with the rest?'

'It doesn't,' Joe said.

'Bet Lawlor's wishing he'd laid claim to it. He didn't know what a skim stalk was, by the way. In case you missed that.'

Joe smiled and shook his head.

'Didn't dash back to the city first chance he got.'

'Staying power,' Joe agreed. He knew they were talking about Laurie, or rather they were joking about her.

She was grateful for the firm footing they were on, even if her new boots made her feet and ankles feel like they'd been dipped in cement. Her phone buzzed with a text from Milla. Sal's report was through. Then a text from Ted alerting them to an updated exhibits list back from Forensics. 'Ask and you shall receive.'

'Fingerprints?' Joe said.

'Copper wire. From Chris's van.' She pinched the image on her phone, peering at it. 'Looks like a match for Powderhill.'

'Steady,' Joe warned. 'Copper wire is copper wire. Like I said, lots of thefts around here. Chris won't be the only one with it in his garage.'

'All right. But *if* he rigged that crossbow, what was his motive?'

'Unless he had a vendetta against Lawlor, I don't see him finding time to lay traps out by the woods . . .' His voice trailed off, brows meeting in a frown.

Laurie was getting used to his silences, knew when they signalled deep thought. She was about to ask him to share what was on his mind when he parked up, cutting the engine. They were some distance from Bobby's place.

'Stretch our legs?' He didn't wait for a response.

Laurie cleared the empty sandwich packages into the glove compartment, following him into the fresh air where the wind did its best to put her back inside the car, slapping against her chest and legs. Joe was moving in the direction of the trees up ahead that climbed into forest so black it was hard to believe it was three hours before sunset. 'Oi! Use your words!'

He didn't stop or turn, just circled his right arm to alert her to movement in the trees coming their way – a blur of red, sending up an arc of soil. The speed with which he'd reached the foot of the trees made Laurie very aware Joe was a runner and she was not.

An attempt at wire fencing had died a death to the right of where he stood, wooden posts sagging until they gave way altogether. The woods looked about as inviting as a short walk down a stabby tunnel. No picnics here, unless they were making horror movies about that now – *today's the day the teddy bears have a pickaxe* . . . The sky lurched where it met the tops of the trees. She could hear animals rustling and creaking, wind muttering.

'Hey, Jaxon.' Joe propped his palm on the nearest tree trunk, standing loosely as if he didn't want to spook whoever *Jaxon* was.

A scrawny kid on a red bike. Tracksuit bottoms, football shirt, beanie pulled tight over a bullet-shaped skull. Freckled face, fierce eyes. He swung the bike about, showing mud stains on the back of his clothes.

'There's a can in it,' Joe said. 'If you tell us what you've seen around here in the last few days.'

'Who's she?' Jaxon jerked his head at Laurie. He looked ten, at a squeak. Tough as nails, though. Like he'd seen it all, and couldn't care less about any of it.

'Laurie,' she said. 'Mate of Joe's.'

'You're a liar.' His stare was a stone thrown at her face. 'Copper written all over you.'

'Fair enough. DI Laurie Bower. Mate of Joe's.'

Jaxon swung a different stare at Joe, less like he was chucking a stone, more like he was skimming it across a body of water. 'Seen him yet? Eric.'

'Yes, in fact.' Joe didn't move a muscle, his voice indifferent.

It lured the kid from the path to the place where they were waiting. His face screwed shut. 'What d'you see? Shot? Or stabbed?'

'Were you out here on Friday?'

'So what?' His scuffed knuckles rested on the bike's handlebars. 'Not my fault I'm suspended. That's on that fat bastard mate of yours.'

Was he talking about Ted Vicars?

'Oscar not with you?' Joe asked.

'He's in school. Gonna tell me, or what? You said you seen him.'

'Eric? At the hospital, yes.'

'What?' Jaxon backed up. 'No, you said—' He eyed Laurie with fear, as if he'd put his foot in a trap. Then he lifted his chin. 'They're all dead. Eric, too. I saw bags being taken out. Three bags. I can count to fucking three, can't I?'

'The hospital has a mortuary.' Joe's voice was cold, bringing the kid up short. Under other circumstances, Laurie would have wanted to talk to him about his interview technique, check whether he understood what an appropriate adult was and why you didn't lure kids out of the woods to talk about corpses, especially not those of other kids. But she trusted Joe. He knew Jaxon, how to talk to him. Had she been on her own, or with one of her sergeants from Salford, this kid would've been a thin streak of dust, long gone. Instead he was standing with his eyes fixed on Joe.

'I was here Friday.' The words left him in a rush. 'Saw him with his gun. Ratting. That daft old bugger too. With *his* gun.' He snorted air down his freckled nose. 'Tied her up, he did.'

'Bobby? Who did he tie up?' Joe threw the questions out lightly, the kid racing after them like a puppy chasing scraps.

'His dog. Old bastard ties her up when he's out with his gun. Should take her with him. She's a collie, knows how to hunt.'

'She's old, though. Like Bobby. Where was he hunting?'

Jaxon pointed towards Higher Bar. 'Eric's dad coming the other way like *Silent Hill*.' He mimed a gun, propping it to his scrawny shoulder. 'Both of them packing it.'

'They each had a gun,' Joe interpreted.

'Yeah but Chris's just a little stick. Bobby's got a fucking *pole*.'

'A shotgun.'

'Yeah.' Jaxon was warming to his theme. 'Looking proper tappy too. Like he's going to *bap* that bitch!'

Joe turned away, shaking his head. The look on his face said he didn't believe a word out of Jaxon's mouth. It made the kid dance in frustration.

'I saw it! Two of them squaring off! Old bastard looking *lethal*. I ain't kidding. He shot at Oscar last Hallowe'en. We're in masks and shit, Eric's mum gives us bags of Haribo but that old bastard says he'll burn Oscar's mask in his drum. He's always burning shit in there. He's batshit, not even joking.'

'So they both had guns, out on the road between their houses on Friday night. Then what happened?'

'Then – nothing.' His shoulders sagged. He threw a baleful glance at Laurie as if he blamed her for losing face in front of Joe. 'Eric's dad goes back to his. Old bastard turns round, heads indoors. I hear her going mental in there.'

'Her?'

'*Isla*. He shouldn't tie her up, it's not fair.' For a second, he was a little kid, lower lip pouting on the dog's behalf.

'What time was this?' Joe asked.

'Well after tea. My mum had stuff to say when I got back but she was leaving for her shift at the garage so I didn't catch it for long.'

'When does her shift start?'

'Nine.'

'Is she still at the garage in Sickleholme?'

'Yeah. Takes her twenty minutes but she always leaves longer for tractors.'

Joe turned to look at the woods before he focused his stare on Higher Bar. Shadows fell across his face. Jax stared, spellbound. After a moment, Joe dug in his pocket, producing a Snickers, which he held out. The kid took it and split the wrapper, eating half the bar in a single bite. The transaction was innocent enough, something they'd done a hundred times before. Laurie couldn't tell whether Joe was bribing the kid or feeding him. Jaxon looked half-starved. For all his gangster swagger, he wasn't far from being feral. He hadn't washed in a while, his legs were bowed and his teeth terrible.

'How often are you up here?' Joe asked him.

'Most days. No school.' He spoke through a mouthful of Snickers. 'Where else'm I gonna be?'

'Plenty of woods down the other end, nearer home.'

'Why'd I want to hang out near that shithole? You bin there, you know.' He ate the rest of the bar ravenously. When he caught Laurie watching, he widened his eyes. '*What*? What're you looking at?'

She shook her head, holding out her unopened bottle of Diet Coke. The kid took it, twisting at the lid with thin fingers. Joe said,

'What else can you tell us about Chris and Bobby? Or Chris and Eric's mum?'

'Piss off, I ain't doing your job for you.' The Snickers had restored his bravado. Just as Laurie was thinking Joe had made a mistake in feeding him, Jaxon broke out a grin. 'Shifting shit through them Travellers you lot won't touch.'

'Who was?'

'Chris was. Piping, lead . . . Whatever he took from houses he worked on. Always someone round here, paying him a visit. Not all friendly, either.'

Joe took a moment, scratching at his cheek. 'This's getting a bit colourful, Jax. Are you sure you want to continue? Only we'll need you down at the station with an appropriate adult if we decide you have something we really need to hear.'

Laurie couldn't believe he was giving the kid a get-out. She was about to interject when Jax lifted his head to give Joe a stare that could've stripped paint. 'You calling me a liar? 'Cos I know Shane Leggitt. And Shane knows Des Morton and we all know what Des'd do to you if he got the chance.'

'He'd have done it by now.' Joe sounded bored. 'If he was capable of it. Are you making a statement or just flexing for DI Bower? Crying wolf again? Because I've real work to do, if it's the latter.'

The kid's face was a fist, knuckles white as he gripped the handlebars. 'I seen him with *dozens*! Travellers, blokes on bikes, in cars down from Sheffield. Seen him dealing right under your noses. *Twats*. You ain't got a clue.'

Joe put his hands in his pockets, resting his chilliest stare on the boy's face. Laurie shivered, saw Jax do the same. 'Someone carried a shotgun into their home on Friday and shot them. Chris and his wife.'

'DS Ashe.'

'It's all right.' Joe didn't look at Laurie, his attention on the boy. 'Jax knows everything. Someone took a shotgun to Eric's mum and dad. Now they're dead. Three body bags. How much of it did you see?'

Jax was swaying under his gaze like a snake in the grip of a charmer, chocolate in the creases of his mouth, tongue flickering to taste it. 'Seen the bags,' he said finally. 'This morning. Heard the shots, Friday night. Two. *Bap-bap*, quick like that. Seen a car drive off. Big, silver.'

'Make?' Joe said. 'Model?'

Jaxon snapped out of it then. 'Get lost. *Copper*. Do your own dirty work.'

'I'll see you at the station with your mum later. Better make it before her shift starts.'

'Piss the lot of you.' Kicking the bike to face the woods. 'Creepy fucker!'

Joe watched him go before he met Laurie's stare. 'I owe you a Diet Coke.'

'You owe me an explanation, mate. But let's start with the Coke. I'll have the one you stashed in the car. What's Jaxon's surname, for the record?'

'Grice.'

They retraced their steps across the field. 'How old is he?'

'Eleven.'

'Looks younger. Isn't anyone bothered by that? Social Services?'

'They get involved from time to time,' Joe said. 'But it doesn't stick. He's not a bad kid, and his mum works all hours to do her best by him.'

'What's his problem with DS Vicars?'

'Ted's usually the one who arrests him. Actually, I'd be interested in what Jax thinks of the Trek Procaliber from Powderhill.'

'Bit out of his league, isn't it?'

They walked the rest of the way in silence, Laurie chewing over what she'd witnessed. Not only what was said about Chris and the dealing, but about Bobby's shotgun and his confrontation with Miles on Friday night. 'How reliable is he – Jaxon? If he says the car he saw up here on Friday was silver, can we trust that?'

'I'd say so.' Joe was on his phone. 'I've asked Ted to prioritise silver cars with the ANPR.'

'These deals he says Chris was doing. If even a fraction of that's credible, it gives us motive. Those shootings were brutal. Exactly what retaliation looks like where I come from. Executions.'

'We need to look into it,' Joe agreed.

'From the sound of it, there's a lot more to Chris Miles than we thought.' She was pressing for a response but Joe held his tongue, reluctant to speculate in the absence of firm evidence, she guessed. But he was one who'd prised Jax open, spilling what the kid had seen, what he'd heard. 'What're the chances of him showing up at the station with his mum?'

'Slim,' Joe admitted. 'But if he doesn't, it'll be because he hasn't any more to tell us. I wasn't joking about his tendency to cry wolf, especially if he needs an alibi for his mum or the school. He wouldn't do that over something this serious, though. He's a decent witness in that regard, won't waste our time.'

'And what's his special deal with you?'

'You know what his deal is.' Joe unlocked the car, pausing to look across its roof. 'He thinks I see ghosts. And that other people see them, around me.'

Adam blamed mass hysteria, triggered by shared trauma. Jaxon Grice hadn't been born when the bus crashed, but he'd been poisoned by the same delusion, regardless. 'And you let him think it,' she accused Joe.

'Sometimes it's easier than arguing.'

'And sometimes it gets you a nice little freaked-out informant.'

'It's been known to keep his hands clean between arrests. Say when he's thinking about switching from twoccing bikes to breaking and entering.'

In the car, Laurie fastened her seat belt. 'Convince him the places he's eyeing up are haunted, do you?'

'Something along those lines.' Joe fired the engine, resting his hands on the wheel. 'It was probably Jax who nicked Chris's bike last summer. It was lifted from the garage at the farm, which means he might've seen stash of some kind, *if* Chris was dealing. And you'll want Bobby in for questioning.'

'I'll leave it to you to persuade him to put some clothes on, spare DC Howden's blushes.'

Joe pointed the car towards Higher Bar. 'Is there a problem with Theo?'

'He's a sensitive flower who happens to love protocol. Nothing wrong with that, but it's a shame he thinks I don't understand the delicate work you're all trying to do around here.'

'I'll speak with him,' Joe said after a pause.

'Not for my sake, if that's what you're thinking.'

'For his, then. He needs to toughen up.'

It made her wonder whether there was more going on with Theo than she realised. This team and its secrets.

'One problem at a time. Let's see what the search has for us. And get a warrant for Bobby's shotgun – I'd like that under lock and key.'

'We won't need a warrant. He'll hand it over if we ask.'

'If *you* ask, you mean. Fine. Since you're confident you have everyone under your spell, I'll just wait in the car for you to sweep it up.'

'No spell,' Joe said. 'Just community relations. Bet there're hardened criminals in Salford who do as you tell them.'

'Safe bet.' He'd averted an argument, again. He really was very good at that. 'Not just hardened criminals who fall into line, detective.'

He glanced across, saw her smile, relaxed his shoulders. 'Got it, boss.'

22.

Bobby German answered the door in his underpants. Joe heard Laurie swear under her breath as she took a step back, Isla pushing her wet nose at Joe's hand.

'You again, is it?'

'I'm afraid so, Bobby. We're going to need your shotgun, and some proper answers this time. You'll want to get dressed, I expect.'

Bobby looked from Joe to Laurie. 'She can have the gun. Rather talk to you, anyway.'

'You'll be talking to both of us,' Laurie said inflexibly. 'At the station.'

'High horse, is it? I'll get my spurs.'

'I'll come with you,' Joe said. 'At least, until we have the gun.'

At the station, Bobby sat with a cup of tea, in his greasy trousers and a greasier jumper. He'd shown Joe where the shotgun was kept, swearing it wasn't loaded – 'Hasn't been in fifty years' – but he didn't have a licence. It made Joe wonder how many more unlicensed shotguns were lying around. Laurie's father-in-law had owned one, he remembered, until she'd checked it in at the station.

'Bobby, we have a witness who saw you with that gun out on the road on Friday. You and Chris facing off like a pair of B-movie cowboys. You didn't mention your shotgun when we spoke yesterday.'

Bobby indicated their surroundings. 'Didn't fancy getting dressed. Knew it'd be a waste of your time.'

'So you're not denying it?'

'No point, is there? You've a witness. Jaxon, was it? As if he's any better, nicking whatever's not nailed down.'

'Why were you and Chris arguing on Friday?'

'Only showing him what a real gun looks like.' Bobby sucked at the tea, licking his expensive dentistry. 'Gets on my wires, firing that piddling popgun in all directions, never hitting owt.'

'What's your real gripe with him? It's not like you to care whether anyone round here can handle a gun.'

Bobby huddled the tea to his chest. He side-eyed Laurie before fixing his stare on Joe. 'Who's looking after Isla? While I'm stuck in here?'

'She's happy. Milla will check on her if this ends up taking time.'

Bobby took this as a hint to move things along. 'Fritzed my electrics, didn't he? Tarting up that palace next door. On purpose, what's more. Middle of winter, buggers my heating. I'd no power for three days.'

'What makes you think Chris did that on purpose?'

'On a kickback from those sods who want me out.'

'Why would you say that?' Joe asked.

'I know what it costs to rewire a house. Not enough to send your mum and dad halfway round the world.' He shivered, looking every one of his eighty-nine years. 'Three days, freezing in my own home. Isla wouldn't stop whining. Why I keep that bonfire going now. In case he tries it again.'

Joe waited to give Laurie a chance to ask questions but she was silent, studying Bobby. Sammi had opted out of this round, staying with Isla. He'd not said more than six words to Joe since his chat with Jaxon out by the woods; he was always quiet where kids were involved.

'What happened up there on Friday?' Joe asked Bobby. 'We know you didn't discharge your gun, it hasn't been fired in a long time. But someone fired a shotgun, twice. Three dead bodies, a family gone. Help us find who did that.'

'All I know's he was on the make.' Bobby rubbed a finger behind his ear. 'Not just next door, right across town. Visitors all hours, night and day. Her looking mad as a snake, or scared out of her wits. Thought she's trying it on, mebbe, covering her tracks. Can't see why he'd kill her, else.'

'Why who would kill her?'

'Whoever done it. *He* was courting trouble, clear as day. But to do her too?' He shook his head, old and exhausted. 'Makes no sense.'

'On Monday,' Laurie said, 'your first thought was that Chris was responsible. "He's not killed them. Not that, Joe." Your words.'

'Happens that way often enough.' Bobby blinked at her. 'News is full of it.'

'You believed Chris was capable of killing his family. That's more than *courting trouble*. What'd you seen to make you believe that?' She leant into his silence. 'Mr German? What had you seen?'

'I'd a dog once.' He ran his tongue around his teeth. 'Before Isla. Same breed but nothing like. Devil in him from a pup. Nowt wrong with that, make a good guard dog, I thought. Only he wouldn't stay put, always after a fight, bringing them back to my door often as not. Poking his nose, yipping all hours, like he couldn't get enough of trouble.' He raised his eyes to Laurie's face. 'That's who Miles reminded me of. Old Tidzer. No doing owt with him, and in the end?' He snapped two fingers, shakily. 'I'd to put him down.'

Joe elected to take Bobby home after the interview. Laurie wasn't keen; she wanted to brief the team on the latest developments. 'Can't you put him on a bus?'

'I can put him in the Tollgate, take him home after we're done for the day.'

'That could be a late night.'

'Granted,' Joe said. 'But no buses run out his way, not in years. Taxi's a long wait. Let me get him settled, see if I can find someone to get him home.'

Laurie watched him walk Bobby out of the station. She felt unsettled, off her game. Possibly because their case was leaning heavily into hearsay evidence from little kids and old men. She wished she'd prised the truth out of Cary Lawlor while she'd had him fidgeting in his seat. She was certain he had more to tell.

In his office, DCI Saxton listened as she brought him up to speed. 'Chris had a lot of cash to throw around,' he summarised, 'more than we'd expect an electrician to make. On the other hand, he was exceptionally busy.' He frowned, folding his arms. 'Though I saw him in the Tollgate a fair amount, for someone with no time on his hands.

But let's not scapegoat a murdered man. How's DC Shaw getting on with the digital forensics?'

'I'm about to find out. Team briefing.' Laurie hesitated, reluctant to say more without Joe here. They were a team. She wanted Saxton to see that, didn't need him imagining this was some city-bred theorising she'd brought to the table.

Saxton pulled on his jacket. 'Mind if I attend the briefing?'

'I'd think it odd if you didn't.' She smiled brightly back at him. 'They need to see their DCI. I'm still a stranger.'

'Not for long. You'll see.'

The briefing took time, the team worn down by the day's grind. Not unusual at this stage, golden hour behind them, shock settling into a grim realisation of the hard work ahead. Laurie knew the importance of making space in the investigation, had put her foot on the ball countless times to bring order when 'fast-track' threatened confusion. But she was having difficulty identifying which track was the fast one in Edenscar, could've used a little of her old team's spicy approach to legwork. They'd been fuelled by caffeine and Monster energy drinks, but it got them out of their seats, unlike Ted Vicars, who looked welded there. At least she knew Milla was digging deep into the tech trail, searching the contents of Chris and Odette's phones, Chris's laptop. Joe had returned from the Tollgate looking tired and edgy. Laurie wondered if he'd had another run in with Brother Buckfast. His left shoulder wasn't sitting straight and he was avoiding her eyes. Whatever it was, they didn't have time for it. They needed to talk to Odette's mum, if necessary circle back to Keith and Beverley. Loved ones usually had more to say on day three or four, as shock morphed into a nagging need for answers.

'How'd you get on with Des?' she asked Ted. 'Did you find out whether his Golf was parked up at Powderhill on Wednesday night?'

Vicars shoved a thumb at the paperwork on his desk. 'Didn't think that was a priority any longer, boss.'

'It wasn't, before we found this new link between our murder victim and Powderhill. Get on it, please.' She waited to see if Saxton had any questions before winding up the briefing. 'Let's see how far we can get with the digital trails and ANPR before the end of the day. But unless our on-loan search team turns up the murder weapon, I'm going to suggest most of you get off at the usual time. Rest and be ready for what tomorrow brings. DS Ashe, a word?'

'She's on to you,' Sammi said.

Joe followed Laurie into her office where she closed the door and fixed him with a stern stare. 'Out with it. Whatever happened in the Tollgate.'

'I paid for a ploughman's for Bobby. Don't think it can be construed as a bribe since he'd already given us his statement—'

'We have time for this? For you to play funny soldiers with me?'

'Told you,' Sammi said. 'She is on to you.'

'What is it you want to know?' Joe asked. 'Let's arrive at it that way.'

'Was Des Morton in the Tollgate?'

'No he was not.'

She narrowed her stare until it felt like being stabbed in the face with a Sharpie. 'Ow,' from Sammi. 'Was his mate Shane Leggitt in the Tollgate?'

'Also no.'

'Who *was* in the Tollgate? And what happened to your shoulder?'

'Give it up, Joe. You won't win this fight.'

'Fred Hallam. His sister Pru is my ex. He's not a fan of the way she and I ended things. I've some regrets about that myself. But nothing happened to my shoulder, except it's stiff from the driving. It gets like this sometimes.'

'Fred Hallam,' Laurie repeated, as if committing the name to memory.

'For operational purposes,' Joe said, 'Fred is not a threat. Just my guilty conscience kicking in.'

'Tell it we're busy hunting those guilty of a serious crime. Not of dumping someone's sister.'

'Understood.'

She searched his face, seemed satisfied. Her patience was thin, and he knew why. The slow progress on the case was getting to him too. To the whole town; the Tollgate had been packed with punters wanting to be reassured their families were safe, looking for a reason why the Mileses were targeted. Anything but a random madman on the loose. Laurie didn't need to be told what the town was thinking, or feeling.

'What's your gut instinct as a local? What was it about Chris that put Bobby and Lawlor on edge? Who killed him?'

Joe needed to impress her. *Too soon to say* wasn't going to hack it.

'Bobby isn't easily spooked. There has to be a good reason for him thinking Chris was someone you wouldn't mess with. I never saw that side of him, but maybe he took care to hide it. Why Lawlor was wound up, I don't know. He can't have seen much of Chris, not being local. And he gave him that second job, either because he trusted him, or felt obligated in some way.'

'Quick question,' Laurie said. 'Do we need to look at Bobby for this? He gave us a motive back there: Chris cutting off his power.'

'Motive,' Joe agreed, 'but not much opportunity. He's eighty-nine, not too steady on his feet. And the shotgun, apart from being the wrong gauge, hadn't been oiled in a while, let alone fired.'

'All right, carry on.'

Sammi said, 'Go back to basics. That set-up in Powderhill was a trap. Who for? And who set it?'

'It's possible Chris laid those traps, but I doubt it. He was busy, that's been established. Powderhill took time and planning. It was a piece of theatre.'

Laurie was watching him intently. Sammi too, lounging into the filing cabinet behind her desk, eyes flicking between Laurie and Joe.

'You want my gut instinct? Whoever killed Chris and Odette, and left Eric to drown, is the same person who rigged Number 28.'

She absorbed this, her expression not changing. 'So the crossbow was meant to kill Chris? Is that what you think?'

'Or it was a warning of some kind.'

'Which he chose to ignore.'

'If he was even aware of it.' Joe rolled his shoulder. 'Why he needed warning, I couldn't tell you. Not with what we have currently. Unless Jax is right and he was doing deals with the wrong people, but that's speculation.'

Laurie drummed her fingers on the desk. 'One problem with your theory.'

'More than one, I imagine. But go on.'

'The skim stalk. Someone broke that window *from the outside*. Chris had access, a legitimate reason to be there. Why draw attention by breaking a window?' She shook her head. 'Still think Jax's going to turn up here to give a statement?'

'You'll be lucky.' Sammi was studying the contents of Laurie's desk. It reminded Joe to check what Theo was up to with the newspaper cutting about her sister. 'Yes,' Sammi said, 'because what you need right now is another wasp's nest to poke. If Theo's screwed up, that's his lookout.'

'Slim chance Jax will show. I'll take that hit, if it happens.'

'We'll both take it,' Laurie corrected him. 'Let's see what Milla has for us in the next couple of hours. She's our best chance of turning up something new, unless the Ripley team get lucky with the weapon search. Everyone's strung out. If we've hit a wall, we'll use it to rest and regroup.'

'I'm happy to pull a late one. No one waiting at my place.' Joe didn't want to go home. 'You're right to say we're strung out, but it'll be like this until we catch a break in the case. We'd all rather be working towards that.'

'Oh, no danger of you and me getting the night off.' Laurie reached for her jacket. 'Odette's mum. Come on.'

23.

The woman who answered the door was enough like Odette to send a chill up Joe's spine. Fair hair, pale skin spoilt by sorrow, swollen eyes. Early forties, at a guess. 'Mel. I'm Odette's big sister. Sorry, Melanie Newell.' She put out her hand, blinking until her face settled. 'Mum's upstairs. I'll get her. Come in.'

Laurie shook the hand Mel held out. She didn't offer it to Joe, but she tried very hard to smile at him. Her mum's bungalow had no log burner, its radiators battling the cold push of the canal. Sammi was dancing his feet to get warm, 'Keep your coat on, if I were you.' It was going dark, the last of the day leaving the sky.

Mel took them to a room whose French windows faced a square of lawn. Chenille sofas, washable rug spread in front of a hearth filled by baskets of toys, plastic lorries, Lego bricks, a wooden play arch strung with cloth shapes. Big TV, coffee table, bookcase, but Joe's eyes kept returning to the toys. One of the baskets had lost a plush lion to the rug. Mel scooped it back with the rest of the playthings. The way she handled it said the lion was Eric's; all the toys were. It struck Joe that the only toys in Keith and Beverley's house were those outgrown by Chris.

Yvonne's grief entered the room a second before she did, like something solid sliding into place, a screen or a wall. Her face was bruised in all the same places as Mel's, her mouth wrung into an empty shape. Mel sat with her on one of the sofas, Laurie and Joe taking the other. Sammi settled on the floor with his back to the whitewashed bricks of the hearth. He was quieter than usual, watching Joe for cracks where pain might slip through. The room was vibrating with pain.

'This is my fault,' Mel said. 'If I hadn't needed Mum to come and get me on Monday, we'd have been able to see you then. It was just so hard seeing them at the hospital. Ricky, especially. Eric, I mean. Sorry.' That word jumping out at her at every chance, not letting her relax for a second.

Laurie spoke a version of the words she'd used with Chris's parents about questions and answers, and not wishing to make their lives harder.

Yvonne listened in silence then said, 'I had the chance to take him. Odette asked me months ago. She said it was all getting too much for her. I said it'd settle down, every new mum feels that way.' A dry sob. 'That's what I told her.'

'Mum, don't.'

'She'd have asked you too, if you'd only had a car, or kids of your own.'

Mel looked wretched, holding hard to her mum's hand.

'When was this?' Laurie asked.

'Back in August,' Mel said, 'when that heatwave was battering us. By September, Etty had him enrolled at nursery. Mum was right, things settled down.'

'If I'd lived nearer, I'd've taken him every weekend.' Yvonne nodded at the hearth. 'He'd have been here now, playing with his toys.'

Sammi stretched his legs on the rug, as if he didn't want Joe picturing Eric.

'Things were difficult for Odette, with Eric.' Laurie watched the women's faces. Yvonne's was more naked than Mel's, primitive in its suffering. 'How were things with Chris?'

'He was no help,' Yvonne said bitterly. 'I knew he wouldn't be, the way he lived before they were married. Thirty-nine and never grew up. She'd to raise him as well as a baby, that's how it looked to me.'

'Mel?' Laurie wanted a second opinion.

'Chris was living at home when they met, that's true. Etty always had her own place, ever since she was nineteen. Bedsits, sofas sometimes.' Her smile was colourless. 'She was always the independent one.'

'She met Chris at the shop where she worked, is that right?' It was what Beverley Miles had told them.

'Not a shop,' Yvonne corrected her. 'Wholesaler's. She managed their stock. He'd come to look at a problem with the air-conditioning.'

'She gave up the job after the wedding,' Mel said. 'They were always going to settle in Edenscar. Etty found the farmhouse, saw its potential. Auction sale because it was in such a state, but she said Chris could fix the electrics and plumbing, she'd fix everything else. She struggled, though. With the house and then with Eric, as Mum said.' Her eyes appealed for Laurie's understanding. 'They couldn't get on with the land the way they'd hoped. Etty said it took all Chris's strength just to keep the rain from inside the house. Not a chance of farming, not that she'd any hope of that, but she'd thought maybe holiday lets. They put in a planning application soon after they bought the place. Chris was keen.'

Yvonne made a dismissive sound. Mel squeezed her hand. 'Outbuildings, shepherd's huts, hot tubs, that sort of thing. But the land wasn't right, or the drainage wasn't. They couldn't get any of it to work the way they wanted.'

'Chris couldn't get it to work.' Yvonne twisted her mouth. 'Boasting about prospects and investments then grumbling in the pub about a losing battle with the land, saying he didn't know how farmers did it – "You can't control a thing round here" – as if he'd expected everything to magically fall into place. He'd never've got that business of his off the ground without her.'

'Etty did help him a lot, but she liked doing it. She'd not have married him otherwise, Mum. She wasn't the sort to make a mistake like that.'

'A mistake like what?' Laurie held Mel's gaze, keeping her voice low, as if she sensed Odette's sister was oversensitive, all exposed nerve endings.

'Falling for someone who couldn't look after himself, or who needed looking after. She wasn't romantic, not like that. She lent a hand but it was because she could see Chris needed a push, after living that long with his parents.'

'Coddled by them, made to think he was better than he was. Perfect, no less. That's how they talked about him, as if he was the catch of the century. Now look!' Yvonne clawed her hand into a fist. 'He couldn't keep his family safe, couldn't even keep a *baby* safe.'

'Mum, *no*.' Mel tried to sound shocked but it wasn't the first time her mother had laid the blame at Chris's door, that was clear. 'We've no idea how this happened.' That appeal to Laurie again, her eyes filling with tears. 'There was nothing in their marriage that could've caused this, nothing big enough. Just the usual little things making life hard sometimes, not *this*.'

Soon afterwards, Mel left her mum to see Laurie and Joe out of the bungalow, stepping outside with them and drawing the door half-closed behind her.

'Sorry, she's struggling. The hospital was harrowing.' She held her hair from her face, steadying her voice. 'I don't want you leaving with the idea Etty was a victim. She'd have hated that almost more than—She was the strong one, you know? Met life head-on, fought its battles. I suppose . . . I was surprised when she married Chris. I'd made up my mind she'd be single for good. It suited her. She never settled for a half-glass, you know? Then we lost Dad, and I was starting over after the divorce, talking about dating again, and she just came out with it one day – "If you can't beat them, join them" – and next thing I know she's talking me into a green bridesmaid's dress even though it's a terrible colour on me.' The words had rattled out of her. She stopped, smoothing her hair over her shoulders. 'I don't want you leaving with the idea she made some big sacrifice by marrying Chris. She went after him, not the other way round. She found that farmhouse, talked him into taking it on, got him to set up his own business. All of that was Etty. Then when Eric came it was different again because he wasn't like Chris, couldn't be organised in the same way, you know? So, yes, there was a moment when it all got too much for her but that summer was so hard. The heat, you must remember it.' Appealing to Joe this time. 'Once it was over and there was the nursery to look forward to, it was better. Ricky loved going there.' Her eyes went through them for a second, into the past. 'Mum's torn to pieces by this, you can see that. She and Etty were finally getting on. Even when we were little, Etty never *needed* her, you know? She was just so independent. After Eric, Mum had a role at last, that's how it felt. Etty was over here with him every other week, wanting to spend time with Mum, finally. I think it's hitting her twice as hard because of that. She's lashing out at Chris because he's closest but really she can't believe Etty was safe all those years on her own in those dreadful bedsits and flats, only to be—' She broke off, shivering. 'When she should've been safest, that's what Mum keeps saying. Settled down at last, with a husband and family to think about. That's what she can't believe. It's like someone took her whole philosophy of life and turned it inside out, trampled on it.'

Wind tugged from the canal. Sammi turned in the direction of the car, trailing his shadow. He looked older, as if these family visits were getting to him.

'I didn't want you leaving without hearing that,' Odette's sister said. 'It's my fault you weren't able to see her on Monday. Sorry. She's much worse today.'

'Thank you', Laurie said, 'for sharing this. We'll be in touch.'

24.

In the car, Laurie checked her phone for messages from Milla. The Ripley team still hadn't found the shotgun, the search called off for another day. 'Looks like we're getting that early night we talked about.'

Joe pulled away from the kerb, pointing the car towards Edenscar. 'Mel doesn't want us seeing Odette as a victim.'

'Why would she? That's her sister. The hospital must've been a nightmare. She'll have those pictures in her head for ever.'

Izzy. The independent one, always, but she'd hated the dark. The thought of her in that morgue drawer had preyed on Laurie's mind for weeks.

'Mel said Odette never needed her mum, even as a child. Could that be true?'

Laurie was silent for so long it made Joe look at her. 'She'll have needed her, just never found the right way to express it.'

'Yvonne blaming Chris. Is there anything in that, d'you think?'

'I think Mel gave us a really good reason for it. But I also know we'll be pulling that reason to pieces soon enough. One for fresh eyes in the morning.'

She needed to process what they'd learnt from Yvonne and Mel, separate it into strands, isolate it from any contagion she'd carried into that home where a mother and daughter were struggling – fighting – to make sense of their loss.

Joe's brain was bending itself around the problem, it showed in his profile. She wondered what he had planned for his evening, if he'd be picking up where they'd left off, doing what digging he could at home. No one waiting for him, he'd said. The car carried a whiff of greasy clothes, reminding her that Joe's evening was ferrying Bobby home from the Tollgate, hoping to avoid a run-in with his ex's brother, or Des. 'Want to get a takeaway and eat at ours?'

'That's kind of you.' Joe glanced at her in surprise. 'Another time, maybe? I promised my gran I'd pop round and see her.'

'After you've chauffeured Bobby back?'

'I sorted that. Ted's giving him a lift.'

'Good. About time he pulled his weight.'

When they reached Peter's house, Joe parked in the spot he'd chosen at the start of the day. Was it really only twelve hours ago? She felt as if she'd been working with him for a week. 'It's been a long day. Make sure you get some rest.' She watched him drive off then turned to the house with resolve. *Adam.* She needed to show her support. No point doing half the job she'd come here to do.

He was in the kitchen, sitting at the table with a greying cup of tea. When he looked up, she saw his green eyes dim with tears.

'Hey . . .' She crouched at his side. 'What's up?'

'Nothing new. Just . . . God, I've missed you.' He pushed long fingers into her hair, pulling her close enough to kiss.

Laurie fitted herself into his lap, smoothing his eyebrows with her thumbs. 'I'm here now. I've got you.'

His hands moved to her hips, holding her hard to the kiss. She pressed back, the chair creaking under them. Footsteps in the hallway.

Adam swore under his breath, breaking the kiss. 'Dad?' He called it loudly enough for Peter to hear if he was in the sitting room. No answer.

Laurie wanted to hold Adam in the chair, but knew she couldn't. 'Let me go and check on him. You take some time out.' She stood, straightening her clothes.

'Actually, I couldn't go to the pub, could I? Just for a quick one. A mate called, someone I was at school with. Ben Ambler. He can't believe the news about Chris. I said we'd raise a glass to him. Doesn't need to be tonight, if you're knackered. You must be knackered.'

'No, it's fine. You should go.' His car was outside, needed in case of emergencies with Peter. 'How'll you get back? If you're drinking?'

'I'll only have the one. Promise.' Adam gathered his wallet and keys, looking like a teenager who'd been promised a night out after a long grounding. 'I can ask Helen to come across? Or Esther?'

'No need. I'm tackling a triple murder investigation and a twitchy team. I think I can manage a couple of hours with your dad.'

Brave words, Bower. She saw Adam off before making her way to the sitting room. The door was open to the cupboard under the stairs. She was about to shut it when she saw Peter in there, staring at the hoover she'd tidied away on the day they moved in. 'Hi, Dad. Everything all right?'

He turned towards her, his face half-lit from the overhead bulb. He looked odd, like two people at once, mouth carved by shadow, eyes wet and red.

'You,' he said. 'Poking about again.'

'I'm not poking about. Just saying hello.'

'In here!' He pointed at the space she'd tidied. 'Can't find anything now.'

'What're you looking for? Let me help.'

'I'd a gun in here. Sixteen-bore, side lever. Sweet sixteen.'

'It's at the police station. That seemed the safest place for it.'

'This is *my* house!' His fist flailed, catching the bulb hanging from the cupboard's low ceiling. 'My gun!'

The bulb swung wildly, crazing his eyes with its white light until she blinked, taking a step back. She reached for his arm, shocked by its thinness but he was strong, pulling her into the cupboard, thrusting his face close, '*Mine!*'

She broke free from his grip, stumbling backwards, heart thudding in her chest. Adam's dad stayed where he was as the bulb slowed before swaying to a halt, draining the light from his eyes and casting his jaw into darkness.

25.

Merry had been busy. Joe found himself staring at a row of what looked like sex toys in lurid shades of pink and purple. 'If these are candles, Gran, I'm not sure you'll be able to shift them at the farmers' market.'

'Novelty candles.'

'The novelty being?'

'Oh you sweet, beautiful boy,' she said fondly. 'Have you really never seen a dildo before?'

Joe burst out laughing, not stopping until he was seated at the table, wiping tears from his eyes. 'Thank you.'

'For what?'

'Reminding me there's more to life than work.'

Merry started packing the candles into an oversized Tupperware. 'You need a hot meal inside you. Fancy a fry-up?'

'Please. Let me help?'

'You'll only get in the way. Sit and share something decent about your day. Not', she clarified, 'whatever's worn you to the wire.'

'I got clobbered by a can of Carling, up in Sheffield.'

'That explains the smell.' She clicked the kettle on. 'Thought you'd been all day in the pub.'

'Only briefly, getting Bobby settled after he'd been at the station.'

'What was he doing there?'

'Giving a statement about Chris.' Joe shouldn't talk about police work. He didn't want to, either. He'd come to switch off, and because seeing Fred in the Tollgate made him miss Pru, the way they'd been at the beginning. Sammi had snapped him out of it: 'She wanted too little of you, Joe.' He wished Sammi was with him now, having a hoot over the novelty candles. But he never came to Merry's cottage. *Maybe that's why you're here,* he thought. *Hiding from Sammi, or from work at any rate.* His head ached. He sniffed at his shirt. 'I should take a shower. Sorry.'

'You sit there.' Merry put a mug of tea in front of him. 'Fried bread?'

'Please.' He propped his head on his hand, watching her crack eggs into a bowl, folding their empty shells.

'How many rashers?' She had the bacon out. 'Two?' She added the rashers to the pan, making cuts in the rinds to stop the bacon curling as it fried.

'Gran, did you know Bobby had a shotgun?'

'Did I? No. But I'm not surprised. I'd have one if I lived up there. Can't trust a thing that passes along that road. How many times have I told you that?'

'Many times.'

'There you go, then.' She added chestnut mushrooms to the pan, dabbing butter into their caps. The smell made Joe's mouth water.

'I keep forgetting to tell you, Nelson sends his best wishes. He said it again when I saw him on Friday.'

His grandmother buttered two triangles of white bread before adding them to the pan. 'Did he, now.'

'Said all the boys chased you, back in the day. Terry Doyle, Peter Bower. Nelson said he didn't get a look-in, being so much younger.'

'That boy was born old.' Merry turned the bacon with a fork. 'Used to look at the rest of us like the fools we were.'

'Were you fools?' Joe smiled. 'I can't imagine it.'

'That's the trouble with you youngsters.' The pan spat. She shook a spot of hot fat from her hand. 'You can't imagine we were ever young and fast on our feet. Sharp as knives, the lot of us.'

'I can imagine that. And it's how Nelson remembers it, too. He said you ran rings around the rest of them.'

They tucked into the food, Joe eating hungrily, aware of his grandmother watching him. She liked to see him eat, always had.

'What were you doing all the way out at Middlestone Hall?'

'Asking about Tom Sangster.' He spoke around a mouthful of fried bread. 'Our local weapons expert.'

'They're saying it was a shotgun killed the Mileses.' Merry loaded fried egg on to her bacon. 'All except Eric.' She watched him with pity on her face. 'You've had a hard day of it, my darling.'

'I've had better,' he admitted.

She put out a hand, gripping his wrist in her strong fingers for a second. She never made a fuss, hadn't made one seventeen years ago when he'd asked her to tell him what no one else would, or ten years ago when he'd said he wanted to join the police. Mum wailed, begging him to reconsider. Dad shrugged, refusing to make a fight of it. But Merry told him to sit down and sample the gingerbread men she'd iced to look like those who'd died in Eyam, the plague village. Her hobby at the time – local history rendered in edible form.

'What's the gossip? About Higher Bar. People must be talking.'

'Flapping, you mean.' She speared a mushroom on her fork. 'Like crows. Take care when you're out there.'

'Flapping about what, exactly?'

She clucked her tongue, as if he ought to know better than to ask daft questions. He thought of Jaxon Grice, standing with his bike: *'Seen him yet? Eric.'* He'd been certain Jax would turn up at the station because he wouldn't be called a liar by anyone, least of all a copper. Just a chance he knew what went down at Higher Bar, if not on Friday then in the weeks leading up to the murders.

Joe finished his food, taking their plates to the sink, trying to get rid of the beat at the back of his skull, scouring the plates until Merry said, 'I'd like some pattern left on those, my darling,' at which he stopped and rinsed the sink. He shook wet from his hands, taking the towel she offered. 'You won't mind if I make a couple of phone calls?'

'Work calls?' She shook her head, but didn't try to fight him.

Joe took his phone to the back step, dialling Nicola Grice's number. When she didn't pick up, he remembered she was working the 9 p.m. shift at the service station in Sickleholme. She'd have gone to work whether or not she'd seen Jax, couldn't afford to lose her job. Every chance her son was home with his feet up, pleased to have stood Joe up. Ted was right about that much, the kids round here were bred like bricks. He considered driving to Nicola's place to be sure Jax was safe, but knew the reception he'd get. The Grices lived on the same estate as Des. He'd be lucky to get out with his tyres intact. The sensible thing to do was go home and sleep. On impulse, he texted Laurie: 'Same pickup time tomorrow?'

'Sure. How's your evening going?'

'Good. Yours?'

Her response took so long he was braced for a lecture about boundaries and leaving his boss to enjoy whatever personal life she could fit around the edges of their work. She must've changed her mind, though. The text when it came was just three words: 'Yeah. Good. Night.'

26.

Laurie rubbed her thumb at her phone, half-wishing she'd sent her original text to Joe. Or Rez, maybe. 'My evening? Starting to think Adam's dad would like me dead. Might be going mad, though. Best factor that in.' How would Joe have responded to that? With his signature calm, a polite enquiry intended to uncover the extent to which she was becoming contaminated by this place. Rez would've been less polite but just as sceptical. In any case, her evening hadn't been that bad, not in the context of her day. After the interlude under the stairs, she'd taken Peter to bed. He kept thanking her as she led him up the stairs – 'Sorry,' over and over until her eyes filled with tears of pity. He wanted his life the way it used to be, his home free from lodgers, his privacy restored. She was an outsider here. It was a role she'd known all her life, only outgrowing it when she found her feet in Salford. When Isabel was first sinking into addiction and Laurie was the only one shouting for a lifebuoy, their mum had chided her, 'She's coming out of her shell. Let her be. It's good to see her enjoying herself. We can't all be workaholics. You should try it yourself some time.' When her sister's addiction took hold, that too was somehow Laurie's fault, as if she'd put the thought into Izzy's head with her worrying. She didn't want that reputation here in Edenscar, with Peter's family. She should've been better at managing his moods, having researched his condition in detail, but none of the articles or textbooks had prepared her for the hard fact of living with someone in such rapid decline. The way he kept changing hit hardest. God knows she was used to dealing with people who did that. Not just Izzy. Thirteen-year-olds who swung between little kids and hardened criminals, heroin addicts who couldn't stay the same person for more than five minutes at a time, lawyers who turned the charm on and off. She felt for Peter, but he scared her. The way his illness drew everything into its orbit, the past rushing in without warning before retreating again, the tug of it as slow and irresistible as the tide.

When Adam came home from the pub, he found her sitting with a cup of green tea. The kitchen was spotless because it couldn't answer back, had been dealt the full force of her need to restore sanity and order to her day.

'You're a domestic goddess, Lore.'

'And you're drunk. I hope you didn't drive.'

'Not drunk,' he protested. 'Just happy to be home.'

He *was* drunk, should not have been driving, could easily have hit someone on these roads and the headlines wouldn't have been 'Local man caught drink driving', but 'Murder DI's husband drunk in charge of a vehicle'.

'How was the pub?'

'Rammed.' He propped his fist to the table, smiling at her with his curls in his eyes. 'Only been home a week, but it's like I never went away.'

She returned his smile reflexively, but the pit of her stomach knotted against the idea this was *home* for him. Not the city, not her home, but here. She watched him pull a chair out and sit. 'Who was in the pub? Anyone you know?'

'Just Ben and a few blokes from school. Everyone's talking about Chris.'

She got up to put the kettle on. 'What're they saying?'

'Never anything to suggest a problem in the marriage, how solid they were as a couple.' Adam traced a pattern on the table with the ball of his thumb. 'He and Odette always looked happy. In love.'

Laurie made a cup of tea, taking her time over it to let Adam get the rest of the gossip off his chest. Not only because he needed to, so he could go to bed with a clear(ish) head. Because she wanted to know what people were saying, things they were unlikely to tell the police but which might be significant. 'Higher Bar's a fair way out. Did they spend much time in town?'

'Chris did; that pub was his local, Ben said.' Adam cocked his head at the ceiling. 'How's Dad? Your evening okay?'

'In bed. He was fine.' She handed him the cuppa with a smile. 'So everyone liked Chris? They saw a lot of him?'

'Yeah.' Adam's eyes dropped. He was holding something in, reluctant to share the less savoury gossip.

'Or saw too much of him, maybe?'

'Ben wasn't a fan, from what I could tell.'

He pulled a face, drank a mouthful of tea. She waited, knowing there was more he wanted to say. He'd analysed this town after the bus crash. He'd be doing the same now, couldn't switch off that part of his brain any more than she could switch off the detective in hers.

'What was Ben's problem with Chris, did he say?'

'He wasn't going to diss the guy under the circumstances, just implied Chris could be an awkward git when he put his mind to it. Which of us can't, though? Ben was putting them away, all of us having a session.'

'It didn't ring true to you?'

'Not saying that. Chris *was* a bit of a punk at school.'

'Nearly burning down the science lab?'

Her husband gave a brief grin. 'Since he became a dad, though?' He drew a cross over his heart, 'All about work, according to Ben.'

Someone else who didn't want to speak ill of the dead but who'd had a problem with Chris. 'He wasn't the only electrician round here, was he?'

'No, just busier than anyone else. People trusted him, I guess.'

'So no enemies?'

Adam's face tightened. 'I wasn't there to interrogate anyone, Lore.' On the side of his mates, just at this minute.

She'd pushed it further than she should. She climbed to her feet, taking her cup to the sink. She should have left it there, didn't know why she started the second half of their conversation: 'Your dad said something funny the other day.'

'Dad says a lot of funny things.'

Laurie turned to see him run a hand over his face, tiredly. 'He said he was going to tell you a secret about me.'

'What?' Adam peered at her. 'What secret?'

'That's the funny thing. No secret. Just what I said about Izzy after that scene at our wedding.' She waited but he was silent. 'I was upset. We all were. You remember.' She dried her hands on her jeans. 'I said I wished she'd make up her mind whether she wanted to live or die.'

'Lore . . .' Adam stretched out his hand.

She shook her head, swallowing around the grief in her throat which came so quickly, easily, as if it'd been waiting for the right words to summon it. 'Your dad called me a bitch, threatened to tell you what I'd said. As if he thought you didn't know, as if it would change how you feel about me.'

Her husband dropped his hand to the table. After a beat, he said, 'What're you doing?' His shoulders had stiffened and his face too.

Laurie's thumbs pricked warningly. 'I'm just telling you what your dad—'

'No.' Adam shook his head with drunken vehemence. 'You're making it about you. It's not about you. He's up there, scared and sick. Losing his mind.'

'That's true. You're right. I'm sorry.'

She should've taken his hand when he held it out. His eyes were cold green glass. He was Peter's son, not her husband. He was Addy.

'Don't make this about you,' he warned. 'The way you did with Isabel. Dad's right about that.'

It landed like a punch. 'Excuse me?'

'What d'you want me to say, Lore? We've talked about this often enough. Dad's right. You know he is.'

He needed it to be true, needed this much of his dad to be unchanged: someone who spoke his mind, handing down judgements a less confident man would keep to himself. Adam was scared. His dad was dying and instead of making it easier, Laurie was making it worse. She hadn't meant to make it worse.

'Come on, Lore. He's not saying anything you've not said yourself.'

But this was *private*. Her pain, her sister. Nothing to do with him or his dad, who'd looked down his nose at her for years, trying to get her drunk to prove his point, pushing drink at her as if he had to find the edges of her resolve, all the small places where her grief met her anger, threatening to crack her apart. 'Can you stop?' she asked Adam. 'I need you to stop.'

He did, blinking at her with his eyes glazed by drink. *He's drunk. Let it go. He doesn't mean it.* Like Isabel. Every time she said Laurie was a bad sister, accused her of not caring or of caring too much, phoning in the middle of the night begging for her help only to scream at her when she tried to give it. *She didn't mean it. He doesn't mean it. Let it go.*

'I'm just reminding you none of us is perfect.' Adam looked on the verge of tears. 'Dad certainly isn't. But he's *dying*, Lore. These are the end days. Everything he says and does is the *last time*. Last time he'll pick a fight, last time he'll be a grumpy sod, find fault with our career choices, try to wind us up.' He passed a hand across his face. 'What kind of son would I be if I judged him for what he says now? I came to mend fences not dig up old grievances. Can't we leave the past alone? It's just that. *Past*. And I know I make my living digging there, but I can't be a therapist to my dying dad, I just can't. It isn't fair, isn't why we came.'

The past didn't care why they'd come. You couldn't put it in its place, the way everyone advised. The past didn't have a place, any more than fear did. It was everywhere, all the time. Here in this kitchen with them right now, and out there in the night, in the pub he'd left and on the long road up to Higher Bar Farm where it had walked in on a family as they settled down to their evening.

She held out a hand to Adam. 'Team hug, come on.' It was an old joke. She didn't much feel like making it, but she couldn't afford to fall out with him. There was too much to do. And it hurt, seeing him like this.

He hugged her, stinking of beer. It made her think of Joe with Carling on his collar, standing at her side as they watched Sal Thomas take apart what was left of Chris and Odette. She shuddered and Adam mistook it for arousal, the last thing she was feeling. 'Lore . . .' His mouth on her neck, hands on her breasts.

She wanted to push him off, tell him to take a shower first at least. In Salford, she'd have done that and he'd have laughed, persuaded her into the shower with him. Here, the shower was over a bath in the only room with a loo which Peter might need in the night. She could hear him, shifting in his bed. Adam's hands were inside her clothes, his mouth sloppy on her throat.

She was very aware of the windows behind them, the way light carried in the darkness, wished she was in the city at the top of a high-rise, anonymous. Just a shadow moving in a tower of shadows while cars swept past below them and over to the east trains took strangers away.

27.

Wednesday. Day three of the investigation. That sense of time falling through their fingers, the case slippery, no handholds. Laurie and Joe walked into the station at 7.05 a.m., expecting to be the first, but Ted and Theo were hard at work wrestling a flatscreen TV into position near the evidence board. Saxton nodded a greeting before turning his attention to Milla, who had managed to connect her iPad to the TV despite the technical challenges, bringing up a grainy black-and-white image of someone's back bedroom seen from an odd, high angle.

'Did we miss a memo?' Laurie said. 'What've you got for us?'

'Knew you and Dash would be in early, boss. The memo went to everyone else.' Milla was bright-eyed with a breakthrough. 'Chris's laptop. Started ringing alarm bells with digital forensics thanks to the number of times he'd wiped the hard drive, or tried to. You know how sticky that stuff is. I've a friend in digital forensics, Tee.' Her blush said more than a friend. 'They spent last night digging into it, and this's what they found. Put it together with the rest of what we have' – she nodded at the paperwork on her desk – 'and it starts to look like a serious lead. Chris installed a lot of CCTV, for business clients mostly, but a few personal ones too. Some of the paperwork didn't stack up until Tee recovered this from an attempted hard drive wipe.'

Everyone's attention was on the TV screen.

Laurie said, 'Tell us what we're looking at.'

'Footage recorded with or without the homeowner's permission, although the angle suggests a hidden camera. Even if he had permission to install it, I can't believe anyone gave him permission to watch what it recorded.'

Milla pressed Play. She was right. Unless the couple in the back bedroom relished an audience, they wouldn't have wanted anyone seeing their short-lived lovemaking. Not a married couple, or not married to one another. Too clumsy, and much too furtive. 'Cameras of all kinds,' Beverley had said. 'Photos, pictures.'

Chris Miles, Peeping Tom. Pricey telescope not for stargazing but spying. Until someone put a stop to his games. This discovery changed everything. No more random, senseless killing. No wrong-place-wrong-time narrative. Chris left a door open, let this nightmare in. Saxton folded his arms, giving a small shake of his head. Ted made a sickened sound. The room felt too hot, the air too dead. Laurie wanted to fling open a window, let a cold lick of sunshine inside.

Joe turned to Milla. 'You said you had more?'

She nodded, closing the bedroom footage and opening a new clip. 'Not what it looks like from that first film. At least, I don't think so.'

Three further clips, captured on CCTV mounted outside a doorway, inside an office. General shiftiness suggested callers who shouldn't be calling, threatening body language, cash being palmed. Laurie didn't recognise anyone onscreen but Joe did. And Ted and Saxton, the three of them exchanging glances, and names – 'Is that Derek Symonds?' the last person Chris called before his death, 'Wait, was that his wife in the bedroom?' And, 'That's deffo Ben Ambler,' Adam's mate from the pub, starring in what looked like an amateur bid at benefit fraud which nevertheless brought the fine hairs up on the back of Laurie's neck. These men lived right here in Edenscar. Each clip was short, no longer than half a minute. How many hours of surveillance to capture those fifty incriminating seconds?

'Who edited these?' she asked.

'I think it must've been Chris.' Milla finished with the footage, set her iPad down. 'There's no evidence anyone else had access to his laptop, the only prints are his. And these files were well hidden, split into different folders, tucked away.' She took a breath. 'I'm still working through it, but from what I've found so far he emailed the clips to his clients. Each email asked for an invoice to be paid. He attached the invoice and embedded the clip in the email signature. Subtle, but I doubt anyone overlooked it. For one thing, the invoice was always bogus, identical to one the client had already settled. If anyone queried why he was resending the same invoice, he referred them to his signature. No further pushback after that.'

Dead silence in the room, the kind that said everyone recognised this as a turning point in the case. Milla picked up the paperwork she'd been sifting through since Monday. Bank records, accounts Chris had kept, his latest tax return.

'No paper trail for the second payment, but cash deposits match the bogus invoices in every case I've tracked so far. Set that against his bank records? He was bringing in over double what he was legitimately earning.'

There it was, then. Their victim had been a blackmailer. *One* of their victims. Laurie glanced at Joe, seeing in his face a reflection of her own conflicting emotions. Relief they had hold of a solid motive at last. Revulsion at Chris Miles, and a sad brand of anger that his nasty little sideline had brought devastation on his family. 'Do we think Odette knew about this?'

Milla shook her head. 'No way to know. Might've been why they were fighting, *if* they were.'

Laurie looked at Theo, wanting a contribution from everyone in the room, a way to bind them together. 'Nothing from the mums at the nursery about an unhappy home life, that's right, isn't it?'

'Nothing to suggest Odette knew about anything like this,' Theo said.

Ted had made a fortress of his face as soon as he started recognising people in the clips; she wondered how many were his mates. She glanced at Saxton, who was managing to look simultaneously wretched and unsurprised. He gestured for her to take the lead. She let the silence build for a time, so they could process what they'd learnt. They had their focus now, a clear direction of travel.

'Good work.' She nodded at Milla. '*Great* work. Let's have copies of that list, please. I want to know exactly who Chris was extorting, and for what. Ted can cross-check the names against ANPR, look for anyone with a silver car—'

'I still think that source stinks,' Ted said.

Jaxon Grice, he meant.

'The same source gave us Mr German's shotgun,' Laurie reminded him, 'and his stand-off with Chris on Friday. Corroborated by Mr German.'

'Just saying, if that little toerag turns up here with anything approaching a useful statement, I'll eat my hat and everyone else's.'

'In that event, I'll supply the cutlery.' She nodded at the TV. 'Let's get these men in for a chat, find out about Chris's MO. And I'd like Mr Lawlor back. See what he knew about this, if anything. Any chance he's on the blackmail list?'

'Not so far, boss. But I'm still digging.'

'Good, keep us posted. Joe, do you want to fill us in on the copper wire?'

'Boss . . . Cary Lawlor confirmed Chris was one of the last people inside Number 28. Tests pending, but there's a chance the wire used to rig the crossbow matches copper wire found from Chris's van. Given what we now know about his sideline, that looks suspicious.'

'Does it?' Ted was still nursing his grievance against Jaxon.

'DS Vicars has a point,' Laurie said. 'Rigging secret spy cameras is a bit different from rigging murder weapons. Hard to blackmail someone with a bolt through his neck. But all theories welcome at this time.'

Laurie shut the door to her office, turning to face Joe. 'You and I need to prioritise these interviews. Not just with Lawlor. Anyone identified in that footage. Derek Symonds, Ben Ambler. And we need to decide how much we're sharing with Chris's parents at this stage. They might have light to shed on their son's sideline.'

'They might,' Joe said. 'But nothing we saw on camera justifies one murder, let alone three.'

'So we haven't seen the worst yet. Milla's hunting that down. We wanted a motive. Blackmail is a very strong motive. Chris might've thought he was on to a good thing, a safe way to pay for his parents' holidays, but if he picked on the wrong person at the wrong time? Few of us like being spied on. And no one likes an unexpected invoice.'

'I'd like to think most of us wouldn't reach for a shotgun.'

'You're an optimist,' Laurie said. 'You want to watch that.'

Sammi bit his thumbnail, hiding a smile. 'She has a point, Joe.'

'Yvonne was right, then. About this being linked to Chris. But she can't have suspected blackmail or she'd have pointed us that way.'

Laurie nodded. 'There's a chance Odette found out. Bobby said he heard them fighting, could've been about this.'

'His parents might know if Chris had a history of spying, on them or their neighbours. But we're going to need something better than benefit fraud or the CPS will laugh us out of the room, don't you think?'

Laurie was about to answer when Ted knocked on the door.

'ANPR match.' He held up a printout. 'Bullseye.'

28.

'Roland Orme. Fifty-seven. Property developer, living in Sheffield. This is the man who hired Chris to rewire the house next to Bobby's. He's been trying to persuade Bobby to sell for six years.' Laurie pinned Orme's picture to the board. 'Thanks to Milla's great work, we know he's on the list of those Chris was blackmailing. Thanks to Ted's diligence, we know he drives a silver Mercedes GLA. And thanks to ANPR, we can confirm he was on the road between Edenscar and Sheffield late last Friday night with his high beams on.'

Everyone's eyes were on the little balding businessman in the photograph. Laurie tapped the man's forehead with her index finger. 'Joe and I are going to pay Mr Orme a visit. Ted, let's get the precise route he took on Friday. Timings, sightings, anywhere he stopped along the way.' She turned to face Theo. 'I want to know what links he has to the local area. When was he last in the house Chris rewired? When did he most recently offer money to Bobby, and how much? Does he have a history of leaning on people the way he's been leaning on Bobby? Oh, and does he have a licensed shotgun and if so, make and model.' To Milla, 'Keep tracking his online footprint. I want him hunted into every murky corner. The guv's twisting arms to get us warrants but in the meantime, be imaginative.'

She nodded at the team then pointed Joe towards the car park, briefing him en route as to what she wanted from the day. 'Orme's in a fancy part of Sheffield, not much chance of getting canned but keep your eyes peeled. I've a feeling he's about as respectable as Jim Chancellor, Mr Salt of the Earth, who pretended to be developing properties in Deansgate when for decades he'd been rinsing money for people traffickers.' She slung her bag across her body. 'That ended in a couple of big arrests, no murders, but I trust these people less than their brochure promises: *Building the homes we'd like to live in ourselves*. Except they never do. Always in some mock-Tudor pile their parents swooned over.'

'That sounds like Orme's place.' Joe had been digging online. 'Five double bedrooms, detached. High security if the photos on Zoopla are telling the truth. Masquerading as privacy, but motion-sensitive CCTV on all sides.'

'Good, let's hope there's footage of him arriving home with a shotgun on Friday night. That'll save time.'

As they reached the pool car, Joe hesitated. 'It's going to take the best part of an hour to get to that side of Sheffield at this time. Are you sure you don't want to call ahead, see if Mr Orme's home?'

'Give him notice of our arrival? I'm going to assume you're joking. I wouldn't take a marked car to a man like that.'

'What makes you so sure he's a crook? Whether or not he's a killer.'

'Gut instinct,' Laurie said shortly. 'And long experience.' She looked Joe over, as if sizing him up for the task ahead.

Did she wish she had one of her Salford detectives in tow? Was she worried Joe might give Orme the benefit of the doubt, or otherwise flounder in the big bad city? 'Prove her wrong.' Sammi played a tune on the roof of the car. 'Come on.'

'His house's on Zoopla,' Laurie said. 'Does that mean it's on the market?'

'Archived listing.' Joe unlocked the car and they climbed in. 'He bought it at the back end of last year, can't have told them to take the photos down yet. It's possible he's made alterations, might even have decommissioned the CCTV.'

'Doubt it.' Laurie settled into the passenger seat. 'Property developers are a paranoid bunch. That's why my gut's telling me this might be our man. Bet his finances aren't too happy, why lean on Bobby otherwise? For the sake of a pair of holiday homes in a location like that? And if he put Chris up to a campaign of harassment, cutting off the heating in an old man's house? That's nasty.'

'If he did,' Joe agreed.

'Plus he's hiding out in a mock-fortress with silly security and probably some of the worst interior decor money can buy. Jim Chancellor had a floor-to-ceiling portrait of his family *sitting on horses*.'

Sammi burst out laughing on the back seat.

'That does sound naff,' Joe agreed.

'Roland's going to have a chandelier in the kitchen. Bet you a tenner.'

'A chandelier?'

'In the kitchen,' Laurie said darkly.

The chandelier wasn't in the kitchen but close enough: in an L-shaped dining room leading from the kitchen where Roland Orme took Laurie and Joe after inspecting their warrant cards via gate-mounted CCTV. Inside his mock-fortress, he offered coffee, which they declined, Joe taking his cue from Laurie.

'I was due to come your way later this morning. If you'd called ahead, I could've arranged to pop into the station in Edenscar, saved you the trip.'

Orme smiled, his teeth rivalling Bobby's for brightness. He pronounced it *Enscar,* suggesting he'd spent time there. Wasn't surprised to find detectives on his doorstep before 9 a.m., but with the kind of face that'd schooled itself not to show emotion. He faked surprise quickly enough once his brain caught up with the fact he shouldn't be looking like someone who expected police on his doorstep, at any hour. Since the surprise was about as authentic as his teeth, Laurie discounted it. His face was all forehead, sleek hair dyed an unlikely shade of mink. Vain, with a short man's habit of putting his shoulders back to gain height. He hated Laurie on sight. For being taller; she got a lot of that.

'You're here about Chris Miles?'

'Why would you say that?'

Orme slid his eyes to Joe. Trying to share a male-bonding moment but getting his machismo bruised on the brick wall of Joe's most neutral expression. 'I heard the news. Shocking. Especially his little boy.'

'I'll be honest, Mr Orme.' Laurie stood under the fuck-off chandelier. 'We're not here to find out how shocked or otherwise you are by the news of a triple homicide in *Enscar*. You were there last Friday. Your car, the one parked in your drive, was seen on the A57 shortly after 9 p.m. that night.'

'Quite right.' The accusation slid straight off him. 'I was there on business, meeting a client about a potential development in the Hope Valley.'

'We'll need details of that. Your client's name and address, the time of your arrival and when you left.'

'Of course. I'll write it all down.'

'Did you see Chris Miles that day?'

'Not at any point, no.'

The smile hung from his face so complacently Laurie had an urge to punch it into his back teeth. She decided to cut to the chase. 'We're here because we have reason to believe Chris was extorting money from his clients.'

Silence, underscored by the glassy lack of expression on Orme's face. In the L-shaped dining room everything was a different shade of white – chalk-coloured cupboards, bone-white tiles, parchment blinds. She wondered if Joe was seeing what she was: the contrast between this sterile space and the farmhouse kitchen where Chris and Odette were gunned down.

'Was Chris extorting money from you? We know you paid several invoices for work you hired him to do in your house next to Bobby German's. The house you've been trying to buy for the past six years, despite Mr German's insistence he isn't interested in selling.'

Orme put his index finger to the pale marble counter where a serving hatch had been fitted between the kitchen and dining room. He was watching Joe for some reason, but he was hearing Laurie. She could see her words reflected in the reconfiguration of his face. He didn't look like a killer. A sleek little otter of a man in a fancy waistcoat. Joe didn't give an inch under his scrutiny. In the car, he'd wanted to talk about Cary Lawlor and Jaxon Grice, but she'd shut him down: 'One thing at a time. I need you focused on Orme. We don't have anything like enough for an arrest but we need to move things forward and fast. I'm going to shake this tree, see what drops. I need you watching with me. Clear?'

Orme's finger slid back and forth on the polished counter, calculating the extent to which he was screwed; she'd seen it in a hundred faces. Those who lacked his wealth usually made the calculation sooner, reaching for a weapon if they had one, taking to their heels if they didn't. Orme's calculation involved how soon his lawyer could be here, how expensive that would be, what work might be lost if he was tied up answering questions for any length of time. She knew precisely when he reached his decision because his face relaxed, his forehead smoothing to a mask that said *expensive lawyer incoming*.

'Quite right. Mr German has no intention of selling, to me or anyone else. I'd given up asking. And quite right about Chris, who attempted to extort money from me on more than one occasion. Submitting invoices for work already done and paid for. I have a full paper trail. My accountants can send you anything you need to see.'

'That would be everything,' Laurie said.

'I'll make sure they understand the urgency.' Orme lifted his finger from the counter and inspected it, pulling his shoulders back as he smiled at Laurie. 'Chris was a first-class cutthroat. He offered to run a campaign of intimidation to drive Bobby out, shutting off the power during a cold spell, imagining I'd admire his spirit of enterprise and pay him for it. I didn't, of course. I condemned it in the strongest possible terms, and instructed him to restore the power immediately, warning him I'd inform the police.'

'Did you?' Joe asked. 'Inform the police?'

'I did not, DS Ashe, no. It wasn't necessary, as Chris did as I asked.' After a meaningful pause, 'We have a mutual friend in Nelson Roache, I think?'

Joe's expression didn't change. 'Was Mr Roache aware of this campaign of intimidation against Bobby?'

For the first time, Orme's face flickered with uncertainty. 'Of course not.'

'Then why mention him in connection to this enquiry?'

'I was merely making conversation.'

'This isn't a conversation,' Joe said coldly. 'We're conducting a murder investigation. Do you own a shotgun?'

It was outside the brief they'd agreed in the car, but Joe was improvising and he was good at it. Really very good.

Orme swallowed convulsively. 'I do, as it happens. Yes.'

'What bore?'

'Twenty.'

'Licensed?' Joe asked next.

'Of course.'

'Where is it?'

'In my safe. With the firing mechanism removed.' Orme was recovering his composure, but on his guard against the pair of them now. 'Ammunition stored separately. In a locked container, in line with police guidelines.'

'When was the last time you fired it?'

'Some time in April, I expect. Out in your neck of the woods. Nelson's friends organise the odd shoot, as I'm sure you know.'

Joe made a note of this. 'What did you shoot?'

'Grouse, I expect. Or muntjac. I can't remember. Whatever we were hunting, I didn't hit anything. I go for the camaraderie more than the sport.'

'Just a group of friends hanging out in the woods,' Laurie said, 'shooting defenceless animals. I'm getting a warm glow.'

There was a second when Orme was going to offer his opinion on the value of hunting, some pious cant about animals having no natural predators in the UK and therefore no opportunities to experience the 'thrill of the chase', or the role hunts played in protecting agriculture and the environment from pests and overpopulation. In the end, he said nothing.

'We'll need to see it,' Laurie said. 'The gun and the licence.'

He led them to the safe. The route passed through three rooms on the ground floor, two of which had fuck-off chandeliers. Laurie made a point of raising her eyes, in case Joe wasn't paying attention. The shotgun was exactly as Orme described: locked in a safe, its firing mechanism removed and stored separately. Ammunition in another place, also under lock and key.

'We're taking all this. You can sign for it.'

'Happily,' Orme told her. 'Whatever I can do to assist. Chris may not have been the most moral of men, but he didn't deserve what befell him. Nor did wife and child.'

Had she thought him *pious*? If Roland Orme got any holier, he'd need a halo. A nice shiny white one to match his interiors.

'We'll be in touch. You'll need to make yourself available on our request, at the police station in Edenscar.'

'Of course. You have my number?'

'Oh I think so.' Laurie cocked an eyebrow at Joe. 'What do you say, DS Ashe? Do we have Mr Orme's number?'

Joe had the shotgun tucked into his armpit, muzzle pointed to the ground. 'I'd say so, DI Bower, yes.'

From the doorstep, Orme watched them go. 'How long before he calls the Police Commissioner, do you think?' Laurie cracked her knuckles. 'Either directly, or via your mate Nelson.'

'Hard to say.' Joe was negotiating the tail end of the rush hour, queuing to get on to the A57. 'But I believed him about the blackmail. He didn't think enough of Chris to feel threatened by him, certainly not enough to kill him, or not for whatever went down at Bobby's.'

Laurie was inclined to agree. 'Wouldn't want to get his hands dirty. But you never know. Blokes like that have all sorts of weaselly deals going down. You owe me a tenner, by the way.'

'That was a dining room,' Joe said. 'Not a kitchen.'

'It had a serving hatch.'

'Kitchen-adjacent, at best.'

'Diet Coke from the service station, and we'll call it quits.'

Joe accepted this compromise. Laurie checked in with Milla, was told Orme had sent through copies of every invoice he'd received from Chris, confirming his accountants would give the police full access to his financial records.

'Is it just me, or is he a bit too eager to lend a hand?'

'He's covering his tracks,' Joe said. 'Like a hunter.'

Laurie listened to the tough sound of the shotgun case shifting in the boot. 'You said whoever went after Chris and Odette was hunting. But you don't think Orme had the motive to kill?'

'Based on what we currently know?' Joe shook his head, but his profile was tauter than usual. 'I'm open to being convinced.'

'He has money, clearly. It's possible that means he wasn't intimidated by Chris's tactics. Depends what he was blackmailing him for, though, doesn't it? Did you believe him about Bobby's place, that it was Chris's idea to cut the power?'

'I did, actually. He seemed genuinely disgusted by the idea of trying to freeze an elderly man in his own home.'

'He's not the only one,' Laurie said. 'Chris Miles was a piece of work.' She waited for Joe to agree or disagree but he was silent. 'Someone with less money than Orme might've found it harder to forgive whatever form the blackmail took. Those cameras could've caught anything. Drugs, sex, violence. Secrets. That kind of invasion of privacy could tip the wrong person over the edge.' The thought of a hidden camera in Peter's house made her sick, the stain of last night still fresh on her skin, their fight then Adam's drunken groping, her submission for the sake of peace. 'Blackmailers are like arsonists. They get addicted to the risk, to seeing things go up in flames. Makes them want to do worse.' She thought of Orme's arrogance, that lawyered-up look on his face. 'There was *something* there. He was too pleased with himself, like he'd got away with it.'

Joe's phone was ringing. He pressed the hands-free pickup. 'Ted, I'm with the boss. We're headed back.'

'That's good,' Vicars said. 'You can talk Nic Grice off her high horse.'

'What's happened?' Joe's voice was sharp, his eyes on the road.

'She's accusing you of scaring off her precious son. He's not been seen since you had that chat out by Higher Bar. Wasn't home all night, she says.'

'Have you got anyone looking for him?'

'Not yet. He's been gone longer than this, come back under his own steam.'

Ted was complacent – no surprises there – but Joe's profile was carved with worry. 'We should find him. He's a potential witness in a murder investigation—'

'He's a wind-up merchant. Chances are he's taken himself off on purpose after you put the idea in his head he's a big deal when we both know he's a pig-headed little bastard who loves giving trouble.'

Laurie said, 'DS Vicars?'

'Yes, boss?'

'Do your bloody job and find Jaxon Grice. I'll expect an update by the time we're back.' She ended the call, looking at Joe. 'You're freaking out. Why?'

'An eleven-year-old is missing. Was missing overnight. That's a legitimate cause for concern.'

'You thought he'd come to the station yesterday to give a statement. If he didn't, it'd be because he was strutting, pretending he knew more than he did.'

'I was wrong.' Joe's hands tightened on the wheel. 'I should've taken him in yesterday.'

'Why didn't you?' When Joe stayed silent, she said, 'Because you thought you knew how to handle him, thought you were the wild-kid whisperer.'

Joe still didn't speak. She had the impression he was listening to a second voice in the car, or he'd jumped ahead of her, knowing what it meant. A missing kid, another child's life in danger. Her chest clenched. 'If he saw something on Friday night at Higher Bar, or if our killer *thinks* he saw something—'

'Thanks', Joe said drily, 'for spelling it out.'

'We should've taken him in.' She was appalled at herself. 'That wasn't just on you. I was there, the SIO. I should have taken appropriate action.'

Joe put his foot down, reverting to silence. A scrawny eleven-year-old, half-starved, chocolate at the edges of his mouth. Talking like a gangster about guns – *a stick, a pole, bap-bap* – and she'd let him turn his bike around in the dirt and head back into the woods, alone. What the hell was wrong with her?

29.

At the station, Laurie briefed the team on their visit to Sheffield. Orme's shotgun was logged, but no one believed it would be linked to Higher Bar. The murder weapon was twelve-bore, Orme's was twenty. Joe was having difficulty keeping a lid on his darker thoughts. All the way back from Sheffield, Sammi had speculated about Jax, about blackmail and murder weapons, until it was hard to concentrate on the road or Laurie. She was angry with him, again. And with herself, which in some ways was worse. Neither of them deserved to get off lightly for letting Jax go. In his office, Saxton asked questions to which neither of them had adequate answers: 'You believed he was a witness but you left him to his own devices? I'm finding that hard to fathom.'

'My mistake,' Joe said. 'He's not always the most reliable witness and his version of events was inconsistent. I thought if we pressed him, he'd double-down and we'd be wasting time. But I should've brought him in.'

'Nice try,' Laurie said in an arid voice. 'But I'm the SIO. I was there, heard everything DS Ashe heard. It was my call. I called it wrong.'

Saxton studied them. 'Well, I can't say the hair shirts suit you, but we are where we are. Let's find him. Joe, you know his hiding places, lead on that.' He nodded at Laurie. 'Stay with Higher Bar. This might not be connected. Jax could've spooked for any number of reasons. Joe's right to say he has form.'

In Laurie's office, Joe said, 'Give me a couple of hours to see what I can find? If he's still missing after that, we can call in extra hands.'

'No, thanks. He's eleven. There's a killer out there. You call in the extra hands now, or I'll ask Saxton to put someone else in charge.'

'Ouch.' Sammi leant into her filing cabinet. 'You took that in the chest.'

'Fair enough. You're right.' *She's right, Sammi.*

As he was leaving, Laurie said, 'Joe,' and he turned, steeling himself for more of the same, or worse. She shook her head at him. 'I'm pissed off with myself. Well, with both of us. But I didn't mean to give you both barrels. One of those was for me. Watch yourself out there, and keep me posted.'

On the Wakefield estate, parking was limited to a handful of spaces between rusting caravans and cars. Joe parked some distance off, knowing the pool car was a red flag; he was enough of a red flag on foot. Sammi kept step with him, 'Lighten up. Feeling guilty isn't going to get him home any faster.'

Joe took out his phone, pretending to be on a call. 'What was I thinking, do you know? Leaving him like that, walking away.'

'Same as Laurie. He's a tough nut, wouldn't crack if you'd lifted him.'

'Eleven years old.'

'Remember what you were like at that age?'

Joe was silent, remembering.

'Still thinking I was alive, on and off. Couldn't accept this was me now.' Sammi stretched his arm, turning it so the sun hit his wrist, shining from his skin, sleek with muscle beneath. Joe could smell the fresh mint of his breath, feel the brush of cotton where the hem of Sammi's sweatshirt touched his knuckles.

'You're so real today. Does that mean I'm worse?'

'Means you're tuning in. Using all your senses. Because you're closing in on this case.'

'Am I? Doesn't feel like it. I lost a child. We've no serious suspects—'

'The only danger's if you start wallowing in self-reproach. Animals don't do that. They're too smart.'

'All right. Well, keep me posted on that.' Joe ended the call and Sammi lapsed into silence, staying at his side.

Behind the Wakefield estate, the woods rose up, spiked tips of larches like razor wire at the horizon. That was where Jax would be, assuming he was safe – deep in the forest. It was where he lived, more or less, on that bike of his. Different to the one he was riding last time they ran into one another. The way the kids rode bikes around here, nothing lasted very long. Nelson had set up a club to provide new bicycles as they outgrew their old ones, a way of keeping kids active, coming up with the idea after the summer spate of thefts. Joe wondered if the red bike was one of those from the club. Nelson took no credit for the idea, but it was his money that'd paid for the first dozen bikes, and kept the club running.

Nicola Grice answered the door in the jeans and logoed fleece she wore to work at the service station. She did not look pleased to see Joe, but she invited him inside, afraid of being judged a bad parent. Joe didn't judge her, knowing how hard it was to hold a family together around here. Nicola worked three part-time jobs (when she could get them), never had a moment to herself.

'He wasn't home for his lunch, or tea. I left it out when I went to work, had to go early because of the road closures. Thought he'd be here when I got back, wanting whatever cakes were being chucked, past their sell-by dates. He always waits up for that.' She sounded worn down, dragging her fair hair behind her ears. Her eyes were small and brown, but with none of her son's light, that fierce stare Jax gave to the world.

'His friends haven't seen him? Oscar, or the others? No one's seen his bike about the place?'

Jax often left the bike at the side of the road when he was with his mates, hanging around the shops or taking a chance on a free bus-hop into Sheffield.

'Bike's been gone longer than he has. He keeps it in the woods, I think.'

'Can you give me his phone number?'

Nicola recited it and Joe put it into his phone, dialling the number. The call went straight to voicemail, an automated message suggesting the battery was dead or the phone switched off. Unlikely a kid his age would switch his phone off.

'He'll have let it run down,' Nicola said. 'He only ever charges it here.' She'd been avoiding looking at Joe, her eyes anywhere else. Now she fixed her stare on him, fearfully. 'They're saying you were the last to see him. I don't want that to be true. Don't want to hear you saw him – *see* him. Don't tell me if that happens. I don't want to hear it. I'm not another Han Cooper.'

'I understand.'

Guilt rose like acid in his chest; he had to swallow to make it go back down. He explained all the reasons why it was too soon to be worrying about Jax, wishing he'd brought Theo, a safer pair of hands when it came to reassuring anxious parents; Joe just made them worse. He put a call through to the team at the station, speaking with the police search advisor, requesting family support for Nicola, before saying his goodbyes.

He was halfway back to his car when Sammi, sounding like Laurie, said, 'Incoming!'

Joe swerved, narrowly avoiding taking the hit in his left shoulder. Instead it exploded across his chest – a clod of dried earth and builder's sand compacted into a handy, bruising missile.

'Fucking pig!'

He shook the shoulders of his jacket as Sammi hissed a second warning, seeing what Joe only half-registered at the periphery of his vision: Des and Shane with a third friend whose name Joe knew but couldn't recall since his brain was occupied with calculating the distance to his car and whether or not he'd make it before the three had him on the ground, which was clearly their intention. 'Carl Fulton.' Sammi, naming the third man. '*Run*. They're not after a chat.'

Joe took to his heels, hoping he had the speed to make it to safety. Either by accident or design, the trio had cut off his route, closing in like a pack. He was faster than any one of them, on a good day. But this was their turf and they knew it, splitting up in a bid to block his route. He sprinted, nevertheless.

'Joseph?'

A silver Audi was slowing to a halt up ahead. Joe switched direction and ran towards it. The driver had the passenger door open – 'Hop in' – scooping him from the road like a stranded action hero. Not that he felt particularly heroic, struggling to fasten his seat belt, catch his breath and thank Nelson, all at the same time.

'Was that Des Morton leading the pack? Animals.' Nelson glanced at the dark stains on Joe's shirt. 'You're a mess. Are you hurt?'

'Only my pride. And the pool car, if I leave it for any length of time. You'd better drop me there, if that's all right?' He told Nelson where he'd left the car and they circled back via a long route designed to fox the unfriendly forces.

'You were lucky to find me out this way, doesn't happen often. Tommy and I are looking at woodland for sale. Tommy's keen we don't let it fall into the wrong hands.' Nelson chatted away, giving Joe the chance to regroup. 'He's all for making a stand against the taming of our landscape, says he's seen too much of that in Italy, wildfires, tourist impact. Wants to preserve the ancient spirit of this place. Animals in the woods, not just those on foot endangering our local constabulary. Here you go. Car looks safe. You're fit to drive?'

'Definitely.'

'Well, shout if you need to come out this way again. I'll be your backup, if that's what it takes.'

Joe thanked him, pausing as he climbed from the car. 'I don't suppose you saw Jaxon Grice when you were up in the woods?'

'On any number of occasions. But not recently. Is there a problem?'

'He's not been home in nearly twenty-four hours. There's an alert out. Were you and Tom Sangster in the same part of the woods earlier?'

Nelson shook his head. 'Too much ground to cover. There's a chance Tommy saw him – he was scouting the bike trails. You'd be best off asking him directly. I can call him, get him to confirm one way or the other?'

'I'll call him, thanks. And for the rescue.'

'Get yourself out of here, would be my advice. That looked like a hunting party out for your hide. Take care, Joseph.'

'I will. Thanks again.'

Joe drove the pool car to a safe spot a mile away, parked up and scrolled through his contacts for Tom Sangster's number. The call went to voicemail.

'Mr Sangster, this is Joe Ashe. I was just speaking with Nelson, who suggested I get in touch about a missing child you may've seen. Could you call me back as a matter of urgency? Thank you.'

Sammi sat in the passenger seat, shaking his head. 'You'll have bruises. That was a brick he threw at you, good as.'

'I'm fine. Just need a clean shirt.'

But Sammi wasn't happy to leave it at that. He twisted in the seat to meet Joe's eyes. 'You need to stop pretending he's just a bit of local colour, start making an official record of all the times he's tried to screw you over. That way when they find you with your skull caved in, they'll know whose door to go knocking on.'

'Cheery of you. But it's been seventeen years. He'd have done it by now if that's what he wanted.'

'I'm serious, Joe. We're not kids any more. He's a thug and he hates you. Not names-on-the-bus hate. Skim-stalk-to-the-back-of-the-head hate.'

'I'll deal with it.'

'You'll need to.' Sammi's eyes flashed.

'Leave it with me. And tell me why I'm thinking I need to find Tom Sangster.'

'Because you didn't know he was back in the country. And because of the crossbow. Oh, and by the way?'

'Yes?'

'Nelson drives a silver car. Just throwing that into the mix.'

'Thanks.'

'Hey.' Sammi held up his hands. 'Don't shoot the messenger.' He stretched in the seat. 'Enough shooting around here already.'

30.

'You have Derek Symonds for me?'

'Boss.' Milla pushed her headphones to the back of her neck. 'He's waiting by the front desk when you're ready.'

'Good work,' Laurie said. 'Get together everything you have on him and Chris, and join me in the interview room. Where's DS Ashe?'

Joe had been gone nearly two hours.

'I'll put a call in, boss.' When she joined Laurie and Derek Symonds in the interview room, Milla said Joe's voicemail was on, but he'd been in touch with the PolSA searching for Jaxon Grice. 'I asked him to check in, soon's he's free.'

Derek Symonds didn't look like a serious suspect in a triple homicide, not least since he had an alibi for Friday night, but he knew how Chris operated, could shed light on the seedier side of his business. Unlike Orme, he wasn't wealthy, nor had he been impervious to attempted blackmail. He began by expressing regret at his failure to alert the police sooner, and dismay at the idea (his own) that Chris must have tried to extort money from the wrong man, or woman: 'He'd try anything, honestly.'

Symonds was a big man, not tall but broad, with an open face and square hands he held up at intervals, as if calculating the dimensions of the interview room for a refit. 'Started as a joke, that's what I thought. Said he'd left a camera running by mistake in the show house, caught a couple "trying out the master bedroom, if you catch my drift". We'd a laugh about it.' His face crunched with regret. 'He was a good sparks, we don't have that many round here and we all knew he was struggling. We felt sorry for him, happy to put work his way. Only these past six months he started chucking his weight around, turning down jobs he didn't like. Bloody ruthless, he was, when you got right down to it. If it'd just been money' – shaking his head – 'but he got a kick out of it. Making us sweat at the thought of what he'd do if we didn't pay up.'

'Us?' Laurie echoed. 'You know other people Chris was blackmailing?'

'At least three of us. I'll give you names if I have to, though they won't thank me for it. We feel proper Charlies, letting him do that.' He squared his jaw against the memory before letting it go. 'He put in CCTV for me back home, a freebie for the work I was passing his way. Only then he decides I need to see what he's caught on camera and put it like this – me and the missus won't be going on that cruise this year. Given as how it's clear who she'd rather be going with. He shouldn't've had that footage, let alone saved to his laptop. Backed up on fancy flash drives. Felt sick when he showed me mine.'

He dug his hand into his pocket and pulled out the device, putting it on the table. The kind of flash drive sold in bulk online, weighing less than twenty grams. The first line of Derek's address was printed on it in small, neat letters. Laurie's heart sank, knowing it meant they had a whole new search ahead of them, Chris's laptop the tip of the iceberg. How many of these did Chris have? And where had he hidden them? Nothing in the logs about flash drives, she'd have remembered.

'I paid in cash,' Symonds said miserably, 'and he handed it over, no word of apology. Don't ask me why he went for me instead of her. Except I'm a softer touch. Spying, on those of us daft enough to let him do work in our homes.' He frowned at his empty hands. 'I say *daft*, but you can't blame us for being trusting. You don't expect people to do that, not spying and that. Well, do you? I reckon he was hooked on it. On the secrets. Ben says he was like that at school, sneaking up on people, spreading whispers. He loved attention, did Chris. Do anything for it.'

Sticking his finger in a socket, nearly setting the school's science lab on fire. When Adam shared that story, Laurie pictured a rowdy kid, a show-off. But this fitted with the evidence from Chris's old bedroom, those sketches of the children's faces. Snatching at secrets, stories. Obsessive, addicted. It fitted with what Yvonne and Mel said too. Chris couldn't control the land up at Higher Bar, but he could control people. With his flash drives, his blackmail.

'Do you think Odette knew anything about this?' she asked Symonds.

'I know she did, heard her and Chris fighting over it.' He flushed. 'That makes it sound like *I* was spying but he was loud, on his phone. Worse than if he'd been having an affair, that's what she said. Spying on other people's affairs.'

Bobby thought Odette was having an affair. Maybe he'd heard her use that word, but in the context Derek was describing, it had nothing to do with her own fidelity.

'We'll need the names of everyone who was a victim of his blackmail.'

'I'll write them down. But if you're thinking one of us would've killed him, you're barking up the wrong tree. We don't deal with our problems like that, not round here. My wife's having a bit of a fling, so what? And the others? He hadn't anything on us big enough for murder. Odette was nothing to do with it. Nor Eric – we all knew he was in that house. None of us'd harm a hair on his head, not even on Chris's. He was a rotten piece of work, but to go up there with a gun and blast the whole family to bits?' He shook his head.

His secret was small, 'a bit of a fling'. It didn't follow that every secret Chris threatened to expose was inconsequential. Or that his other victims shared Derek's opinion of what justified wholesale slaughter.

Once the interview was over, Laurie asked Milla to follow up on the names Symonds had supplied. They headed back to the incident room together.

'What about that flash drive? I'd been hoping all the evidence would be recovered from Chris's hard drive. Wishful thinking, clearly.'

'The flash drive was news to me.' Milla pushed her fringe from her eyes. 'If that's where he was storing the clips, we need to go back over the evidence, look for where he might've hidden more sticks. Loads of ways you can hide or disguise them, too.' She pulled a face. 'Sorry, boss.'

'Let's get all hands on that. We need to find *all* the blackmail material Chris was hoarding. Somehow I don't see Derek Symonds as our killer, do you?'

Milla shook her head. Derek's flash drive contained the footage they'd watched at the start of the day: Mrs Symonds and her visitor, identified by Derek as a local and discounted as a suspect after it was confirmed he'd left on a cruise, without Mrs Symonds, before the time of the murders.

'Let's focus on the new names Derek gave us. Start with anyone on the ANPR list from Friday, or with a licence for a shotgun. If that gives us nothing, we'll think again. And, yes, check in with Evidence about flash drives.'

Something Symonds had said struck a chord in Laurie: he'd insinuated that the killer was not a local. If that was true, it was time for her to make contact with DCI Reza, see what he could tell her about the current shotgun-toting crowd with business out in the Dark Peak.

'Any sign of DS Ashe?'

Theo raised his hand. 'He phoned in hoping to catch you, ma'am. He's following up a lead in Ilkley and could you call him back?'

'What's in Ilkley?'

'Big houses and a bugger-off moor.' Ted was eating lunch at his desk, an egg bap (the smell was a punch in the nose) filled with something crunchy that might've been salad but was more likely to be crisps.

Laurie didn't have the energy to ask for a proper answer to her question. She went to her office for privacy, shut the door and speed-dialled Joe, who picked up promptly enough. 'What's in Ilkley?'

'Tom Sangster. There's a chance he saw Jax in the woods earlier. And he's our crossbow expert. I thought we might pick his brains about that copper wire.'

'This could've been a phone call, couldn't it? Ilkley's going to take you ninety minutes, both ways.'

'I couldn't reach him by phone. How're things at the station?'

Laurie looked through her window to where Ted was picking egg off his tie. 'We're a whirlwind of activity. Derek Symonds confirmed Chris was blackmailing anyone who gave him work round here, saving his spy reels to USB sticks by the look of it. Milla's chasing them to ground. How was Jaxon's mum?'

'Unhappy. His phone's dead. I've given the number to the search team.' Joe sounded distracted, heavy traffic on the road.

'Get back here as soon as you can. Don't waste longer than you need to on that bloody crossbow. We've two clear objectives: find the killer and the kid. PolSA's looking for Jax. I need you on Higher Bar. If you weren't already halfway to bloody Ilkley, I'd tell you to turn back.'

Next, Laurie dialled a number she knew by heart. 'Bloody hell, Bower. It's not even been a week.'

'Hey, boss. Miss you too.'

'With a triple murder to solve? I doubt it. You holding up? Sounds nasty from what I've heard. A baby?'

'And his parents. We're looking for someone with a twelve-bore shotgun and a very cold heart. Speaking with lots of locals but I'm wondering if we need to widen the net.' She explained her thinking, how it was possible the killer was local to Manchester rather than Edenscar.

Rez heard her out in silence. 'Speak with Saxton, get him to put in a request for our help. He'll have called in a few favours already, I bet. You're not doing this as a team of six, or however many you have there in Edenscar.'

'*Enscar*. And it's a case of however *few* we have, not many. Extra bodies from Ripley, mostly for the searches. Complicated just today by a missing kid. Did I really say I'd be bored here?'

'How's Adam, and Peter?'

'Bad, and badder. No, that's not fair. It's getting worse faster than we thought, which, you know, might prove a blessing in the long run.'

'And the Team of However Few? Made many allies?'

'I thought so. But he's pissed off to Ilkley for some reason I don't think's clear even to him.' She shook down her shoulders. 'Thanks for listening to my cranky Ted Talk. Give my best to the gang.'

'Which one? We've so many here. Assuming you don't mean the Z-Team?'

'Ha. Thanks, Rez. See you.'

31.

Tom Sangster lived on the edge of Burley Woodhead in a house that enjoyed a high degree of privacy thanks to a long drive with potholes of the kind guaranteed to make Laurie curse. The house was old, although not as old as Middlestone Hall, with views towards the Vale of York and surrounding moors. Flanked by forest that reached to the back door; Powderhill on a grand scale. Paddocks, meadows, even a stream. None of it especially well kept. Joe wondered whether this was deliberate on Sangster's part, a celebration of the natural landscape. It made him wonder what the house was like inside, whether Sangster drew the line at letting Nature do her worst to his bricks and mortar. He was given no opportunity to find out. As he parked, a man strode from the woods with an axe in his right hand that appeared at a glance to be bloodstained. 'Whoa!' This was Sammi. 'Joe?'

'Detective Sergeant Joseph Ashe?' The man pointed with the axe-head. 'Nelson said you might come calling.'

'Mr Sangster? Yes, I tried phoning but—'

'No signal out in the woods. And it's Tom, please.' He swapped the axe to his left hand, holding out his right for Joe to shake. 'Good to meet you at last. Nelson speaks so highly of you, I half-wondered if you were a figment of his imagination; rare for him to praise someone your age. The price of being a child entrepreneur, always looking for enterprise in the youth of today.'

His smile was friendly, his build athletic. Tanned, toughened skin suggested he spent much of his time outdoors. He was a talker, barely drawing breath as he led Joe to the edge of the meadow that'd once been a lawn. 'Taming the undergrowth. *Ribes rubrum*. I like to leave nature alone as a rule but it's proving hard for wildlife to get through. Just lending a light hand.'

Redcurrant juice on the axe, not blood. He stooped to wipe its blade clean on the long grass before striding on, Joe keeping step at his side, to the nearest outbuilding: a woodshed with a padlock on its door.

'You won't mind if we stay out here, will you? Takes more effort than you might think, keeping this place looking as if I do nothing to maintain it.'

He dug a key from the pocket of his waxed trousers. A heavy-duty canvas jacket fitted his frame so closely it might've been made to measure, like Roland Orme's waistcoat, but Sangster's jacket was a great deal more practical, patched with secure-looking pockets. He unlocked the shed, clicked on a light to illuminate a neat space where his gardening tools were kept. Across three walls, a series of nails and hooks held everything a self-respecting woodsman might need to lend a light hand to nature. It smelt of creosote and lubricating oil, like the shed where Merry's hobbies sprawled and multiplied.

Sangster took up an oiled rag, began cleaning the axe blade. 'Sorry to put you to the trouble of tracking me all the way out here. You must be run off your feet. That business at Higher Bar.' He shook his head. 'Appalling.'

'It is, yes. Complicated now by the disappearance of another child.'

Sangster looked up, shock turning his eyes a darker shade of hazel. His hands halted on the axe. 'Another child?'

'Jaxon Grice. Do you know him?'

'Of him, certainly. Well, by repute.' His hands began moving again, cleaning the blade on autopilot, his gaze fixed to Joe's face. 'There was some trouble, wasn't there, last summer? Bikes being taken?'

Joe nodded. 'Jaxon's been missing twenty-four hours now.'

'That's a worry.' He reached to secure the axe in a cradle of nails before giving Joe his full attention. 'How can I help?'

'It's possible you saw him when you were with Nelson earlier today.' Joe named the woods. 'You were scouting the bike trails, he said?'

'Looking for damage, yes.' He wiped his hands on a clean cloth.

'Some of those nail traps laid in the summer were lethal. Lucky no one was badly injured.'

A couple of mountain bikers had been seriously hurt, in fact, one still recovering from a bout of sepsis after his calf was torn up by a trap.

'I didn't see anyone out there this morning, but there was an abandoned bike. I was tempted to take it to the skip at the top of Wakefield Road, you know the one? Assumed it'd been dumped but it wasn't rusting, just muddy. So I decided it must belong to someone, left it for them to collect.' He frowned, working the cloth between his fingers. 'A red bike. That's significant?'

'It might be, yes. Can you give me an exact location?'

'In those woods? I can do my best.'

Joe attempted to call up a map on his phone, but Sangster had been right about the lack of signal out here. He pulled out his tablet, sketching an outline of the woods in question, before handing the tablet and pen across.

'Remember that camp we built in those woods?' Sammi was examining the tools strung from the woodshed's walls. 'Could've used some of these, back then. You got splinters from breaking up firewood.'

Joe was watching Sangster work on the map. He needed Sammi to keep the memories to a minimum, wouldn't have minded his thoughts on Tom since he was finding the man hard to read. 'Ask him why he's buying the woods,' Sammi said.

'Nelson says you're considering buying woodland, is that right?'

'It is.' Tom was drawing landmarks on the map, neat and precise. 'Someone needs to make a stand against urban sprawl, don't you think? I fell for Edenscar the first time I saw it as a small boy. Used to build camps in the woods,' he smiled.

'Don't you dare tell him we did the same, Joe. That's private. You and me.'

'Lots of woodland for sale,' Joe said. 'And development slated for the area.'

He was thinking of Roland Orme's expansionist plans. The man's mock-Tudor pile couldn't be more different to Tom's overgrown acres.

'I don't know, Joseph. I'd like to bring an energy back to Edenscar. The way it made me feel as a youngster, all that adventure on our doorstep. Wildlife, insects, forest for miles.' Tom gestured towards the sprawl of trees behind his house before focusing on the map again. 'Everything's over-sanitised now. There's a reason we speak of unspoilt nature. When we overreach, we run into trouble. But we seem to want everything on our doorstep these days, nature be damned.'

Joe heard him out in silence, processing the long speech while he waited for the man to finish drawing the map to where he'd seen the red bike. Jax's bike, too much of a coincidence otherwise. Joe's head was ticking, not helped by Sammi pacing, eye-rolling at Sangster's proselytising.

'I know scores of others who feel the same,' Tom was saying, 'in case you're thinking I'm a one-off. Developers would have us believe unspoilt land is a wasted opportunity, that the green belt needs browning. But look at this woodland.' He handed the tablet to Joe. 'In desperate need of custodians to keep it special. I may beat back the odd bramble but I know my place, wouldn't dream of trying to tame ivy, or bracken. Can't be done. Those woods are what they are.' His eyes softened, showing Joe the boy he'd once been. 'People have tried to put down paths for centuries but it reverts to forest. Some places aren't meant to be tamed.'

Like Ladybower. The reservoir gave the illusion of obeying engineers, boiling down those monstrous plugholes. But water, like forest, is never tame.

'What time was it when you saw the bike?'

'Early. Not long after first light. I needed to be back here to try to make up for the time lost when I was in Italy. Nelson's gardeners keep his place in shape, but I'm a one-man band.'

Joe needed a phone signal to get the map to the team searching for Jax. 'Do you have Wi-Fi in the house?'

'On a good day, yes. But right now I'm waiting for a man to come and fix the connection. It's been out since I got back.'

'No working phone line of any kind?'

He shook his head. 'You're best off driving back to the main road, picking up a signal there. Sorry not to be more help.'

'You've been very helpful. I'd better get going.'

They walked back to Joe's car. When they reached it, Tom said, 'Ever get to the bottom of that business with the crossbow?'

'Not yet. Wouldn't mind your eyes on it, next time you're in Edenscar.'

'Of course. Good luck finding that young man. Let me know if I can help in any other way.'

'You can get your Wi-Fi fixed, for starters.' Sammi kicked at the overgrown verge. He didn't like Tom Sangster, for whatever reason.

Joe didn't have time to quiz him about it. He needed to get the map to the search team, and himself back to Laurie.

32.

'What's the weather like in Ilkley?' Laurie was working through the lists of Chris's blackmail victims when the call came from Joe. 'Only it's pissing down paperwork here. I need you back.'

'I'm headed your way now. Tom gave us a lead on Jax, spotted his bike in the woods earlier today. I've let the search team know.'

'Good. What's your ETA?'

'Eighty minutes? If the Snake Pass is clear.'

'I'd tell you to put your foot down, but I don't want to be taping off trees. Get here as quickly as you can without taking any stupid risks.'

She didn't know why she bothered with the warning; Joe was far too cautious to need or warrant it. She handed Milla her share of the list. 'I'm not seeing anything we haven't already checked. Are you?'

'Maybe.' Milla hesitated. 'Cary Lawlor?'

'What about him?'

'Didn't he say he'd been trying to get Chris to fix a broken extractor fan at the cottage in Powderhill?'

'How I remember it. What've you found?'

Milla showed her an invoice dated three weeks ago, for the fixing of the broken fan. A pricey job, close to £500 including labour and VAT.

'That's it? One invoice? I thought we were after people he stung twice for the same job of work?'

'We are, but since we're not getting far, I thought I'd include everyone he did work for in the last six months. This stands out because Lawlor never said the work was done, just that he *wanted* it done. The guy who boarded up the window said he could smell the rat from outside, tried turning on fans in the bathroom and kitchen to get shot of the smell, but neither was working. He reckoned they'd been out of action for a while, judging by the build-up of mould in the units.'

'And yet Mr Lawlor settled this invoice.'

'Yep. I'm thinking maybe he *was* blackmailed?'

'Chris did the original rewiring job,' Laurie said. 'Which means he'll have been in that cottage for weeks. A long time to resist his favourite pastime of putting in cameras.' She was remembering the sickened look on Lawlor's face as he stared at the exhibits seized in Powderhill. Was that fear they'd been seeing, or guilt? 'Find out what you can about his finances and business, ahead of Joe's return.'

'Already done, boss.' Milla fished a folder from under her iPad with a grin. 'Figured I'd shred it, if you didn't fancy him as a suspect.'

'Right now, I'd fancy anyone with a trigger finger.'

Laurie took the folder, opening it. Milla said, 'This's interesting,' pointing to a page where she'd highlighted contact between Lawlor and a local developer, sourced from an article about second-homers bringing money to the local area.

'Oh, hello again, Roland Orme.'

An unlikely team, the lanky Londoner and the sleek little Sheffield otter. But circumstances threw people together, say if both men were blackmailed by Miles: Orme for the pressure put on Bobby to sell his house, Lawlor for whatever Chris uncovered when he was playing games in the cottage in Powderhill.

'One more thing,' Milla said. 'When I was looking through the paperwork sent over by Orme's accountants.' She separated out the relevant sheet. 'He paid a local garage for a set of tyres about a month back. Unusual to need a full set in one go; roads round here are bad, but not that bad. When I asked for the reg, the car wasn't Orme's. He drives a Mercedes, this was a Golf. New tyres were fitted at the roadside because it was on bricks, up at Wakefield Road.'

'Are we talking about Des Morton's car? The one Sandra Buck swore she'd seen outside Lawlor's cottage?'

Milla nodded. 'Black Golf GTi, untaxed until a month ago. Des paid the tax in cash as far as I can tell, around the same time he got the new tyres.'

'Four tyres, plus roadside work? That wasn't cheap. And *Orme* settled the bill.' Laurie frowned. 'Why? Does he have any connection to Des we know about? They're not family. Unlikely friends, I'd say.'

'No connection I could find, boss. Maybe it's a charitable thing? Like Mr Roache and the bike club?'

'The only charity Orme supports is saving his own skin. No, this wasn't an act of generosity. It was payment of some kind, for something. And given what we know about the sort of work Des does, I doubt very much it was legal services. DS Vicars!' Laurie called across the room, gesturing for Ted to join them. 'Did you get anywhere finding out where Des Morton's car's been this last week?'

'Getting around to it, boss. I'd've been out that way Monday, but the news came in about the murders. Everything diverted in that direction.'

'You failed to carry out an order from your DCI? Is that what you're saying?'

'I was chasing ANPR all afternoon,' Ted protested. 'Didn't think Des was a priority in light of what was happening up at Higher Bar. If I could've kept on top of Powderhill *and* the murders, of course I'd have done that.'

'*Of course?*'

Ted tried a smile. 'What can I say? I'm a people pleaser.'

'Name one person who's pleased with you right now.' Laurie waited, then shook her head. 'Get hold of Des. I want to know why his transport bills are being paid by Roland Orme. And why, as now looks likely, his car was parked up at Powderhill the night someone rigged a deadly weapon in Number 28.'

Joe returned from Ilkley in a compressed mood, too silent for Laurie's liking. Word had got around about Jax's disappearance, locals volunteering for the search. He had a reputation as a troublemaker, but a missing kid was a missing kid.

'They found his bike,' Joe said. 'Exactly where Tom Sangster said it was.'

'Good, that'll help with a structure for the search. Did you eat lunch?'

'Not yet. How're things here?'

'Gathering pace.' She filled him in on the development with Lawlor and Orme. Joe wasted no time seeing what she'd seen: an unlikely connection but one which might make sense of the motive behind the murders.

'Neither man's local.' He reached for Milla's paperwork. 'That could mean they didn't know about Eric, thought they were eliminating a threat in Chris then Odette walks in, has to be dealt with.'

'Cary as the shooter?'

Joe looked sceptical, probably remembering the man's squeamishness over the dead rat. She didn't blame him; she was up to her throat in doubts of her own.

'What does Saxton have to say?' Joe asked.

'About what you'd expect. Not enough for a warrant, barely enough for an interview given we've already questioned him once. Lawlor has no licence for a shotgun. We've no evidence he was in the vicinity on Friday.'

'Except Chris was in his place right before it was turned into a death trap. He's been desperate to get in there since Monday, spent a night in the Tollgate which, without wishing to sound disloyal to a local community hub, has an average star rating on TripAdvisor that would shame our custody cells.' Joe studied the paperwork. 'Why would he limit the availability for holiday lets? He told me the place was a money pit, but he's not allowed the agency to let it out more than once or twice in the last four months.'

'Agreed that's odd, but the team's been back over that place. All prints accounted for. Nothing suspicious. No hidden cameras.'

'Chris could have removed them once he'd got what he wanted. Why don't we take Mr Lawlor to Powderhill, see what he's like when he's inside the cottage? Maybe we'll find out what he's so twitchy about.'

'It's a plan,' Laurie said. 'You need to eat first. And explain the grubby shirt. You didn't look like that when you left the station this morning.'

Joe rolled his left shoulder, returning his attention to Milla's paperwork. 'Des's car was put back on the road by Orme. What's that about?'

'Ask Ted. I've put him in charge of finding out.'

'From Des? Good luck with that. He wasn't in a chatty mood when I saw him earlier.'

'Oh, that's how your shirt got in this state?'

'So Sandra could've seen Des's car that night. And we know Orme has links with Lawlor.'

'You're triangulating suspects? Roland Orme, Cary Lawlor and Des Morton? I wouldn't add Des to a threesome without considering the cost, and I'm not referring to a new set of tyres. He's a thug, but I doubt he's the brains of any operation.'

'They didn't need brains. Orme is smart. Lawlor too, enough to be making serious money in London for a second home out here. If they involved Des it was because they had a use for him. Muscle, or wheels. Or a scapegoat.'

Laurie watched Joe's eyes move over the paperwork. 'DCI Saxton would like to remind us that Roland Orme is cooperating with our investigation. Cary Lawlor looks tangential to everything, at best.'

'You don't like them for it?' Joe said. 'I do.'

Roland Orme's arrogance, the readiness with which he threw Chris Miles under the bus, knowing murdered men can't answer back. Deluging them in paperwork from his accountants, forgetting the invoice lurking from the garage that put Des's car back on the road. Confident no trail would lead to his door. Because he wasn't involved, or because he had an alibi lined up? Lawlor was alibied to his eyebrows but that was the great thing about partnerships: you spread the risk, doubled your chances of getting the job done, at least until one of you cocked up.

'Lawlor's in the pub,' she told Joe. 'I'll dangle his keys, you get a sandwich inside you, and we'll see what happens.'

Cary Lawlor looked surprised to find both Laurie and Joe keen to accompany him to 28 Powderhill. Surprised and alarmed. *Good.* Laurie could work with that.

'Couple of questions first, if that's okay. At the station. Just squaring things away for our DCI.'

She'd asked Milla to turn up the heating in the interview room; the air was stifling, like breathing desiccated pine needles. When

Laurie produced the bogus invoice from Miles, Lawlor turned the same institutional green as the walls.

'I think I mentioned Chris fixed a fan for me?'

'An expensive job,' Laurie said.

'Two fans. One in the bathroom, one in the kitchen.'

'Two fans. But here's the thing: neither one is working. So when you paid Chris five hundred pounds, it wasn't for fixing fans. What was it for?'

'The fans *were* fixed. But then they broke again. You know how it is in these cottages.'

'I don't, actually. Where I come from we ask for our money back when that happens. Did you ask for your money back?'

He licked his lips, thinking. She expected him to employ Orme's tactics – dead men can't talk – and thought a little better of him when he shook his head. 'I didn't ask for my money back, no.'

'Why not?'

'I just—I never got around to it, I suppose.'

Joe said, 'Was Chris blackmailing you?'

'No.' He shook his head. 'Absolutely not.'

'Here's the other thing,' Laurie said, 'when someone's asked whether a murdered man was extorting money from them, typically they express surprise at the idea of the murdered man being a blackmailer. You didn't. Why not?'

'Well, because he *was* murdered. I assumed blackmail was a motive you'd uncovered.' His sweat was a sour taste in her mouth. If he wriggled any worse, the chair would need a new seat.

'Let's move on to your business dealings with Roland Orme.'

'Who?'

'Much better.' She pointed an approving finger. 'Almost convinced me you didn't know him. But Mr Orme generously submitted paperwork to assist in our enquiries. Your name is on one of those pieces of paper.'

After bruising himself on her silence for half a minute, he spread his hands. 'I *was* in touch with a property developer, a while ago. I can't remember his name, it might've been whatever you said. Roland Orme?'

'It was.' Laurie put the printout where he could see it. 'An email from you to Orme, saying how good it was to meet him and requesting the information the two of you discussed. Dated six weeks ago.' The heat made the lights soupy, bulbs fizzing like flies. 'Is that jogging your memory?'

'I think we must've met at that sales meeting about the woodlands.' Lawlor wet his lips from a glass of water. 'He was developing properties in the area, I was looking into that, as you know. I expect I made contact for that reason.'

'And what was the upshot of that contact?'

'Nothing. Nothing I can remember.'

She wanted to give him a set of pens and invite him to write, *I'm a big fat liar* on the walls, but he was within shouting distance of asking for a lawyer. She didn't want to push him over the line, not yet. And while Joe remained as cool as ever, her shirt was sticking to her skin. She began gathering paperwork. 'Why don't we give you a lift to your cottage?'

'No need, I have a car.'

'No trouble.' Joe tortured the floor with his chair before standing.

Lawlor stared up at him with a mouthful of excuses but if Laurie's silence was a brick wall, Joe's was a glacier, smooth and unscalable.

In Powderhill, Sandra Buck was a diminutive figure standing halfway between her cottage and Number 28, Nancy rooting around at her feet. Sammi, who'd been watching Lawlor closely during the interview, said, 'He's going to chicken out. Refuse to go in there. Wait for it.'

Laurie walked across to speak with Sandra, leaving Joe with Lawlor, who said, 'Actually? I think I'll leave this to the cleaners. The agency can make a list of what needs doing, advise of any damage.' His eyes tracked in Sandra's direction before coming to land on Nancy. The dog's tail was rigid. She was making a sound that in another dog would've been a bark.

'Is there a problem?' Joe asked.

Lawlor dragged a hand across his upper lip. 'I can't stop thinking about that rat. In the *wardrobe,* for pity's sake. I doubt the smell's ever coming out.'

His stare left Nancy, travelled past the steel storage container at the side of his property, out to the foot of the trees. Sammi said: 'You need better dogs than Nancy out here, Joe. Sniffer dogs.'

'DI Bower?' Joe called across to her. 'Mr Lawlor's decided he doesn't want to go inside the cottage.'

Laurie left Sandra's side and strode back to where they were standing. 'Are you wasting police time, Mr Lawlor?'

'No, I'm just realising this's a job best left to the agency. It's not as if I can get to work on it myself. I don't have the necessary equipment apart from anything else, cleaning products and so forth.'

'Nevertheless,' Laurie said. 'We should take a look inside. As we're here.'

Lawlor's face was green, ghastly.

'What is it you're afraid we'll find in there?' Joe asked him.

'Nothing, I just . . . I don't want to smell that rat.'

'I'm smelling something,' Laurie said in a bored voice. 'How about you, DS Ashe?'

'Something's not right,' Joe agreed. 'But I think Mr Lawlor's keen to help us. He put up with a night in the Tollgate, which can't have been ideal.'

'Of course I want to help.' He put his hands into his pockets, eyes twitching from Joe to Laurie and back. 'It's just that I don't know anything—'

'When did you buy that storage container?'

'What?'

Joe nodded to the side of the cottage. 'It wasn't there on Thursday night, when DS Vicars and I were dodging bolts in your bedroom.'

'I—Wasn't it?'

'Let me guess,' Laurie said. 'Something else you don't remember.'

She was looking at Joe, wondering no doubt where he was headed with the question about the storage. 'She's not the only one,' Sammi murmured.

'We've seen containers like that before. At Higher Bar Farm.'

He didn't take his eyes off Lawlor, catching Laurie's fast intake of breath before she said in a flat voice, 'Three containers. Identical to yours.'

Joe wondered if she remembered where they'd seen a fifth of the same kind, jemmy-proof. 'That's seriously high-spec for a holiday let. Why would you need to offer that level of security to your tenants?'

Lawlor said faintly, 'Some of them bring bikes, outdoor equipment . . .'

'And some don't come at all.' Laurie folded her arms. 'We know you put a halt on the holiday lets, the agency confirmed it. So what's nine hundred quid's worth of armoured box doing out here? Taking a spa break all on its own?'

'I tried to cancel it.' He was right at the edge of his endurance. 'The storage box. It should've been delivered weeks ago but there was a delay and when I tried to cancel they said it was too late. I knew you'd think it odd, with the timing, but I told them I didn't need it any more.'

'It's why you needed it in the first place that interests me. Chris had pricey electrical equipment. What do you have? An Alessi kettle?' She held up her hand. 'Before you waste more of our time, try to remember we found the key to your door *under a rock*. You weren't interested in security a month ago. What changed?'

'Mr Lawlor,' Joe said. 'Get it off your chest. You'll feel better, I guarantee.'

'I don't know what it is you think I've *done*!' His voice rose, making Nancy lift her head in their direction.

'I think you were talked into something,' Joe said. 'By Roland Orme or Chris Miles. I don't think you wanted to but they were persistent, wore you down. Now you're out of your depth and could use some help. Let us help you.'

'It was Roland Orme.' The words jerked out of him. 'He said we'd make more money using the place to . . . that the rental market was a joke, over-saturated. I'd made a big mistake buying here, too far from anywhere, nosy neighbour putting people off. He had a similar problem with the neighbour at the place he'd done up out by—' Lawlor gestured, looking desperate.

'Out by?' Laurie echoed.

'Chris Miles's place.' His face cracked right across with despair.

'This is the house owned by Roland Orme near Higher Bar Farm?'

'Yes.'

'Orme was having trouble finding tenants, so he was making money from the property in other ways. And he suggested you do the same, here in Powderhill.'

'*Yes.*'

'What was his proposal, exactly?' Joe asked. 'What did he want you using the place for?'

Sammi said, 'Storage containers. You're a genius, Joe.'

Hardly. A genius would have added it up two days ago.

'As a warehouse,' Lawlor croaked. He cleared his throat. 'There's demand, he said, for empty properties out of the way of most people.'

'Warehousing what, Mr Lawlor?' With each question, Laurie's voice was getting tighter and less patient.

'He didn't specify. I got the impression . . . At least, I don't *know*, but from the way he said it, I thought maybe drugs.' His face collapsed with shame, or guilt. 'Even weapons of some kind. Not that'd I *ever*—I said no to that, of course I did.'

Joe had his phone out, dialling the station. Laurie said, 'Orme was using his house at Higher Bar to stash drugs and weapons?'

'I don't *know*, that's the thing. He said he had people lined up with . . . with specialist interests, he said.'

'What sort of interests?' Laurie demanded.

'He didn't go into detail, just talked about a portfolio of options, unspecified, that he was able to offer those with the right kind of money.'

'What did you imagine he meant?'

'Like I said, drugs. Nothing too—Weed, maybe. People like to come here to relax, don't they?'

'This is why you limited the availability on the agency's site, and purchased a nice big theft-proof storage box?'

'The container was Orme's idea. He sent me a link to an online shop.' Lawlor threw a bitter glance in the direction of the steel box. 'Stupidly expensive but he said it was the best on the market.'

'I'll bet. You don't want to cut corners when you're stashing illegal substances, or firearms. That's what you were signing up for, wasn't it?'

It was a confession too far for Lawlor. His face zipped shut. 'I'd like a lawyer, please.'

'Oh, let's not start making lists of what we'd like. Mine would bring you out in a rash.' Laurie stared him down. 'When did Chris find out about this? He caught you on camera, didn't he?'

Nothing. The forest was doing more talking than Lawlor, wind muttering through its branches.

'Did he pick you off one by one? Or as a couple? Cute little matching flash drives, that's what the five hundred pounds was for, wasn't it? Did he hand the footage over once you'd paid up? Or did he realise he was on to a good thing, bigger than anything else he was dabbling in around here. Half a grand is nothing to men like you and Orme. Which of you was first to see it wasn't going to stop – you, or Roland? From the sounds of it, he knows some nasty people. People you were happy to go into business with, when it came to making money from your failed holiday let. People who'd take a threat to that business very seriously.'

'I have a right to a lawyer.' He wiped sweat from his upper lip. 'I think I should call mine before I answer any more questions.'

'I think you're right. It's why I'm about to caution you, Mr Lawlor.'

Between her caution and Joe's call requesting sniffer dogs – in Powderhill and at the house next to Bobby's – Lawlor looked finished. When he was stashed in the back of the car, Joe lifted a hand in response to Sandra's troubled wave. She wouldn't have to worry about being alone out here, not for a while anyway. The dog handlers would keep her company and Nancy too, who was burrowing her way into the rubbish, white tail raised like a flag.

33.

'*Five* storage containers,' Laurie said when it was just her and Joe. 'The fifth's at Orme's place, next door to Bobby's. We saw it there on Monday. Do you think Roland's on commission from the company that makes them?'

'It suggests a serious business venture,' Joe agreed. 'Nothing speculative about that amount of hardware. He was definitely expecting deliveries.'

'Boys and their boxes.' She shot him a look. 'Good catch.'

'Teamwork.'

'Don't ruin it by being modest.'

'Boss.'

'Or by sucking up. Tell me what we need now.'

Joe didn't miss a beat: 'We need the flash drive Chris used to blackmail Lawlor and Orme. We should search that room at his parents' place, lots of boxes there. We need a warrant for the house next to Bobby's. The murder weapon would be a bonus. And' – his cheek thinned – 'we really need to find Jaxon Grice.'

'Not our job,' Laurie said firmly. 'Let PolSA do their thing. We're finally getting close to our killer, or killers. Eyes front. Come on.'

A quick debrief with the team served up a large helping of dead ends: the crossbow wire was too old to be a match for the wire from Chris's van; nothing useful on the Travellers Chris might've been dealing with, and no murder weapon.

'These high beams seen on Friday around the time of the shooting.' Saxton had the ANPR report, flicking through its pages. 'Tempting to think that'll set us on our killer's trail; I know you've put a lot of manpower that way. But boot prints were found in the kitchen at Higher Bar Farm, isn't that right?'

'And in the hallway,' Ted said. 'Both Chris and Odette wore boots, like the rest of us round here. Most of the prints are a match for theirs. The others look like deliveries; we're still ruling those out. All this rain hasn't helped. No matches for Lawlor. We found posh walking boots in his car, distinctive tread; no matches with any of the prints taken from Higher Bar. High beams were almost certainly Orme's. Trouble is, his story about a meeting holds up. We spoke with the company he was visiting, who confirmed it was a late one. Orme was there until eight, then they all went to the Fox for drinks. Tallies with ANPR, almost to the minute.'

'On the subject of Orme.' Saxton put the paperwork down. 'As requested by our SIO –' a nod to Laurie – 'an arrest is going to be made in the smart end of Sheffield to bring him in for questioning. I've added my weight to the request for sniffer dogs and warrants, and to let forensics loose on Lawlor's car, and Orme's. Until he graces us with his presence, all hands on the search for this alleged flash drive. Failing that, solid evidence of any kind would be a good start.'

Not the greatest pep talk of all time but he was right. What they had wouldn't prop up a wonky table let alone satisfy the CPS. In the absence of the murder weapon with Orme or Lawlor's prints all over it, the flash drive was their best bet. Joe could be right about Chris using his old bedroom as a hiding place, although the thought of being back there made Laurie crave an armoured box of her own, its lid deadlocked against memories – hallucinations, whatever – of Izzy. No time in her schedule for distractions of that kind.

Rain was falling when they left the station, the soft vertical kind that invited you to tip face to it. Laurie pictured it falling on Beverley and Keith's house, running down the windows like unstrung beads.

In the car, Joe's attention kept straying to the back seat until she wanted to turn and check who was creeping up on her. She'd insisted on driving to give his shoulder a rest, was beginning to wish he was at the wheel with no choice but to watch the road. 'Will you stop doing that?'

'Doing what?'

'Making me wish I had eyes in the back of my head.'

'You don't wish that? I do. Would've saved me two shirts this week.'

'Oh, so you do still have a sense of humour. Starting to think you'd left it in Ilkley.'

'If anywhere, I left it on Wakefield Road.' Joe rolled his shoulder. 'Just wish we had news for Nicola. Beyond a recovered red bike.'

'Why would a kid like Jax abandon a bike?'

'He wouldn't. It's why I'm worried the news won't be good.' His fingers moved thinly across his phone. His face said no new messages.

'In the words of my boss back in Salford? You don't have sufficient information to be worrying about that yet. Let the search team finish up for the day. They could still find him, or he could stroll into the station for the satisfaction of seeing the looks on our faces.'

'I'd settle for that,' Joe said. 'To know he's okay.'

The house where Chris Miles spent the first thirty-eight years of his life smelt of bonfires. The smell hit them as soon as they stepped from the car. Burning paper and plastics, poisonous. Soot and sparks from the rear of the house. Joe lengthened his stride, 'Keith. He knows. He's burning everything from that room.'

No answer to their knocking, even when Laurie added, 'Police!' to the mix. The noise brought the neighbour, Joe saying, 'We need access,' Laurie at his heels, through the house and out the back where a fence separated the two gardens. Joe took the fence in two easy moves, Garden Olympics, going for gold. Laurie followed, a shot at bronze, landing to see him snatch up a blanket and fling it over the short steel incinerator where Keith was poking a stick – 'Stand back' – smothering the worst of the flames. Green blanket, from the single bed in the room with the decals on the window. Laurie looked in that direction, seeing Beverley's face zigzagged by Orion, blurred by smoke. Scattered all over the grass were toy cars, action figures, pebbles and shells – the whole of Chris's magpie collection, bundled in the blanket and brought down here to be burnt. 'Private bonfire,' Keith said, 'not illegal.'

'Disposing of evidence in a murder enquiry is very fucking illegal. DS Ashe, do you want to make the arrest or shall I?'

Joe checked under the blanket to be certain the fire was out. Percussive spit of rain hitting the sides of the incinerator. Keith holding an ugly length of wood in his hand, charred where he'd used it to poke at the fire.

'Put that down,' Laurie snapped, 'before I add common assault to the charge.'

'We understand you're upset.' Joe switched from action-hero mode to his most Zen-like calm. 'Talk to us about why you're burning Chris's things.'

He pulled the blanket free, letting the rain finish what was left of the fire; it was falling too lightly to do further damage. A sweet smell, wet and charred, drifted up from the incinerator. Laurie's eyes were watering.

'Nothing there of any relevance to your case,' Keith growled. 'All personal things. Our business, not yours.'

'You burnt a sketch your son made of me. That feels fairly personal.'

All right, *not* his usual disguise. Joe fixed Keith with an ice-water stare. Laurie saw the man shrink, but his fist tightened on the charred length of wood. Animal response, every cell in his body wary of the threat Joe posed.

'We can talk about it out here –' Joe's voice was a good match for his stare – 'with your neighbours listening. Or inside the house. I'd like Beverley to be part of the conversation.' He waited a beat. 'Let's see if we can avoid any arrests.'

Laurie held out her hand as he stopped speaking, waiting as Keith made up his mind to surrender his weapon. The wood was hot from his hand, sticky. She tossed it to the far end of the garden, following as he walked up the lawn to the house, kicking cars and pebbles from his path, savagely, with the toe of his shoe.

Beverley was waiting in the kitchen, moving to make space for the four of them around the table where a coffee pot sat next to a steel rack of cups. 'Sit,' Laurie instructed, nodding at Joe, who headed for the stairs, gloving-up as he went.

The bedroom had been stripped so thoroughly it was like stepping into a wind tunnel. Desk, bed, shelves, all empty. Sammi strolled to the window, peering down at the incinerator. 'Anything salvageable in there?'

Doubt it. He used an accelerant.

'It stank. Those sketches won't even be ash . . .' He turned on his heel to study Joe. 'Cheer up. Flash drives take a lot longer to burn.'

Joe checked under the bed and desk, running a hand around the room's plug sockets in case they were being used as hiding places. He straightened, moving to join Sammi at the window. *Nothing, but I don't think he kept the sticks here.*

'Based on what?' Sammi said.

Let's take it to Laurie.

Sammi fell in, following him back to the kitchen where he pulled himself on to a counter to watch. 'Nothing,' Joe said in answer to Laurie's glance. 'Everything's been stripped except those decals.'

'Why?' She directed the question at Beverley. 'What were you afraid of?' She held up a hand before Keith could cut in. 'Mr Miles, I'm asking your wife. You'll get your chance to answer my questions at the station. Trust me on that.'

Beverley moved her face painfully. 'We've been meaning to do it for a long time, I told you that.'

'No. I'm sorry, but no. You heard something, or you found something. It made you afraid that on top of losing him and Eric, you were going to have to listen to people saying Chris was to blame.'

The kitchen stank of the bonfire. It was all over Keith's clothes, soot sticking to his skin. His face was flushed, like a bad case of sunburn.

'Chris was shot first.' Beverley tongue moved against her teeth. 'That's what the post-mortem said. How could he be to blame when he died first?'

She looked at Joe as she said it.

'DI Bower isn't suggesting Chris killed anyone,' he said. 'But I think, all the same, you're afraid he was responsible for what happened on Friday.'

Keith made a violent sound, turning his head away. Sammi said, 'Ask him about the souvenirs.' Like Joe, he'd seen into the incinerator, knew Keith had been burning more than Chris's childhood treasures. The tiki statue, Hollywood sign, Swiss cowbells – it was all in there. 'You weren't just burning Chris's things. You were destroying souvenirs from holidays he paid for.'

'Did you know that?' Laurie fixed her stare on Beverley. 'Your husband was out there burning the mementos you brought back from all those trips Chris paid for, with the spare money he suddenly had.'

'Don't speak to my wife that way!'

'You know what, Mr Miles? You're right. I don't want to speak to your wife in any way that causes her more distress than she's already in.' Laurie pointed a finger at him, her eyes like agate. 'You're the one who can put a stop to that. By swallowing your pride or your shame or whatever it is and telling me the simple truth. Your son liked spying on people. Yes or no?'

Keith bit his mouth shut. Beverley said, 'Yes.' She let out a weary sigh, as if a wound had been lanced deep inside her. 'Since he was a child. Spying. On us, on neighbours. They found him sneaking around the holiday homes down the bottom of our road, taking photos through windows. He denied it. He was good at covering his tracks, always very good at that. But we knew. We did know, Keith.'

Her husband wouldn't look at her, or at any of them, sitting rigidly at the table. A grieving father, whose guilt was almost certainly going to destroy him. Sammi lifted his head to give Joe a speaking look. He felt a familiar heaviness in his throat. Chris had covered his tracks, as his mum said. Right up until last Friday night. Kept his secrets safe, but not his family. Pushed his luck with the blackmail until Odette and Eric paid the price.

'Chris liked spying,' Laurie said. 'Did he also like blackmailing people?'

'We never knew that.' Beverley shook her head quickly. 'Not until Keith heard about people being questioned. Derek Symonds and the rest. All those Chris had done work for.' Her voice caught. 'Those he'd said were so pleased with the cameras he'd put in—' She broke off with a hard sob.

'That's when it fell into place,' Sammi finished for her. He put his head down. Grieving mothers always made him miserable.

'A specialist team is going to examine the contents of that incinerator,' Laurie told Keith. 'It would save time if you'd tell us whether anything you burnt might conceivably be a motive for the murders.'

Keith unclenched his jaw to say, '*Nothing*. Not a thing to be proud of, but nothing worth killing over. Scribbles and photos, years old. *Years*.'

'It's true.' Beverley twisted her hands into a clumsy prayer shape. 'I—We wouldn't have burnt anything like that. Keith's angry, but neither of us want to get in the way of what you're doing to find whoever did this.'

'He'd not have brought that here,' her husband said ferociously. 'He'd've known what I thought of it. Of *him*. That's what all the holidays were for, and the rest of it. Trying to make us proud after the shame he put us through as a kid. He'd not have dared bring anything like that in here.'

'You were right, Joe.' Sammi slipped from the counter. 'I'll catch you later. Go for a run maybe, get some fresh air.' He was gone a second later.

Laurie asked, 'Did Chris ever mention a man called Roland Orme?'

Keith and Beverley shook their heads. 'What about Cary Lawlor?'

'He did work for him.' Beverley wiped her eyes. 'Up near the woods, a holiday home.'

'Did Chris talk about him at all?'

She shook her head. 'He never talked about any of those he did work for. Only the work itself, and then only when cameras were involved.' She raised red eyes. 'As if he was trying to tell us. As if he wanted us to stop him, the way we did when he was a boy. But he wasn't a boy.' Her hands lost the prayer shape, fell apart. 'He was a grown man. A *father*.'

The sound that came out of Keith was primal. Beyond grief, beyond rage, a howl that emptied out his throat and left the kitchen echoing, its windows scarred by smoke.

In the car, it was a long time before Joe or Laurie spoke. They'd made no arrests; Keith and Beverley had volunteered to give full statements at the station. Joe had arranged for Theo to collect them.

Laurie said, 'Any chance of forensics recovering a flash drive from that mess?'

Joe shook his head. 'I think Keith's right. Chris wouldn't have hidden anything in that room. The stakes were too high.'

'So where's the bloody flash drive? It's not in Evidence, I checked.' Laurie put some of her frustration into the driving, slowing down to piss off a Land Rover. 'You don't think Lawlor's lying and it's stashed in his sock drawer up in London, or at the bottom of the Thames?'

'Chris didn't hand over that footage for five hundred quid. He must've known he could make serious money from it. A prize of that kind? He'll have hidden it somewhere safe.' Joe checked his phone, a muscle stressing in his cheek.

'Still no news of Jax?'

'Nothing.'

It'd be dark in a matter of hours, already the sky had that hard metallic sheen. A second night in the cold, assuming Jax was alive. Neither of them said it, but the knowledge sat in the car with them, like an unwanted passenger. Laurie needed to keep Joe's thoughts away from Jax, or away from the dark at least.

'What's your latest theory on that bike in Lawlor's bathtub?'

'Stolen goods, surely?' Joe propped his head to the window. 'If the place was being used as a warehouse, as he's admitted.'

'And the traps? The crossbow? That's a weird warehouse. Functional weapons, I'd understand, maybe even a booby trap to put off trespassers. Not forgetting whoever smashed that window from the outside. If we didn't know better, I'd think it was an insurance scam. Windows done like that in Salford are usually for a racket of some kind.'

'What if the bike was a lure? Kids like Jax lift bikes on a regular basis. And you'd need to be a kid to get through that window.'

'Someone to blame for a break-in, you mean?'

Joe thought about this then shook his head. 'Too elaborate for insurance fraud, you're right.' He checked his phone again.

She could talk him into the middle of next week and his mind would still be on Jax. 'How long until the sniffer dogs get to work?'

'Hopefully by the end of the day. They're prioritising Jax. Any dogs we get are likely to be for that purpose.'

'All right, let's you and I try a different dumb animal. Des Morton. Saxton's working on the warrant to search his Golf, but nothing's stopping us from getting a head start. I'd like to ask Des a few questions about his dealings with Orme, see what he knows about this warehousing business.'

'You'll find it easier to get answers out of him if I'm not in the interview. Maybe run that one with Ted?'

'Good, because I was going to suggest you check in with PolSA. You're not getting any rest until you do, face it. Contact Jax's mum, see if she's thought of anywhere else he might be. Talk to his friends. Oh, and check with Bobby in case he's spotted the kid hanging around up at his place, where we saw him yesterday.'

34.

'What's my problem with Joseph Ashe?' Des screwed his face into a scowl. 'You saw him in the 'Gate, making Molly and Tyler's mum cry. He gets off on people's misery, winds them up about their dead kids. You seen the state of Han Copper? She's a wreck, thanks to him. He's a *freak*. Shacks up with Fred Hallam's sister, when we all know he fancies men. How're we supposed to trust the police with that in charge?'

'You've put a lot of thought into hating DS Ashe,' Laurie said. 'That's clear. Is there a special reason for your animosity? Other than the fact you're a bigot who likes to throw his weight around?'

Under the strip-lighting in the interview room, Des's long face was all jaw, bunched with malice. 'You deaf, or what? I *just told* you my problem with him. It'd be your problem too, if you lived round here.'

'I wasn't asking about DS Ashe until you decided to make this about him. I was asking about Roland Orme. Why he paid for a full set of tyres for your car, and gave you cash for it to be taxed and put back on the road.'

'Now you're just making shit up.'

No point turning the interview room into a sauna for Des, who'd just shed a layer to show her what a man he was. She slapped a bagged sheet of evidence on the table. 'Your prints on the skim stalk used to smash the window in Powderhill. Am I making that up?'

Des kicked back in the chair, putting his stare on the ceiling. He thought he was a hard man but Laurie could see the cracks in him already. He was hungry, for starters. She'd heard his gut rumbling as soon as he stepped into the interview room. And he was sobering up. He'd been at the bar in the Tollgate, ordering a second pint when she and Ted scooped him up, didn't get to drink it despite having paid for it; the first ten minutes were taken up with him moaning about that. He was pissed off about the lack of progress to find Jax, Laurie believed that much. He was an antagonistic arsehole but he cared how the police deployed their limited resources, even if he didn't have the vocabulary to articulate it in those terms.

'You're wasting police time,' she told him. 'We should be out looking for a killer and a kid from your estate. Do us all a favour and answer my questions so you can get back to your pint and we can bring Jaxon home to his mum.'

'With Ashe in charge? Only way she'll see Jax again is if he talks her into believing in his ghost.'

Ted Vicars leant his bulk forwards. 'You're saying you know where Jaxon is, Des? Is that what you're saying?'

'No.' Flickering, as the channel changed behind his eyes. 'Just your freak friend never found a kid alive in his life. Only hangs out with dead ones.'

'You're saying Jaxon is dead, Des?'

'Fuck's sake!' He thumped the heel of his trainer on the floor. The cracks in him were a mile wide. Laurie had broken tougher witnesses on her tea break.

'It's not going to look good', Ted said, 'if word gets round the Wakefield you were stringing us along when we could've been getting Jax home to his mum. Might get you barred from the 'Gate. They've barred men for less.'

Des stared at him for a long minute before switching to Laurie, who gave him the same stare with interest. And then he cracked. 'You want to know what the fuck's going on? Orme's pissing about with blokes from Sheffield. *Salesmen*, he calls them. They come into the pub, selling security or spare staff. Some're legit, but most aren't. Shifting ammo or guns for gangs up in Manchester and Leeds, Bradford, wherever. Safer to stash stuff around here, where everywhere's a second home and you lot think badger baiting's a crime.' He bared bad teeth at Laurie. 'If you were doing your jobs, you'd be all over this. Orme paid me to take shit up to his place in Higher Bar, and out to Powderhill. So what? I took it, dumped it, done the window like he asked. End of.'

As confessions went, it was a big one, dumped all over the room like a job lot of silage, spilling its stink into the corners.

'What did you take and where did you put it?'

Des gave an approximate inventory: traps, snares, crossbow. All left on the kitchen floor. He denied taking any of it upstairs, didn't rig the crossbow, looked blank when Laurie suggested that. But he put the mountain bike in the bath.

'Why?'

'Because he paid me.' Spacing the words apart, as if Laurie was the one having difficulty following things.

'And you don't ask questions? Just do as you're told by the little man with the fancy waistcoat and a wad of cash?'

She let him see what she thought of that – a big bloke like him running errands for Orme – and it had the desired effect. He cracked again. Joe had been right about his patience. Soap bubbles had more staying power than Des.

'Wanted me to put it about, didn't he? That there's a bike worth thousands up in Powderhill if anyone's got the balls to go get it.'

'Why would Orme go to that trouble? Did you ask him?'

Des shrugged. 'None of mine.'

Laurie had been grappling with why Orme chose him for this task. A huge risk, surely, to trust a man like Des. But at the same time she could see how his palpable lack of curiosity might have appealed, not to mention his criminal record should it come down to a case of his words against Orme's; even on an off day, Orme was a thousand times more credible. Too bad about his arrogance, believing himself safe in Sheffield, thinking nothing out in the sticks could bring that life crashing down around his ears.

'You told Jax about the bike?' Ted demanded.

'No.' That flickering again. 'But word got around.'

For the first time, Des looked uneasy. Understandable, given the wrath coming off Ted. She hadn't known he was capable of generating heat of that kind. Des would have kept his mouth shut, she realised, if it wasn't for Jax. Another mistake Orme had made, imagining a man like Des Morton didn't draw lines, consciously or unconsciously, like everyone else.

'You tell kids to go robbing in a house where there's a rigged weapon?' Ted radiated contempt for Des's cowardice.

'Nothing was rigged when I was there. Just a load of junk, and the bike.'

'And a smashed window only a kid could fit through. May as well've fed him through it yourself. Now he's missing, and guess what? There's a killer on the loose. Nice one.'

'That's nothing to do with me. Nothing to do with those places—'

'Give me strength.' Ted bunched his fists. 'You're a brain cell shy of an ostrich, Desmond, always have been. But if you think those storage scams aren't connected to the fact Jax is gone? You're taking the piss.'

Morton looked from one of them to the other, his face working thickly. Laurie didn't have time to tell him what she thought of him. She read him the charges he was facing, left Ted to do the honours, and went in search of Joe.

'If Jax knew about the bike, why didn't he take it when he had the chance?' Like Laurie, Joe wasn't sold on Des's version of events.

'No idea. Unless he could sense it was a trap. Des is about as subtle as a fist in the face, and Jaxon's a bright kid.'

'There isn't any way Des arranged those traps or rigged the crossbow. Not his skill set.'

'Agreed. He's a stooge, and an alibi; Orme's covering his arse. But that doesn't explain what he was hoping would happen.' She perched at Joe's desk, thinking out loud: 'Assuming *Orme* rigged that crossbow. Why? Was it Jax he wanted dead? Why risk a lucrative business venture for the sake of killing an eleven-year-old?'

'It makes no sense,' Joe agreed.

'I guess we'll find out.' She worked an ache from her neck. 'You should go home, get cleaned up. I want you in this interview with Orme.'

'About that.' Joe used his bomb-disposal voice, the one that said he knew there was a risk of explosion.

'Oh, you are not about to tell me Orme wasn't home. That no one can find him. That the interview's screwed.' She pinned him with a stare. 'I don't want to hear anything even vaguely resembling that.'

In recognition of this, Joe was silent.

'Fuck's sake.' She pushed her hands into her hair, massaging her scalp. 'We should've brought him in when we had the chance. Just like Jax. This rate you and I'll be lucky to have a job by the end of the week.'

'There's an alert out,' Joe said levelly.

'It's him, isn't it? Our killer.'

'No murder weapon,' he reminded her. 'And no demonstrable motive. Without that flash drive, we're throwing sand.'

'So why's he absconded? Explain that.'

'Oh he knows he's in trouble. He'll have heard about the warrants, that we have Lawlor in for questioning, maybe Des too. He keeps his ear to the ground. And he's dealing with some very nasty people. If they've got wind of the fact we're on to the warehousing racket, it's possible he's avoiding them, not us.'

'Or they found him first and shut him up.'

Joe appeared to debate this with himself. He wore that distracted look he'd had in the car, tuned to a frequency she couldn't hear. 'We'd know about it, if that were the case. Little point keeping it quiet. They'd consider it a warning for anyone else involved in the same racket; I doubt Orme's the only one.'

'Unless Higher Bar was the warning. Chris had more of those storage containers than anyone else.'

'Empty,' Joe reminded her. 'Apart from the telescope. No evidence anything was ever stored there. From the look of it, he was getting ready to go into business with Orme's lot. Why kill him at the outset?'

Laurie worked the knots from her neck. 'Unless he was muscling in on Orme's patch. That's what the blackmail was about, Chris demanding a piece of the action. Orme sees how sneaky he is, untrustworthy, decides to take him out of the picture before he can make worse trouble. Encourages him just enough to keep Chris happy, provides the storage boxes – "here's your handy starter kit" – then chooses his moment to strike.'

'Where does Cary Lawlor fit into that?'

'Orme collects stooges, that's clear.' She paced, walking the theory like a pet dog to see if it would play ball or sit on its haunches, refuse to move. 'Paying Des for the taxi service up to Powderhill, and to be a big mouth on the Wakefield estate. No way Des pulled the trigger in Higher Bar, though. That's well above his pay grade. Lawlor, on the other hand? If he was backed into it by Orme? I can see him panicking and shooting Odette, can't you?'

'It's a stretch.' Joe rubbed a thumb at his temple. 'No evidence Lawlor knows one end of a shotgun from the other. That kind of familiarity? Still feels like a local to me. Lots of locals grew up around guns. My gran, for example. Not', he added, 'that I'm proposing her as a suspect.'

'Or my dad-in-law for that matter, not just because his shotgun's stashed in the station.'

The pet theory had lost her interest, lying at her feet with its tongue lolling. She felt a throb of anger under the frustration, wanted to nurse it to full-blown rage, needing more than frustration to get this done.

'No news of Jax, I suppose?'

'None.' That muscle played in his cheek, tightly. 'Search party's taking sniffer dogs into the woods where they found the bike.'

'That's it, then, for the day. Nothing we can do until we've got hold of Orme, or found the flash drive, or miraculously stumbled on the murder weapon.'

'I might join the search for Jax, if you can spare me.'

She shook her head. 'Go home, get some rest. We both need it. Don't worry about giving me a lift, Ted's already offered. Let's start again at first light.'

35.

Laurie had hoped for time alone with Adam after work. Back in Salford when a case hit a wall, she counted on him to help her regroup. Here it was different, and not just because of Peter. The town was full of strangers, everyone waiting for news of Jax, their local lad. South Yorkshire Police were hunting Orme, whose Mercedes had been snapped heading in the direction of Bradford. She needed to keep her focus narrow. Here, in Edenscar.

When she reached the house, Peter was at the dining table with Helen, who nodded a greeting, then asked Adam if he needed a hand in the kitchen.

'I'm here now,' Laurie said. 'Let me help.'

The three of them worked as a team to keep Peter calm, making the meal feel like family time. It wasn't until Helen and Adam took the empty dishes to the kitchen that he looked at Laurie with his old rancour.

'Everything all right, Dad?'

'I'm not your dad. If I was, I'd have taken you in hand years ago.'

He wasn't faking his illness, she knew that. He had a complicated disease that knocked him about from past to present, ricocheting off the people he'd been; they were all different people at different times in their lives. Isabel had been a good little girl once upon a time, neat pinafores, dolls' tea parties. Laurie had loved poetry, philosophy. Peter was dying, couldn't help who he'd become. Not like Chris Miles, who went looking for trouble, or Bobby's old dog, the one he'd had to put down. Peter's eyes strayed across her shoulder – 'Helen?' reaching a shaking hand for his daughter. 'I'm here, Dad. Addy's making tea, then we'll sit together.'

Laurie stepped back to make space for them, watching as Helen took her father's hand, chasing the ghosts from his eyes to make him calm again. In the kitchen, she tried to do the same for Adam but he stepped wide.

'You okay?'

'Actually? No.' He was pissed off. It didn't happen often, but no mistaking when it did. 'You have to question people, I get that. But a heads up might've been nice. Saved me looking like a twat.'

'What're you talking about?'

'Ben. You couldn't have warned me you were going to quiz him over a couple of invoices he paid Chris? I have to hear about it from him?'

'I wasn't the one making the phone calls—'

'I know.' His eyes chilled to green glass. 'He said it was a detective constable, made a joke about not warranting senior attention. This's a guy I've known since I was *eleven*. We were drinking in the pub the other night, we just lost one of our oldest friends—'

'Well, I'm sorry for embarrassing you.' She was sorry, but not enough to apologise for doing her job. 'I'm sure Ben understands what we're trying to do, which is finding whoever killed Chris and his family.'

Adam made a weary sound and turned away.

'Seriously?' she demanded. 'I was doing my *job*. I'll be doing it for the next six months, since that's what we agreed. I won't have time to manage your mates' tantrums while I'm trying to find killers and missing kids.'

'Fine. Get on with it. I'm surprised you're not out there right now, searching for that boy.'

'Jaxon Grice. That's his name. The search is being conducted by a specialist team who don't need me under their feet.'

'Really? Ben's joining the search right after he finishes work today.'

'Yes, Adam? Your mate Ben is a liar. There were volunteers helping with the search earlier today. Now it's limited to specialists. I imagine Ben's down the pub, telling everyone what an arse-ache your missus is. Which is fine, I'm used to it. Just don't start taking the word of people like that over mine, all right? That feels like a fair request, from where I'm standing.'

She rarely lost her temper, could nurse a low-level mood for weeks before it reached a state of white-hot rage. But she'd reached that right now. Here in this house where each day brought fresh evidence her husband wasn't the man she'd married, the man she'd thought he was, but an overgrown infant indulged by his sisters, in thrall to his bullying dad. It was on the tip of her tongue to tell him exactly that — demand to know where his empathy was, not to mention his common sense. She was saved from that mistake by her phone ringing. *DS Joseph Ashe*.

'I have to take this.'

She walked past Adam into the hall and from there to the front door, needing to breathe air that wasn't crisp with her own anger.

'Give me good news,' she instructed Joe.

'Jax is at Bobby's place. Safe and well, from what I can gather.'

'Thank God.' She tipped her face to the dusk, shutting her eyes for a second. 'Is he able to answer questions?'

'From what Bobby says it'll depend who's asking them. I should come clean — I've only just heard this news, and from Bobby not PolSA. They don't know as yet. You're the first call I made.'

'Flattering, but forget that. Call it in.'

A tiny pause, punctuated by the pig farm's soundtrack. 'I will,' Joe said. 'But you and I need to be the ones who go over there. Bobby says if he sees a marked car or strangers, he'll bolt. He's barely able to sit still as it is.'

'What happened to him, does Bobby know?'

That same pinched pause before Joe said, 'He's saying he was hunted.'

'*Hunted?*'

'In the woods. Might be an idea to have those boots handy.'

36.

Bobby opened the door in an ancient towelling bathrobe belted over his oldest trousers. He looked haggard, putting a finger to his lips to warn Joe to tread softly inside the house. He didn't like seeing Laurie on the doorstep but Joe had explained he wasn't able to keep this between the three of them. He'd been about to take a shower when the call came through: 'You'll want to be here –' hoarse whisper in his ear – 'soon's you can.' Joe hadn't recognised the voice. 'I'm sorry, who is this?' Until Sammi at his shoulder said, 'Bobby.'

'Just get yourself over here. And don't come all sirens, lights blazing. He'll be gone again if you do.'

'Are you able to tell me what's happened?'

'He's here,' Bobby whispered. 'Nicola's lad.'

Joe had reached for his car keys, wanting to run to Higher Bar and see Jax for himself. Not buried in the woods, or at the bottom of the reservoir. *Safe*.

'He'll bolt,' Bobby warned. 'Had to talk him into seeing you, doesn't want his mum or anyone else. In a proper state, he is, never seen anything like it.'

'Does he need an ambulance?'

'Not like that. *Scared*, Joe. Out of his wits. Don't know what's spooked him, only that he's saying he was chased up in the woods.'

'Chased? By whom?'

'Doesn't know, or won't say. *Hunted*. That's the word he used. Come quietly, and on your own.'

'I can't do that,' Joe had said. 'It wouldn't be safe for any of us. I need to call it in, get the search team—' At that point Bobby had hung up and Joe, after debating the matter with himself (well, with Sammi) had called Laurie.

Bobby held the door wide, gathering the bathrobe to his chest. If he was looking his age so was Jax – barely scraping eleven, and as if he'd spent the last forty-eight hours running. Tracksuit bottoms caked in mud, football shirt ripped at one shoulder, scrunching himself into the corner of Bobby's couch. Blood had dried in thin scratches across his face.

'Fuck's she doing here?' His stare was the same as ever, instinctively hostile, but his voice shook. A kid's voice, none of the usual bravado in it.

'It was me or your mum,' Laurie said. 'And Bobby told us you're not ready for her to be here.'

'She even miss me?' He had to push the words past chattering teeth.

'Yes, she did. She hasn't been into work.' Joe knew this would hit home. 'Waiting by the phone for news.'

Jax scrubbed a hand under his nose, turning his head to listen for cars or footsteps, strung out on adrenaline. When Isla padded into the room, he pressed himself deeper into the couch. The old collie went to his side, standing patiently until Jax pushed the fingers of his left hand into her fur, holding his right arm awkwardly, curled into his chest.

'You look like you need someone to check you over,' Joe said. 'Those scratches are nasty.'

'Wouldn't let me put anything on them,' Bobby said. 'Arm's the worst, where he was shot. I've a first-aid kit, most of. But he won't let me near.'

Shot? Joe crouched on his heels a short distance from the couch. 'You going to let me take a look? Or wait for the paramedics?'

Jax slitted his eyes for a second then thrust out his right arm. His sleeve was torn between his shoulder and elbow. Blood had soaked through, drying in rusty patches.

'You okay if I do this? Or would you rather it was DI Bower?'

Laurie had the first-aid kit. Jax eyed her, but shook his head. 'You do it. Don't care, anyway.' He lifted his chin but it was unsteady. He was approaching the end of his endurance.

Joe asked Laurie to make a sweet cup of tea, Bobby saying he'd show her where the mugs and milk were kept. Jax was less tense when the room wasn't full of people. 'I'll need to cut this –' the torn sleeve – 'that okay?'

'Mum'll kill me. Brand new, for my birthday.' He looked close to tears, thrusting his fingers more deeply into Isla's fur, toughening his voice before he spoke again. 'Fucker's got my phone and bike, too. She'll kill me.'

'Unlikely, with all the police around. We've got your bike safe, don't worry about that.'

He considered the boy's shirt, knowing forensics would want to take his clothing into evidence, doing his best not to touch it as he checked the extent of the damage. An angry-looking graze scored Jax's upper arm where a projectile of some kind had torn a path through his skin. Not through the arm itself, fortunately. But it looked nasty, lots of dirt in the wound.

'D'you know who did it? Shot at you?'

'Some fucker in the woods.'

'What kind of gun did he have?'

It didn't look like bullet damage. Pellet? An airgun, or—

'Not a gun.' Jax squinted at the arm, then at Joe. 'Fucking *arrow*. Fucker shot me with an arrow. Kept shooting, waiting for me to run. I'm running but I'm falling and he's *waiting*. Each time. For me to get up and run again, try to get away.' He swallowed a furious sob. 'Sure he'd kill me when I couldn't get away. Could've killed me, easy. But he's waiting, like he wanted the fun of it, of chasing me. I couldn't even *see* him!' He scrubbed a hand under his nose, blinking back tears. 'Never let me see him. Just fucking trees everywhere and I lost my bike, came off it. Dropped my phone but he wouldn't let me go back, kept pushing me on, fucking *firing* at me, at the trees, making sure I ran where he wanted.' He shuddered, his chest hiccupping. 'Even after he stopped, I didn't dare come out. Got myself dug in, out of sight, but heard branches snapping, knew he was out there.' He slipped his hand under Isla's collar, holding her close. 'Fell asleep in the end. Don't know how long, except I was knackered. Hadn't had any food since that Snickers you gave me.'

Seeing the childish tremor in his lip, Joe was so angry his vision blurred. The light in the room was white-edged, pulling out all the places where Jax was just a boy, hurt and bewildered by the last few hours.

'Our age,' Sammi said, 'remember?'

Joe remembered. The rush of it, how the world could pivot from sunshine to dark clouds needling rain, the slip and slide of his feet through bracken, deeper and deeper, sudden splashing of a cratered puddle, fear forged into a battle cry before hunger blotted it all out.

'Damn, Joe.' Sammi's voice was soft. 'You really do remember.'

Let me do my job, Sammi.

The crown of Jax's head held the pattern he'd been born with, a blond cowlick. For all his fierceness, the way he ran them ragged over the summer, he was a child. The idea of someone hunting him through a forest, firing arrows to make him follow a path of their choosing, was barbaric.

'What sort of arrows, could you see? Long ones, or—'

'Short.' Jax sniffed. 'Sharp.'

'Like this?' He showed the photo on his phone of the crossbow bolt dug from the wall in Powderhill.

'Yeah. Exactly like that.'

'What time was it when you last heard him?'

'Dunno. Lost my phone, didn't I? Still light, though. That's why I stayed put. Wasn't gonna risk it.' He shivered again. 'Those woods are rank after dark.'

And frightening. Full of rotting paths, places where water turned the ground to sucking mud. 'What happened then?'

'Came here. Through the rest of the woods.'

'That's a long route. Why not go home?'

'No bike and phone, looking like this?' He indicated his arm, and his clothes. Shook his head.

'Your mum's been worrying about you. We all have. People joined the search to find you. Everyone wants to get you home safe.'

The boy bent to bury his face in the dog's fur.

'Your mum's not going to be angry, just glad you're okay.' Joe gave him a moment longer to comfort himself with Isla. 'You were in the woods above the Wakefield estate, is that right?' Jax shook his head, hard. 'That's where we found your bike.'

He looked up, confused then enraged. 'Piss off, I wasn't there. *Powderhill*. Those woods. That's where he was hunting me.'

'You didn't see him? He didn't speak to you?'

'Nothing, but fuck off if you don't believe me! Go and see for yourself—Fucking *arrows*!'

Joe waited for the storm to leave the boy's face. 'All right. Look, I believe you. You don't scare easily. And you're bleeding. Anyone can see this was bad. It's only that I need all the facts so I can do something about it.'

Laurie returned with a mug of tea, wincing when she saw Jaxon's arm. 'That looks like a job for a doctor, not a detective.'

Jax bent his head over Isla, fussing with her fur again. Joe suspected he was close to tears, fearing – or just feeling – Laurie's sympathy. He straightened slowly, stepping back from the couch. They left Jax to drink tea and eat biscuits, Isla curled at his side. From the kitchen, they kept an eye on the pair.

Laurie said, 'The team's on its way, with his mum. Paramedics, too. I've warned them to take it gently. He's going to have to be interviewed, though.'

Joe could see Jax at the station, reverting to silence as a defence mechanism, keeping himself safe from their questions. Joe had seen him cry; Jax would want to fix that, make sure his legend was intact before he went anywhere near his home or his friends.

'He needs food,' Laurie said, 'and sleep. They'll keep him in hospital overnight. Get some meds inside him, treat those injuries. He needs looking after.' Her phone rang and she frowned, carrying the call to the back door. 'DI Bower.'

'Bobby,' Joe said, 'thanks for looking out for him.' He touched a hand to the man's elbow. 'Are you okay?'

'Up most of the night,' Bobby grumbled. 'Couldn't believe my eyes. Last time that little bugger knocked on my door's Hallowe'en, trying to scare the life out of me. Thought for a second he were at it again, looking like that.'

'He's a mess,' Joe agreed. 'Did he tell you much about what happened?'

'Less'n he told you just now. Didn't mention arrows to me. Mind, he was in a state when I found him out there. Pushed past to get at the sink, drinking from the tap like a dog.'

Dehydrated. Exhausted. Injured. It would be a while before they were able to interview him. Sammi circled the kitchen, his eyes on Joe. More memories, this time of the aftermath from the rescue, detectives lining up to ask Joe what he knew of what caused the crash. Sammi at the foot of his bed like a bodyguard, telling Joe to ignore them, go back to sleep. Joe wondering why no one was asking Sammi to tell them what happened since he was fighting fit, on his feet, while Joe lay in the bed, dazzled by drugs, unable to form a sentence.

Bobby was watching the boy on the couch. 'Seen hunted animals all my life, seen 'em and smelt 'em. That boy? Was *hunted*. Lucky to get out alive, I reckon. You want to catch whoever did it. Give 'em hell.'

'We will, Bobby.'

'DS Ashe?' Laurie beckoned from the doorway.

When Joe was out of earshot of Bobby, Laurie said, 'South Yorkshire Police are reporting another sighting of Orme outside Bradford. Looks like we'll have him in custody by the morning.'

'*Good.*' Joe spoke with more force than usual.

Very likely the sight of Jax made him want Orme in handcuffs at a hard table, with or without his solicitor present. She felt the same, not least when she remembered what Lawlor told them about Orme's portfolio of offers at Higher Bar and in Powderhill. She had to unclench her teeth to continue: 'People with specialist interests. Is that what he meant? *Children?* Was someone trying to catch that kid and . . . sell him? Trade him?' It was unfathomable, almost unthinkable.

Joe's eyes were marked with darkness. He moved his head, smoothing a thumb at his mouth to make it less grim. 'Maybe, but I doubt Lawlor imagined anything like that. He'd have been a lot more freaked out, if he had.'

'How did Orme get all the way to Bradford if he was chasing Jax through the woods earlier today?'

'A lot earlier. Jax says it was still light. He was hiding for hours, then asleep a long time after that.'

She searched his face. 'You believe him about the hunt, the arrows?'

'You don't? What's your explanation for how he got cut up like that?'

'He was in the woods, certainly. Lost his bike and his phone. Knew he'd be in trouble when he came home. Saw the squad cars, the scale of the search.' She held Joe's gaze, wanting them to at least consider this version of events before they ventured down the nightmarish path of *bespoke portfolios*. 'Let's say he spent the night hiding out, caught himself on a few brambles then came here to someone he knew would buy it – "daft old bugger", isn't that how he referred to Bobby? You're the one who told me how often he likes to cry wolf.'

'You saw his arm,' Joe said. 'That wasn't brambles.'

'Okay. But it's a stretch to say *arrows*. Unless word got around about the crossbow Des dumped.'

Joe tilted his head, physically withdrawing. He couldn't believe she was entertaining an alternative theory, where a kid's imagination was fired by a set of straightforward criminal circumstances they could tackle to the ground and contain, not a monster roaming wild. He put his hands in his pockets, bringing his shoulders up as he met her eyes. 'Let's go and see for ourselves, in that case. The woods at Powderhill, that's where he's saying he was chased.'

'I'm not giving up my sleep the night before a major interview to traipse around a bloody wood. And neither, before you get any funny ideas, are you.'

Joe's eyes turned achromatic. *Defence shields activated*. 'You've seen the state of him. That doesn't make you angry?'

'It makes me furious, since you ask. But he's badly dehydrated, hasn't eaten in a couple of days, terrified he's in trouble with his mum.' She tried to hold him with her stare. 'We cannot afford to lose focus. We've Lawlor's statement on Orme. Des's, too. And a couple of very hopeful sightings to suggest we're close to having Orme in custody. Finding Jax was our priority an hour ago. Now it's nailing Orme and his accomplices for the murder of that family. We're close. You can feel that.'

'Close to something, certainly.'

'And we're a team. Stay with me, detective. *Focus*. Yes?'

37.

They stayed at Bobby's house until the search team arrived with Nicola Grice and a pair of paramedics. Jax looked like he might bolt as Bobby had predicted, but in the end he let his mum pull him into a hug every bit as fierce as the one Laurie had needed from hers after Isabel was lost to them; she had to turn away, the heat of tears in her eyes. Joe drove her home in silence. She was afraid his head was in the woods, searching for evidence to exonerate Jax. When they reached Peter's house, she turned to face him, 'Get some sleep, that's an order. See you at first light.'

'You don't want to work through? Prepare for the interview? Orme's going to give us a run for our money, I'd lay odds on it.'

'I'm not arguing, just saying you need sleep. Have you seen yourself?' She pulled down the mirror, showing Joe the shadows under his eyes. 'And please, for the love of God and the sake of Saxton's blood pressure, find a clean shirt.'

Joe watched Laurie walk into the house. Then he reversed from the driveway and pointed the car towards Powderhill. 'Oh, don't you dare.' Sammi moved from the back into the passenger seat. 'You heard what she said. *Go home.*'

'Would you go home if you thought the woods were full of arrows? That's *evidence*, Sammi. Orme didn't just kill Chris and Odette and leave Eric to drown in the bath. He tried to kill Jax. Chased him down like an animal.'

'You're not thinking straight—'

'You know I figured out where I heard that *yark* before, the sound the crossbow made right before the bolt was shot? You've heard it too. Out in the woods when we were kids. *Hunting.* It's been going on for years.'

'No one ever shot at us, Joe. If that's your theory.'

'I don't have a theory. Not yet, anyway. You might help me, instead of playing Laurie's deputy.'

'All right.' Sammi stretched his legs in the footwell. 'Arrows in the woods, Jax being chased, what else? He's tougher than we were at that age. Worst we ever did was nicking milk off doorsteps, never have dared do half the stuff he's up to. Everyone knows it, too. He's the poster boy for juvenile crime around here.'

'Meaning we shouldn't believe a word he says? You were there. You saw the state of him—'

'I get it. You know I do. He's a lost boy, our age. The age we were when the bus crashed. But Joe, you're knackered. She's right about that. And even if she wasn't, she's your boss. You need to do as she says.'

'Since when have you been the voice of reason?' Joe demanded. 'You're usually the instinctual one in this team.'

'Take a minute', Sammi said, 'to think about that.' He was looking down at the curled shape of his left hand, as if he might be holding a phone. Sammi hadn't held a phone in seventeen years, for the simple reason ghosts don't own phones.

Joe glanced to see what he was doing and felt the car drift before he pulled it straight, cursing under his breath. 'What're you doing?'

Sammi held up his hand, unfurling his fingers to show a glossy black bug nestled in his palm, red markings across its back. 'Name it. And watch the road.'

'Red-and-black froghopper.' Joe kept his eyes front.

'In Latin?'

'*Cercopis vulnerata.*'

'When did we last see one?'

The bends in the road were as familiar as the creases in Sammi's palm: heart line, life line, fate line.

'August, the summer before the crash.'

'Where did we see it?'

'The woods behind Powderhill.'

'What else did we do that summer?'

'Built the camp in the woods.' Joe sucked a breath, held it, let it go. 'Stayed out all night. Set fire to a load of marshmallows, trying to toast them.'

The memories came easily, like sleep tugging at the end of a long day.

'It's *been* a long day,' Sammi said. 'Jax is safe. They're going to get Orme. Big interview tomorrow, you need to get it right. Go home. Get some sleep.'

Joe slowed the car, turning it at the next junction, away from Powderhill towards his flat. 'Come with me, tomorrow?'

'If you need me, which you won't, if you've slept properly. And with Laurie in your corner.' Sammi ran the window down on the passenger side. Then he stretched his hand, and the froghopper leapt from his palm into the night.

38.

Laurie woke with a hangover, of the alcohol-free variety. She hadn't fallen from the wagon, just lost her footing trying to navigate the switchback atmosphere in Peter's house. Adam was pre-grieving, unable to manage anything for himself. Helen had stayed over, which was lucky, since Laurie had no idea where to find Peter's razor or keys or any of the other things he insisted on seeing as proof his house hadn't fallen into the hands of thieves. She cooked breakfast while Helen smoothed her dad into the day. A born doer, Adam's sister, the kind that made everyone else stop doing and stand aside, afraid of getting in her way.

'He can have these' – handing Adam a big clutch of keys on a brass ring – 'if it makes him happy. But keep the razors out of reach, obviously.'

'Thanks.' Adam folded himself forward into a hug, somehow managing to look small with Helen's arms around him.

Laurie's phone buzzed to say Joe was outside.

'Sorry to run out on you again.'

'You have to,' Helen said briskly. 'Leave everything here to me.'

In the car, Laurie looked Joe over, pleased to see he'd caught some sleep and was wearing a crisply ironed shirt. 'Big breakfast?'

'Not bad, thanks. Coffee on the back seat.'

She scooped it up. 'Hope you left room for a breakthrough.' When he looked at her, she gave her shiniest smile. 'Day four. About time, don't you think?'

'Orme?' Joe suggested, looking hopeful.

'Still in the wind, as far as I know. No, this one's all ours. I'll tell you when we get to the station.' She hugged the coffee to her chest. 'Need to check Evidence first, make sure I'm not imagining things.'

'Fair enough.' Joe reversed past the potholes in Peter's drive and turned on to the main road. He was smiling, her energy infectious.

The sun slanted through the car's windows, catching the copper of the cup so that for a single fanciful second she was holding a fiery chalice.

Milla was at her desk, headphones around her neck, looking up when she saw Joe. 'It is true you found Jax?'

'Bobby found him. Well, Jax found his way to Bobby's, but yes. He's safe.'

'Thank God. That's something, at least.'

'No news on Orme, I take it?'

Milla shook her head. Her desk was spread with photos of what looked like party bag gifts: plastic unicorns, metal dog tags, cartoon characters, even a fake fingertip with a polished nail. 'Novelty flash drives,' she explained. 'I thought since we're getting nowhere finding the boring kind, Chris might've used something like these. Didn't want the search to overlook anything.'

'Nothing from that bonfire at his dad's place?'

'Nope. And nothing from anywhere else he was hanging out. D'you think there's a chance he gave it to Lawlor, or even to Orme, and they lied about that?'

'Why kill Chris,' Joe said, 'if that was the case?'

All the same, it was starting to look as if they'd dreamt up the flash drive, a pocket-sized piece of wishful thinking on which they'd hung the full weight of their chances at a conviction. Laurie came back from Evidence with a pair of sealed bags, her smile undimmed. Joe felt the breakthrough – whatever it was – nipping at the back of his neck. He couldn't sit still, watching as she walked to the whiteboard and started rearranging the information pinned there.

'What's happening?' Milla hissed in a whisper. 'Is she okay?'

'She's great. I think we're about to find out why Salford's counting the days until they get her back.'

Sammi said, 'You're drooling, Joe,' but he was caught up in the excitement too, turning to watch Laurie expectantly.

She finished with the board. 'Come and pick holes in this.'

Chris Miles had been moved from the central spot he'd occupied since the blackmail was exposed. In his place, wearing her wedding dress and smiling for the camera, was his wife, Odette.

'Keys.' Laurie held up the two bags from Evidence. Each had a key ring inside, loaded with the usual assortment: car, house, garage, cupboards. One key ring was black faux leather with Chris's company logo printed in peeling gold, the other was an acrylic cube filled with purple glitter.

'The storage boxes at Higher Bar came with heavy-duty Chubbs welded with individual security IDs; I took a close look at the firm's website.' Laurie separated out the keys on the acrylic cube. 'They look exactly like these.'

'*Odette* had the keys to the storage boxes,' Joe said. 'Not Chris.'

'More than that.' Laurie put the key ring down, folding her arms. 'The farmhouse was her idea, that's what her sister said. Outbuildings as holiday lets, except they couldn't make that work. The way Mel described her, Odette was resourceful, independent. I can't imagine she sat back when things started to go south. She was struggling with Eric, we know that. But she was the strong one in the marriage, used to taking charge.'

'She worked in stock control,' Joe remembered. 'At a wholesaler's.'

'Perfect credentials for Orme. Better qualified than Lawlor, in fact.'

Odette beamed at them from the wedding photo, all white tulle and roses. She'd left home at nineteen, fended for herself, never needed her mum's support even as a child, living in bedsits, on sofas. Not like Chris, who was still with his parents past the age of thirty-eight and who, according to his mother-in-law, would never have got his business off the ground without Odette.

Milla frowned. 'Do you think she knew about the blackmail?'

'I think she's the one who locked that telescope away,' Laurie said, 'as soon as she realised what he was up to. I think it took a while for her to catch on – we know he was good at covering his tracks, and she had Eric to look after. But as soon as she found out, she took charge of his mess. And he was grateful; this was always an obsession with him, not a way to make money. That came later, after he started feeling guilty about spying again, needed to appease his conscience with those expensive holidays for his mum and dad. We know they argued. I expect she was furious – about the spying and the blackmail – but I'm also willing to bet she didn't waste any time restoring order, finding a practical solution to their money problems. One which her nearest neighbour had tried and tested.'

Roland Orme with an empty property at the end of her road, scouting for people who might be persuaded to open their houses to his disreputable friends. Had she justified it to herself as another kind of stock control, the only way to make money from that house after they were forced to abandon their legitimate plans? She wouldn't have liked Orme, would have seen straight through his sales pitch, but what choices did she have left?

'If you can't beat them,' Joe remembered, 'join them.'

Odette's words to her sister, when she surprised Mel by marrying Chris.

'She'd had a miserable summer,' Laurie said. 'Then things started looking up in the autumn. Mel assumed because of the nursery, how well Eric was settling in, but that's around the time Orme was working on Lawlor, same sales pitch.'

'And it's when her mum suddenly started seeing a lot more of Odette and Eric,' Joe said. 'Weekly visits.'

'The search for the flash drive's been focused on Chris,' Milla said. 'His old bedroom, his van, but if *Odette* hid it . . .'

'We've been looking in the wrong places,' Laurie agreed.

The incident room door breezed open behind them.

'DI Bower, DS Ashe. My office.' Saxton pointed, striding in that direction.

'This isn't good,' Sammi said at Joe's shoulder.

'He'll cheer up', Milla suggested, 'when he hears your theory about Odette.'

'Bottle that optimism,' Laurie advised. 'We might need it.'

Magnus Saxton was in full Viking guise, looking like someone had upset his runes or run his longboat ashore. He stood by the window, arms folded, face carved with wrath. 'Bradford have Roland Orme. They picked him up about an hour ago.'

Laurie said, 'And that's bad news?'

'Bradford's ROCU's had him in their sights for over a year.' Regional Organised Crime Unit. 'We're an outreach project as far as they're concerned, a spot of speculative expansion. The serious action's in the city. They don't want us taking our rural pitchforks to their carefully tended patch.'

'We're investigating three murders,' Joe objected. 'Don't we get priority?'

'Repeat after me: "Not without solid evidence."'

Frustration turned the air jagged, threatened to suck the energy out of their morning. 'About that,' Laurie said. 'We may have a new lead.'

'You don't sound frantically convinced.' Saxton looked from her to Joe.

'It could give us the flash drive,' Joe said.

'That would be timely, certainly. But until *may* and *could* become *have* and *got*, I can't help you. The storage box next to Bobby's place was empty, nothing in the house we wouldn't expect to find in a failed holiday let. Bradford, on the other hand, have plenty with which to charm the CPS. Their cup runneth over, in fact.' The lines on his face deepened. 'You should know they're claiming Cary Lawlor as their witness, not ours.'

'They're welcome to him. He's less use than a snooze button on a smoke alarm.' Laurie squared her shoulders. 'Orme *owns a property* next door to our crime scene. There's every chance he talked our victims into being part of his scheme. They have matching armoured boxes, for god's sake. Unless Bradford think that's a cute neighbourly coincidence—'

'Or they want the murder solve as a bonus prize,' Joe put in.

'*That*—' She pointed at Joe. 'Is that what they're after?'

Saxton put his hands up. 'I sympathise with every sentiment. Trust me. But the best I can offer right now is a remote seat at the ROCU interview.'

The wrong side of the glass. No access to the suspect, no influence over the interview. Orme could walk right up to a confession about what went down at Higher Bar and the Bradford team would miss it.

Different priorities. The CPS would rank a murder solve higher than a conviction for handling stolen goods, but they'd go with whichever had the better chance of sticking. Saxton was right about that.

'Happy for you to take the remote monitoring, guv.' Laurie schooled her face to a bloodless expression. 'We'll go after the evidence.'

'Joe, I'll let you get on.' Saxton kept his eyes on Laurie, letting her know she wasn't dismissed; he had more to say, for her ears only.

She sent Joe what was left of her breakthrough smile – 'Be with you as soon as I can' – watching as he went.

When it was the two of them, Saxton said, 'Welcome to the bowels of the pecking order. Your first time down here since you were in uniform, I expect.'

Laurie stuck with the smile. 'Who's leading in Bradford?'

'Nolan Ricketts.'

'I know Ricketts.' No history there, but no chance of a quick phone call to an old mate either. Ricketts kept a tight lid on his team.

Saxton was watching her face. 'Tempting to take this to DCI Reza, see what trees he can shake. Don't.'

'Is that advice, guv, or an order?'

'Whichever works.'

'Any chance of a look at the charge sheet from Bradford?'

'If you want to rub salt in your wounds, go ahead.' He went to his desk and twitched the paperwork from a folder, passing it to her. 'One more thing. It's been suggested a specialist interview adviser manage our strategy for Orme, after Bradford have finished with him.'

'I hope you turned down this shitty suggestion. Guv.'

Saxton waited, presumably for her to burn through the anger to a place where she embraced the bottom of the heap, bowing and scraping with the rest of the yokels. He'd wait a long time.

'We interviewed him once and got nothing, so what? That's how it goes. Or our pitchforks are a bit rusty, in which case—'

'For the sake of both our careers, I am not letting you finish that sentence.'

Shame as she'd had some great suggestions about where the SIA could shove their pitchforks. 'Orme is mates with Nelson Roache.

Did this land on Alan Worricker's desk overnight? Because if the police and crime commissioner's getting in the middle of my case, I'd like to know about it. Roache has the ear of the PCC, that's what I've heard. Friends with Joe, too.'

'That' – Saxton pointed a finger at her with the precision of a sniper – 'is why we're standing here instead of hunting for your hard evidence.'

He was warning her off. Joe's friendship with the local bigwigs was not to be exploited for the sake of discovering why the PCC were saddling them with an advisor whose chief specialism was going to be winding her up.

'So we're to await the arrival of this guru' – she tucked her fists into her armpits – 'and hang on his every word, is that the plan?'

'We're to work with him to strategise our approach,' Saxton amended. He managed a look of apology, sympathy, whatever. 'It could be helpful.'

'It's an insulting pain in the arse, guv.' She scanned Orme's arrest sheet for light relief. 'Let's not dress it up.'

Saxton gave a dry laugh. 'I hope you're up to speed on the PEACE framework, as this looks like being a back-to-school day.'

Laurie came out of Saxton's office looking as if she'd set it on fire, virtual steam rising from her shoulders. Joe was tempted to go and check the guv was in one piece. Even Sammi shifted a foot away. 'Everything all right?'

'Everything's great.' Her eyes blazed briefly before she blanked her face. Whatever went down between her and Saxton, she wasn't going to let it derail the morning. 'Where're we up to with the flash drive?'

'I spoke with Mel. She's at her mum's place, expecting us.'

'Send Milla, and Theo. He can charm Yvonne into letting them loose on the house. Milla knows what she's looking for.'

'What're you and I going to be doing?' Joe asked. 'Licking our wounds?'

Laurie held up Orme's arrest sheet. 'We're going to the woods.'

39.

In Powderhill, the sunrise was swallowed by forest. Middle of the night on replay. Joe parked up, glancing at Laurie. The worst of her temper had burnt itself out and she was eyeing the woods with misgiving. 'Not too late to back out,' he said. 'I've got this. Orme's in custody. Jax is safe. It doesn't need two of us to look for bolts that might not even be there.'

The charge sheet was soggy with ROCU's self-satisfaction at catching their man red-handed with stolen goods of the kind guaranteed to excite the CPS. Drugs, ammunition; Christmas come early. Right at the bottom: a carbon fibre crossbow. No one in Bradford was excited by this — a twelve-bore shotgun would have been different, maybe — but the crossbow had leapt out at Laurie and Joe.

'If it turns up conclusive evidence against Orme?' She released her seat belt. 'It'll make my day, and Saxton's too.'

Above them, the sky was bright. But where it hugged the trees, it was a different story, dingy and indistinct. 'Mrs Buck's up early. She looks upset.' Joe climbed from the car before Laurie could raise an objection.

Sandra was on her doorstep in a turquoise tracksuit, empty lead in her hands. 'She's never done this, Joe. *Never*.'

'Nancy?'

'Gone in the woods after a rat, nearly as big as her. I've called and called, but she won't come. I'm scared for her. What if someone's put traps down like the ones you took from that place? What if she's lying in a trap and can't bark? Or someone's taken her, for company or ratting? She's a good girl, a good ratter.'

'We'll look for her,' Joe promised. 'Go inside, it's not that warm out here.'

Laurie was waiting for him at the side of the car, stamping her feet, hands hidden up the sleeves of her jacket.

'What if *he's* taken her?' Sandra wailed. 'Whoever took Jax?'

'Jaxon's safe with his mum. Nancy's just nosing, like you said.' He held out his hand for the lead. 'If we see her, we'll bring her back.'

First three hundred yards weren't so bad, that was the story Laurie told herself. A nice stroll along firm forest floor, trees giving out the scent of silver birch. She assumed it was silver birch. Her phone had a strong signal, her new boots liking the terrain. Further in, they found a sign like the one above Higher Bar: *Woodlands for Sale*. It'd been taken down, or torn down, lying half-hidden in the undergrowth. Joe stopped, listening intently. Laurie did the same, hearing birdsong high above them, leaves ticking as a sharp breeze dropped through the branches.

'Woodlands for sale.' He turned to face her, eyes fathomless in the half-light. 'You know what I think? This was a land grab.'

'Explain?'

'It's a bit Wild West, but bear with me. Think of it like the turf wars on your patch back in the city. We talked about those, not that long ago.'

'You think *gangs* are hiding out here?' Preferable, in a lot of ways, to wildlife. Less chance of her legging it, for starters.

Joe had shrugged himself narrow. 'I didn't see the connection at first. Woodlands can't be developed, no profits to be made, certainly not the kind worth killing for. But when I googled *woodlands for sale*, it was under Rights and Covenants: "The sporting rights are included in the sale." For "sporting", read "hunting". That stag I moved off the road, remember that?'

She remembered. The size of it, blocking their way. Joe's neat swerve. Her palms were damp with the sensation of a near-miss. 'Hard to forget.'

A crow cawed above them, setting off a chorus. She'd have preferred sirens, or traffic. She'd changed her mind about the terrain, hating how the forest floor felt like sponge under her feet. 'What's that stag got to do with Orme? Or the murders?'

'I'm not certain. But I'll tell you what it has to do with Jax.' Joe twisted Nancy's lead in his hands. 'The bike in the bathtub was for him, Des admitted that. He broke a window small enough for a kid Jax's size to climb through, let the whole estate know there was a bike there. But Jax and his friends never nicked bikes for money. They nicked them to ride, typically in the woods.'

The look on his face sent shivers down her spine. He was grim with this theory of his, believing in it beyond any shadow of a doubt. 'Go on.'

'I think Jax was meant to take the bike and race it in the woods. For sport.'

Leaves stirred. Somewhere, a light pattering of stealthy paws. If they stood here long enough the wood would come alive. Claws and teeth. Life and death. She shivered in spite of herself.

'Orme wanted to hunt Jax for sport, that's what you're saying. Or someone wanted to, and Orme was facilitating it.'

'A portfolio of offers,' Joe reminded her. 'For people with specialist interests. Not just stashing stolen goods, in other words.'

It sounded incredible. Medieval. But kids were chased all the time in cities. For county lines, or by rival gangs. Did it make a difference that the chase Joe was describing took place in a forest? Between trees like these, dense with shadow, razored with brambles? Hadn't they come to search for bolts fired from the crossbow found in Orme's car?

'That display, the traps and snares, that was his *portfolio*?'

'Even chance Chris had cameras hidden in the cottage,' Joe said, 'and cleared them out before he was killed. If he caught Orme talking with one of his special interest clients, showing off his hardware, explaining how the hunt would work? That's sensational, certainly worth killing for.'

Laurie, her blood thrumming, was aware of being deep in his thrall. Like Keith Miles just before he gave up that length of charred wood.

'The whole set-up was theatrical. And Orme's a showman, you said it yourself. Fancy waistcoats, chandeliers. Everything he does is for show.'

'Hunting school kids for sport.'

She struggled to bend her brain around the idea. Here in the woods where Jax was made to run for his life and where the creaking of trees was like footsteps, or floorboards. Less terrible than the alternative, the *specialist interest* she'd feared, kids trafficked for sex. On the other hand, *that* was familiar. She could fit it in a box. This? Was horribly new. She could smell honey, hear the slow drone of insects in the bracken. Every hair on her neck rose in primitive, watchful protest.

'A game,' Joe was saying. 'To entertain his wealthy clients. A bespoke portfolio offer. He'd had a run-in with Jax, maybe. Knew he was fearless, thought he wouldn't be missed.'

Kids as disposable. She was familiar with that idea, commonplace in the city. She thought of Jaxon's scrawniness, bad teeth, bowed legs.

'Something like it's been going on a long time,' Joe said. 'At least, I think so. The Lawlors were scared by shadows out here. We assumed they were easily spooked, but perhaps they saw something, or someone. When I was a kid, I used to play in these woods with my best friend.' His stare went deep into the forest, where trees converged, the gaps between them were too narrow for anyone but kids to slip through. 'We'd hear people shooting at squirrels, foxes. Then the game got bigger. Muntjac, red deer. Stakes have to keep rising in a game like that. More dangerous, less legal. Adrenaline junkies need that escalation. Orme figured out how to feed their thrill-seeking, and how to monetise it. Woodlands for sale, a private space where they can pit themselves against whatever animals they're prepared to kill for sport.' He started moving. 'First one to find an arrow gets a Diet Coke.'

'His bike was found miles away, wasn't it? Why're we not in those woods?'

'Because Jax told me this is where he was hunted.'

Laurie, striding to catch up with him, missed her footing and went down as a big bug of some kind sped past her cheek. She was fighting her way back on to her feet when Joe crouched, putting a hand on her wrist. She felt a fool, 'I can manage, thanks. Might want a refund on these boots—'

His grip tightened. 'Stay down.' His voice was a hiss, his body tense.

She squinted, following his line of vision to the torn trunk of a tree where, at roughly head height, a bolt was quivering. Not a bug, a *bolt*, shot from a crossbow. Exactly like the one fired from the bedroom behind them, where a rat was flung into a wardrobe to die a slow, painful death.

40.

Joe kept his grip on Laurie's wrist a second longer before he released it. The forest was holding its breath, everything suspended when the bolt landed. Birds rattling from treetops, mice scurrying for safety then nothing. Silence. Only Joe and Laurie were out in the open. And whoever had fired the crossbow. Whoever was hunting them. Not Roland Orme, who was in custody after drawing their fire; that crossbow in the boot of his car had stopped them digging, convinced they'd found their man. But *their man* was standing a matter of feet away, armed to the teeth.

Laurie whispered, 'Where is he? Can you see?'

'No.'

'Well, can you *hear*—?'

'No.'

They fell silent, listening with their whole bodies for the sound of the hunter. Nothing. Just the deathless hush of the trees.

'Next time I have a bright idea off the back of a bad mood,' Laurie hissed, 'it's your job to talk me out of it.'

'Roger that. But shall we shelve the disciplinary until later?'

Laurie had taken out her phone, cursing at it under her breath. 'No bars. We're literally twenty feet from where I last had a signal. How's that even possible?'

There wasn't any satisfactory answer Joe could give. He was saved from attempting one by a second bolt striking the ground close to Laurie's left boot.

'Okay, we need to move.'

They stayed close to the ground, scanning for cover. Laurie wanted to head back the way they'd come, towards a phone signal and the car, but that plan was swiftly abandoned after a third bolt came so close Joe felt its breeze against his throat. This wasn't sport, or not only that. Sport in the way Chris and his family had been sport, maybe. Sport with no survivors.

'Trust me,' he told Laurie. 'Stay close.' He led them deeper into the woods, demanding answers of Sammi in his head: *Where is he? How close?*

'Effective range for a crossbow? About forty yards. Fifty if he's good. He's fifty yards to your south. Tracking you, though. You'll have to keep moving.'

Thanks, figured that much out for myself.

Laurie moved with him, shoulder to shoulder, her breath between her teeth. That first bolt would've struck her if she hadn't slipped. The thought was a cold spot in Joe's chest, recalling a headline he'd read online, 'How to take your target practice to trophy taking'. Laurie was this maniac's idea of a trophy. Joe, too. *Who the hell is it, Sammi? Who's hunting us?* 'You know who.'

A fourth bolt had him swerving, Laurie at his heels, the smell of bleeding from the tree where the bolt struck – larch, its sap citrusy.

How're we getting out of this?

'I don't know, Joe. But you'd better figure it out. That last shot hit a lot harder than the rest. He's thirty yards away, max.'

Joe knew where the hunter was driving them, could see it in his mind's eye: a thick twist of trees spiked by brambles. Jax's scratched face sprang to mind; the boy was chased until he found a burrow where he dug deep, waited for the night. Joe changed tactics accordingly, Laurie synchronised at his side, focused on following him as closely as she could, trusting him to get them out because this was his home turf. He grew up here, with Sammi. Knew the secret paths, places where leaves lay deep enough to hide in, where streams ran dry in summer, wet in winter, tall trees whose root systems hollowed out the forest floor to make shelters, hiding places. This was his turf. Not the hunter's, or not only his. Joe's home ground. *Damned if he's having this*—'Good. Now shut up and fight back.'

He gripped Laurie's wrist, pressing it warningly right before he pulled the pair of them off the path the hunter had set them on, into a tangle of trees to their right. She probably thought he was mad, restricting their freedom, making it much harder to make a run for it. But he knew what he was doing, knew this path. All of his body remembered it, from the thud of his feet to the throb of his throat.

Down into the trees, her breath hot on his neck, a quick catch of fear in it. The same fear was running like ice through his blood. If he got this wrong, they were dead. Worse, he'd have killed them. Driven them to a dead end, no hope of rescue or escape.

Branches scraped against their clothes, snagging like fingers. Thank God for the rain, making the ground silent. Their feet skidded as the path dipped, delivering them fast to the knot of undergrowth twenty feet below. Joe pushed his way inside, holding back branches for Laurie.

They were hidden, at last. So deep inside the wood, he could feel its heartbeat. No sound, no movement. *Dead end*, his brain kept repeating stupidly. End of the road. Dead. End. The silence felt huge. He could taste water like iron in his mouth, sharp glass stinging in his palms.

At his side, Laurie tensed, her eyes finding his through the darkness. Her face was taut and pale, her mouth set in a tough line. Her eyes asked questions, but he shook his head, still listening. *Sammi?*

'He's lost you. But he's tracking back. He knows you know. Only one of you is getting out of here alive.'

Dramatic, Joe thought drily. *And* two *of us. I'm not leaving Laurie.*

'You've brought her to our old camp. Didn't think you'd ever share this place with anyone else.'

Life and death. That's allowed.

Sammi fell silent. The whole forest was silent. Until a shrike gave a shrill cry above them, the sound falling through the leaves to where they were crouched. Laurie smothered a curse. Joe shook his head at her, counting time, listening for the sound of the hunter. He saw her check her phone. No signal. Watched her scanning the undergrowth for a weapon. What could they use against a crossbow? Nothing. They'd have to sit it out the way Jax did, wait for dark or someone at the station to raise the alarm when they failed to turn up for the interview with Orme. *Why was that crossbow in his car? Orme ran an enormous risk. For what, or who?*

'You know the answer,' Sammi said. 'You just don't want to believe it.'

The silence stretched, almost to the brink of being comfortable. The shrike didn't cry again, must have moved on. The sun found its way inside, leaking in patches across the forest floor, but not into the tight spot where they were hiding.

Eventually, Laurie whispered, 'He's gone, surely?'

'I doubt it,' Joe whispered back. 'He's waiting, same as us.'

'For what?' She rolled her neck. 'Forget I asked. Bright ideas? I could use one, round about now.'

'He gave up on Jax when it got dark.'

'So we're going to be here all day?'

'You had plans?' he joked, in a bid to make her smile.

She did smile. 'The SIA is going to be pissed off.'

'There you go. Silver lining.'

'And I win the Diet Coke. That was my neck nearly found the first arrow.'

'You're a winner. All I've got to show for myself is another grubby shirt. Third in three days—'

They tensed in the same second, at the sound of movement coming down the slope towards them. Laurie's eyes were wild until Joe shook his head.

He'd have to be uncanny to find us here.

'You think you're the only uncanny one?' Sammi was watching through a gap in the leaves. 'He knows these woods, at least as well as we do. Better, since he's been playing here a lot longer. Joe, you need to go.'

We'll be an easy target—

'You're a *sitting* one, right here.'

Joe was about to signal to Laurie to move out when he recognised the sound of the footfall coming towards them. An unhurried pattering, low to the ground. *Nancy*. The dog had her nose down, tail pointed. Following their scent without any difficulty. Leading the hunt right to them. *Yark—*

The bolt struck her flank, spinning her from her paws on to her side. She made no sound beyond panting, high and hurt, scrabbling in a semicircle, stirring up soil and leaves.

Boots slid down the slope towards them, black-toed, laced to the calf. The gap in the leaves didn't show any more than that.

The hunter's tread was light and purposeful. He stopped at the side of the dog, watching as she struggled, showing one bright eye, baring her teeth at her attacker. An ugly dog, beautiful in her bravery. The nose of the crossbow grazed the bolt in her side, the hunter poking at the edges of her pain. Something inside Joe snapped at the sight. Sammi said, 'Joe, *no*, wait—'

But he didn't, couldn't. Rested on his heels for a second before putting all his weight into his shoulders as he thrust forward, through the branches into the half-lit patch of wood where the hunter was waiting.

41.

Laurie had known what Joe was about to do a split second before he did it. Felt the tension ripple through him, fear churning into fury. They'd run out of options. One of them was going to have to take an appalling risk. Her fury wasn't far behind, seeing Sandra's dog shot so heartlessly. But it was Joe who barrelled from the bushes to tackle the hunter to the ground, hitting him low in the legs, toppling the pair of them backwards, the thud shaking the ground, travelling up the trees to scatter birds in a squall of alarm. She shoved free of the undergrowth, swerving the action to get behind the armed man who was using the crossbow to beat Joe bloody before he rose to his feet, the weapon's nose swinging in her direction with a terrible, majestic inevitability. Gleaming flight rail, gloved finger on the trigger. *Isabel*. Her sister aged sixteen, smiling with a silver trophy in her hands.

Thunder filled Laurie's skull as her right shin, acting independently, kicked the hunter's knee, spinning him off his feet into the dirt where Joe rolled on top of him, grabbing the crossbow with both hands and holding on even when the man wrenched the weapon upwards to get it out of his reach.

An awful sound crunched from Joe's shoulder but he didn't let go. Laurie reached in to spray the hunter with as much PAVA as her thumb could give her, making him scream, the pitch of it high and wild. *Great* sound, the best she'd heard out here. She wanted to go on hearing it. More PAVA, bonus feature. As he folded, she fed him her free hand in the form of a fist.

By the time he was face down on the forest floor, she had the plasticuffs out, hauling his wrists behind him, ripping the cuffs as tight as they'd go. Kicking back, she stood over him, boots planted either side of his waist. Waiting – *hoping* – he'd give her an excuse to use more of the adrenaline which was making her shake. Seeing that baby face down in the bath. Eric Miles, snuffed out.

42.

'You okay?' Laurie demanded, her breath ragged.

'Mmm.' Joe fought his way on to his knees.

'That sounds like a no.'

She started towards him, he held her off with a look. 'I've put my shoulder out. Unless you're offering to put it back in, don't touch me. It's dislocated.'

A small word for a world of pain. But what mattered was the hunter face down, gargling PAVA. Cuffed, in custody. Joe repeated the words like a mantra to keep the worst of the pain at bay. His left arm was blazing from the tips of his fingers to the top of his shoulder. He gathered its wrist and elbow, cradling its dead weight in his lap. 'Check on Nancy?' Laurie did, stripping off her jacket to cover the little dog. 'Is she dead?' Joe felt sick.

'No, just in shock. Like you, I expect.' She considered the awkward slope of his shoulder. 'Ambulance could take a while, and that's after I've found a signal. I should put it back in.'

'Assuming you know what you're doing.'

'When have I ever not known that?'

The next ten minutes were the longest ten hours of Joe's life. Not helped by the knowledge that with two working arms he could have carried Nancy to a vet, or kept a proper watch over the hunter while Laurie got the dog to safety.

When the shoulder was back in, she stepped wide, keeping one hand on his elbow to support the arm's weight. 'All right?'

'Mm-hm.'

'Are you going to throw up?'

'No.'

'Pass out?'

'No.'

'Right. Let's turn him over, shall we?'

She straightened, stepping to where the hunter was spitting irritant spray. She rolled him on to his back with her foot, so they could see his face.

'Told you,' Sammi said.

43.

Nelson Roache was keen to cooperate. He said as much to DCI Saxton and to Laurie before repeating it to Joe. 'What sort of shape are you in, Joseph? You look dead on your feet.'

'I'm fine,' Joe said in his even way. 'If you could please answer DI Bower's questions, I'd be even better.'

Laurie watched Roache give a slow nod. He was right, as far as his observation went. Joe looked terrible. Bruises on his cheek and jaw, pinpoint pupils from the painkillers given by the paramedic who'd congratulated her on putting his shoulder back in. She'd wanted him stood down, sent home to rest. It was Joe who pointed out that, of the two of them, only he'd spoken with the man who'd fired a bolt into Sandra's dog, and tried to fire bolts into them. Nancy would live, thanks to Joe's care of her while they were waiting for backup to arrive. The man who'd fired the bolts didn't speak a word while they were waiting, not even when Laurie read his rights before arresting him for attempted murder. She hadn't recognised him. It was Joe who'd given her the man's name. He gave it again now, facing Nelson Roache in his plush sitting room at Middlestone Hall.

'Tom Sangster tried to kill me and DI Bower earlier today. In the woods behind Powderhill.'

'So you said.' Roache creased his brow, looking from Joe to Laurie. 'And you believe he may've done worse?'

'Definitively. We believe he shot Chris and Odette Miles, leaving their infant son Eric unattended to drown in the bath.' The chill in Joe's voice froze the back of Laurie's neck. 'We know he chased Jaxon Grice, discharging a weapon at him designed to cause serious injury or death.'

Roache looked shaken, she had to give him that. His face hollowed, mouth opening. 'That *child*? He shot at him?'

'Disappointing, isn't it?' Laurie said. 'When those we trust turn out to be people who should be under lock and key.'

'Indeed it is.' Roache looked appalled.

Joe moved his neck away from the soreness in his shoulder. Despite the painkillers, the dislocation had to hurt, just not enough to stop him wanting to see this through. Tom Sangster was in a police cell, so silent he may as well have been vacuum-sealed. The answers they needed weren't going to come from him.

'And Roland Orme?' Laurie asked Roache.

He spread his large hands, frowning. 'Isn't it the case he's been arrested in Bradford? Charged in connection with properties in Powderhill?'

'How do you know that?'

He shifted his gaze from Joe to her. 'I'm afraid you aren't going to approve of my answer, Detective Inspector.'

'I don't approve of much I hear during murder investigations, Mr Roache. Just answer my questions.'

'Of course. As I say, I'm keen to do whatever I can to resolve this matter to your satisfaction. That these men were my friends . . .' He shook his head, a bleak brand of anger in his eyes. 'Orme contacted me late last night, wanting me to put him in touch with Alan Worricker.'

'The police and crime commissioner?'

'The same. When I asked why, he said he'd managed to get himself into a "*ridiculous situation*" – his words – involving a pair of empty properties in the area. He said nothing about stolen goods, or weapons of any kind.'

Laurie let that rest, wondering whether Joe was taking any of this at face value. He'd been in touch with Roache most of his life, but whether he knew the man was another matter.

'You have business dealings with Mr Orme. Correct?'

'Currently? No. In the past, he and I have discussed the purchase of woodlands.'

'Similar to discussions you were having with Tom Sangster, then.'

Nelson shot a troubled look at Joe, appeared on the brink of asking again if he was well enough to be here. He was invested in Joe's well-being, that much was evident, but there was a flavour underneath it which Laurie didn't like.

'The three of us are old friends of some years' standing. You're right to say that rankles, in the light of the reason you're here. The issue of woodlands came up over a supper, a long time ago. Two, three years? Roland's a developer. Tommy and I were arguing against his ambition to build more houses in the area, trying to explain the benefits of keeping the land as nature intended.'

'Red in tooth and claw?' Laurie suggested.

Roache gave a short-lived laugh. 'Tommy's mantra. He was always very keen on hunting. Insisted I'd enjoy it, if I'd only let myself. But I grew up in a different class, couldn't see the attraction the way he could.'

'You and he went on a hunting trip to Poland,' Joe said neutrally. 'Where you killed a number of wild boar.'

'We did,' Nelson conceded. 'Tommy's birthday gift to me. I told him it was overgenerous, failed to put my foot down.' A flush marked his face. 'Despite good reasons to be proud of my roots, I find myself inclined to defer to those of a higher social status, like Tommy. I'm ashamed of that instinct, all the more so in the light of what you're telling me he's done.'

'Did you know he'd bought the forest behind Powderhill?' Joe asked next. 'With the aim of turning it into a private hunting space for friends and clients? That aim being some distance from the legal use of woodlands.'

'I did not. The purchase alone is news to me. He certainly never disclosed it during our discussions. Nothing was ever said about a purpose of that kind.'

His answers were considered, his expression unwaveringly grave. A good witness, if Laurie could take anything he said at face value.

'You told DS Ashe that Sangster was in Italy last Friday. In fact, he'd returned to the UK two days before.'

'I apologise for the misunderstanding, although as memory serves' – a gentle tone for Joe – 'I only said I *thought* he was in Italy. There was no intention on my part to prevaricate or mislead.'

'He was close to bankruptcy. Were you aware of that?'

Roache shook his head. 'Certainly not. At least, I knew things weren't going well for him, here or in Italy. But I'd no idea how bad it was.'

'A lot of money to be made from illegal hunting,' Joe said. 'We know he was investigating the importation of animals for this purpose. Lynx and wolves from Sweden, where they're culling due to overbreeding. Cheaper to hunt indigenous animals, however. That's how he thought of the kids from the Wakefield estate.'

He held Nelson's gaze, appeared to be waiting to see who'd be the first to break eye contact. Roache just looked straight back at him.

'It's appalling, Joseph. I've said as much. I grew up near the Wakefield estate, know exactly how it feels to be looked down on by men like Sangster.'

'And yet you were friends,' Laurie said. 'How'd that happen?'

'As I say, a regrettable instinct on my part to seek the approval of men like that. Combined, I suppose, with a corresponding desire on his side to exploit the friendship for his own ends.'

A flavour of bitterness in his voice; if this was an act, it was Oscar-worthy. She didn't like, though, a distant alarm bell sounding in her head.

'In what way did he do that? Exploit your friendship.'

'I've made a number of modest investments over the years to help him out. Most recently, I was funding his interest in saving our woodlands from developers. That, at least, was my understanding of what he was doing.' He looked from Joe to Laurie. 'I can see neither of you is impressed, and on the face of it I've been a fool, thinking he was ever my friend. Gullible, too, going along with his plans without digging deeper into what he was hiding. I wish I had satisfactory answers to your questions, but I am being candid. Not seeking to excuse my snobbery, or stupidity. Answering to the best of my knowledge.'

Not afraid of looking a fool, no trace of arrogance. That shovel beard was handy, could be hiding a multitude of micro-expressions. Laurie would have liked him clean-shaven, exposed.

'And Orme? What part did he play in this? To the best of your knowledge.'

'From what you've said, he appears to have been busy with his own lawbreaking, although I wouldn't rule out the idea of a partnership. He was always very impressed by Tommy's plans. The pair of them spent more time talking together than the three of us ever did.'

True, on the face of it. They'd found evidence of numerous phone calls and emails between Sangster and Orme, few between Roache and the other two. Laurie studied the man's face, trying to see beneath the surface. 'You're the one with the connections to the police and crime commissioner.'

'Yes, for my sins.' He sounded beyond bitter, actively betrayed. 'That does appear to have been another factor in the friendship. Friendships.'

'Have you spoken to Alan Worricker about any of this?'

'I contacted him as soon as I heard from Orme last night, didn't want to trouble Magnus Saxton at that stage, since I'd no suspicion it was connected with your murder investigation. Alan said he'd make a note of the conversation, advised me to put it in writing, which I did.'

Another incontestable truth. Nelson had filed a report of the conversation early this morning. Either he had a hard-on for early-morning admin, or he was an expert at covering his arse. Saxton had warned her about shaking this tree, but since the rest of the forest was giving them zip, she'd take her chances. She put a photo down in front of Roache. 'Do you know what this is?'

'It appears to be a piece of Lego?'

'It's a flash drive,' Joe said, 'disguised as a Lego brick. It was hidden in a basket of toys at a house in Macclesfield belonging to Odette Miles's mother.'

Laurie said, 'Her son-in-law filmed your friends Roland and Tommy discussing plans to turn the woods behind Powderhill into a deadly assault course for boys like Jaxon Grice.'

Roache picked up the photo delicately, studying it with distaste. 'You believe this is why that poor family was slaughtered?'

'Your friend Roland has admitted his part in the plan, warehousing weapons and traps. He's claiming he was threatened by your friend Tommy and feared for his life.'

'That poor woman.' Nelson shook his head, staring at the photo of the flash drive. 'Losing her daughter and grandchild.'

His sorrow was authentic, Laurie had no doubt, conscious of his daughter Maggie watching from the silver frame at his elbow. What had her death done to him? Laurie's dad was long gone before Izzy died. A blessing, her mum always said.

'Your friend Tommy's place in Ilkley is an arsenal. Multiple weapons, all with ammunition. Have you been to his house?'

'No, I haven't.' He returned the photo to the table, lifting his gaze to meet Laurie's. Sharper than before, a cutting edge to it, cold against her skin. 'Nor was I aware of any unlicensed weapons in his possession.'

'How about cages?'

Another photo for him to study.

'Were you aware of those? Galvanised steel, the kind you'd keep prey animals in. Or small children.'

He recoiled, as anyone would, from the idea of kids kept in cages. 'No. Absolutely not. And to be clear, had I any notion whatsoever of these plans you're describing, I'd have been straight on the phone to the police.'

Alan Worricker, he meant.

No twelve-bore shotgun in Sangster's arsenal. Without the murder weapon, the CPS were doing their favourite dance: shaking heads and dragging feet. The flash drive told a good story, but there was no evidence Sangster ever set foot inside Higher Bar Farm. An initial search of the land behind Powderhill had turned up the bolts fired at Laurie and Joe, as well as a number of trees injured by similar bolts fired at the approximate head height of Jaxon Grice. Sangster himself said nothing. Not to his solicitor, nor to the police. He sat in silence, eyes reddened by the irritant spray, face vacant. Nothing Laurie said, or Joe, or Saxton, drew a flicker of response. Even the specialist interview advisor admitted defeat. Nelson Roache had looked like their best bet of gift-wrapping Tommy for the CPS. But he was either in the dark, or doing a really good job of pretending to be. There was nothing for them here. Middlestone Hall was a dead end. Tomorrow, it would be a week since Eric and his parents were wiped out. What did they have to take to Mel and Yvonne, to Keith and Beverley, but this shabby little tale of greed and privilege?

'What's the story with you and Roache?' Laurie asked when they were back in the car. 'Not the generous benefactor line you spun before. The real story.'

'Why're you asking?' Joe winced as he fastened his seat belt. His shoulder was hurting worse than he remembered from the last time he'd dislocated it.

Laurie was driving, since she wasn't in a fog of strong painkillers. 'Just wondering why he hates your guts.'

Joe felt his eyes go wide with shock. He stared until she glanced across at him.

'All right, you didn't know. I wondered.'

'Why would you say that?'

'The way he looks at you. *Looked* at you. You've seriously never turned back after you've said goodbye, caught him glaring?' She had turned back, that alarm bell sounding loud and clear. 'Surprised you couldn't feel it, half a dozen knives quivering in your back. I've not seen animosity like that in a long time.'

Joe looked at her blankly before shaking his head. 'You're wrong.'

'You said his daughter was your teacher. She died on the bus, that's his beef with you. Like Des and his brother. Seth, was it? You survived, Maggie didn't. You said some people blame you for the crash. Well, if they formed a club, Roache would want to be president. And not just because he loves a loud tie.'

'He's been kind to me,' Joe protested. 'Kinder than just about anyone else around here. Maybe he was disappointed by the uncomfortable questions I had to ask when he's dealing with the fallout from two toxic friendships—'

'Toxic friendships?' Laurie echoed. 'Teenage girls have toxic friendships. Grown men screw one another over. Clearly that's what was going on between Orme and Sangster. I'm wondering if that's the extent of it.'

Joe rolled his neck. 'You think Nelson is, what? The local kingpin? That Sangster and Orme were his stooges?'

'You don't like that theory? Admittedly, I'm telling it to you in a pool car rather than a creepy wood. Probably lacks impact for that reason.'

'It has impact, just no solid structure. Where's your evidence?' Before she could answer, he added, 'No disrespect, but isn't this more or less how you came by your reputation in Salford? Unmasking the local philanthropist? Jim Chancellor, was that his name? Mr Salt of the Earth. Everyone else was taken in, but you saw through him. Are you sure you're not on high alert for a pattern that's not there?'

'Interesting speculation.' Laurie steered the car around a pothole, easily. 'All right, why did Orme have a crossbow in the back of his car? Answer me that.'

'It was Sangster's, obviously. Part of the arsenal he was relocating to Powderhill for the Dark Peak's version of the Hunger Games.'

'As soon as I saw that charge sheet, I was itching to get into those woods. Where, to be clear, wild horses wouldn't have dragged me if I'd thought the killer was still at large. And if you hadn't been so determined to clear Jaxon's name.'

'What's any of that got to do with Nelson?'

'It's common knowledge how you feel about the kids in this place. If the bike was a lure for Jax, maybe *he* was a lure for you.'

Joe's head was starting to hurt more than his shoulder. 'I'm following less than twenty per cent of this. Can you speak plain English?'

'I keep coming back to that crossbow. Not the one in Orme's boot, or the one Sangster fired at us. In Powderhill, right at the start of this. Forget who rigged it. Who was the intended victim?'

'Chris, surely?'

'Nope. I refer you to the broken window, and the fact he was gunned down in his kitchen. If Sangster was prepared to take a shotgun up to Higher Bar, why mess about with wires and improvised traps? That crossbow was intended for Jax, or for us. If he wanted to hunt Jax, why kill him? That leaves us and by *us*, I mean the police. Since I wasn't here at the time, I'm wondering if we need to call that an attempt on your life.' She indicated left, turning in the direction of the station.

'That's crazy,' Joe said slowly. But he'd suggested it himself, at the start of all this.

'Is it? You've literally just survived an attempt on your life. What makes you so sure it was the first?'

He shook his head, struggling to know how to answer. He'd suggested it, but he'd never believed it. In the end, he said, 'This is Edenscar, not Chicago.'

'Lots of strong emotions here, that's what you told me. And you're right in the middle of them, that's been obvious from day one.'

Joe sifted through the onslaught of emotions – shock at her accusation, frustration at his inability to articulate a counterargument – telling himself to stay calm. Nothing to be gained by losing his temper.

'It's frustrating, not having solid evidence against Sangster. And Orme's charge sheet threw us. But you're reaching, you must see that.'

'You want me to tell you what I'm seeing?' Laurie pulled in to the side of the road. She parked up and turned to look at him. 'Two men who knew how to play us, maybe three. Orme's cutting deals left and centre. No one can get a word out of Sangster. These men push buttons for a living. Orme's a palm-greaser, Sangster likes to play for high stakes. Master manipulators, the pair of them.'

'I'm not disagreeing with any of that. It's when you cast Nelson as the master puppeteer that you lose me.'

'Just because he wasn't pushing any of your buttons back there doesn't mean he isn't into the same game. We know Orme manipulated Lawlor. Maybe Nelson's manipulating you. Your sense of fair play, your need to atone. You told me you joined the police because you didn't know what else to do with the guilt of being the sole survivor of that crash. Have you ever told Roache the same thing?'

'Have you, Joe?' Sammi propped his chin to the back of Joe's seat, interested in his answer.

'He's been kind to me, for years.'

Laurie dismissed this, rejoined the traffic. 'So he gets off on controlling you. Winning your trust, lowering your defences, then seeing you in danger. From what you've said, he's controlled your career since the start. Made certain you made detective, which, in case it escaped your notice, is a risky business. Plenty of opportunities to lose your life, or break your bones.' She nodded at his shoulder.

'Just because you put this back in,' Joe said, 'doesn't mean you have to try to find out which other parts of me give under pressure.'

She shook her head, driving in silence. A little further along the road, he tried again: 'There's nothing connecting Nelson to Chris—'

'Agreed. We have Sangster for the killings. He's the hunter, and the weapons man. But that doesn't mean Roache is in the clear. Could be he's playing a long game, have you considered that?'

Joe considered it, or tried to. His head wasn't as clear as he needed it to be. Sammi was lost in thought, no help there.

'A long game with whom? Sangster and Orme are going to prison. We've enough to get Sangster for what happened in the woods, to us and to Jax. Orme was fitting half the town with armoured boxes—'

'Oh he's going to prison,' Laurie agreed. 'I'd like to know the full story, though. Wouldn't you? Sangster has such a hard-on for hunting he can't keep it in his pants even when we have a suspect in custody? You know what I think?'

'I'm discovering it.'

'I think Sangster disgusts Roache. The same as Orme disgusts him. The pair of them are impulsive, incapable of playing a long game. Nelson's cutting ties, serving up their heads to cement his position as your benefactor and as the police and crime commissioner's good friend. And to exonerate himself from suspicion.'

'Wow,' Joe said politely when she stopped. 'I guess I've been missing a trick or two around here. Good job you're staying to put me straight.'

'I put your shoulder straight. Didn't I?'

'You did. So you *are* hanging around?'

'Six months, that was the deal. Hasn't even been six days.'

'True.'

Longest six days of his life was how it felt right at that minute.

Laurie shot him a look, shaking her head. 'Okay, shame on me for spoiling the moment. We took the killers off the streets. We'll find the evidence we need. Look how we found that flash drive hiding at Yvonne's place. Cheer up.'

Sammi agreed: 'Cheer up, Joe.'

You don't feel it? The prickle in his palms. *We're missing something.*

'She's put you on edge, but she's said sorry. You're knackered. You need to get home, ice that shoulder. Things'll feel better then.'

Joe leant his head to the seat rest, watching the forest at the side of the road, spilling long shadows into the car, over the backs of his fingers, tangling around his feet. Sammi was right, he was knackered, could hardly see straight. But it was there all the same, the ticking that never went away, the sense something vital was missing, a piece of the puzzle or a piece of him. Missing, or gone.

44.

'Gran, you've known Nelson Roache a long time. Do you trust him?'

'That's a strange question. Why wouldn't I?'

Joe shifted his shoulder, cautiously. 'Laurie has a theory, says Nelson hates me. Blames me for the bus crash.'

'He's been decent to you, hasn't he?'

'Always. Put in a word when this shoulder looked like I'd fail the medical.'

'You're not far from that same place now, by the look of you. Drink that tea and take yourself to bed.'

As it wasn't even 7 p.m., Joe ignored the second half of this statement. He needed to get the day straight in his head. Sammi had gone quiet on him, as if he'd taken all the talk about people living in the past personally.

'You told me once he was "always an ambitious boy". Nelson. What did you mean, specifically?'

'Just that.' She stirred her tea, watching him with concern. 'Look where it got him. Not many from that end of town living the high life, then or now. He *got on*, that's what, didn't settle for what life handed him.'

She admired Nelson, he'd known that for years. But there was something else, under the admiration. Joe was finding her unusually hard to read. He'd never known her to be secretive, although she must have secrets. Everyone did.

'Laurie thinks he's playing a long game.'

'Sounds like *Laurie* might be stirring things.'

The acid in her voice made his teeth hurt. 'I doubt it. Not her style.'

He thought of Sangster's sermon about lost childhoods, his nostalgia for the good old days when kids roamed wild, living by their wits. He'd taken that notion to its extreme: hunting kids for the thrill it gave him. Was he glad when the Higher Bar killings spread fear in this place? Hoping to make a fortune pandering to people who considered hunting the sport of kings. Primitive, thrilling and formidable. Nostalgia repackaged as an excuse for violence—

His phone was ringing . He reached for it, his heart sinking when he saw the name on the display. He pulled his body upright in the chair, finishing his tea before answering the call. 'Ms Cooper, is everything all right?'

His grandmother shot him a furious look of warning, pointing at his shoulder and the bruises on his face.

Zoe's mum said, 'Joe, you have to come.' Her voice was thinned to a razor. Not marked by grief, but terror.

He came to his feet, frowning. 'What's happened, can you tell me?'

'They said—You *have* to come. Please.'

45.

Hannah Cooper came to the door with her mouth pulled sideways by distress, a clear warning in her eyes. Well, Joe had known what he was walking into. He was only surprised it hadn't happened before. Des Morton and Shane Leggitt were in her sitting room, Des with a tyre wrench in his right hand. He pointed it at Joe, then at the sofa. 'Sit the fuck down.'

Hannah reached for Joe's left hand, stopping short, fingers outstretched. 'Don't be scared, darling.'

'*Darling?* Oh shit – are you two fucking?' Shane hooted with laughter.

'Sit the fuck down,' Des repeated. 'If I've to tell you a third time, it'll be with this.' Swinging the wrench to point it at Joe's left shoulder. 'You've brought a shit heap of trouble down on me, and this time you're going to pay for it.'

Hannah moaned with fear. Shane's grin curdled, glee turning to disgust. 'She's old enough to be your mum, you sick shit.'

Joe ignored him, keeping his eyes on Des. 'I've called it in.' He used his flattest voice. 'Everyone at the station knows I'm here. You're already facing charges over the handling of stolen goods. If you want to make that worse, go ahead. I'd be happy to see you off the streets for a bit.' When Shane took a step forward, Joe swung his stare that way. 'You too, since you're joined at the hip.'

'What happened to your face?' Des demanded, as if Tom Sangster had cheated him out of the job which was rightfully his: smashing Joe's face, breaking his shoulder, firing bolts at him. 'Who did that?'

'He's in custody for three murders, including a baby's. And for the attempted murder of three others, one of them a child.'

Joe had reached the end of his patience with people like Tom Sangster and Des Morton, who thought this place belonged to them, tried to shape it with their thuggery, refusing to move on. People who made a life's work of digging the dead.

'So go ahead, do whatever it is you had planned for the evening. But I give you fair warning, I'll press charges. Oh and I'm wearing a body cam.' He drew their attention to the BWV camera. 'Which has been recording since I stepped out of my car and will continue recording during whatever fun and games you had in mind.'

He'd never spoken to Des like this before, always avoided conflict, let his guilt take a front seat. Des had been counting on having an easy time knocking him about. *Enough.* Apart from anything else there was Hannah to think of, standing by the side of the sofa, her face ashen, stare fixed on Joe's left side.

'Well, come on.' He looked from Des to Shane, and back. 'One of you must want to hit me enough for it to be worth a prison sentence. No? In that case, Ms Cooper would like you to leave her house.'

Shane had been keen to go as soon as he saw the body-worn video camera, Des less so, but the sound of sirens settled the matter. The pair of them went, Shane without a backwards glance, Des with a look that said this wasn't the end of it. Joe hadn't expected an end to it, just a reprieve in which to reassure Hannah she was safe, and to redraw the battle lines between him and Des. He needed to move on, put the past behind him, focus on what mattered.

'I'll thin out, then, shall I?' Sammi was on the sofa where Des had wanted Joe to sit, his eyes shining with sadness. He was solid enough to put a dent in the sofa cushions. He had a shadow, and a pulse; Joe could see it, beating at the base of his neck. He was Joe's best friend, ally, confidant. *Don't you dare. I'm not ready for that. Give me time. Let me build up to it.* Sammi nodded, shutting his eyes. He looked as tired as Joe felt.

'Sit down,' Joe told Hannah. 'I'll put the kettle on.'

The squad car brought Ted and Theo. He spoke to them on the doorstep, letting them know the danger had passed. Theo looked into the house before searching Joe's face. Joe shook his head warningly, and Theo stayed silent.

When they'd gone, he went to the kitchen to make Hannah's tea. The heating was on, food in the fridge from the online delivery he'd organised the last time he was here. Otherwise, the kitchen showed the same signs of neglect as the rest of the house. He did what he could to reduce the risk of vermin, clearing food waste, wiping everything down with disinfectant. A pile of post had been pushed to the back of one of the counters, mostly junk mail but a couple of the envelopes looked official. He was torn between respecting Hannah's privacy and checking she wasn't about to be evicted or taken to court for unpaid bills. One of the envelopes had been hand-delivered, her name printed in small neat letters.

'You know that writing,' Sammi said alertly.

Joe picked up the letter, testing its weight. The envelope had been opened, its contents falling to the counter with a sharp *tick*. A flash drive. Not disguised as Lego or anything else, identical to the one brought into the station by Derek Symonds. Except this had the first line of Hannah's address printed on it. In the same block capitals Chris used to address all his blackmail victims.

Sammi said tersely, 'You need to leave. Now.'

Joe stood staring at the flash drive before scooping it into his hand. He'd asked Chris to come here a month ago because the house was so cold, to check the heating system in case of an electrical fault. Chris refused to charge for the work, calling it his good deed for the day. Joe turned to look at the boots abandoned by the back door. He'd seen them last time he was here, while they were searching for the car whose high beams he'd watched on the road up at Higher Bar.

'*Joe!*' Sammi urged. 'Get out of here.'

He moved in the direction of the front door, finally, but he was already too late. Hannah was on the sofa in the room where he'd left her, hands full of shotgun: twelve-bore, muzzle facing out. She lifted her gaze to Joe's left side, then to the fist he'd closed around the flash drive.

'He sent that.' Her voice was dull like her eyes, as if a film had formed over their cornflower blue. 'Chris. He said he knew all about us. You and me.' She stared at the place where she saw her daughter at Joe's side. 'He took pictures of us.' She raised her eyes to his face. 'She wasn't in the pictures.'

Sammi strode across the room to stand between the shotgun and Joe. His face was drawn deep with lines Joe had never seen before.

'Ms Cooper,' Joe said. 'Can you put down the gun, please?'

'You're taking pictures,' Hannah said in the same dull voice. 'Right now.' She meant the BWV, the camera lens facing her from the lapel of Joe's jacket.

'I can switch it off. Let me switch it off.'

He started to move, stopping when she swung the shotgun up, pointed squarely at his chest. Sammi stood in the way but he wasn't as solid as usual; Joe could see straight through him to Hannah's tight face.

'She wasn't in the pictures!' Her voice was trapped between a snarl and a wail. 'Just you and me. He wanted money, I didn't care about that. He stole her from here –' hitting the sofa with a fist before gripping at the gun again – 'from *me.*'

The shotgun was heavy. Joe saw its weight in her face but he also saw her strength, the sinews in her forearms, tendons in her neck. A tall woman, slender but strong. A farmer's daughter. He pictured her in the muddy boots, striding with deadly purpose on Friday night. Carrying the shotgun to Higher Bar Farm as the family settled to their usual routine.

'She was here,' he said. 'Zoe. The last time I came.'

Monday. Three days after the murders. Hannah had begged him to come, her grief worse than usual that night.

She nodded. '*Yes.*' Then she said, 'It's how I know he's all right. Eric. He's with his granddad, or his mum. With *you.*'

Joe's skin contracted, the cold burn of ice in his veins. *You did this,* he thought. *You drove her mad.*

'Shut up,' Sammi snapped. 'Concentrate. You need to make this stop.'

'Not if you shoot me,' Joe said.

Hannah stared at him, the shotgun gripped hard in her hands.

'If you shoot me, Eric will have nowhere to go, and neither will Zoe.' A keening came out of her, like no human sound he'd ever heard. 'They need me. *You* need me. Let me help.'

Her finger was tight on the trigger, her face tighter still. They stared at one another across the wasteland of her sitting room, across the years between then and now. The reservoir's water seeped in, icy fingers closing around the fist where Joe held the flash drive. Zoe Cooper was here.

'It's not working. She's going to fire that thing.' Sammi stood between him and the gun, facing Zoe's mum. If she fired, it would pass through his chest and into Joe's. A twelve-bore slug at this range would put a hole through both their bodies. Even if Sammi were alive, it would kill the pair of them. 'It's not working, Joe.'

'Hannah, you need me.' He drew a breath. 'And I need you.'

For the first time, her face wavered. The muzzle dipped a fraction, no longer aimed at his chest. Pointing at his thigh. The shot would take his leg off. Still fatal, given how quickly he'd bleed out, just a little longer to die.

'You think I only come here to bring Zoe, when you're desperate to see her. But that isn't true, or not the whole truth. I come because I have to try to do some good. Make a difference, however small. Without that? I haven't anything. There isn't anywhere else for me to go. I'm trapped on that bus, for ever.'

Sammi turned to face him. 'Oh God, Joe.'

'I'm on that bus and I'm drowning.'

'Stop it. You're breaking my heart.'

Tears shone in Sammi's eyes. He held out his hand and Joe took it. His other hand held the flash drive, Zoe's cold fingers wrapped around his.

'Why was I saved?' he asked her mother. 'If I can't make a difference?'

'I killed them,' she whispered.

'I know. I know you did. Let me help you.'

She ignored this, her eyes distant, face fixed in the past. 'I killed him, for what he did. Her, for leaving Eric to drown. She *left* him – "He's in the bath, alone" – as if that was my fault! I'd never have left Zoe, ever. Not for a second.'

But you left Eric.

'It only takes seconds for a baby to drown. I knew he'd be gone before I could get to him. He's safe now, though.' Her eyes glistened. 'With you.'

She'd left Eric to drown because she believed in an afterlife, in ghosts. This was *his* fault. Again.

'Joe,' Sammi warned. 'Stop it. Make it stop.'

'She's here.' He held up his hand, fist closed around the flash drive. 'Zoe. She's here and she wants you to get help. To put down the gun, and ask for help.'

'I tried to die,' Hannah said. 'More than once. I thought I'd find her that way, but she isn't there. She's with *you*.' Her face twisted. 'She's always with you.'

Joe slowed his breathing. Zoe's cold fingers clutched so hard he felt the flash drive pressing its shape into his palm.

'Why won't you let her go?' Her voice rose. 'You won't let any of them go!'

'I don't know how to. I need help too. We both need help. If you'll put down the gun, I'll get us what we need.'

Sammi said thinly, 'Joe, you do know the BWV's recording this? That you'll be on record?'

Alive, Sammi. I'll be alive. The muzzle was level with his kneecap. Not necessarily fatal, just half his leg gone.

'I'm not leaving here,' Hannah said savagely. 'It's her home! I won't go to prison! I'd never see her again.'

'I'll visit. I'll bring her whenever you want.'

She stared at him. He tried to find the words to change the course of what was happening because of him. Again, because of him.

'Zoe drew a cat on the bus window. Did I ever tell you that? She was with Ellie Howden, who drew Theo. Zoe drew a cat. Did you have a cat?'

Hannah's face flickered. 'She wanted one.'

The muzzle was below his knee now, at his ankle.

'She still wants one,' Joe lied. 'There are so many things she wants, to see and to feel. Things she wants *you* to see and feel.'

How would it feel to lose a foot? A burst of pain, but he'd live. Wake in a hospital bed, Sammi at his side. He'd be able to work again, in time.

'She wants you to hold her, if you're saying goodbye. Will you hold her?'

A cheap trick. He hated himself for it, but her fingers opened on the shotgun as he reached for the muzzle to swing it wide, snatching the barrel from her grip, rolling out of range as she lunged for him, hands grabbing at empty air, voice rising, calling her daughter's name over and over until Joe wanted to cover his ears.

'Will you empty that fucking gun?' Sammi sounded out of breath.

When Joe had done as he instructed, he lifted his head to see straight into his best friend's eyes. Sammi was so close, only inches away. Joe could feel his breath against his cheek. Near enough to touch if he could only do it – put out a hand and reach for Sammi, the way Hannah had reached for Zoe. Risk clutching at empty air, the death all over again of the person he'd loved most in the world.

'Call it in,' Sammi said softly. 'It's over, Joe.'

46.

Hannah Cooper was not a name Laurie knew. She wasn't on the list of witnesses or suspects, or among the blackmail victims as far as they'd been able to discover, no invoices or emails had been sent to her by Chris Miles. She wasn't a mum at the nursery, or someone who'd been in touch with the family in the days leading to their deaths. She'd have remembered this woman's face. Haunted and intense, the way her neck stretched tautly forward, those blue eyes staring straight ahead, through solid walls and closed doors, to a place no one else could see.

'Her daughter, Zoe, was on the school bus with Joe.'

Milla was at her shoulder, watching the woman on the other side of the glass. Their killer, sitting alone with the light in her lap, hands clasped.

'Joe was the only person she'd ever accept help from. He *did* help, or he tried to. Those things she said to him, when she was holding him at gunpoint . . .'

Milla shook her head, trapped between misery and indignation for Joe. Hannah Cooper closed her eyes and started swaying, her expression unnervingly devout, like a woman seated in a church, not an interview room.

'How is Joe?' Laurie asked. 'Have you seen him?' She hadn't. She'd been sitting down to supper with Adam and Peter when the call came through.

'He's been with the guv since he brought her in.'

'Who's watched the BWV footage? Apart from us and the guv?'

'Theo.' Milla paused. 'And Ted.'

'How're they taking it?'

'Not well.' She hadn't moved her gaze from the woman swaying in the chair. 'She lost her little girl. How could she let someone else's baby die?'

In the incident room, Ted was at his desk. He turned away when he saw Laurie, jaw bunched. Theo climbed to his feet, holding her gaze. 'Ma'am.'

'How are you both? DS Vicars?'

'About what you'd expect.' Ted tidied his desk with blunt shoves of his fingers. 'After finding out one of your team's been winding up a madwoman.'

Laurie left a short pause for his pain before saying quietly, 'Ask Milla to show you the footage Chris recorded.'

Ted looked at Milla, who nodded. 'Dash didn't do anything. He just sat there, never said a word. It was all in her head.'

'Everyone deals with their grief in their own way,' Theo said. 'Joe wasn't encouraging Zoe's mum. He was making space for her way of mourning.'

His expression gave Laurie goosebumps; the same evangelical look was on Hannah Cooper's face. His sister died on the bus, she remembered. He'd been halfway to hero-worshipping Joe before this. It was only going to get worse.

He turned his back to the others, addressing her in a low voice. 'Joe doesn't deserve to be vilified for this. Everyone who's lost someone knows how hard he works to make that loss easier to bear.' He was talking about Isabel.

She had almost forgotten the newspaper clipping she'd found on his desk while hunting for whiteboard pens; a problem to be tackled another time, she'd thought. She couldn't work up the energy to be indignant with Theo and anyway he was right, Joe didn't deserve it. He wasn't responsible for anyone else's delusions. That glimmer of Izzy in Chris's bedroom was her problem, not his. She considered the new shape of the team – Ted's rigid jaw, Milla's misery, Theo's fanaticism – and it struck her, forcibly: she'd been assuming she was the outsider here when it was Joe. It had always been Joe.

'DI Bower?' Saxton, beckoning from the doorway.

'We'll speak later,' she told Theo, nodding at Ted and Milla before leaving the incident room for Saxton's office.

Joe was seated at Saxton's desk, in the clothes he'd worn to Middlestone Hall. Dark suit, white shirt. She could see where the BWV had left a small, shiny indent in his lapel. He glanced up when she came in, but didn't speak.

'I'll let DI Bower take your statement,' Saxton told him. 'Ted and I will take Hannah's.'

'She'll need someone with her,' Joe said. 'She's vulnerable.'

His voice was the same, rock-steady, but he looked like he'd been dug from a ditch, pale and muddy-eyed.

When Saxton went, Laurie drew out a chair and sat beside him. She put out her hand. After a second's hesitation, he took it. His fingers were thin and cold.

'Not how I imagined you spending your evening, but at least you're in one piece.' She gripped the fingers warmly. 'Someone's offered you a hot cup of tea, I hope. You're giving me frostbite.'

Joe broke a smile at that. 'Tea would be great.'

'Good. Let's make this as painless as possible.'

When they both had a cuppa, she rattled through the formalities before asking, 'Did you know Hannah owned a shotgun?'

Joe shook his head. 'No. I knew her dad was a farmer, but I wasn't aware of any weapon in the house.'

'You'd been there before?'

'On multiple occasions.' He drank a mouthful of tea. 'I'll give you a list of dates and times.'

'You kept a log?'

'No, but my memory's good. And my gran will know.' His mouth moved towards a smile, stopping short. 'She probably did keep a log.'

'She disapproved of you visiting Hannah?'

'She said it wasn't helping anyone.' He held the mug between his hands, blinking his eyes into focus. 'She was right.'

Every word was an effort. The painkillers had worn off, his pupils no longer pin-heads. He was holding off a crash, but it was coming. He'd been through too much in the last twelve hours. She was in deficit herself, skin-of-her-teeth, and she'd not been held at gunpoint.

'Did you have any reason to suspect Hannah was dangerous?'

'No. She was always very quiet when I saw her.'

'No history of violence?'

'Only towards herself.' Joe put the mug down, rubbed a hand through his hair. 'She tried to take her own life, three years ago.'

'Are you able to give me a rough date?'

He gave her an exact one: 'October sixteenth, 2022.' He met her stare head-on, managing not to flinch. 'The anniversary of the bus crash.'

Laurie made notes, conscious of how near they were to the room where Saxton and Ted were interviewing Hannah. She found herself praying for a confession. With a confession, they wouldn't have to show Joe's BWV footage to anyone else; it could stay inside the team.

'How did she know Chris Miles?'

'That was me.' Joe's voice was run through with self-reproach. 'I asked Chris to take a look at her boiler because it was so cold in the house.'

'Did you have any reason to suspect he'd install a camera, or try to threaten or otherwise extort Ms Cooper?'

'None.'

'Did you have any reason to suspect Hannah of wanting to harm Chris and his family?'

'None.'

Exhaustion like fever rose from him in waves. He looked impossibly young and bruised. For the first time, she saw the boy from the bus made to fight for his life only to have his bravery recast, fired into shame. His survival should have been a cause for celebration. Instead, it was met with suspicion. Miraculous, mysterious. The detective in her wanted to solve that puzzle, lay all the ghosts to rest.

'I just' – Joe had his eyes down, fingers curled around the mug – 'want to do my job.' His voice shook before he pulled it back. 'I was trying to do it, tonight.'

Guilt had its hooks in him, deep. He'd lived with it a long time, but this was different. This was going to drag him under and drown him.

She waited a beat before moving on. 'The aggravated assault tonight. What precipitated that, do you know?'

He straightened in the chair, forcing focus back into his face. 'Two things, I imagine. Des and Shane invading her home, threatening violence. And the BWV, which reminded her of Chris's filming.'

'How did you de-escalate the situation?'

'You know how.' Joe looked at her, eyes burning blackly. 'Everything I said is on the BWV.'

'I've watched the footage. What I saw was a woman who would have pulled that trigger had you not defused the situation. No question whatsoever in my mind.' She spaced the words apart, stressing each syllable: 'She would have pulled that trigger. So let me reword the question, detective. What strategy or strategies did you employ to de-escalate a lethal situation?'

'I told her what she needed to hear.' Joe drew a breath. 'I said I'd visit her in prison, that I wanted her to get help.' He let the breath go. 'And I said I needed help too, which was what she needed to hear.'

'It wasn't the truth?'

Laurie had to ask. If she didn't, someone else would.

'It was a version of the truth designed to de-escalate—' He stopped, steadied his voice. 'It was what she needed to hear.'

Easy for Joe to slip out the back, dodge the gamut of the team's attention. Instead, he went in the direction of the incident room, going first to Ted. 'How is she?'

Ted looked surprised but after scanning Joe's face, he nodded. 'She's doing all right. Full confession. Doctor's coming to look at possible meds.'

'Thanks.' Joe touched a hand to his elbow. 'I appreciate that.'

It disarmed Ted, who said gruffly, 'You take care, all right?'

Theo next. Joe squeezed his shoulder, asking if he was okay. Theo's eyes were shining, his nod emphatic. It was astounding to Laurie that only four years separated them. Joe looked a generation older.

'Dash.' Milla pulled him into a hard hug, drawing a laugh from him.

'Oh, okay. Thanks.' He set her at arm's length with a smile, but he was closer to tears than he'd been at any point during the interview. Time to go.

In the car park, Laurie said, 'Remind me to keep you away from magnets. Core of steel, that's you.'

'Oh, sure.' Joe blinked at the night sky. 'Drop me at my gran's?

She's been texting like mad since I left her place. I'm bound to be in her bad books.'

By the time they reached Miriam Ashe's cottage, it was approaching dawn, birds already stirring in the trees. The street was deserted, no lights in any windows apart from the cottage where Joe was expected.

Laurie parked a short distance away. 'One last thing.' Passing him the clipping from Theo's desk.

His grey eyes lifted, full of apology. She shook her head.

'Not a lecture on team discretion. A word of warning about guilt. I let it ride me, for years. Before Izzy died, and after. Didn't do a bit of good, for me or anyone else. I'm not talking about Hannah, or Eric. October sixteenth, 2008. You didn't cause that crash. No, Joe –' because he'd opened his mouth – 'listen to me. You were a kid. The driver was trained to cope with kids. It wasn't on you.'

He smoothed the news clipping with his thumb. 'Theo blames himself for his sister being on the bus, says she tried to get out of the trip by hiding her bag. He found it, thought he was being helpful. Don't judge him too harshly, will you?'

'I'm not judging anyone. But I am serious about the crash. Whatever went wrong, it was not your fault. I'll prove it, if you like.'

'How?' Joe asked, looking genuinely curious.

'I'll reopen the investigation, if I need to. Go over every damn fact. Things change, you know that. People remember stuff, new tech makes sense of skid patterns – happens all the time. I'll prove you didn't cause that crash.'

'In six months?' Joe raised his eyebrows, almost smiling.

'You're forgetting my reputation.'

There was more she wanted to say. Words he could get hold of when he was trying and failing to sleep, turning the evening's nightmare around in his mind. *I just want to do my job*, he'd said. She wanted to tell him how her sister's long death turned her into someone she didn't like, impatient and intolerant. That when she finally put the guilt away, she became a better friend, better wife, better detective.

'You know, Joe, sometimes our job isn't saving other people. It's saving ourselves. You want to do your job? Start there.'

Joe watched her go, standing with Sammi at his side. The dawn was lit with silver, making cut-outs of the cottages. Somewhere the low churring song of a nightjar spun itself into silence. When the car was out of sight, Sammi said, 'She means it. She's going to be digging your dead for the next six months.'

'What it looks like,' Joe agreed.

'Any thoughts on that?' Sammi turned to face him. A smile lifted the edges of his mouth but his eyes were serious, troubled.

Joe tilted his head to the sky, filling his lungs with cold, clean air. 'Maybe it's time.' His ribcage unlocked, for the first time in hours. It felt good.

'She'll change everything.' Sammi bit his thumb knuckle.

'Yes.' Behind them, a small cloud of starlings rose, wings dipped in the first fragile light of the day. 'I think it's time.'

Acknowledgements

This book is brought to you by a host of wonderful people who inspired, enthused, endured, edited and championed me until *The Drowning Place* found its ways into the hands of readers. Special thanks to: my agent, Veronique Baxter, and the team at David Higham Associates; my editor and publisher, Katie Ellis-Brown; Liz Foley, Mia Quibell-Smith, Graeme Hall, Anouska Levy, Sam Matthews, Sam Rees-Williams and Hannah Telfer at Vintage; Vicki Mellor, who first encouraged me to create this series; my mother, who took me to Eyam as a child, where I met the ghosts who have haunted me ever since; my sister, Penny, who has read nearly everything I ever wrote and was still excited to learn of this book. During the writing, a number of my friends were subjected to my excited mutterings and unsettling silences: Simon Bewick; Julie Akhurst and Stephen Brown; Jane Casey; Anne Cater; Alison Graham; Mick Herron and Jo Howard; Lindsay Jackson; Erin Kelly; Vaseem Khan; Paddy Magrane; Abir Mukherjee; Tim Rideout; Sarah Ward; Lucie Whitehouse. In response to my odd but exacting commission, my son, Victor, drew a brilliantly dark map of the Peak District. This book is dedicated to Lisa Shannon, who gave me the great gift of her friendship, and that can of Carling which so nearly clobbered DS Joseph Ashe outside the Northern General Hospital, Sheffield.

[Harvill credit page TO COME – allow 2pp]

[About the author TO COME – allow 2pp]